THE WARRIOR WITHIN

BOOK ONE OF THE WARRIOR SERIES

BROOKE CAMPBELL

Copyright (C) 2021 Brooke Campbell

Layout design and Copyright (C) 2021 by Next Chapter

Published 2021 by Next Chapter

Edited by Chelsey Heller

Cover art by CoverMint

Back cover texture by David M. Schrader, used under license from Shutterstock.com

Mass Market Paperback Edition

To Terri Nelson. Every day, for a million reasons, I choose you.

ACKNOWLEDGMENTS

I would be horribly remiss if I didn't thank the following people—in no particular order of importance. You know why you are on this list and have earned my gratitude. My uber-talented and gorgeous sister Yvonne, Grandma Campbell who passed along her love of reading and endless boxes of bodice-ripping romances, my mentor and fellow author Christy English, Patrice Schwermer, Chelsey Heller, Shannon Quinn, and E.J. Thinker. If I've forgotten you, feel free to dip me in chocolate and feed me to the lesbians.

1

TWILIGHT FAN CLUB

*B*obbing my head to the hypnotic beat, I make my way around the dance floor, my eyes full of the mass of sweat-slicked bodies writhing under the strobe lights. There is some serious eye candy here tonight. Carefully, I continue along the long side of the L-shaped bar to the short hall leading to the smaller bathroom, counting on a shorter line. Don't ask me why the area's most popular nightclub only has one stall on this side, but most people know about it and opt for the larger bathrooms on the other side of the dance floor. To entertain myself in line, I turn around and face the greater room. My body sways slightly to the beat. *I miss dancing. I wish...*

No. No sense getting caught up in wishing.

But the thought sours my enjoyment of watching the dancers. Instead, I turn my attention to the people clustered around the bar, entertaining myself with the *gay or nay* game. Okay, maybe it isn't especially politically correct, but it amuses me. HoneyBears, the area's only gay bar, is famous for cheap drinks and amazing music. They draw huge mixed crowds every weekend. Visually, I make my way down the bar, noting to myself *gay* or *nay,* while balancing on the cane as I keep the rhythm.

Unexpectedly, my eyes snag on the sexiest woman I have ever seen sitting at the far corner of the bar. My mouth goes dry. Statuesque, she towers at least a head over those around her. In the flickering light, I can only tell her hair is dark, shaved close on the sides with perfectly messy curls on top, as if she just ran her hands through it. Dressed in an inky sleeveless mock turtleneck that emphasize a long neck and powerfully built frame—holy cannoli, is she a hot, hot, hottie. Contrasting sharply with the black top, her flawless skin glows pale. Talk about butch. At a glance, I'd assume she was a man. *Oh, Gaia. You are so my type.*

My breath hitches. I swear, she is staring right back at me, smirking like she just heard a joke. *No, not at me. Someone's behind me, right?* Casually, I turn around, but I'm the only one paying attention to her. When I look back, she nods once as if in confirmation, and my breath leaves me.

I swear, if she isn't a lesbian, I'm going to cry.

A devastatingly handsome man walks up to Hottie. They talk, but Hottie keeps staring back at me. Through me. I could seriously get lost in that woman's intense gaze. I resist the urge to look behind me again. Handsome follows Hottie's gaze and I squirm under his hostile scrutiny. He's casual in ripped jeans and a faded black T-shirt with a Led Zeppelin album cover on it, but only a fool would dismiss the danger rolling off him in waves. He's lean and clearly strong, with chiseled cheeks and piercing eyes. A chill goes through me despite the heat. Thankfully, after a long second, the man dismisses me, and I let out the breath I was holding. Grabbing a martini glass from the bar, he heads across the room.

The line moves, and I step back several paces into the darkness of the hall, giving me the relief of anonymity. But Hottie keeps staring in my direction as if she can still see me. Surely, she can't. My mind runs away with an image of those intense eyes probing mine as she bends to kiss me, and my pulse races before I can blink the illusion away. A sexy grin stretches across Hottie's face. I start to return her smile and stop myself just in time. *Ridiculous. She isn't grinning at me.*

A small group of laughing women join me in the back of the line and my view is broken. All three of these pretty women are very drunk and clearly having a blast. Watching them, I wish I was out with my best friend Emma tonight instead of being the designated driver for my coworkers.

Finally, I give up on being able to see around the women. Probably for the best, anyway. *Hottie is so far out of my league, I'm not even in the stadium.*

I turn and face the cute woman in front of me. She's young, petite, and wearing darkly provocative eye makeup. She has on a tight pair of cut-offs and a tighter cropped top. A belly button piercing flashes— no really, it must be an LED light—on her flat stomach. I look down at my own outfit and stifle a sigh. Of all the women in this club tonight, why on Earth was that sexy woman looking at me?

My coworkers and I went out for a casual dinner after work before coming here. I didn't know this is where we would end up, or believe me, I would have dressed differently. While my T-shirt is a pretty green, it is two sizes too big, with *Visualize*

Whirled Peas emblazoned in large white letters across my chest. Not exactly club attire. And to top it all off, I've tucked it loosely into baggy jeans that don't flatter my figure at all, but leave room for a knee brace. The result is that the T-shirt balloons out, making me look larger than I am, thanks to the two best things my mother gave me. Completing this stunning outfit is a worn pair of dark brown Clarks that are very good for my feet and back, but look like boats. It feels like my ponytail has come loose.

Yup, sex goddess, that's me. Fashionista Emma would be horrified if she saw me here now.

And completing the ensemble, there's the cane. Navy, with bright flowers, it doesn't blend in so well. I hate how people look at me when I have it. All the questions even strangers feel free to ask. *You poor thing! What happened? Do you need help? Ugh.* I tried to convince myself it was an accessory, but times like this, I wish it were easier to hide. *Who am I kidding? I wish I didn't have it at all.*

The woman in front of me goes in after two others emerge holding hands. I don't even want to think about what they were doing in that disgusting stall. Yuck.

When it's finally my turn, I take a quick second to refresh my ponytail, tucking wisps behind my ears, stifling my hope that I'll see that butch again. Yet, on my way out, I can't stop myself from seeking her.

My heart sinks when I can't find her. *Why so surprised?* It just confirms what I suspected all along. People like that aren't interested in people like me. *Move along, hot women, move along. There's nothing to see here.* The dejection that blankets me takes a long minute to shake off. Maybe I'm not as resigned to singlehood as I thought.

After the relative quiet of the hallway and bathroom, the thumping music and flashing lights are starting to give me a headache. I pick my way along the bar, trying to anticipate the erratic movements of the writhing crowd.

Suddenly, a shrieking woman tumbles backwards off her stool right at me. Instinctively, I twist and lurch away, wrenching my bad knee and my back. I lean heavily on my cane when the flailing woman manages to kick it out from under me, and the cane flies out of my hand. Trying to remain upright, I flail my arms. Staggering backwards, I run into a solid barricade. An arm sweeps across my abdomen and lifts me flush against a hard body, as if I'm a rag doll. The tall stranger's arm holds me so high on my abdomen that my double Ds are propped on top of it, like a shelf. But all thoughts are chased away by a nerve pulse shooting down my leg, and I spasm and gasp with the white-hot pain.

"I have you, I have you, shhhh." Soft breath and a deep voice caress my ear. An enticing scent calms me somewhat, but my focus is scattered. "Are you hurt?"

All I can manage is a jerk of my head as the nerve zings again, coiling around my foot like a live wire.

"*Merde.*" Disjointedly, I note the slight accent and recognize the French curse. "Can you sit?" At a second jerky nod, I'm lifted effortlessly onto a stool. In dismayed shock, I recognize my savior. *Figures Hottie would have to see me like this. Gah, she's strong.*

My teeth are clenched in pain and I'm trying not to draw attention to myself. I mumble, "My cane, I-I

5

need my cane." I hurt so badly, I can't even think beyond getting out of this place.

"I will get your cane. Right now, you just keep breathing, in and out, good." She takes a few deep breaths with me and I train my focus on her emerald eyes. Once she sees I'm breathing more deeply, she squeezes sideways beside me, signaling the bartender. Facing the dance floor, I can't hear or see what she's doing. Every bit of me is focused on trying not to cry. *Only drunks cry in bars. Remember? You are having fun tonight.*

I'm staring blindly down when a figure approaches and I look up into steely eyes. *Super.* Mr. Danger looks me over critically, eyebrows knitted, and I shudder.

He turns to Hottie, anger punctuating a British accent forced through clenched teeth. "Bloody hell! I hope you know what you're doing, mate."

Relax. It's called pity. She couldn't possibly be attracted to me. Give me a minute and I'll be on my way.

Hottie maneuvers around, holding a glass of what looks like a soda. She hands it to me, a fat straw swirling as if it's just been stirred. "Drink this. It will help."

When another shot of pain passes, I blow out my breath. "Thanks, but I don't want any alcohol." I try to push her hand away. She is so strong that all I end up doing is pressing my hand against the back of hers. Her cool skin is like satin over steel. I let my hand drop, and I can't stop the jerk when the nerve zaps me again. My shin is alive with pins and needles now.

Hottie ducks her head so our eyes meet and hers are intense. Like dark evergreen forests with streaks of sunlight peeking through. "*Oui,* so I noticed. No alcohol, I promise. Besides, you look very *thirsty*." Towering over me, a woodsy, sensual scent envelopes me. Cologne? Pain momentarily forgotten, the smell tightens my abdomen. I take the sweating glass as she turns to him. "It is under control, Niall. Let the others know that I will be a while."

Niall walks away, shaking his head. I can't believe how thirsty I am all of a sudden. When all I taste is soda, I'm relieved. *Gah, I'm so thirsty*. I chug half the glass. "Thank you."

Hottie nods and keeps staring at me like she's trying to read my thoughts. *Thank the goddess that can't happen*. A few more deep swigs and I lean back into the bar. The nerve pulse isn't as sharp and my knee doesn't seem to throb as much. I feel my face and shoulders relax. I take another long drink and a deep breath. When the shooting pain stops abruptly, the relief is so profound that tears pop into my eyes and I gasp. Despite blinking rapidly, one tear escapes. I stop breathing altogether when she cups the side of my face and her thumb wipes the tear away. I have an insane urge to rub my face in her hand like a cat. The gesture is so intimate that I squirm self-consciously. She drops her hand and gestures to the glass. "Finish that."

"What do you mean, you noticed?" I'm a little slow catching up, but she seems to know to what I'm referring. There are only a few swallows left and I drink them down. Just like that, my headache dissolves and the tingles in my leg disappear. I feel almost normal. *Weird. I've never had pain just go away like that*.

A sultry look comes into her eyes, distracting me. "Oh, I have been watching you for a while now. Hard not to. With a face like this lit up by laughter—" she spreads her hands in a can-you-blame-me gesture. I'm really out of practice because that can't mean what it sounds like she is implying, but my cheeks heat anyway. I mean, *look* at me. "Especially judging the condition of your...friends...you surprise me. You are different."

Yeah, I'm different, alright. I don't know what to say to that, so I don't say anything. Nervously, I tuck a stray lock of hair behind my ear a couple of times. I can't believe how much just sitting here has helped me. *How is that possible?* I actually feel better than before that drunk fell into me. At that moment, the memory of what happened floods me. I have been so fully distracted by the pain that I forgot. In my mind's eye, I see myself flailing my arms and hopping around like a crazed bird, and then tripping right into this sex-on-a-stick woman...I cover my face and groan into my hands. *How humiliating. If it weren't for this knee, I never would have lost my balance. Gods, I hate this body.*

She takes hold of my wrists and gently pulls my hands away from my reddened face. "I believe you are being too hard on yourself. Did you ask that woman to fall off the stool into you?"

Oops. Guess I said some of that out loud. "No, no. I just looked ridiculous. Gods, I hope I didn't hurt you when I ran into you." She shakes her head, looking amused again. "Look, thank you. For everything. But I'm fine now. I'll go back to my coworkers and you can go back to..." I trail off. For some reason, I started to say *the hunt*. Though she seems calm, she's as intense as her friend, Niall. As if underneath the veneer, she is coiled for...violence.

8

"Please, do not apologize for something you cannot help. Everyone looks ridiculous when they fall, *n'est pas*? Besides, you saved me the trouble of figuring out how best to approach you while simultaneously setting me up to be the hero. I should be thanking you." She smiles and it transforms her face. *Just wow.* Then she gets serious again. "Can I ask you something?"

"Um, sure, I guess." I frown, figuring it's going to be about the cane or the knee brace. Her hands are resting on my knees, so I know she feels it.

That's why I'm floored when she comes out of left field. "Why do you hide your incredible body? Because when you were pressed up against me, mmm, believe me, I felt every luscious curve." Her eyes heat and her accent thickens with the seductive words.

My mouth drops open. For real. Cheeks red, I snap it shut. My 1950s pin-up body doesn't fit today's ideal of lean beauty. Besides, who would want a crip like me? Ignored is easier than rejected, so I hide.

I'm grasping around for something to say, tucking my loose hair behind my ear a few times. Watching my struggle, a slow, sexy smile spreads across her face. "What is your name, *belle*?"

I blink. Twice. *Beautiful?* I blink again and shake my head. *Stop. She probably calls all women beautiful. It isn't personal.* "Ah, my name is Libby."

Her face lit up with mirth, she gives me a short bow and says, "A pleasure to meet you, *Libby*." She rolls my name around her tongue like melting chocolate, and I think it's the sexiest sound I've ever heard, my name on her lips. "I am Jo."

"Hello, Jo." I laugh at the rhyme, and that's when it hits me how tired I am. Had it been up to me, I would have left hours ago, but since I agreed to be the designated driver, I need to wait. I thunk my forehead. "My friends are probably wondering what happened to me."

"Libby, these *friends* are beyond caring about anything. See for yourself." She wraps her arm around my back and presses me forward so that I can see around the people at the bar to our table. The action is so familiar that I'm momentarily overwhelmed. I'm entranced by her sexy scent and inhale deeply. With effort, I pull myself together enough to focus on the table. Several people have joined them, and the party is raging on just fine without me.

I straighten and look up. Jo lowers her head and cinnamon-scented breath fans my cheek. I wonder if she's going to kiss me. Gah, I want her to kiss me. Her eyes are hypnotic. On another deep inhale of her delicious scent, the butterflies dive deep.

Gulping, I break eye contact, and lean back, babbling like a scared teenager rather than the experienced 27-year-old I am. "Obviously, my co-workers are okay. They sure look like they're having a great time. I guess they don't miss me." It's been a long time since someone showed interest in me, and unless I am way off, she is. *But she can't be!* And I have apparently forgotten how to flirt. Mortification colors my cheeks. *What is wrong with me?*

Her smoldering expression clears, and she straightens and steps back. I relax, albeit disappointed, smoothing away hair that tickles my cheek. "Do you live nearby, Libby?"

"Um, no, actually I live about 45 minutes south of here. Down 81."

A broad smile brightens her face. "As do I. Will you allow me to help you?"

I don't know what she is talking about, but I find myself agreeing. "Yes." Then I can't help myself. "But you have already done so much, you don't have to—"

"This is not about what I have to do, Libby, rather what I *want* to do. If you will allow me."

I'm still not sure what she intends to do, but strangely, I feel safe with this complete stranger. "Sure. Please."

"Excellent. Do not move." She pats my knees and I watch her weave her way through the crowd, texting on her phone. A quick look around finds Niall standing at a table not far away, watching me pensively. I feel like making a face at him, but the childish impulse passes, thank Gaia. In this lighting, he's almost painfully white, even more so than Jo. I glance around at the handful of equally pale, ridiculously attractive people. *It's the Twilight Fan Club gone seriously wrong. Lay off the plastic surgery, folks, and get some sun. It's kind of pathetic.* Suddenly, Niall doubles over with laughter.

Yeah, I know. The idea that she's into me is hilarious, am I right?

On her way back to me, Jo studies the floor, and a few feet away she ducks down and comes up holding my cane. She moves like my cat, lithe and quick. I could watch her body move all night. Gods, what I wouldn't give to watch that sexy body move to music. Any music.

Somehow, I manage to smile. "Thank you. Really. You didn't have to."

"Come, before you fall off this stool from sheer exhaustion."

I pat the bulging pocket where my keys rest. "Oh, believe me, I'd love to but I'm the DD tonight. I have to wait for them to finish partying."

"*Oui*, so they earnestly informed me. I sent for a car to take them home."

Does she mean a taxi? Uber? Should I pay for it? "Um. Okay." It hits me that I've crossed over that fatigue line. *Geez. I may not be safe to even drive myself home.*

"You do not have to, Libby." *I must have voiced my thought again. I really am tired.* She smiles enigmatically. "Louis will take you home. Tomorrow, when you are ready, he will bring you back to your car." She stops the protest rising on my face. I get the impression she's angry with me. "Did you not agree to allow me to help you, Libby?" For a second I think I see a flash of red in her eyes, but I blink and it's gone and I'm sure my tired brain conjured it. I swallow and reluctantly nod my acquiescence. It's not often I accept help, but tonight, I know I need it.

She keeps hold of my cane, having no trouble cutting through the crowd, and I focus on following in her wake to the door. However, I'm not too tired to notice the tight buns in those fitted designer jeans. *Holy Hairballs!* She stops when Niall meets up with her and they have a quiet conversation. He actually winks at me as he walks by.

It is such a relief when we step outside into the quiet. I lift my face to the night sky and fill my lungs with the cooler air. My ears ring.

"I regret that I am unable to personally see you home this evening, but I invited people here and I must play host. However, I trust Louis with my life and I hope you can forgive me."

"Oh, there's nothing to forgive. You've done so much." I'm disappointed she isn't coming with me, but I hold my tongue. We come from vastly different worlds. She could have anyone. And she probably can't wait to get back to her friends. "Goodbye. It was nice to meet you."

An energetic 50ish gentleman wearing a smart black suit and a kind smile hurries to us, and Jo hands him my cane. He bows to Jo, then to me, and steps discreetly away to wait by a huge black SUV parked on the street. This must be Louis.

Jo lays her hands on my shoulders. "This is not goodbye, sweet Libby with the sexiest-yet-carefully-concealed body." I'm fully blushing now, her seductive smile warming me to my toes. "*Au revoir*, until we meet again." She brushes her lips across my forehead, helps me up into the SUV, and turns. She and Louis speak in low voices and I touch the spot she kissed. Once settled into the buttery leather, fatigue covers me like a blanket. I rouse myself as Louis hands me my cane, and then his card, which I tuck it into my pocket. My eyes lock on Jo as he closes the door. I can hardly believe what's happened tonight is real, and I'm afraid I'll never see her again. Reluctantly, I tear my gaze away to give Louis my address for his GPS. When I look back, Jo hasn't moved. Bathed in streetlight, she stands like a fabled goddess of war in marble, watching us roll down the street.

2

AM I DROOLING?

*T*wake from a deep, nearly dreamless sleep to birdsong and a breathy purr. Whiskers tickle my ear. I squirm away and open my eyes to sunshine peeking around plum-colored blackout curtains covering the two windows over my head. Darcy's whiskers trail up my cheek and I can't help but smile, especially when the tips of his ears come into my peripheral vision. "Mornin'," I reach out and scratch under his chin. The purr ends in a plaintive meow. "Now, that's pitiful. Just a sec, little man."

I roll to my side as he leaps from the bed with a solid *da dump* that belies his delicate frame. I notice it's after 11. As I didn't get in until close to 2 this morning, I am grateful I slept so late. I steadily push myself up until I'm perched on the side of the bed. It takes several deep breaths for my body to settle. Slowly, I take stock of my joints, tentatively moving my feet and legs around. My knee remains less swollen than it has been for the past two weeks, and I feel some of the normal stiffness in my lower back, but otherwise, it isn't bad. Considering the jarring fall I took last night, I'm relieved. Frankly, I should feel much worse and I don't really understand why I don't. But I chalk it up to one of those quirks of a complex immune system. Half-heartedly I do some stretches a physical therapist once gave me to help loosen my back before shuffling to the bathroom, trying not to trip over my tuxedo as he weaves figure eights around my legs.

By the time I make coffee, my back and neck are less stiff. As I wait for the fragrant brew, I lean against the counter, thinking about last night. *Jo.* Oh my, was she provocative. The whole fantasy package. Strong, tall, intense, mysterious. And, since we are talking fantasy after all, rich doesn't hurt, either. I mean, she had her driver take me home.

Oh, crap. My car. I yawn widely. *Yeah, it can wait.*

Darcy rubs against my leg and voices his frustration, interrupting my thoughts. "Oh, excuse me! Would you like some food, Darcy?" Laughing, I push away from the counter, and get the can I'd opened the day before. "All right, little guy, here ya go." I scoop the remainder of the smelly food onto a small plate and place it on the cracked linoleum. He chews wetly, his deep purr rumbling out as he devours it.

The coffee pot beeps and in moments I have my favorite bright lavender mug fixed just the way I like it. My dad and I found the little pottery where I bought it on a weekend getaway to visit the caverns in Luray back when I was a teenager, and I've used it almost daily ever since. I alternate between sending small puffs rippling across the creamy surface and taking tentative sips of the slightly sweet brew as I pad barefoot through my small contractor-grade, off-white apartment.

I draw curtains and spin open the plastic blinds

on the windows in the front living room. Two narrow panes bookend a large square picture window. The remaining two windows are in the only bedroom. The two sets of windows stand at either end of the narrow, carpeted apartment, allowing for a bit of a cross breeze when the wind is just right. One of the things I love about the apartment is being able to have so much natural light in both main rooms. The apartment isn't much, but the picture window boasts a wide sill, deep enough to serve as a window seat which sold me on it. Plump cushions in pinks and oranges cover the sill. Before Darcy can settle in like a sultan, I do, enjoying the already slanting sun. I inhale deeply and let it out slowly. I'm so glad it's not a work day. I finish my coffee daydreaming about Jo.

Deciding it's time to get moving, I search for my purse, suddenly remembering I shoved it in the glove box when we got to the club last night. Grabbing my jeans from where I draped them last night, I fish out the card Louis gave me. The logo is vaguely familiar. In stylized black font, "JN Conglomerates" also rings a faint bell. Under that is his name and a phone number. No job title, no address, no email. I shrug, grab my phone and call.

He answers on the first ring, sounding very formal and very French. "Louis Bisset, at your service."

I barely remember him speaking at all last night, so the musical accent takes me by surprise. Louis' accent is thicker than Jo's and I'm grateful he's fluent in English. My five years of French classes were a long time ago now, and it's true what they say—if you don't use it, you lose it, and I'd be hard pressed to have more than a casual conversation now.

"Hi, Louis? This is Libby. Um, you brought me home last night?"

"But of course, *mademoiselle*. I have orders to be at your service today." Humor in his voice lightens his formal words.

"You know, Louis, just a lift back to my car would be more than enough. I know it will take a chunk of your time. When would you be able to get me?"

"I happen to be in the area of your apartment complex and can be there at a moment's notice. You have only to say when."

"Well, then, how about give me 30 minutes?"

"But of course, *mademoiselle*. It will be my pleasure." With that, he hangs up.

Feeling bemused, I head for the shower. I steal a few minutes to shave, which is a dire need, while I let conditioner sit in my hair. Afterwards, I comb out my towel-dried hair, but don't take the time to style it. Instead, I pull the auburn waves into a thick ponytail that hangs down to my shoulders. Finished dressing in denim shorts and an extra-large T-shirt that reads, *Don't Believe Everything You Think,* I grab my Asics and go out to the living room to put them on. I expect Louis would be on time, and, in fact, I am still tying my right shoe when there's a knock on my front door.

I follow Louis, who's wearing another smart black suit, to an idling SUV parked in my spot. I'm not a car girl—all I can tell is that it's a huge Lincoln. He opens the rear passenger side door, so I slip into the cool interior and sink into the comfortable seat. If I'm not mistaken, this is the car I rode in last night, though I was too tired to appreciate its luxury at the time. I may drive an ancient Toyota, but I recognize quality. I smooth my hands over the soft leather and indulge myself in appreciation of the sleek polished wood and shining chrome. It's pristine, and I'm glad I don't have anything on the bottom of my shoes. I'd be terrified to drink, or, goddesses forbid, eat in here. After a few minutes of this awed inspection, I just stare out of the spotless windows, not sure what to say to Louis or if it's even proper to talk to him. I feel way out of my element. I sit on my hands before I tell myself I'm being foolish.

My mind wanders and I wonder how late my coworkers got home. Dinner was fun, marginally, but I don't think I will join them again. I heard things I didn't want to know about people I work with and for. I hate gossip.

It's a relief to interrupt my thoughts as I direct him to the parking lot where my car is parked. I make myself wait as he comes around and opens my door, and I thank him. He waits by the SUV while I get into my own vehicle and start it. I am reminded forcibly of my father, who always waits at the door to be sure my car starts, and so I feel a misplaced affection for the proper Louis. Inside my car, it is hot as blue blazes and I quickly bring down the windows. At this time of day, it will be a while before anything other than the winds of hellfire come out of my vents, so I don't even bother turning on the feeble AC yet.

I call out my thanks to Louis and give him a little wave as I back out of the space. Raising a hand, he watches me pull out of the lot as he talks intently into a cellphone.

A part of me—okay, a big part of me—hoped Jo would show up instead of Louis today. I'm still feeling tired when I get home, so, stifling my disappointment,

I make myself a sandwich and settle onto my squishy couch to lose myself in a book while I eat.

I wake with a start, the e-reader forgotten beside me, and Darcy darting to the bedroom. As I gather my wits and try to figure out what woke me, it comes again: three quick raps on my door. Surprised to have a visitor, I open the door to a young man in a white two-piece uniform. His flower-covered name tag reads Harry. He holds a white porcelain bud vase with a single white rosebud. The vase is wrapped with a wide royal blue ribbon, tied into an elaborate bow. The effect is stunning, and I find myself just standing there taking it in.

Harry clears his throat. "Are you Libby?"

"Yes."

"Well, then, this is for you." He's smiling as he offers it to me, and I take it automatically. He turns away, whistling.

I close the door in a daze. I've never gotten flowers before. Thrilled, I hold out the vase in front of me, turning it this way and that so I can look at it from all sides. The partially opened bud is spotless and the silken petals are edged in delicate peach. A card is tucked into the bow. When I pull it out, I just hold it for a moment, savoring the feeling. My name is in a slanting hand I don't recognize. *Not Dad, not Emma, not Sarah.* I run through the short list of people most likely to send me flowers. Certainly no one I work with. Stumped, I decide to satisfy my curiosity. I pull a small card out of the envelope and in the same slanting script are the words:

For a most memorable evening, my humble gratitude. Until next time. -Jo

I pick my mouth up off the floor and read the card

about fifteen bazillion more times. *How did she know where I live? Oh...Louis. Of course.* I feel a moment's embarrassment for my low-rent apartment and raggedy car, but that chicken has flown the coop. I wonder if Louis was talking to Jo as I drove away.

I shrug. If it's meant to be, and all that. I can't do anything about it now.

And why would I? For heaven's sake, I'm not pretending to be someone I'm not just because I feel unequal. I'm not ashamed. If Jo doesn't like it, she won't pursue me. I don't like how much that idea saddens me. I need to toughen up. *I am enough, just as I am, today, right now. I don't need a relationship to make me whole.* Yet, she did send me a flower. For a while, I just bask in the simple delight of it.

Sunday was uneventful. I spent the day resting, reading, and watching Roku on my TV—a typical day off for me. This morning, I awaken early, feeling refreshed. I'm off Mondays and don't have a plan for the day. I'm watching a pair of fox squirrels chasing each other round and round the trunk of a maple in the apartment complex's central yard when I have a sudden urge to go for a walk. *A run would be better.* A wistful urge to do what I used to be able to do punches me in the gut. I'm shocked to feel my eyes tear up. I blink several times rapidly to clear them and get moving.

I decide on what to wear while slathering toast with butter. I eat it, then force down my morning pills. I dress quickly, checking my appearance in the mirror. At 5'6", with my curves, I cross the line into dumpy in baggy clothes. I admit, I like my hourglass figure. I just wish women I'm attracted to also did. So I never let it show anymore. I mean, what's the point? *Not that anyone will ever notice.* Sigh.

Then Jo fills my mind. She definitely noticed. And she liked my curves. Or so she said. I look at the rose on my bedside table and smile.

I gather my hair into a high ponytail to keep it off my neck, enjoying how the periwinkle top complements my blue eyes and brings out the pink tones of my skin. Overall, my skin is somewhat pale and freckled (thanks to my red-headed mom), but smooth and clear. I don't usually wear makeup other than a little mascara on my naturally long lashes, for which I can (and frequently do!) thank my father. Poor guy. He has endured comments about them since his boyhood.

I slide a black neoprene brace over my left knee. Tying my walking shoes poses a bit of a struggle with the morning stiffness in my lower back. As always, I manage.

Mourning my former runner's body, I soldier on, promising myself a cold drink if I can make it to the gas station. No sidewalk means my back is increasingly unhappy getting jostled around on the uneven side of the road, and I'm happy I brought the cane. Summer traffic is sparse this time of morning and I enjoy birdsong along the way.

As they have been wont to do lately, my thoughts return to Jo. Friday night was one of those once-in-a-lifetime opportunities. I wonder if I'll see her again. I really, really hope so.

When at last I step through the gas station door, the blast of cool air dries my sweat and goosebumps spring up on my arms. I hobble to the drink fountain. I've just finished filling a cup with ice when a tall figure appears beside me, a little too close, an unforgettable sensual scent curling around me. Startled, I look up into intense green eyes.

It's as if I conjured her from my thoughts and I have to blink several times to know she's real. As if it were possible, she looks even hotter in the daylight. About my age, maybe a little older, she has strong cheekbones, an angular nose, and luscious narrow lips —*am I drooling?*—that are currently drawn up in a wide smile. She is completely yummy in a perfectly tailored tan suit accented with a dark green silk tie.

"Jo! I...what are you doing here?" My memory didn't exaggerate. She is 100% my type. My fantasy in the flesh. My cheeks heat and I nervously tuck stray hair. I can't take my eyes off her.

"I was pumping gas when I saw you walk in."

I stare at her mouth. *Oh, Gaia. I'm in trouble.*

"Of course. Sure. I was hot so I was...getting a drink."

"*Oui?*" My mouth goes dry as she reaches for me, pulls my ponytail forward, and runs her fingers through it. I shiver at the intimate contact. When she opens her palm to reveal the leaf she removed, I feel stupid. *Get real. She wasn't flirting.*

I take two steps back and flounder for something to say. "Um, thank you for the rose. It's beautiful."

"I am happy you like it." She steps forward and crowds my personal space, again, so close the fabric of her suit pants brush against my bare thighs. Her deep forest smell sets butterflies aflight in my abdomen. To my utter amazement, my panties dampen. My eyes widen and my cheeks grow warmer as I realize how turned on I am just by being near her. *Geez, I know it's been a long time, but pull yourself together, girl.*

Jo's eyes flash and a slow smile spreads across her face, and I could swear she knows exactly the effect she's having on me. Instinctively, I know she has a wealth of experience, and I feel like an awkward rube. Her confidently sexy smile makes my nipples tighten.

Determined to stand my ground this time, I clutch the cup until the plastic crinkles. Her hooded eyes are so passionate, I'm shaken. I'd swear I could detect a sheen of crimson, too, but I know that can't be right. It's just my overstimulated brain.

Before I can form any words, she takes a deliberate step back. I expect to feel relief when she leaves my personal space, but instead, it feels a little wrong, somehow. *Gah! This is crazy.*

"I am more sorry than I can say that I must leave you, but I am late for a meeting. It was...enlightening to see you again, *belle*. I look forward to the next time." With those words, she spins on her heels and walks out before I can even process what just happened.

3

NERD CITY

a bout an hour later, as I lather away the sweat, my thoughts are still of Jo. This is how pitiful my life has become. A hot woman stands close to me and I practically have an orgasm right there.

I find myself humming Fleetwood Mac's "Think About Me." The walking (and—though not literally this time—running into Jo) energized me a little. My lower back has loosened up significantly and I enjoy being more limber as I rub lotion into my skin. For a moment, I imagine Jo smoothing her hands over my body and bring myself forcefully back to the present.

I sink into my couch, and brush some color on my fingers and toes. Pleased with the result, I prop my lavender-tipped feet up on the coffee table to dry and settle in to the deep cushions to read. After I read the same paragraph several times and still don't know what it says, I give up. Puffing in frustration, I black the screen and toss my e-reader onto the couch beside me, my eyes falling on the rose I carried out this morning. I just can't stop thinking about Jo. As if the sexiest woman I've ever seen showing a little interest in me is strange! Okay. Who am I kidding? It really, really is.

In my teens and early twenties, thanks I guess to my shiny hair and a ready laugh, I received admiring looks and even dated a few times, though nothing serious as I was more focused on school. I dressed differently then, too, showing off my early blooming curves and accentuating my smaller waist. I've dated a little since then, but none of them really seemed to appreciate me, or held my attention.

Not like Jo.

When I attended James Madison University, my friends and I would travel to a gay bar in Washington, DC to dance our asses off. I wouldn't sit down the whole night. Women would crowd around us, and let's just say I really let loose when I dance and leave it at that. However, now just the idea of shaking my booty sends phantom nerve pain down my legs, and on the rare occasions when I do go out, I tend to stay at the table rather than risk the dance floor.

Believe me, I'm grateful I had those experiences. But this is my new reality. It's been a long time since anyone other than close friends or Dad has looked at me with anything other than pity. It's taken a long time, but I've learned to stop crying over what I've lost and accept it.

Mostly.

When the doctor told me I had Ankylosing Spondylitis I was floored. My mother's much older brother had it. They were estranged, thanks to my mother, and I was just a kid when he found out he had it. I had the impression that it was an older man's disease. Color me surprised to learn that it can actually strike men and women, and at any age. Like most people I knew, I thought of arthritis as something old people developed. But that is only one of many types.

My eyes had been opened in the most painful way. I could be looking at life in a wheelchair in the not-so-distant future. At the very least, I may never have a truly pain-free day again.

My thoughts turn to how Jo leaves me speechless and off-center. I shake my head. I'm out of practice, but well, it's just not like me. I pride myself on my independence and control. Feeling flustered is new to me, and I don't think I like it.

Darcy leaps down from the window seat and up onto the coffee table. I shift to keep his hair off my toenails. My mind fills with Jo's striking features...and impressive strength...lifting me effortlessly. *Stop that.* I shake myself, decide my toes are dry enough, and carefully stand. It's time to bake.

I find myself humming a senseless tune as I go through the familiar motions of mixing chocolate-chip cookie batter, my mind replaying Jo at the club, and then again at the gas station. I stare through the pass-through island and out the picture window. When the oven timer goes off, I jump. I've zoned out staring out at the Red Maple across the parking lot. Laughing at myself, I pull out the tray, slide each golden cookie onto a cooling rack, and scoop out the remaining dough. Before I finish, my cell rings.

I "dash" into the bedroom and pull my phone off the charger, smiling when I see who's calling.

"Hello!"

"Hey, girl! What are you up to?" Emma's voice reflects her usual cheerfulness. We've been friends since middle school, and in all those years, I've rarely seen her without a smile.

"Hey, Em! Nothing much, I'm just baking cookies. But since I don't want to eat them, I thought I'd take them next door for my neighbor's kids. Want me to save you a handful?"

"When a bell rings, do angels get their wings? Heck, yeah, I want some. Listen, come have coffee with me this afternoon and you can bring them then." She doesn't have to say where. We only ever go one place for coffee.

"Hey, sure, that actually sounds great. Say two o'clock?"

"Done. See you then!"

I want to tell Emma about Jo, but what is there to tell her? I certainly can't tell her about...

Yup. Flustered. And I definitely don't like it.

———

I step into the cool, bright interior of Perk U Up with a smile on my face. My closest friend and I try to get together at least once a week, but with one thing or another, it has been nearly three weeks since we met up. Definitely too long. And, though I feel embarrassed about my adolescent-like behavior, the truth is, I need her perspective on whatever may or may not be happening with Jo. Emma is one of those rare people you can trust to tell you the truth.

I do a quick scan, but don't see her. I order a house brew and splurge on steamed milk. After paying, I choose a two-top table in front of a window so Emma and I can people watch. As the server brings my coffee, Emma breezes in on a gust of warm air. I'm not the only one to notice, believe me. Emma is a rare beauty, and when she comes in a room, it's like the air changes, brightens. Eyes all over the room follow her. No one is immune to her genuine smile and infectious laughter. Loads of wavy blond hair, big sparkling blue eyes, an athletic build, and a movie-star smile complete the picture. But I know that inside is a heart of gold. Her parents raised her to believe that true beauty lies within and she lives that belief. She is in love with life, and known among her friends for fairness and generosity.

Emma and I met after my family relocated when I was in 7th grade. We didn't have any classes together that year, but we both joined the volleyball team. I was the new kid and already had eye-catching boobs I had to stuff into a suffocating sports bra (what sadist came up with that particular torture device?). I didn't fit into a group of already-skinny girls hellbent on fitting into tighter and smaller attire. They weren't particularly hostile to me—we were a strong team after all, and Coach would have benched them if they had acted out—but they snubbed me in the halls.

Not Emma. Emma walked away when the gossip started and over to me, to chat me up. She insisted I sit with her at lunch. She told me about her parents. I told her about my mother. She invited me to her house for sleepovers, and understood why I couldn't ask her over. As you can imagine, she was popular with everyone without even trying, which the other girls envied. But they couldn't risk ostracizing her and alienating the boys. Ah, teenage angst.

Today, Emma's long, tanned legs are encased in pressed white linen shorts that hang to mid-thigh, which she paired with a cool sleeveless ocean-blue silk top. Honestly, I don't know how she keeps linen looking so good. It's like magic. I have a linen skirt I love, but as soon as I sit down, the wrinkles are there to stay. Her recent pedicure looks great in strappy white sandals, the candy-apple red matching her lips and shiny purse. She looks like money. Yet, now that she has to earn her own way, I'm guessing this outfit came from the Junior League consignment shop she helps keep in business downtown.

After paying, Emma spins with a whirl of her shoulder-length hair and glides to the table, smiling her million-dollar smile. I stand and meet her for a quick hug.

"Girl, you are looking so good! I love the color of that dress and it sure brings out your eyes, but seriously, honey—it looks like a gorgeous pear-shaped sack and makes you look way bigger than you are. You have got to stop hiding your *ass*-ets." She emphasizes *ass* with a wicked grin and wiggle of her own as she lowers gracefully into the seat across from me.

I roll my eyes. This isn't a new line of conversation. Remember, she knew me before neoprene.

"Gosh, I just love your backhanded compliments, Em." I bat my eyes at her and cup my face in my hands. "Am I glowing?" I slide a baggie of cookies across the table to her. "Here you go, though for that comment, you don't deserve them."

"Oh, stuff it. You know I love you." We both laugh. After taking an appreciative sniff at the opening of the bag, she rolls her eyes heavenward in bliss.

"So how come you can have coffee this afternoon?" Emma has a 9-5 job working as an assistant to a financial advisor. Normally, she only gets an hour for lunch at most.

"Francine had to do something and decided to forward her calls to the answering service. I was able to get away for a while." She brings her hands down on the table decisively. "Tell me why you had to bake today." I love to bake, but Emma knows it often means I'm stressed. I blow a lock of hair off my face and tuck it tightly behind my ear, smoothing it a couple of times. Her eyebrows raise in interest as she knows this is a dead giveaway that I'm nervous. My cheeks redden and I drop my hand guiltily. "Okay, now I am really intrigued! I want full details!"

"Okay, so yeah, I guess something happened." I clear my throat as she rolls her eyes.

"Duh. Talk."

"So, you know I went to dinner Friday night with my coworkers, then to HoneyBears so they could drink, and I could, well, you know..." I trail off as the cashier brings Emma's coffee.

When she walks away, Emma picks back up. "Drool over all the lesbians? Yeah, I know. And?"

"And...I met the hottest woman I've ever laid eyes on!" My cheeks hot, I tell her about just how we met.

"Oh my gosh! Libby! Were you hurt?! What did she do? What did you do?" Emma is bouncing up and down in her excitement.

"Yeah, actually, it stirred up my back pretty badly, but she bought me a soda. And after I drank it and rested, my pain, like, vanished. Emma, she...she is so hot, and she seemed worried about me, and she made sure I got home safe, and she is *amazing*!"

"Hallelujah!" She claps her hands together and rubs them gleefully. "I've been waiting for something like this to happen! Finally! I want all the details. What does she look like? What's her name? What does she do? Where does she live? When are you two going out on a date?"

I wish I had answers to all the questions Emma

fires at me. "Her name is Jo, but that's all I know. And I doubt we'll ever go out, because she is so rich and incredibly hot. Oh, Emma, I just have to tell you that she's so perfect. Muscular, like she lifts weights, but not too much, you know? Tall. At least 5'11. Her eyes are this incredible shade of dark green with gold streaks with a ring of evergreen around the iris, and they are so *intense*. Like she could see *through* me and knew what I was *thinking*." I pick up my coffee and take too big a gulp. I sputter and hold the napkin to my mouth.

"I think I need to point out that your eyes are, in fact, glazed over." Her voice is so dry I have to laugh. "What did you talk about?" Seeing my look, her face gets serious. "Tell me you at least gave her your phone number."

"Um, not exactly? But we didn't really talk. I was really hurting, see. I had nerve pains in my leg, and I wrenched my bad knee, and I was really tired. And you should have seen the outfit I had on. Nerd City."

"Wow, I can't believe you felt better so quickly if you had nerve pain." She pauses, waves it away. "Anyway, alright, let me get this straight. You met the woman of your dreams, and she said...not much...and you said...nothing...and then she had someone else drive you home. Did I miss anything?"

I toy with my mug, spinning it in slow circles. The napkin is already in shreds. "Nope. I'd say that's about accurate. Oh! She did send me a flower."

"She sent you a flower?"

"Yup. A delicate peach and white rose. With a blue ribbon tied around the vase. And the card said she would see me again. And, oh my gosh, I ran into her at the gas station this morning! But she made me so nervous. Obviously, she knows where I live, but it never occurred to me to give her my phone number." I thunk my forehead. I definitely don't say anything about Jo's eyes looking red. Emma'd think I was really off my rocker. "Oh, Em. I'm such a loser." I slump back in my chair, feeling pretty miserable.

"Now you stop that right now, young lady." I hear echoes of her mother in her tone. "I won't hear that kind of talk about my best friend. You are definitely NOT a loser, as you know when you are in your right mind. Horribly out of practice, I'd say, but definitely not a loser. So what are you going to do about it now?"

"Do? What can I do? She is so out of my league and I looked ridiculous, and I was hurting and both times I was flustered, Em. I was so *flustered!*" I prop my elbows on the table and drop my face into my up-turned palms. "I had no idea what to say. It's like my brain goes on vacation around her."

"Libby." I don't move. "Elizabeth." Yup, definitely channeling her mother. I huff and sit up. "Honey, you have to lighten up on yourself. So you met an amazing woman and you couldn't think of anything eloquent to say. There are worse things, you know."

"Like what?"

Without missing a beat, Emma begins counting off on her fingers, "You could have drooled all over yourself, you could have told her your life story in a breath, you could have ripped your shirt off and screamed, 'Take me now you big hunk of love!', you could—"

"Okay, okay. I get the picture," I shush her before people start looking, shooting her a grin of gratitude for giving me some perspective. "What can I do? Or no. Gah. Why bother? She won't be interested in me once she knows what I have is permanent." I am dangerously close to whining now.

Emma looks at me with one beautifully shaped eyebrow cocked. "When you went to the bar, did you by any chance wear a brace?"

"Yeah, I have for weeks now. And she knew it was there because she had her hands on my knees at one point, and she also definitely saw it today."

"And we already established that you had your cane with you, right?"

I wave my hand dismissively, not getting her point, "Yeah, both times."

Emma looks smug. I must really be tired because I'm still not following her train of thought. But she just stares at me and finally it hits me. Why would Jo have done all that if she weren't interested?

I laugh. "Okay, okay, message received."

"Here's what you do. You wait." She crosses her arms.

"I wait."

"Yup. And in the meantime, let's talk about this wardrobe." Emma has that determined gleam in her eye that always means I'm going to be giving in to her soon.

Here we go again. "Em, we have been over this a million times. I'm just not comfortable wearing tight clothes. As a professional—"

"Bull," she cuts me off. "Absolute stinking piles of bull."

I fold my arms.

"Go on, grouch all you want. You *know* you are full of it. You are so afraid of rejection that you make sure no one notices you." She leans in. "Well, I see you. And so did Miss Hot and Gallant. Libby, honey, you are beautiful, inside and out. And it's way past time you let me take you shopping." She drains her coffee. "You are 27, not 87. So you have a disease. Does that mean you have to give up and check out of life? No. Enough is enough. Do it for Jo. Actually, no. Do it for you! Do it because you deserve to look your best. Do it because you deserve to take a chance."

I blink the moisture from my eyes and sniffle. *Man, did I need to hear that.* "Okay, Em. I hear you. Yes. Let's do this."

She claps her hands in delight. "Excellent! Tomorrow you are mine! Consignment shops be ready! Besides, I need a new dress." She waggles her eyebrows and her eyes sparkle.

"Oh?" I know that look. "And what is his name and when are you going out?"

"Gosh, what makes you ask?" She laughs. "His name is David. We met at the grocery store of all places." She looks truly amazed. Clueless. "Let's see, he's a CPA, 5' 10", brown hair, brown eyes. He is sexy in a geeky way, and is taking me to dinner Saturday night. So I need a new dress and probably new shoes. And definitely a pretty bra!" She laughs.

"Deal. Text me." I rise slowly, pushing off the table and the back of the chair. Emma watches, but knows not to try to help. I return her fierce hug and we are still saying our goodbyes as we go in different directions out the door.

4

WHAT AM I MISSING?

*L*ast night, I dreamt of a tall statue sculpted from pure white marble. Its face was in shadow, but no matter how fast I ran, it stayed just out of reach. The images and sense of frustration stay with me. I don't have to guess what that dream was about.

Emma texts me in the morning. Her boss is seeing clients out of town, so she has a few hours free. We have a great time shopping, just like the old days. After a little coaxing and redirection, I get into the rhythm of finding styles and cuts that flatter me. As more of my shape is revealed, I begin to feel pretty again, and some of my old confidence comes back. I end up spending far more money than I originally planned—almost my entire quarterly bonus.

Then we go to a lingerie shop, and I top the spree off with a gorgeous bra and lace panty set that is almost the exact color of my eyes. Despite sticker shock, I can't resist. I may have to eat PB&J or ramen for a few weeks, but it's worth it. It's hard to find a good quality bra for my size without paying a small fortune, and the girls haven't looked this good in years. Maybe no one but me will see it. But I'll know. While I'm in a spending mood, I bite the bullet and select a couple of less expensive everyday bras that will work under any shade I wear. I can't remember the last time I bought a bra, if that's any indication of the shape the ones I have are in. Emma finds a gorgeous set that makes her just as happy, and we call the day a rousing success. Too excited to wait, after she leaves, I dart back into the dressing room to put on a new outfit.

Juggling bags, I'm humming cheerily as I walk out. The heat oppressive, I hurry down the strip mall sidewalk. Almost to my car, I have to stop to avoid a group of people coming out of a Chinese restaurant. I'm waiting for them to disperse, my arms getting heavier and beginning to wilt in the heat, when a sexy familiar voice seems to whisper in my ear.

"Those look heavy, Libby. Allow me." And then she's lifting the bags from my arms. Dressed in yet another expensive tailored black suit paired with a gray and black striped tie, Jo looks every inch the executive. A fantasy involving a conference table flashes in my mind and I shake my head to dispel it.

Flustered, I try to protest. "Jo! Oh, I can carry these. No. You don't have to. I..." I trail off when she's holding all of them and looks at me expectantly. I blink stupidly. "Ah..."

She smiles, slow and seductive. "Your car? I assume it is nearby?"

"My car! Yes. Right." I lead her the short distance to the Corolla. I get the back door unlocked and cringe as the metal shrieks. "You can just drop them back here."

The open door is at my back and Jo leans in front of me to lay my bags on the seat. A nude lace bra drops out of a bag onto the stained floor, and I hastily grab it and jerk it behind my back, my cheeks flaming. When Jo straightens, she doesn't back away, her eyes smoldering. She looms over me.

"I would very much like to watch your bra hit a floor, Libby, but not that one."

I swallow hard at the blatant innuendo. The rich fabric of her suit brushes against my bare arm, scattering goosebumps. "Ah..."

"What is wrong, Libby? You seem...flustered."

I drag my eyes from her mouth and look in her eyes. Backlit by the sun as she is, I could swear they look red. But I blink, and all I see is green. And they are glittering with humor.

She fingers the fabric of my cap sleeve. "You look fetching in this outfit, Libby. Good enough to eat, one might say."

"It's new," I whisper.

"*Oui?* Blue suits you. Brightens your eyes. *C'est belle.*"

"Thank you."

"I must have your phone number."

"Okay." I clear my throat. Somehow, I manage to give her my phone number correctly and she programs it into her phone, then tucks it inside her suit jacket. "Where—" but my voice dies as she reaches for my face. Her fingers glide across my forehead and smooth a lock of hair behind my ear. I shiver as her fingers trace the rim of my ear, not only because they feel cool against my overheated skin. Her eyes darken in response and my mouth goes dry as her fingers curl around my ear. It takes a supreme effort not to move. She drops her hand, and the breath I didn't know I was holding leaves me in a gush.

"You were saying?"

Like I can remember anything when you touch me and look at me like that. "Um, I was, I was wondering..." *Pull it together, Weaver!* "Ah, what you do?"

Amusement lightens the intensity in her eyes. "You might say I am in the blood business. In fact, I have blood repositories serving several of the largest hospital conglomerates in the country. I was on my way from a meeting when I happened to glance over and see you."

I feel like I missed a joke. "That's...impressive. I'm so glad to see you again. I wasn't sure..."

Looking irritated at the interruption of her ringtone, she pulls her phone back out.

"*Oui...*" She speaks rapid French and I can't follow it, but whatever the conversation is about, it makes her angry. The relaxed demeanor of moments ago disappears in spring-loaded tension and a venomous tone. Danger emanates off her in waves and the hair on my neck stands on end. I'd give anything not to be on the receiving end of that. Her eyes flash red.

I shake my head at myself. *What's wrong with me? Her eyes aren't red!*

Frowning, she hangs up. "I apologize, Libby, but something needs my immediate attention and I must go. *Au revoir.*" She disappears so fast, it must really be an emergency. I look wildly around the parking lot, but all I catch is a flashy yellow sports car peeling out into the street.

I get to the office at 1 pm. Thankfully, there is a lot of work for me since my boss was busy showing places all weekend. I desperately need the distraction. I like Jenny's remote office because it's quiet and I can focus. A year ago, she rented this space on the north side of town, near her own home.

I'm able to compartmentalize, and in the five hours I'm scheduled to put in, I catch up on most of the paperwork. I only stay over an extra hour to get it all done. It's easy work and doesn't pay much, but she just about lets me work whatever hours I want as long as the work gets done. And the quarterly bonuses she insists on giving me really help. A couple of years ago, I needed a job with limited, flexible hours that allowed me to sit or stand as I needed, and didn't include heavy lifting. This job really has been a gift.

When I get home, I'm exhausted in more ways than one, but I make myself put all my new clothes away. It feels good as my drawers and closet fill up with the pretty new shades and styles that fit. Surveying them, some of my old confidence comes back. Grinning, I put the too-large clothes in bags to donate. Emma was right. I've been hiding long enough.

———

The rest of the week was typical and pretty boring. In my life, that's a good thing, because no flare-ups means I was able to catch up on much-needed rest.

As it has all week, my mind is filled with Jo. I crave to know her, to touch her. But some things just don't make sense. And why hasn't she called or texted? I gave her my phone number. The rest, as far as I'm concerned, is up to her. However, I just may

die of lust waiting for her to make another move. Unbidden, I remember Jo's fingers on my skin, the heat in
her eyes. I imagine how it would feel to have those fingers on other parts of me.

My cell pings in my pocket and it startles me so
much I drop the paring knife I was using to slice an
apple and it nicks my finger on the way to the cutting
board. A bead of blood bubbles up and I thrust it into
the sink and turn on the tap. As I hold it under the
cool running water, watching the water dilute and
wash the blood away, I am forcibly reminded of the
flash of crimson I've seen in Jo's eyes. There's no
denying it now. It's been there too many times to
discount.

What am I missing?

I don't know how long I have been standing there,
lost in my vivid imagination, but I finally turn off the
water and dry my hand. The nick is tiny, and since it
stopped bleeding, I don't worry about putting on a
bandage. Pulling the phone out, I see Emma's text. I
texted her earlier wishing her luck on her date
tonight.

Luck? Yes, he'll need. (devilish grin) Whatcha doin?

Indeed. Poor sod. Nothin. Plans today?

Spa day w/Mom!

I smile. I'm glad she enjoys that kind of thing. A
day spent packed in mud with strips of seaweed
wrapped around my face and body just gives me the
heebie jeebies.

Make him work for it tnite ;) Dets ltr!
U get dets on Jo when I get urs!

Wha? Blackmail! No fair. But Hooray! Sun?

I tell her that's fine and we reestablish our standing brunch date.

The rest of the day I spend on the couch with Darcy, reading. I've always been a big reader. When I was little, Dad would read to me every night. We both loved Harry Potter. My dad still gives me chocolate if he senses dementors are lurking.

Towards evening, I feel restless and pull out some of my jewelry-making supplies. I decide to make a couple of fun pairs of earrings to go with the new-to-me clothes. Soon, I have several pairs of earrings. I climb into bed early with a contented smile on my face.

––––––––

I call Dad after my now-routine morning jaunt to the gas station.

"Hey, Dad!"

"How's my little girl?"

"Good. You?"

"You've got good timing. I just finished a run and I'm feelin' fine."

"Cool. Whatcha up to today?"

"Figure I'll cut the grass, do a little weeding in the flower bed. The usual. Now, how are you, really?"

I may put on an act with most folks, but I don't with Dad. "Really? My back and knee hurt. I'm exhausted. But the flare I was in seems to have passed. I have blood work next week, and the week after I see the rheumatologist."

"Sweetie, you know, if you want me to go with you..."

The familiar offer makes me smile. "Thanks, Dad. I'll let you know."

"What have you been up to? Anything fun?"

"I've started walking every morning."

"I'm so glad!" And I know he is. We used to run together regularly, and I know it bothers him that I can't anymore, almost as much as it weighs on me.

"Oh, and Emma and I went shopping." I smile, thinking of my new clothes.

"What all did you get?"

I laugh. "Try a whole new wardrobe! All thrift stores, of course. Everything fits."

"Oh, honey, that's great! Tell me, is it some*one* or some*thing* that brought that on?"

"You know, Emma's been working on me a long time, but I actually..." I'm suddenly shy to tell Dad.

He laughs. "And what's her name?"

After I tell him what little I know about Jo, I share a story from work. He tells me anecdotes from his own job, and I laugh until my stomach hurts. When we end the call on *I love you's*, I feel lighter.

———

I dress for brunch in a flirty skirt. Feeling attractive, I excitedly rush out of the door.

There aren't many places in this small town that open for brunch, and Pawley's offers one of the two available Sunday brunches. Their competitor downtown heavily advertises an adult brunch. Pawley's has a generally quieter crowd, which Emma and I prefer. After a few passes around the lot, I give up and take one of the available handicap spaces in the front.

I vacillated when my doctor offered handicap tags to me, but as her nurse told me, I might as well take something good out of the diagnosis. And believe me, there are days when I really need it. Times like this though, when I don't even need the cane, I accept my gratitude for the boon.

It takes only a moment to spot Emma waving at me from a table and I let the hostess know. She jumps up and we exchange quick hugs. I settle into the chair opposite hers and grab a menu. It doesn't take me long to decide—I always seem to get the same thing—so when the waitress comes a minute later, I'm ready. We place our orders and the waitress darts away. The place is hopping, but the music isn't so loud that anyone needs to shout.

"That outfit is perfect. I envy your curves—you do that V-neck credit. On me, it would look ridiculous."

This is an old refrain. This stunning woman wishes she had my curves. "Oh, please. Nothing would look ridiculous on you." Before she can answer, I head her off. "How was the infamous Spa Day yesterday?"

"Wonderful! It was wonderful. We had so much fun. Mommy got the cutest new 'do and it takes years off her face. And now we have matching manis and pedis!" She waves her fingers at me and I admire the shiny pale pink. Emma prefers bolder shades, but her mother's coloring demands delicate tints. Emma usually makes up for it by painting on a layer of glitter a day or two after their spa days.

"Do you have a picture of her hair?" I ask.

She gasps in mock shock. "What do you think?" Emma grabs her cell and quickly swipes to the picture. She passes it to me.

Emma takes entirely after her father in looks. Like Emma, when he walks into a room, everyone—and I mean everyone—comes to a gaping standstill. But not so with her mom. Emma's mom is, frankly, plain. Her brown hair and eyes are unremarkable, and she looks perpetually washed out. And Emma's father is hopelessly in love with her. Mrs. O'Shae is one of the kindest, most generous people I have ever met. Unless she is in Mom-mode, that is. As I gaze at the photo, I see her love of life shining from her eyes. Her hair is cut into soft layers and golden highlights brighten her face. I hand the cell back, gushing, "Emma, your mom looks amazing!"

"I know, right?! I'm so glad I talked her into it. You should have seen the look on Daddy's face. I will just say that I got out of there as soon as I could!"

I laugh with her. "I'm so glad. How is your dad's business doing?" Her dad, the Irishman, owns a primarily online importing business, but keeps a small storefront with handmade Irish goods in the neighboring city. Emma worked there through high school and I hung out there a lot over the years.

"You know how it is. Not much demand for wool items around here now, but folks are always coming in for chocolates, Celtic crosses, claddagh rings, and so forth. Online, he still does plenty of business."

"I'm glad to hear it. So, alright, out with it. How was your date with David?"

She gets a sweet, dreamy look. "David is such a gentleman. And so sweet! He held open doors for me. He even stood up when I went to the bathroom!"

Before I can reply, our waitress comes, laden down with our dishes. She refills our coffee, then heads away. For a minute, Emma and I concentrate on eating.

"I'm so glad you had a great date. You really seem to like this guy. Are you going out again?"

"Yes, in fact, he called and asked me out for dinner again tonight! Isn't that amazing?"

"Oh, honey, I'm not surprised in the least. You are the total package after all: beauty, kindness, intelligence, generosity—"

"Oh, stop. Anyway, we really hit it off and I have a good feeling that tonight will go well, too."

"Emma, that is really wonderful. You deserve so much happiness."

"Okay, so I told you my news. Now it's your turn! What's going on with Jo?"

I frown, wishing I had something more exciting to tell. "Well, I've run into her a few times."

"Yay! Do you have a date planned yet?"

I roll my eyes. "No. She always seems to be in a hurry. It's really frustrating."

She frowns. "That's disappointing. But, listen, girl, I predict that the next time you see Jo, she will ask you out on a date." She taps her chest. "I have a feeling."

I've learned to trust Emma's feelings. "Thanks for the vote of confidence, Emma. I appreciate it."

The waitress returns with our checks. Emma insists on paying for mine, and I stifle my argument. We've been over it many times, but the fact is I can't afford to rebuff her generosity. Instead, I thank her and soon we are out the door.

"Em, thanks for everything. You really are the best friend a girl could ask for."

Her brilliant eyes wide, she shakes her head. "I don't know what I would have done if it weren't for you, either, Libby."

With promises to text each other with any developments in the romance department, we part ways.

5

WELCOME BACK

*U*gh. This Tuesday is already shaping up to be a rough day. I woke up late and missed walking in time to have any hope of meeting Jo. My first step out of bed, my bare foot hit a soggy hairball Darcy apparently lost in the night. I spent 20 minutes scrubbing the carpet before I even had coffee. The last two nights, I've dreamt of menacing marble statues with fiery red eyes. I wake from the dreams, shaken and fearful. I don't know what to think about them.

I run to the library because I'm craving the feel and smell of a hardback, but they don't have anything new I'm interested in and I leave frustrated. Then I stop for a rare fast-food lunch and spill "special sauce" on my shirt. In the restaurant's bathroom, I try to scrub the spot out of the blue top, but all I end up doing is smearing the stain.

I'm wondering what I did to piss off a goddess as I drive to the lab in nearby Blacksburg where my rheumatologist sends me to get my bloodwork done to see how the meds are doing. Feeling grumpy, when I arrive, I say the Serenity Prayer and ask for a change in attitude. I walk to the clinic to find the doors are locked. Belatedly, I read the sign: "Closed for Lunch 12-1." A look at my phone; 12:45. I blow sweaty hair off my forehead and stalk around the building. The clinic only takes up a corner of the red brick four-story. The rest is all offices. On the opposite side of the building, there's another entrance. The lab has an interior door, and I intend to wait out of the heat for the lab to open.

Stepping inside, I am immediately cooler. I lift my ponytail off of my neck and fan my overheated face. After a second of searching, I find a tissue in my purse and dab at my forehead and upper lip. I hate being sweaty. I don't see a trash can, so I stuff the limp tissue in the bottom of my purse with a slight feeling of distaste.

The hall is lined with windows into conference rooms. I don't see any doors. All the rooms are dark-ened except one, about midway down, across from the bank of elevators. With time to kill and feeling nosy, I step closer. Seated around a large table, men and women dressed in an expensive professional style all focus on a speaker I can't see. Getting a prickly feeling on the back of neck, I scan the faces, my eyes finally landing on a familiar intense gaze.

I blink in shock, my heart lurching in excite-ment. Beside Jo, I recognize the man from the bar, also staring at me. Nate? Neil? No, something British. Niall. He inclines his head in the barest nod to me. Jo surges to her feet. Everyone at the table turns to her and she speaks, though I have no idea what she says. She disappears into the building. Feeling hopeful, I gratefully dart beyond Niall's re-lentless sight and search for a door. I find one beside the clinic. I wait, breathless with anticipation for it to open.

Suddenly, Jo rushes through the door. I walk over to her, smiling my amazement.

At the same time, we both say, "What are you doing here?"

I laugh. "You first."

She just quirks an eyebrow at me.

"Okay, then. I'm here for blood work." I point at the clinic door. "I came early, and they were still locked up for lunch. I decided I'd wait inside, out of the heat."

"And I am here for interminable meetings." She runs her hand through her hair, and now I know why it always looks that way. *Yummy.* Humor plays across her face. "I am afraid I shocked them when I left so abruptly." But she just shrugs, unconcerned.

Then I realize Jo is fixated on my hair. I touch it self-consciously thinking of the sweat that likely curled the ends, but when I feel the ribbon, I know why she is staring. My cheeks redden. I put the ribbon around my ponytail this morning because it matches my shirt perfectly and looks cute. I wouldn't dare to wear it if I thought I'd see her, though.

"*Oui*, by your pretty pink cheeks, I can see that it is from the rose I sent. You honor me." She brings a hand to her heart.

I don't know what to say, but I am clearly embarrassed and uncomfortable, and maybe that says enough. She looks me up and down, taking in the blue V-neck showing cleavage, down to my painted toes peeking through my sandals. My hand automatically flies to cover the stain on my shirt, and she laughs.

"You caught me on a good day." She looks down

at her dove gray suit and crisp white shirt. "I often have a coffee stain somewhere." I can't imagine her ever spilling anything.

"Oh, I think you'd still look good if you had coffee stains all over the place." I'm surprised to hear that come out of my mouth, and it must show because she laughs again.

"Yet again, we meet and I am regrettably in a rush. I must apologize for not being in touch. Obviously, the fates are talking and we cannot ignore them. Have dinner with me."

My heart is racing. "Okay."

Jo looks at the large platinum watch on her wrist. "*Merde.* I called this meeting and they are already running over the time I allotted for them. I will pick you up. Tomorrow? Are you free?"

I can't even be coy. Of course, I'm free. And if I wasn't, I would change those plans. "Yes, yes, I'm free. I'd love to. What time?"

"Six. Dinner attire should do, nothing formal."

"Okay, got it, dinner dress, not formal. Thanks. I will see you tomorrow." I can't stop the smile spreading across my face.

She strokes a finger down my cheek. "Until then, Libby." The door catches behind her with a decisive click.

A hand on my cheek, I walk to the clinic door and check in with the receptionist. I realize for the first time that part of the clinic is set aside for blood donations. A quick glance around and I find the logo and "JN Conglomerates" from Louis' business card. I don't know how I could have missed that before.

After my bloodwork is drawn, I can't help going

back to see if Jo is still there. The conference room stands dark and empty.

Still, walking to the car, I can't believe how completely my day has turned around. Not only did I see Jo, but now we have a date.

I have a date.

I have a date!

It's all I can do not to squeal before I get in, and I let it go as soon as the door is closed. I look around, but it doesn't seem like anyone heard me. I crank the windows down to let out the searing heat, and I'm so excited I text Emma before I pull out of the parking lot.

News of the best kind!

My mind is so full of what I should wear and how Jo looked in that suit that I'm home for 15 minutes before I remember to check the message that came in while I was driving.

OMG Don't hold out ona gurl! Jo? Date?

Dying! Tell!

Yes Jo, Yes date, tmw, NEED dress! I'M dying!

YES! Tmw? Yikes! Shop tnite. 5:30. Be ready!

There is nothing like having someone to share my excitement, and I've always been able to count on Emma for that. I don't need a brace today and I'm really hoping I won't need one on my date tomorrow. I resolve to be very careful. Not that I do something to it each time it swells or my back gives me pain. It could be the weather, my hormones, or something I ate last week.

I piddle around, sort of touching things but not really doing anything, and Darcy follows me with his eyes, his tail twitching, my excited energy making him tense. Finally, I force myself to sit down and rest.

——————

Emma just keeps saying we will know the dress when we see it. We've been to two large thrift stores with no luck, and are on our way to one more. Emma insists our luck will change and the perfect dress is waiting for me there. However, when we walk in, I don't have my hopes up. The genteel older woman behind the counter tells us that they close in 15 minutes, so I feel rushed before I've even started. I'm coming up empty at the racks in my size when suddenly, I hear a familiar squeal. I hurry over to Emma, who's holding the most beautiful little black dress I've ever seen. My heart skips a beat, imagining myself in it. Emma nods. I nod. She squeals again. I grab the dress and rush to the dressing room. As I step carefully into the dress and pull it easily over my hips, I already see that it's going to be perfect. I call for Emma, and her eyes light up and she shrieks. We both start jumping up and down like teenagers.

I can't believe how I look. It fits so perfectly, like it was made just for me. The hourglass-shaped bodice flares below my hips into in an A-line. The snug padded bodice covers the girls well enough that I won't need a strapless bra. An artfully placed slit allows for a flash of thigh when I move just so. It is modestly sexy and very feminine. I'm thrilled.

Once I'm home, I hang the dress on the back of my closet door. After I climb between the sheets. I lay there, admiring my dress and imagining what Jo will say when she sees me wearing it tomorrow.

When I close my eyes, I see Jo as she was today. I imagine running my hands through her hair. I wonder what her lips would feel like on mine, on my neck, on my...anything. Finally, I have to force myself to think of mundane things so I can sleep.

At some point in the night, it started raining. The change in weather makes me hurt, but it is manageable. Opening the blinds reveals streaked windows and gray skies. Not exactly the kind of weather I want for my date, but that is hours away. I'm sure it won't rain all day, and even if it does, I won't let that dampen my good feelings.

I have a date with Jo!

I can't stop thinking about Jo. About what might happen tonight. Doubts creep in. I try not to have expectations that would leave me disappointed. Jo could be boring or be unforgivably rude to the waiter. She might not like me after she knows me better. Maybe I will embarrass her. This line of thinking just makes me more anxious. Thankfully, work keeps me occupied. By the time I leave work, the rain has stopped, and I'm ready to be home and start getting ready. On the muggy drive, I mentally go through what I would like to do before Jo arrives. I'm overdue for some serious personal grooming.

I decide on my grandmother's pearls. The choker has two rows of evenly sized freshwater pearls on a thin band of black satin. Dangling from the center is a large teardrop pearl topped with a diamond. When I hold it up to myself in the mirror, the teardrop settles into the hollow of my throat. I will wear drop pearl earrings. I spend some time in front of the mirror playing with different hairstyles.

In the shower, I shave myself silky smooth. Every part of me I can reach gets lavender-scented lotion rubbed in. I can definitely use the calming properties of the scent. My stomach is unsettled, and I wonder if I'll even be able to eat. I haven't felt this nervous since my very first date. Telling myself I am being silly doesn't make much difference.

I get my hair and makeup done first. Just in case, I secure the bun with about 20,000 bobby pins. Applying a delicate line of black liner, my hand shakes and it smears. Cursing under my breath, I look myself in the eyes. "If she doesn't like you, that is her loss. You are pretty and kind and loved and loveable." Despite feeling a little silly, the pep talk helps, and my hands are steadier as I fix the damage and brush on multiple coats of mascara.

I put on my sexiest underwear and a silky robe. Excitement bubbling, I can't help preening. I make myself laugh, striking poses and doing a catwalk across my room to the mirror. I've got an '80s mix streaming, and I (gently) dance around my room and belt out the lyrics to Def Leppard's "Pour Some Sugar on Me." I'm feeling desirable. It's been too long since I felt this. I could get used to it.

Emma texts me, wishing me luck. All I have left to do is slip into the dress and shoes. Carefully, I step into it, then stand in front of the mirror. A smile spreads across my face. "It's been a long time. Welcome back."

At 5:55, I step into my shoes. I'm just turning off Madonna when there are two raps on my door. I make myself take a deep inhale through my nose to dispel the butterflies before I open it.

Jo is dressed in a thin charcoal suit made of some sumptuous material and a collarless button-up shirt. The top two buttons are undone, and now I am, too. The blue silk shirt is so pale, it's almost white. One hand is casually tucked into her pants pocket, the other cradles a tube of green paper. The effect is so effortlessly dashing, my heart pounds so that I'm sure it's audible. Peeking from the tube is a glorious gerbera daisy. *She can't possibly know it's my favorite flower.* Long vibrant pink petals surround a sepia center. When she doesn't offer it, I look questioningly up into her face. Smiling, I blush. If she had written me a sonnet, I couldn't have been more flattered. Jo is struck dumb by the sight of me in my pretty dress. As she slowly looks me up and down, a completely forgotten thrill of power washes over me.

"Is that for me?" I gesture to the flower.

She recovers quickly and offers the bundle. "*Oui,* it certainly is."

I lift the showy bloom to my face and breathe in. "It's beautiful. Thank you. I love it." There is an intensity in her eyes that I'm coming to recognize and my heart stutters. I clear my throat. "Ah, please, come in while I take care of this."

Jo follows me into the apartment. My confidence evaporates, leaving me nervous again. I've never had a date here. Thinking Jo is in the living room, I raise my voice over the running water. "I'll only be a minute; I'm just going to put this in some water. I can't believe you got me a gerbera daisy." *Aw damn. I'm babbling.* I turn from the sink intending to take a quick peek at her through the pass-through, but she is standing directly behind me and I almost ram into her instead. Her closeness startles me, and my breath comes quick and short as I look up at her. "They're...my...favorite."

"You are breathtaking." That low, deep voice settles in my belly, and her scent surrounding me sets butterflies diving. Jo reaches up and smooths a stray hair behind my ear. I shiver. My mouth has gone dry. "And you smell divine."

"Lavender." Clearing my throat, I continue in a voice more like my own. "That you smell. Lavender. Thank you. So do you. Look amazing." She inclines her head slowly, and I think she's going to kiss me. Oh, how I want her to kiss me. "Uh, just a sec!" I spin back to the sink and surreptitiously grip the edge. I'm panicked at the thought of her kissing me. But, oh, how I yearn. I squeeze my eyes shut and order myself to calm down. I don't pick up the vase until I'm sure I won't drop it.

I've got it clutched in front of me like a shield when I turn. However, Jo backed off and I feel foolish. "Oh, um, I'm just going to put this on the coffee table." She steps aside, a puzzled expression on her face. I've pulled myself together by the time I set the vase down and grab the little silver purse I'm using tonight. "I'm ready."

Jo opens my door. "After you, *belle*." Blushing again, I follow her to a sleek black sports car. Jo opens the door for me, and I thank her as I ease into the luscious leather seat. There is so much technology inside, I am reminded of the cockpit of a plane.

"Music?"

"Sure. There isn't much music that I don't like."

She touches a button and familiar jazz notes fill the air. "Oh, I love Diana Krall."

Jo throws me a look of approval. "I hope you are hungry, but not starving. I made reservations for us in Roanoke."

"No worries, there! Obviously, I'm always ready to eat." As it comes out of my mouth, I wish I could stop the self-deprecating attempt at a joke. I try to recover. "Where are we going?"

She gives me a small smile. "I know what you mean. I, too, am perpetually hungry. Our reservations for this evening are at Chad's. Have you been there?"

"No, I haven't. But I've heard lovely things about them. I'm excited to have an opportunity to go. Thank you." *For...everything.*

We pull onto the interstate and Jo glances at me with those heated eyes. "In case I have not yet, let me make it clear now. This is a long-awaited pleasure."

Uncomfortable with her intensity, I let Diana's voice fill the air. "So, no Louis tonight?"

"No. I love to drive a good car."

I place my hands on the seat and rub the soft leather. "It certainly is comfortable." Passing a tractor trailer, Jo hits the gas. The engine roars to life as we leap forward smoothly. "Wow, powerful, too. Must be a thrill to drive. I can see why you love it."

Jo glances at me, again, one hand on the steering wheel, the other resting on her knee. *She's effortlessly sexy.* She gestures to the dashboard. "Would you like to drive?"

I put my hand over my heart. "Oh, no, this is too nice. I'd be afraid of losing control."

"Ah, but is that not part of the fun? Losing control?"

"Oh, gosh no. Give me safety and dependability."

Jo laughs, and the sound makes something in me relax. "Now why does that sound like a challenge?" She meets my eyes. "I do love a challenge."

Wait. What? Somehow, I don't think we're talking about driving. *Holy hairballs.* I swallow hard.

She laughs. "You intrigue me. I want to know everything about you."

Oh. Well. "I don't have anything to hide."

"Be assured, I intend to learn everything about you, Libby."

Now why does that send delicious shivers down my spine?

6

A STERN TALKING TO

The sun hangs low in the sky and backlights the Blue Ridge as we get to Roanoke. When Jo opens my door, I admire the sunset. "Beautiful," I murmur.

"*Oui*, Libby, you are." Jo cages me with her hands braced on the car for a pounding heartbeat, then takes a deliberate step back and sweeps her arm out to the side. "Shall we?"

I'm blushing fiercely as I fall in beside her. Jo places her hand on the small of my back. Feminism be damned, I love the possessiveness of that gesture. She opens the door to the restaurant, and I'm moved by all these examples of her gallantry. I smile my gratitude and she dips her head.

We are seated at a small table in a cove of windows. Jo pushed in my chair before seating herself. Candles on the tables and low lighting set a romantically intimate tone. A pianist plays jazz. I'm touched that Jo would bring me to a place like this. I've never been made to feel so...special. I know it must be in my face. I can't hide it. I expect to wake up at any moment.

At Jo's direction, the waiter brings a chilled bottle of sparkling mineral water and Jo pours a measure into both of our water goblets. She toasts. "Here is to learning about the beautiful Libby."

"And here's to finding out all about the gallant and charming Jo." We tap our glasses and sip, then spend a few quiet minutes looking the menu over. There are no prices. I guess it's like they say—if you have to ask, you can't afford it. I remind myself that Jo chose the restaurant and must be prepared for it.

There are so many tantalizing options I have a hard time deciding. When I finally do, I look up to find Jo gazing at me.

"I find it endlessly fascinating to watch the emotions cross your face. No artifice."

Oh, geez. "Yeah. I mean, I'm a terrible liar and have always been told I wear my heart on my sleeve." Sadly, *her* face is inscrutable.

"It is not bad. In fact, I find you refreshing. Many hide their true feelings or behave...differently around me. I appreciate that you are...you." She has leaned forward, laying her arm near enough to touch my hands resting on the menu. My skin tingles.

The waiter walks up to take our orders and I drag my hands into my lap. We both order steak. I order mine medium, but Jo asks for rare. As I hand over the menu, I nervously settle my hands back in my lap. I want to touch her so badly, it's an effort not to wring them. *Get a grip!* Once the waiter leaves, Jo's focus returns to me. "Tell me about yourself."

"Gosh, that's kind of a long story!" I laugh. "Where should I start?"

"Tell me about your family."

"Oh, boy, cut straight to the hard stuff." She

seems distressed and I rush to reassure her. "No, no, it's cool. Umm, where to start? Well, you know I don't drink. The reason for that goes back to my mom." *Okay, here goes.* "She was an alcoholic. She could barely take care of herself, much less me. It was pretty much my dad and me from the beginning. She couldn't hold a job." *Sometimes, she was violent.* I buy myself a second sipping water.

Since Jo looks thoughtful rather than horrified, I continue. "I've been in Virginia my whole life. We lived in Richmond when I was little. When I was 11, we moved here because Dad got transferred, and a year later Mom got sober. But I learned it was a family disease, that it could be in your genes, and believe me, she didn't make drinking look pretty. So I promised myself I would never take the chance."

"You never drink?" Her look is so intent, I blink and look down at my hands.

"Well, I did once in a while in college. These days, I will have the occasional glass of wine. But honestly, I don't like the feeling. I like to be in control of myself."

"*Oui*, I believe you do, Libby."

Just then, the waiter comes with our food and I am decidedly grateful for the distraction. I focus on my plate and find the presentation a work of art.

"Is something wrong, Libby?" She looks genuinely concerned.

"Oh, gosh, no, I was just admiring the work that went into this. It almost looks too pretty to eat!"

She smiles at me. "*Oui*, almost." Blood oozes as Jo slices her steak and my stomach turns, grateful that mine has just a hint of pink. It's so tender, I hardly need the knife. I close my eyes with the first bite. I've never tasted anything like it. It's a struggle not to moan. I roll the morsel around, savoring the complex sauce. I open my eyes to Jo's heated expression and nearly choke, her own fork suspended before her mouth.

I finish chewing and swallow, hard, mesmerized by the raw hunger on her face. "It's really good," I mumble. I'm startled when she laughs out loud. The rich sound makes my nipples harden.

"You have a gift for understatement." She puts the bite in her mouth and winks at me.

The rest of the meal she keeps me talking. I tell her how great my dad is. She asks me about my friends, and I tell her all about Emma and Sarah. When she asks me about work, I cast about for what to say. I'm not ashamed of what I do, exactly, but I'm not using my degree and it feels a little like a waste. And I'm uncomfortable to admit I only work part-time.

"I work for a real estate agent. I do all her paperwork, maintain the MLS, make appointments for her, answer her email, research properties, that kind of thing." I can feel my cheeks burn. To a rich, successful woman like Jo, I'm sure what I do sounds lame.

"Not at all, Libby." You would think she heard my thought. Guess my face really is revealing. "If you are good at what you do and get some enjoyment out of it, why not? The only thing I wonder is why you work part-time."

Did I say I only work part-time? I can't remember. Crap, I was hoping I could put it off. *Just get it all out in the open now so she can end things quickly.* But I've been having such a nice time this evening...*there's no shame in the truth.* Now, if only I actually believed that.

"Two years ago, I was diagnosed with an arthritic disease called Ankylosing Spondylitis. The joint and back pain can get pretty bad and sometimes there is swelling, but often, the fatigue is the worst part. It makes it hard for me to do all the things I used to do, that other people my age do. I had to quit the full-time job I landed straight out of college. Really, I'm lucky to have found this real estate assistant job." I don't look at her. I can't bear to see pity, shock, or revulsion on that handsome face.

"Libby, look at me." After a beat, I do, and I read only compassion. "What a terrible thing to have happened to you. You are a strong and brave woman."

Okay, I wasn't expecting *that.* Relief relaxes my shoulders, but I immediately shift the focus. "Enough about me. I want to hear about you."

She smiles and spreads her hands. "What would you like to know?"

"Well, I detect a French accent...where were you born? Montreal? France? And how old are you?" She looks to be close to my age, but there is a gravitas and maturity to her that feels much older.

"I was born in the south of France. My mother would tell you I am 30, and as she had the distinct displeasure—her words, not mine—of birthing me, she ought to know. You?"

I nod. My guess was right. "I'm 27, but, hey, no fair. This is your turn. Okay, tell me about your family."

Jo leans back with her glass. "My mother died of flu. She was a beautiful, sophisticated, and genteel woman. She despised my father, and until I was in my

20s, she refused to tell me anything about him. I left France soon after she died. My father is a violent person, and unfortunately, I lost track of him a number of years ago. As far as I know, I have no siblings."

"That must have been hard to lose your only parent so young." I picture my life without my dad, and it just seems bleak.

"We are fortunate to have one good parent, Libby. There are many who cannot claim such riches." She drains her glass, leans forward onto her forearms. "What else shall I tell *la belle* Libby?"

I refill her glass, then mine to give myself time to think. I'm biting my tongue to keep from asking how she moves so effortlessly fast, why her eyes seem red sometimes. There's a hint of a dare in her eyes. *I do so love a challenge* echoes in my mind.

I blurt it out before I can change my mind. "How do you move so fast?"

Jo leans in, lowers her head, and captures my gaze. Her deep voice lowers an octave, her intense gaze probes. "Be careful, Libby."

My heart hammers like a trapped rabbit. "Oh, well, I don't, I mean, look, if it's none of my business, just say so." I look everywhere but at her, kicking myself. Jo sits back abruptly, and her face becomes inscrutable again. I let go of the breath I was holding as a waiter hurries to clear our plates. When he leaves, I feel like I should apologize. "Look, Jo, forget I asked. It isn't the first time my imagination got me in trouble."

"Never apologize for a clever and curious mind. Remember that we all have things we do not wish others to know, *n'est pas*? Some things require a level of trust. Some things are better left unsaid."

"Of course! Yes, I completely agree." The reprimand stings, and I excuse myself, unsure of what else to say. In the bathroom mirror, I stare into my eyes and mentally talk myself down. *If this is the only date you ever have with Jo, it has still been a great one. Now go back out there and tell her so.*

Walking back to the table, I study her. She frowns down at her phone, but it doesn't diminish her attractiveness. *If I never get to kiss Jo, or even better, sleep with her, it will be the greatest regret of my life.* Jo's head jerks up and those startling eyes unerringly find me. There's so much heat in them the butterflies in my stomach go crazy and my vulva actually twitches. *Here goes nothing.*

My mouth dry with nerves, I casually sashay, putting a gentle sway in my hips. When I get to the table, I sink down into the chair and cross my legs deliberately. The slit parts just enough before I tuck my legs under the table cloth.

Jo has the most amazing look on her face. Part passion, part pride, part hunter. I shiver, and I know she notices because a deliberate smile crosses her face and one eyebrow curves up.

As we leave the restaurant, her hand is at the small of my back again. I have to focus on walking straight. When we get to the car, Jo leans down as if she's going to whisper in my ear. I tilt my head and turn my ear up to her, but instead, her lips trace the outline of my earlobe and she breathes into my ear. Moaning, I sway.

"I have been waiting for this." She grasps my chin firmly between her thumb and finger. "You will not run away this time, Libby." I feel her husky voice low in my belly. Jo lowers her head, watching me. I build a protest, but she slowly shakes her head and it dies in my throat.

Then her lips are on mine. They're all I imagined they would be. Soft, strong. She slants my head and her tongue traces my lips, teasing them open. She sweeps in, exploring, conquering. Jo pulls my chin down, opening my mouth wider and deepening the kiss. A moan vibrates, but I don't know if it's mine or hers. The second time, I know it's mine. I've never been kissed so thoroughly. I wrap my arms around her neck. I manage to capture her tongue and suck on it. She groans, grabs the back of my head, and takes control again. At some point, my hands wander to her hair. I am breathless; my breasts ache. Who knew a kiss could be foreplay?

I have no idea how much time has gone by when she ends the kiss and cups my face in her hands. "Oh, Libby. If I had known you could kiss like that, I would not have let you put it off for so long." I giggle and she kisses my nose, then rests her forehead against mine. "If we do not stop now, I just may have to take you in the car. And while I have nothing against car sex, that is not how I want to make love to you the first time."

I untangle my hands from the waves in her hair. Jo straightens and drops her hands. A whispered "okay" is all I can manage.

The ride home, Jo possesses my hand as I rest my head against the seat and let Diana Krall's sultry voice roll over me. It's a while before my heart slows. Jo traces patterns on my palm and wrist, and it is driving me crazy. I've had to give myself a stern talking to because a big part of me really, really wanted Jo to take me in this beautiful car. I've never wanted anyone this much. This amazing woman who kissed me senseless, seems to want me just as much as I want her. Truly, I have nothing to complain about. When she pulls into a parking space, she shuts off the car. We both unhook our seatbelts, but neither of us reaches for the door.

She reaches out to tuck a lock of hair behind my ear. "Are you all right, Libby?"

"Better than all right. Thank you for tonight. The dinner was lovely, and afterwards—" I trail off, grateful for the darkness in the car to hide my burning cheeks. "Just thank you for all of it. I've had a beautiful evening."

"You are a refreshing surprise, Libby." I duck my head at the compliment. Jo captures my chin, tilting it back. Her thumb strokes my bottom lip, the possessive action incredibly erotic. My eyes flutter closed before I open them again and meet her gaze. "I could kiss those luscious lips all night, but your fatigue is palpable, *chérie*."

Jo leans in and gives me a gentle kiss. A goodnight kiss. Releasing my chin, she cups my cheek. "May I call you?"

"Of course. Please. I'd like that very much."

Jo reaches for the car door, and, a little sadly, I wait for her to open mine. My keys are in my hand at the front door when I turn to her.

Watching my reaction, she takes the keys from me. Jo unlocks the door and takes a long look inside. Her demeanor reminds me of some kind of police or soldier. Seemingly satisfied, she hands me back my keys.

Jo kisses the back of my hand in an old-world gesture that stutters my heart. "Sleep well, *petite belle*. Thank you for yet another memorable evening." As she releases my hand, she scans the area. Then she waits while I walk inside.

Turning in the doorway, I cup her cheek. "Good night, Jo." Gently, reluctantly, I close the door.

———

I come jarringly awake when my phone starts ringing. Blindly, I grasp around the bedside table for it. I nearly knock the framed photo of Dad and me onto the floor in my haste, but right it just in time. No one calls this early and I have a panicky feeling.

Finally, I get the phone, grimacing as I sit up too quickly. "Hello?"

A warm chuckle. "Good morning, *ma petite belle.*"

"Jo?" *What time is it?* I look at the clock. 6:34. Sheesh.

"I had a desire to know what you sounded like when you wake up." There's a smile in her deep voice.

"You do realize that I haven't had coffee, yet, right?" She laughs again. It's such a sexy sound that I shiver despite my ire. Darcy rubs against my elbow and meows. I brush him away. He comes back and headbutts my back, and I roll my eyes and huff.

"Is everything all right, Libby?" She manages to sound concerned despite her humor.

"I'm glad you are enjoying this." I pause, trying to catch up. "So, hang on, nothing's wrong?"

"Libby, how could anything be wrong when I have the pleasure of hearing your sleepy voice?"

Oh. She is good. I clear my throat. "And you are completely forgiven. Good morning, Jo."

"What do you have planned today, *ma choute*?" I could get used to these endearments as they roll sexily off of her tongue.

I scrunch my eyes and think. "Let's see. I work, then I will probably just hang out here at home. You?"

"That sounds like a much better day than mine. I have meetings all morning at a hospital in Roanoke and am leaving shortly. Then back to Blacksburg for more of the same."

"That doesn't sound like much fun. I'm sorry to hear that."

"It comes with the business." I listen to what sounds like papers shuffling, and then a briefcase clicking closed. "I should let you go, but I do not want to."

"I don't want you to, either." Darcy yowls from the end of my bed and I laugh. "My cat Darcy, however, would very much like me to get off of the phone and feed him."

"*Oui*, I hear!" She's laughing again, then she sighs. "*Ma chérie*, sadly, I must go. Thank you for coming out with me last night. I had a wonderful time."

"Oh, gosh, thank *you*. I will never forget how special you made me feel."

"Once again, I am humbled by your honesty. You have no idea just how special you are, *belle*. I will carry the picture of you in that dress in my mind all day. *Au revoir*."

"Are you kidding? You were mouthwatering in that suit and it will stay with me a long time." My cheeks get hot. *Where did that come from?* Before I can say anything else humiliating, I sign off. "Ah, goodbye Jo." I hang up to more of her laughter.

Unfortunately, the long hot shower doesn't help

my back, and the pain and stiffness slow me down. By the time I've dressed, fed Darcy, and made coffee, I'm rushing out the door. I walk in five minutes late to work, and as luck would have it, my boss Jenny is there. My desk is in shambles by the time she leaves, and I spend way too much time reorganizing. But even this can't ruin my happiness. Under one misplaced stack, I find her latest to-do list. The rest of my shift goes by quickly. I forgot my lunch, and when one o'clock rolls around, the grumblings of my stomach can't be ignored. I leave, despite not getting everything done. No matter what I do today, I can't get my back to loosen up and it hurts more than it has in days.

I've just made a sandwich when there's a knock on my door. I regretfully leave my sandwich on the coffee table. To my surprise, it's the floral delivery driver again. He is holding out the most beautiful bouquet of gerbera daisies. I'm momentarily stunned.

"Boy, somebody sure likes you!"

I wrap my hands around the large globe and hold it close. "Thank you, Harry." The bouquet is heavy and it's a relief to set it down. The pink daisy Jo gave me last night gets moved to the pass-through behind the couch. My hunger forgotten, I carefully pull off the card and read the familiar slanted script.

For last night and for indulging me in waking you up this morning. I look forward to picking up where we left off on the sidewalk. -Jo

Memories of last night flood me, and it's a good thing I'm already sitting down as I suddenly feel weak in the knees. As I eat, I can't stop looking at the flowers. Inspired, I grab my phone and snap a photo, then text it to Emma. Then I thunk myself on the forehead. *I need to thank Jo!* Unfortunately, nothing stellar comes to mind, and I decide to keep it simple and honest.

Beautiful flowers & ur words leave me breathless. Can't wait 2 thank u in person.

A couple hours later I'm wanting dinner, and gingerly rise from the couch. I start for the bedroom to get my cane when my phone rings. I check the ID and smile wide.

"Hi, Jo." I put the smile in my voice.

"How about you thank me tomorrow night?" she starts with no preamble. "Your text came at just the right time, and I only made it through the end of a frustrating day by imagining you breathless." Her sultry voice gives me shivers.

"Oh, yeah?" Darcy winds around my feet and I stumble, gasping audibly. *Move over sex goddess, I'm here now.*

"Libby, what is wrong?"

I rub my back. "Oh, it's fine, I lost my balance, that's all. I'm okay, really." I kick myself for letting Jo hear it in my voice. I'm afraid of scaring her off.

"How may I help?"

"Just talk to me. That would be a big help."

She makes me laugh talking about her day. Sounds as though a lot of people suck up to her and she isn't very appreciative of that. "Unfortunately, I am between meetings and now must go. Thoughts of seeing you tomorrow will sustain me."

How can I turn her down? There's no way I'm missing out on a date with Jo. "I can't think of anything I'd rather do."

Her deep voice resonates satisfaction. "May I pick

you up at 5:30? After dinner, I would like to take you to back to HoneyBears."

"5:30 is perfect. I'm looking forward to seeing you." Excitement bubbles up at the idea of being with her again.

"Until tomorrow, *ma belle* Libby." And with that, she hangs up.

The last time I went to HoneyBears I was very much NOT dressed in club attire. I want to amend that. I decide against jeans, but that's as far as I get. I hurt too much to focus. Waiting for the oven to pre-heat, my phone pings. I lean against the counter and shift from foot to foot as I read Emma's reply:

Gorgeous! Do I need 2 guess who sent ur fav flowers?!

3 guesses

Um, Jo, Jo, Jo LOL

Gosh, how did you guess?!

What can I say? I'm good.

That's what David says...

gasp I nevr

calling fire dept for ur pants

Ya ya. Brunch Sun?

Yes!

Finally, the oven beeps, and I set a cheap, frozen pot pie on the rack. Bending over sends pains down my leg and I quickly straighten. As often happens at night, I'm feeling worse. Looking through the opening, I realize my blinds are still open. Feeling exposed, I hobble to the window. As I reach for the rod to turn the picture window blinds, I make out the silhouette of a man under the tree. Though it's impossible to tell from here, it *feels* as if he's staring right at me. A fissure of fear runs through me.

But then, he seems to melt into the night, and I write the whole thing off as a trick of my pain-addled imagination.

7

INEXPLICABLY THIRSTY

I get to work on time, but Jenny isn't there to notice. Figures. Jo texted me a simple "good morning and see you tonight" kind of thing instead of calling. The pain gets bad, and the sensation of bugs crawling over my legs is driving me to distraction. I'm so worried about getting through our date tonight. When 1 pm rolls around, I can't leave fast enough.

As soon as I arrive home, I crawl into bed. I'm hoping I can find a position which will make my back, well, frankly, all better. I finally find a good position and fall asleep. I wake up groggy and disheveled, but thankfully, the pain is better.

I stay under the hot water for as long as I can stand. Mascara is all I can manage tonight, and I hope Jo won't be disappointed. I part my hair and do a Dutch braid on each side. After much deliberation, I choose a flippy mini-skirt I rediscovered when I went through my closet and a shimmery tank. The top is glittery and the low cut shows off deep cleavage. Strappy sandals and swingy earrings complete the look.

I'm increasingly nervous. I never even leave the

house when I hurt like this, and I've certainly never been on a date while using a cane. I know she met me this way, but I still worry about what Jo will think. I won't be much fun. I think about texting her to cancel, but I can't bear to not see her.

Jo's knock comes right on time and I push up from the couch with my cane. I don't have to force a genuine smile to see her.

It takes me a minute to decipher why she is looking at me with so much...lust. I literally look down at myself before I remember I'm dressed for the club. "You look edible."

I blush down to my cleavage. *Funny, I was thinking the same thing about you!* She's sexily European in black slacks and coordinated layers in shades of navy.

"Uh, I need my purse."

She takes my elbow. "Will you allow me to save you the steps?"

I have a brief battle with my pride, but Jo hands it to me without a word. She takes the keys from me, a question in her eyes. I nod and step out of the way. Louis waits by the black SUV. I give him a little wave before I concentrate on getting to him. In a moment, Jo is beside me, keeping my embarrassingly halting pace.

Jo keeps the conversation light. She is clearly concerned. This isn't a level of pain I can hide and I squirm uncomfortably. Louis drops us at the door of a local Italian restaurant. I hobble in with Jo at my side and we are immediately seated. When the hostess leaves, I don't even bother sitting. I ask Jo to order me an unsweetened iced tea, and make my way to the restroom. There, I gather my courage to ask Jo to take me back home after dinner. The idea brings tears to my eyes, and I dab carefully at them to prevent ruining my mascara. I envision Jo going to the club without me and meeting someone...healthier. Hard as it is, I just can't fathom going anywhere the way I feel right now.

When I get to the table, our drinks are there. After I sink stiffly into the seat, my mouth suddenly feels dry with nerves and I take a sip of tea. A look across the table doesn't help me decipher her expression, but just having her so close shakes my resolve. *Please don't decide I'm not worth dating when I cancel tonight.* But I have to take care of myself. After a bolstering breath I start. "Jo, I'm afraid I need to ask—"

"I know you are *thirsty.* Are you hungry, Libby? I certainly am." She picks up her drink and sips, looking at me over the rim of the glass. Even in my state, I get the message that she means more than one hunger.

I grab my glass and chug. I don't know why I'm so thirsty. "I don't need to look at the menu. I know what I want." I hope I've left the mad out of my voice, but I'm miffed at her for interrupting me. This is hard enough.

"I know exactly what I want, too." I can't help the grin her double entendre brings to my face. Jo signals the waiter. For better or worse, she seems oblivious to my upset.

We both place our orders and I've lost my nerve. I don't know how but somehow, I will tough it out through the night. Still feeling inexplicably thirsty, I drain my tea. "So how was your day, Jo? Full of meetings, again?" To my amazement, I realize my back actually feels...better.

She's been watching me intently, and now her face relaxes into a smile. "The anticipation of getting to see you tonight made my day wonderful, thank you. Yes, I had a number of meetings, but this is to be expected. When the owner returns, particularly when both of them do, everyone wants to ensure they are noticed. As you may have guessed, I am the J of JN Conglomerates, and the N is Niall. You will officially meet him tonight at HoneyBears. He is the CFO, I am CEO. The employees all want to try to prove their value. But it is the ones who prefer not to be noticed to whom we give the most attention. They tend to have something to hide. Typically, we share travel, but Niall and I are both in this area because the financial department has been throwing up red flags. As you can imagine, that is the department with the most individuals trying to hide. We finally sat down with the project manager and division financial officer today. It was most illuminating." That predatory gleam is back in her eyes, and I feel a moment's pity for those folks. I have an ominous feeling that crossing Jo would be a mistake no one would make twice.

Still lessening pain is improving my whole outlook and focus. Those creepy sensations have stopped, and I feel lighter, more energetic. "I'm glad you are getting so much done. I'm sure that gives you a feeling of accomplishment. Um, where else do you operate?"

"My home base is here. Niall's home is London. But we both travel quite a bit and have properties all over to make managing our businesses more convenient."

Wow. Okay. I can't fathom an exciting life like that. I'd love to be able to travel. But her home base being here makes me extremely happy.

The waiter comes with a fresh glass of tea, which surprises me until I see that mine is empty. *I've really been out of it.* I brace myself for pain as I shift in the chair, but the pain doesn't come. I move again. I laugh out loud. No pain!

"*Mademoiselle* Weaver, if you continue to wiggle in that outfit, I just may have to pick you up and carry you somewhere private."

I feel the heat in her gaze low in my belly. I swallow. Hard. My imagination takes off and I contemplate what it would be like to for her to carry me off and...*Oh. My.* I tuck a few stray hairs.

Just then the food comes and I'm so grateful for the distraction I could kiss the waiter. I dig into my chicken and spinach calzone, and thankfully, Jo seems to occupy herself with her stromboli.

I watch her mouth and have to blink myself back. "So what do you like to do for fun?"

"I confess I do not take much time for fun. I like to be in nature. Spar with my friends. You, *belle*?"

"Mmm, same here. I love to be outside. I used to run all the time and I miss it." After a moment, I shrug off the wistful feeling. "I love reading, crafts. But I'd have to say my favorite pastime is baking."

Jo points her fork at me. "*Boulangère*, interesting. I've never dated a baker. Tell me about your baking."

"Well, I make everything from scratch. I bake my own bread. My snickerdoodle muffins are legendary."

"Is that so? A sexy woman with age-old talents."

Jo sounds impressed, and it gives me a little thrill that she called me sexy. "Where did you learn?"

I laugh. "Oh, I learned from the best: Mama Food Network and Grandma YouTube, with a little of Aunts Betty Crocker and Irma S. Rombauer thrown in."

"You joke."

"'Fraid not. My mom couldn't crack an egg if it came out of its own shell, and box mixes are all Dad can manage. I wanted better, so I taught myself."

Jo slowly shakes her head. "Not many people surprise me anymore."

I duck my head and smooth loose hairs behind my ear. "Oh, I'm nothing special."

"Let me be the judge of that."

I just smile and refocus on my delicious food.

Her eyes sparkle. "I am glad to see you enjoying your meal. You make it look so good, I would love a bite, if you do not mind."

I push my plate to her. "Of course! Help yourself."

"How about you cut what you think would be a good sample and I will try that."

"Okey dokey." Guileless, I pull the plate back. I cut a decent bite making sure to get a piece of chicken and spear it carefully.

As I pass the fork backwards to her, Jo wraps her long fingers around mine and turns the fork. She holds my gaze until the fork hovers in front of her mouth. My heart stutters when her eyes half close, she closes her firm lips over the mouthful, and moans.

Ho. Ly. Can. No. Li. The simple act is so erotic, I'm momentarily stunned. I make a strangled sound and break eye contact with her. I have to. If I don't, I may just explode. I jerk back my hand and drop the fork noisily. I blindly grab my glass and gulp several long swallows. I tuck hair behind my ear as if it's all falling out.

Jo chuckles like the cat that ate the canary. "I agree, Libby. That is absolutely delicious. Any chance I can get another bite?"

"No!" I say, panicked. My vehemence stains my cheeks, and Jo laughs harder.

"Or would you rather have a taste of mine?"

I can't even look at her. "I'm fine, thanks." But I can't stop it. My mind starts playing out both of us naked and feeding each other. I shake my head to clear the image and Jo chuckles wickedly.

"Do not worry, Libby. I will not rush you." I meet her eyes. She's more serious, though there is still a teasing glint. "Much."

I can't help but laugh at her addition. "Oh, well, thanks, I think." I couldn't possibly have any more to eat now. The sexual play gives me a thrill. I feel powerful again that Jo wants me and is...kind of willing to wait for me to catch up. "You seem to like getting me off balance."

"And you seem to like staying in control." She has one eyebrow cocked in challenge.

Yeah. She has me there.

"It is a joy watching you lose the battle." Jo leans forward and rests her forearms on the table. She holds my gaze. "Make no mistake. I will see you completely lose control, Libby."

"You really do like a challenge, then, don't you?" I feel a bit brave, apparently.

Jo straightens her spine and shrugs nonchalantly,

though humor dances in her green eyes. "Consider yourself forewarned, Libby."

Well.

We linger, alternating between learning about each other and teasing. Sexual tension charges the air. When the bill comes, Jo sends a text. She carries my cane since I no longer seem to need it. Louis is smiling beside the idling SUV as we walk out.

Once in the SUV, we reach for each other. She cups the back of my head and kisses me stupid. I stroke her face. Her skin is cool and smooth under my fingers. As the car speeds onto the highway, Jo ends the kiss and I lean back against the seat, trying to catch my breath and calm my body. We talk quietly, Jo trailing those long fingers along the tender flesh on the underside of my arm, inside my elbow, stirring me up once more. I feel it everywhere. It's almost a relief when we pull into the parking lot of the club. Almost.

The cane is at my feet and I nearly grab for it, but decide against it. I really am feeling amazingly better, though I've had the occasional twinge on the ride over. When Louis opens my door, Jo takes my hand and helps me out. She keeps my hand all the way in, past the bouncer.

Jo points out Niall and makes a beeline for the table. As before, he looks gorgeous and pale and dangerous. I stifle a groan. *Okay, behave. Don't be rude... unless he is.*

Jo barks a startled laugh and drops a quick peck on my forehead before continuing to the table, shaking her head and chuckling. I don't have any idea what that was about, but the kiss was sweet, and I'm not complaining.

"Libby, allow me to formally introduce you to my

oldest friend and business partner, Niall. Niall, this is Libby." Jo drops my hand to slide her arm possessively around my lower back. Niall's gaze is so intense, it's all I can do to put my hand out. *Why do you dislike me so much?* After a beat, Niall takes it.

His hand is cold, sinewy, and strong, and he takes mine firmly enough that I know I can't pull mine away. "Don't worry, luv, I won't bite...now," he quips in a thick British accent. With a wicked grin, he lifts my hand and kisses the back as smoothly and casually as Jo has done. Niall continues to stare at me after he releases my hand, as though I am a puzzle he must solve. *Lighten up, man. I'm not after her money or anything.* Finally, he looks up at Jo. She squeezes me gently and kisses the top of my head, and I relax. I get the feeling Jo's pleased with us for some reason.

"I will get you a drink." Jo's words against my ear make me shiver, and her eyes sparkle.

Despite the early hour, the music is good. I'm steadfastly ignoring Niall, which is difficult. He's quite an imposing figure. Tall, blond, and devilishly handsome. My inner sense tells me he's a quintessential bad boy. Add that accent, and I can just bet he's got a trail of broken hearts behind him. Something about his stillness and intensity reminds me of something I saw recently, but I just can't pull it out of my memory. At least Niall isn't staring at *me* anymore.

While there are some very fine-looking women, none here compare to Jo. I check out the different outfits, and while mine isn't the height of club fashion, I'm relieved to see that I'm holding my own. *At least you won't be an embarrassment to Jo this time.* Niall turns to pick up his drink and salutes me with the glass. I smile at him hesitantly. *Okay, I don't know what that was for, but I'll take it. Maybe it's going to be okay between us after all.*

I try a little chair dancing as I let the beat wash over me. Sure enough, my back lets me know it's a bad idea. *Crap. I should have brought the cane.*

Just then, Jo sets the sodas on the table. She pushes one towards me. "I am sorry your back is hurting again, Libby. Here, *drink* this."

I guess I'm not very good at hiding my pain. "Thank you." I'm not the least bit thirsty, but I obediently take a big drink. Niall watches me, shoots Jo a sharp look, and shakes his head, but says nothing. It feels as if I'm missing something, but I can't figure it out and don't know how to ask. The moment passes and taking another swig, I turn wistfully to the dance floor.

"What is your flavor tonight?" Jo studies Niall with humor.

He takes a minute to peruse the dance floor. "I'm feeling like rainbow sherbet tonight."

"Again? It is not like you to have the same flavor twice in a row."

"Aye, you know I like variety, but this one is particularly tasty." Niall licks his lips and Jo laughs. I'm pretty sure they aren't talking about ice cream.

"Are you eating in or taking it to go?"

"Considering the sodding bathrooms here, you can believe I'll be taking it to go."

Yup, I thought that's what they were talking about. *I wonder what constitutes rainbow sherbet?*

Jo yanks on a braid to get my attention, interrupting my thoughts. Standing by my stool, when I turn, she captures my mouth.

I dimly hear Niall. "And that's me off to find me own birdie to snog."

Jo toys with my lips, before forcing them apart. A moan escapes me. She lightly drags her hand along my exposed thighs. Goosebumps raise all over my body and I strain towards her. Jo slants her head and deepens the kiss. I clutch her shoulders. She kisses me with expert attention and I can't believe how much just this affects me.

I try to pull back, but Jo draws me closer, pressing my breasts against her chest. Jo intensifies the kiss, and I can't help but eagerly match her movement. All too soon, Jo eases back. She rests her forehead against mine and we both just breathe for a minute. Now I really feel thirsty, and when she takes a step back, I drain my glass.

Jo, sipping her drink, studies me. Then she seems to come to a decision. "Dance with me." She holds out her hand.

I hesitate, worried about making my back hurt again. But I so want to dance, and I find it hard to deny Jo anything. She raises her eyebrow expectantly and I take her hand. At first, I'm tentative, making small movements. Then the lights, the beat—Janelle Monáe's "Make Me Feel" comes on, and I lose my inhibitions. Jo matches me beat for beat, move for move, our bodies in perfect sync. It's so erotic, I lose all concern about my back. For a while, I'm my old self.

The night continues like that. Kissing, dancing, me falling for her. In the back of my mind, I worry about how deep my feelings have become in such a short time. I barely know her. Niall rejoins us periodically, and the three of us shout small talk, mostly about the music and characters we point out to one another. Their easy banter makes me laugh. As the evening progresses, I feel more comfortable around Niall. He seems somewhat more accepting of me. I'm grateful not to be at odds with such a good friend of Jo's. I've noticed him dancing with the same man several times, who is flamboyant in pink leather pants and has a beautiful boyish face. Rainbow sherbet.

When my yawns nearly take over my face, Jo signals Niall and leads me out. I'm sad for yet another magical night to end. Louis is waiting for us at the curb and I'm reminded of the last time she walked me out of HoneyBears. I'm so grateful we're leaving together this time.

When we get to my apartment, she walks me to the door. I turn towards the parking lot and remember the man standing under the tree. Though I shiver, I remind myself that it was just my eyes playing tricks on me. A worried look comes over Jo's face and she scans the area. I wonder what's bothering her. Instinctively, I shift closer to her. Finally relaxing, she wraps her arm around me, and I lose myself in her eyes.

"Thank you for tonight. I had the best time."

"The pleasure was mine, *belle*. *You* are a wonderful dancer." She grins and waggles her eyebrows.

"Oh, no, *you* are an amazing dancer, Jo. Tonight was..." I don't know how to finish the thought.

"*Oui*. It most certainly was." Jo leans in and I meet her halfway. She gathers my braids and gently tugs my head back. Her lips move against mine. "I cannot get enough of you, *ma chérie*. I find the more time I spend with you, the more I want."

I couldn't agree more.

With that her mouth slants across mine and urges my lips apart. She plunders my mouth, her tongue tangling with mine, leaving me breathless and dripping with my own want. My breasts tingle. She ends the kiss, releasing my braids, and holds me while our breaths even out, her heartbeat slow and steady against my cheek.

How it can be so calm when mine races? She kisses the top of my head.

"Sleep well, *mon coeur*. I will be in touch in the morning. I want to spend the day with you, if I may."

"Oh, I would love that. Um, you sleep well, too, Jo. Thank you, again." I rummage in my bag for my keys.

She gently nudges me aside. "Please, indulge me."

I don't see any harm in it. I hand them over.

Jo unlocks the door, steps in, and looks around for a long minute. Seemingly satisfied, she hands me my keys, kisses my hand, and steps back out. I'd swear she was a cop or something if I didn't know better. "*Bonne nuit, ma petite belle.*"

She is still standing there as I utter my own "good night" and close the door. I lean against it, wishing she had asked to come in or I had invited her in. But I don't want a relationship built on sex. And I really like Jo. I mean, more than just her body. Though what a body. And those eyes. And lips. And hands.

Oh...I have to stop. Shaking my head at myself, I step away from the door. I queue up Troye Sivan's "Heaven", the lyrics echoing how conflicted I'm feeling and my fear. I put it on repeat and crawl into bed.

8

BUT I'M AN ODDBALL

I wake, the pain intense. I try different positions, my sleep fitful. When I can't stand it any longer, I drag myself out of bed. It feels as though hot knives are stuck in my lower spine, sending endless searing pain down my legs. I just wanted to be normal for a while, but I constantly berate myself for dancing. I pace my small apartment, tears leaking as I try to stretch it out.

I get busy to take my mind off of it. I clean Darcy's litter box. I vacuum. When it all just seems to make it worse, I give in, my cheeks stiff with salt. I get out the prescription bottle I only open on rare occasions. I choke down two chalky pills with water. They work fast on an empty stomach, and as I lay down, I'm relieved to feel the pain begin to ebb. I sink heavily into darkness.

———

"Libby. Libby, *belle*, wake now. Libby!" Someone is shaking me and I don't like it, but I can't seem to make my mouth or eyes work.

"*Merde!* How much of this did you take? You must wake, Libby. *Drink. C'est bon,* Libby. *Oui, oui, ma belle, drink deeply.* Good. Now you can sit up, *oui?*"

The cool liquid loosens my mouth and I obediently drink. My groggy brain recognizes her voice. "Jo?" I struggle but all I can manage is a slumped sitting position. The edge of the mattress sinks under her, making it harder to sit up straight. My eyes will barely open and the harsh light makes me blink. I'm terribly confused. "What are you...how did you get in here?" I shake my head to clear the fog, but have to grab her arm when my room lists sharply.

"*Oui,* I am here, *mon coeur.* Finish this, *s'il vous plait.* Good, good. Now you are coming around." She studies me critically. "You had me very worried."

"Why? What's going on? What are you doing here?" My eyes fall on the prescription bottle, and it all comes back to me. "Oh, crap. I forgot how hard they hit me. I couldn't sleep. No matter what I did, it got worse, and I...I knew better than to dance last night." My mouth feels cottony, and I lift the glass and drain it. "Maybe I shouldn't have taken two, but I was desperate."

Jo strokes my hair, her face sorrowful. "It weighs on me that you suffered. I wish you had let me know."

I turn my head into her hand, and she cups my face. "It's not like you could do anything to stop my pain." I've almost fallen back asleep when it hits me again and I startle, struggling to get up. She drops her hand. "Seriously, how did you get in here?"

Jo smiles ruefully, gently pressing my shoulders back. Too tired to fight, I settle back against her. "You let me in. Just in time, too. Your neighbor was about to call the police. But then, I *was* preparing to break down the door. Afterwards, you curled up on the floor and fell asleep. Do you remember Niall?"

"No. Is he here?" When she shakes her head, I blow out a breath. "Wow. Okay. That's pretty scary. I just let you guys in and don't even remember it." I shudder, considering what could have happened.

"*Oui*, it is scary. Particularly when you come to the door dressed as a vixen."

I suddenly realize what I have on. Feeling sexy from our date, I dressed in my silky night dress. I look down and color to see my right breast is all but out of it. I quickly adjust the strap and yank up the sheet self-consciously, even if it's a little late for modesty.

Jo chuckles. "Such a shame to take away tempting treats before they have been sampled." She lays her hand on my head again and slides it down to my cheek. "I started texting you at 7:30. Then I called. I had been pounding on the door for nearly 45 minutes before you opened." She drops her hand to my shoulder and her voice deepens. "I thought something had happened to you. I confess I was beside myself."

I don't know what to say to that. I didn't do anything wrong. But I flash on my mom passed out on the couch, little me trying to wake her, terrified she was dead. I feel awful to make someone else feel even a fraction of that helplessness. "I hate that you were so worried. I'm really touched that you care so much."

She strokes her hand down my bare arm and drops it to her side. "Believe that I do, *belle*, I do. Tell me, do you have a habit of leaving the vacuum plugged in, and in the middle of the room? You nearly fell over it when I was following you back here."

I groan, though I appreciate she is trying to

lighten the mood. "No, I don't. Hey, at least I didn't leave it running! That really would have been something." I pick at the comforter. "Geez, Jo, that isn't like me. I'm lucky nothing happened."

"And nothing did happen, so. We have a day to spend together, and if we stay in your bedroom, I cannot be responsible for my actions."

With a squeal, I shimmy out of bed and dash to the shower. The dregs of sedation give way to feeling energized, and I am amazed how much my back has improved. I guess the pills did their job.

I throw on a pair of shorts and a T-shirt and quickly comb out my hair before I start coffee and join Jo on the couch. A glass of tea waits on a coaster for me and I laugh. *Jo sure is solicitous about keeping me hydrated.* She's texting, and that reminds me that I haven't checked my own phone since last night.

I retrieve my cell and turn it on. Darcy winds around my legs and I squat to give him some love, then walk into the kitchen to feed him and pour my coffee. My phone blows up with notifications. Most are from Jo and I guiltily read her texts. I'll listen to the voicemails from her later. There is also a text from Dad.

Wandering back to the couch, I promise Dad I'll call later. As I put the phone down on the coffee table, I turn to find Jo looking at me. I smile and lean back into the cushion. "Hi, you."

She smiles, too. "Hello, you."

"Thanks for being my hero again."

"Thank you for letting me save the day again."

Darcy jumps onto the couch and stalks across me to settle in between us. He stares at Jo for a minute, then turns his back on her and starts cleaning himself.

One look at each other and we both burst out laughing.

Idly, I finger comb my damp hair. "What would you like to do today?"

Jo tears her eyes away from my chest. Belatedly, I think about how my posture must be making my breasts jut out, and I self-consciously drop my arms. My cheeks color and I fight the urge to cross them over my chest. Jo watches me closely, but doesn't comment.

"Given the night you have had, *chérie*, I think a restful day would be best. Do you not agree?"

Thanks to the pills, I actually feel pretty darn good right now, but unfortunately, I know not to push it. "I guess you're right. Thank you for being so thoughtful. Would you like to watch something on TV? Or talk?"

"How about we talk for a while?" Jo reaches for my hand and Darcy leaps to the coffee table. I scoot a little closer to Jo.

I turn her hand over in mine and study her palm as I trace the lines. "How about you tell me about JN Conglomerates. The name implies you have more than one venture."

Watching me play with her hand, Jo takes her time replying. "*Oui*, JN has more than one focus. In addition to blood banks, we have research units in Europe. England and Germany, to be precise."

"What sort of research?"

"We study blood disorders, naturally. The Germany lab focuses solely on the creation of a viable synthetic blood." She pauses, flexing her hand in mine. I turn it over and begin to trace slow patterns around her knuckles and up and down her long slender fingers, reveling in the smooth cool texture.

I want to know every inch of her.

Jo hasn't said anything else and I look up at her questioningly. When I see the expression on her face, "oh" is all I can think to say. I stop my exploration, pat her hand, and sandwich it between mine. Her eyes have that look I'm learning, tells me I'm having an effect on her libido. I try to look innocent, but am pretty sure I only manage smug. "Sorry, what were you saying?"

She gives me a warning glare, but I just continue to smile at her. Finally, she shakes her head. I'm not sure if I'm exactly relieved. "I was going to add that Niall and I split the travel, though I am pleased this trip required both of us. He is family to me."

"My friend Emma is like that for me. The sister I never had. We've been tight since middle school." She turns her hand and captures mine, tugging me closer. I wiggle over next to her and she releases my hand and puts her arm around my shoulders. I relax against her. "What you do is such a valuable service. I'm always hearing about blood shortages following natural disasters, and synthetic blood would fulfill that need."

"*Oui*, from the OR to the battlefield, and a few places in between. At least, this is the great expectation. We are putting a lot of money and hope into synthesizing an exact replica. It seems we come closer all the time. But enough of this. Tell me more about what you do."

"Well, nothing so important or interesting as what you do, certainly. Let me think." I try to think of an example of my work that isn't shuffling papers and answering email. "Jenny has an out-of-towner who is looking for a not-quite dilapidated cabin in the mountains he can use for a getaway hunting lodge. If we find it, his brother and uncle will buy similar places nearby. My job is to locate three old cabins not too far from one another, and research what my boss needs to do to get them sold."

"That sounds like a lot of computer work."

"It's nothing I mind. I enjoy research. And I already found one possibility up in Pulaski County, so I'll get to drive into the Appalachians. It's been a while. I'm excited to explore again."

"How will you get there?"

That's an odd question. "What do you mean? I have a car."

Jo's look is incredulous. "Surely that dilapidated... vehicle...cannot handle mountain roads?"

"Oh, it's in better shape than it looks." I squirm out from her embrace. *Do you think I'd drive that rusted hunk of metal ANYWHERE if I had a choice?!* It brings back to me how different we are. Perched on the edge of the couch, I start babbling, tugging my hair onto one side and playing with the ends. "You'd be surprised how good those old Toyotas are. They just go and go. Real tough cars. Not like they make them today." I jump up and change topics abruptly. "I'm hungry. I guess I slept through breakfast. Are you ready for lunch?"

"Libby, I meant no disrespect." Standing, she turns me to face her.

Pursing my lips, I lift my chin. "This is who I am, Jo. I drive a crappy car because it's what I can afford. I shop in thrift stores. I have a chronic illness."

Jo's smile is pained. "*Pardonez moi.* I was insensitive and have hurt you. Please believe it was spoken out of a sense of concern." She strokes my hair. "Libby, who you are is kind. You are sexy and beautiful, smart and funny. You have immense inner strength. You are loyal. What do I care how much money you do or do not have?" She taps an index finger on the center of my chest. "This is what I care about, *chérie*. And you do not fall short."

I'm touched speechless. *We barely know each other, how can she see me?* My embarrassment forgotten, I step into her arms, tucking my cheek against her chest. It feels so right in her strong arms. I stand on tiptoe and kiss her. "How can I deny you forgiveness after a speech like that?" *How can I deny you anything?* "For real, I'm hungry. Can I make you a sandwich?" I'm sure she eats much better than what I can offer, but my father raised me to be a good hostess. Besides, I'm curious to see just how willing she is to be on my level.

Jo grins at me. "Lead on. I love a good sandwich."

I get out all the makings I have left for sandwiches, including a loaf of my own bread. Grabbing a bread knife from the drawer, I turn to Jo.

"This rivals a deli!"

Sheepishly, I look at the spread sliding across the counter. Jo saves a packet of cheese from hitting the floor. "Yeah, I guess I eat a lot of sandwiches." Echoing my father, I clap my hands. "Right. I'll slice the bread while you decide what you want on it." I concentrate on slicing four uniform pieces. I don't stop slicing, but I feel her stare. "What's wrong?"

"Is this your own bread you are sharing with me, *chérie*?"

"Yeah. It's a crusty loaf, but the inside is nice and

soft for sandwiches. If the crust is too hard for you, just cut it off." I trim an uneven piece off and hand it to her. I hold my breath as she puts it into her mouth. It's been a long time since anyone new has sampled my baking. Seeing her eyes close in silent appreciation, I grin, then turn back to my task. "I have another loaf in the freezer with a softer crust if you'd prefer that." I risk a glance back at her and she shakes her head. I finish slicing and gather the four pieces up carefully, but pause, trying to figure out the look on her face. Exasperated? "What?"

"You always bake your own sandwich bread?"

"Well, yeah. I have time to, so why not? I told you I love to bake."

"Yes, but..." she trails off, sounding frustrated, and I don't understand. She starts again. "You really have no idea how special you are, do you?"

I roll my eyes. "Keep that up and I'll get a big head. Just make your sandwich already." I place two slices on her plate and focus on making my own sandwich. "You can toast it if you'd like, get the cheese melty." I point to the toaster oven.

"No, thank you. I would like it just the way it is. I want to eat your *pain* soft, as it is intended."

Her native word brings a smile to my face as I carry my plate to the coffee table. Wordlessly, we get down to the business of eating. When we finish, I gather the plates and take them to the kitchen. Jo refills my glass and takes it with her while I grab a handful of lace cookies from the freezer. Since they only need a minute to thaw, I plate them up, then carry them to the living room. My tea is swirling when I walk in, I guess from the movement of carrying it. I shrug it off and take a drink.

Jo picks up one of the delicate cookies. "Need I even ask if this is one of your own creations?"

I laugh. "No." I watch a little nervously as she takes a bite. I'm sure Jo has had better, but I hope she likes it.

"Libby, this rivals the *patisseries* of Paris! If you had not told me, I would never guess you are self-taught. *C'est délicieux!*"

"Oh, please." Still, I go pink with pleasure.

"I wonder what other talents you hide under this modesty."

My blush deepens. Jo smiles wolfishly and leans toward me. My arms go around her neck as we kiss. At some point, we shift so that Jo has me pressed against the cushions on the back of the couch. Her hands cup my face and mine caress her back. When we are both breathless, her mouth begins to wander. She nips at my chin, then leaves a burning trail along my jaw to my ear. I shudder as her breath puffs into my ear and her lips track along the rim. She sucks my earlobe, and I shudder again and groan loudly.

My hands rove the strong planes of her back and I whisper her name. Jo's tongue trails from my ear to my neck, and her lips close on the sensitive skin over my pounding pulse. Her teeth graze my neck and she nips gently as I strain towards her. One hand slides from my face, down to my shoulder, and further down to cup my breast through the layers of T-shirt and bra. I press myself into her and moan. I squirm and my panties slicken. Jo's nostrils flare and she claims my mouth again. I'm quivering and panting and wanting, wanting, wanting. *But is it too soon?* As if Jo's thoughts echo mine, she drops her forehead onto my shoulder and her hand slips from my breast up to grip my other shoulder.

"Libby, Libby, Libby. What am I going to do with you?" I don't think I'm meant to answer, so I don't. She leans away from me after planting a sweet kiss on my nose and pulls me against her. I rest my head against her chest, and she holds me while we both calm down.

I excuse myself to splash my face with cool water. Looking myself in the eyes in the bathroom mirror, I take a deep breath and let it out slowly, then do it again. *Okay, then.*

When I pad back into the living room, Jo is on her phone. I can only tell that there is a serious male voice on the other end, but nothing as clear as a word. It occurs to me that she is probably in high demand. A fresh appreciation for the fact that she rarely has her phone out when she's with me sweeps through me. To give her at least the illusion of privacy while she is on the phone, I take the empty plate, grinning because she ate all the cookies. I wash the few dishes in the sink and start another pitcher of tea. As I work, I hear Jo's voice from time to time, but I don't pay attention to her words. When I'm finishing up, strong arms wrap around my stomach.

"Hi, there." I lean into her. She props her chin on my head and we stand this way for a minute, my arms on hers. "Jo, I appreciate that you are a busy woman, and it means a lot to me that you put your phone down when we are together."

"I never see you on your phone, either."

"Yes, but I'm an oddball. I'm just saying I recognize that you may need to be more available to people."

Jo turns me in her arm, her head shaking. "You really are a remarkable woman, *belle* Libby. I do not know what moon or star or god shined down on me for us to meet, but I want to worship it."

Talk about romantic. I reach up on my tiptoes to kiss her. "If you need to work, I can occupy myself. Or we can watch TV or a movie or something."

"Actually, I do need to spend a little time on the phone. About 45 minutes should do it. Do you promise that you do not mind?"

I trace an X over my heart. "Promise."

I walk to the bedroom to the sound of her chuckles, and call Dad. After we catch up, I put in earbuds. I have truly eclectic tastes in music, and I blast Queen as I remove polish from my fingers and toes. I'm shocked at my body's flexibility after the hell of last night, but I don't look the gift horse in the mouth. I hum along with the music as I brush on the first coat of a color that makes me think of strawberries. It looks good on my longish nails and I admire them, especially the deeper color after a second layer.

I'm propped up against the head of my bed waiting for my nails to dry. Carrie Underwood's "Heartbeat" starts, and I sing along in my mind, picturing Jo and I slow-dancing in a soft summer rain. Something tells me to open my eyes. Jo fills the doorway, a typically inscrutable expression on her face, and I yank the earbuds out of my ears. "Done?"

Rather than saying anything, Jo turns around and walks away. Anxiety builds as I hurry into the living room, wondering what I did wrong. Jo is back on the couch, her phone out of sight. I stand there insecure, waiting for her to say something. Anything.

Finally, Jo speaks. "I walked back there to tell you

I was free but when I saw you—on your bed—you made such a pretty picture, moving your body and singing softly. I had to turn around or I was going to have to have you right then and there."

"Oh." *Was I singing out loud?*

"Libby, come, sit. I just needed to collect myself." She turns to me. "You have no idea the effect you have on me, *chérie*. But you are safe." She pats the cushion beside her.

I sink onto the couch and sip my tea, gathering my thoughts. Her confession sent me spinning and I want to be sure before I say anything. I shift sideways, our knees touching. "Jo, thank you for being patient with me. I want you. So badly, I can hardly breathe sometimes." I put my hands over my heart, then drop them. "But I want more than sex. I've been down that road and am not interested in it anymore. I mean, I'm interested in sex, but—" I stop and close my eyes. When I open them, humor sparkles in her eyes. "You have already come to mean a lot to me. But I need to be sure about what I'm feeling. I need to be able to trust and that takes time. I'll commit to communicating with you, if you can, too. Is that okay with you? Are you willing to try a relationship? Because that's what I'm talking about."

Jo leans forward and takes my hands. I study her face, but I'm relieved when she confirms what I think I see there. "You could not have said anything that would make me think more of you or make me happier. *Oui, chérie*. I will wait. *Oui*, I find I can be satisfied with nothing less than a relationship with you, *belle*."

I grin at her like an idiot.

Leaning against her with her arms around me, we

watch *Downton Abbey* for a while. At one point, Jo releases me to take a drink from her glass. She looks at me, nods her head at my glass. I sigh dramatically, which makes her laugh, but grab it anyway.

We opt to order dinner in. We debate briefly and decide on Chinese. She has a place in mind, and when she shows me the menu on her cell, I swallow hard at the prices, then give her my order.

9

MAGIC KOOL AID

*W*e continue learning about one another while we eat. I lean back, too sated and happy to bother with cleaning up yet.

Jo turns to me and I face her. She is studying me again which makes me a little nervous. "Libby, you are my girlfriend, *non?*"

I like the sound of that. "Yes, I guess I am."

"Can you accept that I am the kind of woman who wants to care for, to protect, my girlfriend?"

Her wording sets off a faint warning bell. "Ah, yes." I pause, wondering where this is going, weighing the value of honesty versus self-protection. "I appreciate it."

Jo smiles and squeezes my hands. Still, I have an ominous feeling and that bell starts clanging. "*Petite amie,* I want to ask you a favor."

"Okay." That doesn't sound bad, necessarily, but something tells me this is going to cost me. I'm waiting for the other shoe to drop.

"Louis is not just a chauffeur. One of his specialties is vehicle mechanics. There is not a car past, present, or future Louis cannot fix. He has stocked all the necessary equipment in my private garage."

"Wow, that's convenient." I'd noticed when we went to get the food that Jo drove a different car today. Something racy and yellow. Her private garage must be well-stocked.

Her grin fades. "The favor I ask of my *petite amie*, my girlfriend, is to allow Louis to look over your car." She holds up a hand, stopping the protest before I can voice it. "And I will not allow *ma petite amie* to pay me for anything." She looks disgusted at the idea, and her steely voice gives no leeway.

The proverbial shoe drops with a resounding thud. My knee-jerk reaction is to refuse. But, and it hurts to admit this, my reaction feels like pride, not common sense. Crap. I'm the first to admit I'm constantly on alert for my car to break down. And it isn't like I can afford to get it fixed. If Jo has the means—which she certainly does—and it is no trouble to her, should I object to her help? Can I afford to? Will it end up costing me in a worse way to be beholden to her?

Gah. This is part of building trust with someone, to take them at their word. Has Jo done anything untrustworthy up to now? Has she manipulated me in any way? I search my memory. *No.*

"Will this interfere with Louis's duty to you?"

Surprise raises her eyebrows. "Absolutely not. His duties will not be affected."

"And will he talk to *me* and tell *me* what's wrong, and what needs to be done?"

"You have my word, *oui*."

"Then I would feel much more comfortable driving it if Louis will look over my car."

Jo's relief is etched all over her face. "Thank you, *chérie*. This makes me feel better about your safety."

"Okay, then, just have him call and we'll set it up." I glance at the front windows and notice it has gotten dark. I rise to close the blinds, but pause. *Is that?* Jo is by my side instantly. As before, the image fades before I really get a hold of it. *It's got to be my imagination.* But Jo stiffens and moves me gently, but firmly away from the window. She closes the blinds and pulls out her phone. Her reaction makes the hair stand up on my neck, but I'm not sure what's going on. While she texts, I wait for her to clue me in.

Jo draws me back to the couch. "You have seen that man before."

So someone really was there. Goosebumps skitter across my skin, but I nod.

"How many times? This is important, *belle*."

"Only one other time. I don't know who it could be. But you know who it is."

"A guess. However, if I am correct..." She pauses, looks indecisive. "If my guess is correct, it would be a very bad thing." Her fingers fly across her phone.

Am I in danger? Is someone watching me? I wrack my brain, trying to think if I've been followed or have seen anyone lurking around. I come up empty. Frankly, Jo and Niall are the most frightening people I have come across, well, ever, but I don't think either of them would harm me. At least, I know Jo won't. *Is this why she's always checking out my place before she lets me in?*

Jo stares at her phone. "My people are looking into it. I do not want you to worry, Libby. I have been concerned that someone would target you to get to me, and now that I know, you will be protected."

I press my hand against my racing heart. "Okay. Okay. Um, what do you mean by that, exactly?"

Jo smiles at me. "I'm proud of how well you are taking this, *chérie*. This is not what I wanted for us, especially this soon. I had hoped to have more time to prepare you."

Okay, *that* doesn't sound ominous. No, not at all. *Prepare me for what?*

"I have enemies, *chérie*. People who would stop at nothing to get to me. I could not have you harmed because of me. It means someone will now be watching over you at all times. But you will not see them or know that they are there. This is what they do—they are the best. They blend, they seek, they eliminate threats."

Yikes. Not sure that makes me feel any safer. *Sounds like special forces.* "So, like, when you go home tonight, someone will be out there, watching? Like a bodyguard?"

"*Exactement.*"

"And when I drive places, someone will follow me?" When Jo nods, I go on. "Will they listen in on my conversations?" *What's happening to my privacy? Will everything I say or do be reported to her?*

"Relax, *ma petite amie*, please. Your privacy will not be invaded. Your detail will maintain a distance. Trust me, *belle*, you will not even know they are there. Come to me."

That doesn't fully put me at ease, but I let Jo tug me in. She shifts us so we are sitting against the back of the couch, and she holds me against her side. I place my hand on her chest and snuggle in. After a minute, I reach for her face and she meets me in a kiss. It is gentle at first, but quickly becomes urgent.

All my fear and need for comfort come out into that kiss and my hand fists in her hair. When we end the kiss, I just snuggle back into her.

"You amaze me with your courage, *ma petite amie*. How are you feeling?"

"Honestly? Scared. Unsure. And my back started hurting a while ago, but I was sufficiently distracted that I didn't care. It isn't too bad. I think it will be okay." *I hope it will be okay.*

Jo leans forward and eases me off of her. She takes my empty glass to the kitchen and returns with it refilled. I try to take it from her, but she doesn't let go. When I look in her eyes, she holds my gaze. "*Drink* it Libby. *All* of it." It's a weird, not wholly pleasant tugging in my head, and somewhat familiar. There's a faint metallic taste under the sweetness of the tea, but that doesn't seem to bother me. I drink the whole glass all at once. Why wouldn't I? When I finish, I hand it back to her. Jo takes it back to the kitchen. When she returns, she sits beside me once again.

"I think it is time that I be going, *chérie*, so that you can sleep. You have a lot to catch up on and you look tired." She captures my gaze again. "*You are very tired, Libby and when I leave, you will sleep a long, restorative, and dreamless sleep.*"

I slump with sudden exhaustion. "I'm more tired than I realized, Jo. I'm sorry."

"Walk me to the door *belle*." Hand in hand, we walk to the door. She kisses me on top of my head. "Please forgive me," she whispers against my hair.

I've locked the door behind her and am halfway to bed when I wonder for what she was apologizing. But the thought can't stay, none do, as I crawl into the sheets fully clothed. I am asleep instantly.

I feed my whining kitty, and then go around opening blinds. I'm braced for someone to be standing there as I turn the rod on the picture window. But no one is lurking outside, and I scoff at myself. I wonder how my new bodyguards fared the night.

I pick out my outfit while the coffee finishes. A swingy short dress in pale blue wins and I pair it with my colorful Naots. I slept hard last night, despite sleeping in my bra and tennis shoes. I shake my head at myself. Man, was I tired. But I feel great this morning.

My steaming mug in hand, I settle in the window seat. I shiver, thinking of someone out there watching me. Meaning me harm. I wonder again where the people protecting me are. I wonder how many there are, if they only work for Jo, where they trained, how good they are at their jobs. A text from Jo disrupts my disturbing thoughts.

Good morning belle. I trust u slept ok?

Good morning good looking. Sure did. U?

Same. Movie later? Miss u already

Hey, that's my line. Movie is great. When? Which?

Matinee, will look at options

Great! Looking forward to it.

I'm her girlfriend. A thrill goes through me. The

next thought sobers me. My car. Does it matter that she can afford it? I could use Sarah's advice. Since we met after my mom started AA, Sarah has been my Al-Anon sponsor, a mother-figure, and my dear friend. Like Emma, I've depended on Sarah to tell me the truth for a long time. And I need to get to an Al-Anon meeting soon, too. With a new relationship, it's important I stay grounded.

I decide to go tomorrow and text Sarah, asking her if she's going. When she tells me she is, I ask if we can meet afterwards for coffee. Happily, she can.

With my bright nails and swingy dress, I feel pretty. I finish up with my usual mascara and thread silver hoops in my ears. Grinning, I make the skirt swish in the mirror. More than satisfied, I head out to meet Emma for brunch.

Emma is in line and we hug. By the time we're done with our mutual admiration, the hostess ushers us to a table.

Smiling, I settle across from my best friend. I put the menu aside. "I don't know why I bother. I always get the same thing. So how are you?"

Emma laughs and puts hers down, too. "Yeah, me too. I'm great, actually! I have so much to tell you!"

"Excellent! I can't wait to hear. And I have lots to tell you, too!"

Just then, the waitress comes with coffee and takes our orders. As she walks away, Emma laughs. "So who first? Should we toss for it?!"

We both laugh and I appreciate her light-heartedness more than ever. "No, you start. I'm dying to hear how you and David are doing."

"We are really hitting it off."

"Well, that's wonderful!"

"After warning David, of course, I took him to my father's shop. And Daddy likes him!" She looks amazed and I totally understand why.

"No way! Really?" She is Daddy's little girl, and in his eyes, no man is good enough for her. Or so I thought.

"Yes, can you believe it? Of course, he doesn't want us to have, well, you know, any fun—" she waggles her eyebrows suggestively "—until, well, probably never!" And she laughs. "But David is such a gentleman. I'm just having the best time with him."

She's looking a little dreamy and I can't resist teasing her about it. "Is that drool?"

"Oh, stop. You know I don't do things like that."

That laughter carries us for a few minutes as we dig into our food.

"I can't wait to meet this guy. He sounds like a keeper."

"Oh, he's so sweet. You'll just love him. He's a good dancer. And he lets me pick what we watch." She laughs and waves her fork. "I'm not stupid, I'm sure he'll tackle me for the remote before long, but it sure is nice now. And he is so attentive. And complimentary." She puts the empty tines of the fork upside down in her mouth and stares blankly over my shoulder.

"Oh, boy. You've got it bad."

"Truth." She shakes herself and cuts off another piece of omelet with the side of her fork. "Okay, girl. Spill!"

I wipe my mouth. "Well, Jo is...amazing. She is sexy and generous and strong—wow, is she strong—and she's so good to me and she thinks I'm beautiful! She's everything I ever wanted and more." Out of breath, I pause as I remember Jo's glowing remarks. "And Emma, Jo's really solicitous. I swear, whenever I'm around her, I just start feeling better. Literally! It's like she's the magic Kool-Aid!"

Something about saying these words sets faint warning bells off in my mind, but like smoky tendrils of a dream, the feeling evaporates. "I really think I could fall for her, Emma. It scares me how hard."

Emma cradles her coffee cup. "Why should it scare you? You can trust yourself, Libby. And from what you've just said, Jo isn't like anyone you've dated before. What has you worried?"

"Well, isn't it too soon? And, I don't want to get my heart broken. But there is something kind of big I should tell you about."

"That sounds a little dire." Seeing I am serious now, she leans back. "What?"

I toy with a square of fried potato. I don't want to worry her, but if I can't tell my best friend, who can I tell? "Well, Jo is, like, insanely rich, right? And apparently someone is...I don't know, watching me or something, maybe to get to her?"

Her eyes are like saucers. "Oh no! That's so scary, Libby! Are you okay? Did you call the police?"

"No, we didn't call the police. I mean, what would I say? And Jo said she'd protect me. Like, I guess I have bodyguards with me 24/7 now." I squirm uncomfortably.

"What? Here? Now?" Emma's eyes dart around the room.

"That's what's so cool. Jo said I will never even see them. That that's part of their training. And she's right—I haven't seen anyone yet."

Her brows knit together. "But how is that possible? And how will you know if they're really protecting you if you never even see them? If you can't see them, aren't they too far away? I've never heard of anyone being *that* good. Unless they're Navy Seals or something."

For some reason, her usual rapidfire style ramps up my anxiety. "Gosh, thanks for making me more nervous, Em."

"I'm sorry, but this is just awful, Libby. You're being very calm about it. I'd be freaking out!"

"I guess I just don't fully understand. It doesn't seem real. And like, why? I mean, I'm nothing special. Not like Jo."

"How dare you say something like that! You are incredible! Where is this coming from? Besides, that's hardly the point. If it's Jo this person wants, it wouldn't matter who you are—you're just the bait, after all." She claps her hands on her cheeks. "Oh, that sounds worse, doesn't it? I'm sorry, Libby, I'm worried about you and it's coming out all wrong. You really trust Jo? Despite this possible danger she's putting you in, do you feel safe with her?"

I don't have to think about that. "Yes, I do feel completely safe with Jo. And so far, I trust her. Look, I understand your concern. I don't know, I'm just tired, I think."

"Listen, I'd really like to meet Jo. Maybe we can have a double date? Wouldn't that be fun?" Her earlier distress seems to have dissipated in the prospect of a double date, but I know my friend. She will continue to worry about me.

"Yes! A double date is perfect!"

Emma lays her napkin on her plate. "Honey, I'm so happy for you. For real. You of all people deserve to be happy and treated well by someone who really cares about you."

"You do, too, Emma. I can't wait to check out your new love and make sure he is good enough for you!"

"Ditto!" Her infectious laughter follows me as we part ways. But so do her concerns.

10

BIG DEAL ABOUT NOTHING

"*U*gh!" I look at my glass in disgust. I was chugging it down when I realized something is wrong with my tea. It has a strong metallic taste, yet it looks and even smells fine. I'm wracking my brain, but I can't think what's causing it to taste off. After another tentative sip, I decide to just dump it and make a fresh batch before Jo gets here.

On the way to dump my glass, I'm happy to note that sitting on the couch has already improved my back. It had become painful during brunch, and I'm grateful it won't be as bad when Jo gets here. I wonder if the intimacy between us will still be there when she comes, or if my imagination has embellished it. She seemed so bothered by whoever was out there.

I grab a cardigan for the theater and drape it over the couch while the water comes to a boil. Before I finish the tea, there's a knock at the door and Darcy streaks by me as I walk to answer it.

The sight of Jo plants a huge smile on my face. She takes one long look at me, heat coming into her eyes. She stalks me inside and closes the door decisively behind her as I steadily backing away. Without taking her eyes off of me, she turns the deadbolt, and before I register her move, she's holding me tight and kissing me with all of the passion we had yesterday. After a surprised squeak, I meet her passion with my own. She drags her lips from mine, across my cheek and down my neck, lingering there. Jo's teeth graze across my skin as she nuzzles my neck. Then she stills, taking several long breaths before setting me away from her and stepping back.

It takes me more than a minute to calm down. I clear my throat. "Well, hi, Jo. Come on in, why don't you? I missed you, too."

Jo manages to look contrite. "Dearest Libby, I have been driven to distraction ensuring your safety. When I saw you looking so...delectable...smiling up at me so innocently, well, I seem to have lost my senses."

"Whatever the reason, that beats a handshake any day."

Jo tips her head back and laughs. "Oh, *ma petite amie*, you delight me." She looks down, surprised, and we both watch Darcy wind around her jean-clad legs.

I beam at Jo. She bends down and strokes his fur. From her crouched position she asks about my brunch with Emma, and I tell her about Emma's suggestion to set up a double date soon.

"I would be honored to meet your Emma."

"Great!" Smiling, I head for the kitchen. "I was just making another pitcher of tea. There was something off about the one I made yesterday. I'll just be a minute."

While I remove the steeped bags, she retrieves the mostly full pitcher from the refrigerator. "What do you think is wrong with it? It appears fine to me."

"Yeah, that's just it. I don't know. It smells fine

and looks fine, but there's a funny taste to it. I just don't want to drink it."

"I am very sorry to hear that. How much of this did you drink today, and when?"

Her voice is decidedly casual, but for some reason, it makes me nervous. And suspicious. "Why?"

"How much, Libby?"

"Why? What's going on?"

"Libby, nothing is wrong. Just answer me, please. How much did you drink?" Jo's face is a frightening blank. Hairs raise on the back of my neck and across my arms.

"Oh, gods, Jo, is it poisoned? Did someone poison my tea? I had like half a glass." I start backing away, clutching my neck.

Jo tugs my hands away and cups my face. "*Chérie*, forgive me for scaring you. No, you have not been poisoned. Relax."

I can't shake the feeling that she isn't telling me something. Still, when she smiles at me and doesn't say anything else, I begin to relax. "Okay. Okay. Um, give me a minute and we can pick a movie."

Jo leaves the kitchen. I blow out a breath and finish making the tea, dumping the tainted tea down the drain and washing it out thoroughly. After stowing a freshly made pitcher in the refrigerator, I walk back into the living room.

"How is your pain today, Libby?"

So we aren't going to talk about it. Fine. She is studying her hands and I can't read her expression. I decide to take her lead and see where she goes. The tension between us makes my stomach ache. "It was starting to get bad by the time I got home, but I guess resting until you got here helped because it feels fine now." I pause. "Thank you for asking, Jo."

"Did you sleep better?" She still isn't looking at me and her body is tense.

I turn to stare out the window. *What have I done to upset her? Was it the kiss? Did I say something wrong?* I twist my hands in my lap and answer with forced cheer. "I slept great, actually, Jo. I'm sorry you've been worrying about me."

At last, Jo scoots over until our knees touch. Her soothing scent reaches out to me, and I turn to her. When I unclasp my hands, she takes one of them, further relaxing me. "Libby, *belle*, forgive me." She reaches out and traces between my eyebrows, smoothing the crease that had formed. "I have upset you and I regret it deeply. Please, allow me to make it up to you."

She really looks guilty and my concern melts. "I think I can manage to let you make it up to me." A faint smile lifts my mouth.

Humor lights Jo's eyes. "You think so?"

"I might be persuaded."

"Would letting you choose the movie be part of that plan?"

"I'd say that is a big step in the right direction." I grin. "Along with popcorn, of course."

"*Naturalement*, of course, whatever my *chérie* wants she shall have."

I look at her. "Really?"

"*Oui*."

"Then tell me what's wrong. What happened in there?" I point to the kitchen. "What was wrong with the tea?"

I almost miss her jaw clench, but that's the only

clue her face offers. "*Chérie*, I will do whatever I feel is necessary to ensure your comfort and safety. I *will* tell you everything, I promise this. However for now, I need you to trust me."

I hold her gaze, though her words don't do anything to mollify me. After a second, I come to a decision. I committed to communication, so it's honesty, or why bother. "Jo, I will allow you your secrets. I respect them, and they are none of my business unless you choose to share them. But I need you to understand that I am less forgiving when they affect me."

She doesn't look away, but she nods. "You are a woman of integrity and I hold that in the highest regard."

"And no one broke in here? I wasn't poisoned?"

"No."

"Are you drugging me?" I don't know what made me ask, but now the answer seems very important.

There's that flash of a jaw clench again, and a slight hesitation. "No."

Gah! What does that mean? I want to believe her. She seems to be telling the truth, but then, I hardly know her. *Maybe I'm just making a big deal about nothing.* At least we seem to be on solid footing again. "Then let's pick out a movie."

Jo buys a giant buttered popcorn and gets me the soda I ask for, too. The rom-com is predictably predictable, but it's still good. I like the actress, and it sure helps to have Jo's arm around me—and our hands meeting in the popcorn tub from time to time. I look over at her once to find her gazing at me and I return her smile. She tweaks my nose, and I giggle before I turn back to the movie.

When it's over, she captures my hand, and we talk

about the movie on the way to the car. It all feels so nice and normal, and I'm contented. No spine or joint pain, no worrying about anything, really. Then it occurs to me that we may not be alone, and I ask Jo about it.

"So do we have protection when you and I go out? I mean, is anyone following us?" We've just made it to the level of the parking deck we parked on, and I look around as if I might see one of them.

Jo seems to weigh her words carefully. "When I am with you, it is not as important to have your guards. They leave when I come, and I call them back when I depart. As someone is always with me, the two of us suffice."

Yeah, I can believe that. It's not the first time I've imagined her as a soldier rather than a CEO. Absent-mindedly, I massage the muscles of her arm. My stomach quivers. "Do you have a regular person who always has your back, or do they rotate?"

I get the feeling from her hesitation that she isn't used to talking about this. "I have a personal body-guard who is nearly always with me." Jo takes both of my hands. "I may have enemies, Libby, but I have a lot more whom I call friends. People I would gladly die for, and they for me. Because I care about you, they care about protecting you."

I voice the crazy thought before I can stop myself. "Um, are you, like, mafia or something?"

Laughing, Jo drops my hands. "No, *belle* Libby, I am not in any kind of organized crime." But abruptly, her laugh cuts off, and she lifts her head as if smelling something. She's on her phone a second later. "Did you catch that?" Phone still to her ear, she bends, and before I can even process it, she's lifted me into her arms and carries me as she sprints to the car. Effortlessly, she gets the door open and lowers me into the seat. "Libby, do not leave the car for any reason. Tell me you understand." I manage to nod. She kisses my forehead, closes the door, and the doors click locked.

I stare at her back, frightened, confused, my heartbeat pounding. *She carried me like I weighed nothing. And how did she move so fast?* I can hear her giving orders, but not her words and the car is so low to the ground, I can't see around her rigid body. Suddenly, she yanks open the driver door and leaps into the seat. I glance back at my window, thinking stupidly that she's still standing there. *How did she do that?* Wordlessly, she grabs my hand as the car lurches out of the parking spot, tires squealing. I grit my teeth as she navigates the levels at breakneck speed, barely slowing down to jettison through the gate and speed down the street.

Once we get to the main road, her speed returns to normal. My jaw relaxes when she kisses my hand before releasing it, then she starts barking into her phone. "Get two to her place immediately. Make sure Aella's backup arrives fast. I am flying solo from Blacksburg." She pauses a moment, listening. "*Oui,* good...that is fine...no, no visual, but I know it was him...*bien sur!* Find out anything you can." Jo glances over at me and gives me a brief smile. "*Oui,* she is shaken, but Libby is fine...*non.* Not now. We will discuss this upon my return. *Au revoir.*" Jo drops the phone into a cup holder and reaches for my hand again.

"Talk to me, Libby. You are pale and your hand shakes."

My thoughts won't stay in one place and I'm seriously regretting all that greasy popcorn. "What...what just happened? I mean, I know what happened, but why? What's going on? I don't know what's going on."

"Can it wait until I have you safely in your home?" Jo glances at me. "I swear I will tell you all I know."

"Okay. Sure. Home. Good. Yes. Good." My whole body starts to shake so hard, my teeth chatter and I clench them hard to control it.

Jo turns off the AC. "Breathe, Libby. Deep breaths with me now. Good. Now that the shock has worn off, the adrenaline is leaving you, that's all. We are almost there. Hold on for me." I focus on Jo's strong, soothing voice.

I seem to zone out on the remainder of the drive and am surprised when she parks in my complex. Jo comes around to open my door, but I feel wooden and she scoops me up. It's a relief to lean my head against her chest as she kicks the car door closed and carries me to my door. She sets me down briefly and I stand there trembling, feeling as if my limbs have turned to lead. A moment later, she's gently laying me down on the couch. I hear water running, and wincing, I sit up when Jo brings me the glass. The shaking has stopped, and my muscles feel like I was hit by a bus.

Jo braces me as I sip the water, studying her. Worry lines crease her forehead. I reach up and smooth them out, one by one. "Adrenaline's a bitch."

She chuckles. "*Oui*, it is. How do you feel? What do you need, *chérie*?"

Nothing. Everything. "Just the truth."

Jo gazes at me unblinkingly. "My father is in town."

"Okay. What does he want?" *With me.*

119

Jo stands, starts to pace my tiny living room. Darcy jumps up onto the couch and slinks over. He climbs on my lap and pushes his head in my hand. Automatically, I stroke him, and it helps both of us.

"You remember I told you that my father was not a nice man?"

"I believe the word you used was violent," I clarify unhappily.

"Yes, and greedy. Self-serving." Jo runs a hand through her hair, leaving a wide curl sticking up. I watch as it flops back down. "I believe that he has come here for me. Or rather, for what I can do for him. He wants money, power. Both of which I have."

"And where do I fit in, since I have neither?"

Jo looks at me sharply, but continues without commenting. "To him, you are a means to an end, *chérie*. I believe he hopes to influence me through you."

Emma was right—I'm the bait. "What happens now?" I'm pleased my voice doesn't quake, but I'm far from calm.

Coming over to the couch, Jo pulls my hands into her lap. "Now that we have identified the threat, we will better be able to safeguard you. For one, Beatrice, one of your day guards, will bring you the Jeep and will ride with you when you go to Pulaski to check out that property tomorrow. She will not interfere with your work, only ensure your safety. Nothing will happen to you if I can prevent it, Libby. You have my word." She gathers me into her arms, and I shift closer. She tucks my head under her chin and holds me. She makes me feel so safe. "You are being very brave, *ma petite amie*, and I am very proud of you." Her lips tickle my hair and she inhales deeply. "You smell so good. You feel so good in my arms I could hold you like this always."

Ditto. Now that the chill has passed, Jo's cool skin soothes my overheated senses. I nuzzle her neck and plant a kiss in the dip at the base. After a beat, Jo shifts us, bringing my head up. I lean in before she does, and I'm not disappointed when she grips the back of my head and holds me there. She slants her head and kisses me with all the passion I'm feeling. All my pent-up emotions transition and I lean into her, pressing her against the back of the couch. I tug up her shirt, needing to feel her skin. I explore the cool, muscled planes of her stomach. I moan and gasp, and I want her so badly, I think I might implode.

Unexpectedly, Jo flips us. She grabs my hands and gathers them into one of hers, pinning them over my head. Her mouth sears a trail down my throat and her lips close over my skin, sucking gently. She straddles my legs, propping herself up on her knees. Holding her body away from me, her free hand massages my breasts through my clothes and I thrust my chest into her hand, silently begging. I want my hands on her and I tug, but there's no getting my hands free of her grip. She chuckles, looking down at me wolfishly. "Not a chance."

I wiggle beneath her impatiently. Her nostrils widen, and her knee urges my legs apart. I spread them without hesitation. Her knee rucks up the skirt of my dress and rubs against me, denim to satin. The friction sends me into a frenzy.

Jo kisses me deeply, our tongues dancing, while moving her knee against me. I go a little wild, writhing and bucking beneath her. Her hand is in constant motion, massaging and pinching, gripping my hips. She strokes my inner thigh. I'm lost to sensations, have no thoughts other than *Yes!* and *More!* and am spiraling fast. Little pants come out like wails. Jo is rocking her knee rhythmically up and down, murmuring in French against my ear and moaning deeply. I begin to feel the gathering and my movements are fevered, desperate. I strain against my hands.

All at once it hits me and I make a startled noise, then cry out her name with the first wave of my orgasm. Wave after wave rocks me, and I twitch with them and suck in air. Jo murmurs encouragements in my ear. When the last wave pulses through me, I go instantly limp as a rug, panting. I'm taken by an influx of emotions, but my thoughts are incoherent and I can't suss them out. She releases my wrists and I drag my arms down while she stretches her long legs out along my own. I get my leaden arms around her and clasp my hands to keep them there. Jo holds me while my breathing returns to normal, murmuring beautiful French in a husky voice.

My breathing evens, and my heart rate does, too. Jo props up on one elbow and gazes at me. With her free hand, she smooths the damp hair off of my forehead and strokes my face.

"Ah, *chérie*. Thank you for that precious gift."

Feeling self-conscious and embarrassed, I try to bury my face in her arm, but Jo won't allow it. I'm no virgin, but I've never lost my mind like that. I made noises I didn't even recognize.

Her thumb wipes at the apples of my cheeks that I know are stained pink. "Look in my eyes and see the truth."

On an inhale, I look into the forest-green of her

eyes. My breath catches. *Who are you? How did I get so lucky?*

Stroking my face, she speaks in reverential tones. "That was beautiful, Libby. It touches me that you would trust me by letting go. I knew it would be incredible, and you surpassed even my imaginings."

"That was...unexpected. I mean, I've had sex before, certainly. But that...I didn't...I mean, we still have our clothes on! Jo, that was...thank *you*."

Jo smiles more than a little smugly. "Just imagine what we will be like with our clothes off, *ma petite amie*." She kisses me again, then rolls me. She has me wrapped in her cool arms and my head is tucked beneath her chin. I'm so sated, so secure, that I drift on a cloud of pure pleasure. *Oh, I wish she would hold me always.* Jo kisses the top of my head and I turn in the circle of her arms, cupping her face in my hand. I swallow my nerves. "Um, that was pretty one-sided, Jo."

"Oh, *mon coeur*, you are mistaken. Believe me, I thoroughly enjoyed myself. How could I not, watching you unravel beneath me? What more could I possibly want?"

I gape at her. I've never been with such an unselfish lover. My previous experiences were tit for tat, so to speak, or there were resentments to pay. But I have to believe her. She certainly looks satisfied.

"Ah, all right then." I stroke my hand down her face and rest it against the center of her chest. My other hand is on her hip. I feel so comfortable here in her arms. Just then, my stomach growls and Jo chuckles.

"I guess it's about time we find some real food,

yes? The popcorn has gone, no?" She tugs on my braid affectionately.

"Yeah, we can safely say the popcorn is history." Jo helps me sit up and I laugh looking down at my rumpled dress. "Well, considering what I look like now, I think eating here would be best. But I can change if you'd like to go somewhere."

"I planned to take you out, but if you would not mind, staying here may be best." I know what she isn't saying. It would be safer.

In the end, we decide on pizza, though it's gourmet pizza, of course. The rest of the evening passes with a lot of cuddling. Jo is gentle and teasing, she tells me lovely things about me and I believe her sincerity. She manages to keep the afterglow alive, giving me the kind of after-sex coddling I've always craved. She makes me feel beautiful and sensual and lovable and whole.

By the time she leaves on a kiss full of promise, I know my heart is no longer my own.

11

I DON'T CARE WHY

*I*t's a bright sunny day, perfect for a drive through the mountains, and though it will be hot, there are puffy clouds and I'm flying high on one of them. Jo called around 7 and we had coffee together right up until she walked into a meeting. Louis wants me to bring the car at 4 pm, which gives me plenty of time with Sarah after the 1 pm Al-Anon meeting.

Since today's trek will probably mean trudging over rough land, I choose jeans, despite the heat, and long socks into which I can tuck the cuffs. I'm still getting ready when there's a sharp knock on the door, and Darcy squirms under the bed.

That must be my guard, Beatrice. Even though I'm nervous to meet her, I'm far too blissful with Jo to be bothered about anything, really. Smiling, I coo at Darcy on my way to the door. I open the door to a pale, petite woman with delicate features. But the softness ends there. Wild blond curls are partially tamed at her nape by a braided cord. And she's tough, in well-used but high-quality hiking clothes.

"You must be Beatrice. Please come in. You are a little early and I'm not quite ready yet. You are welcome to the coffee that's left." I head back to finish getting ready. Besides returning my greeting, she doesn't comment. When I come out of the bathroom, I'm startled to find Beatrice in my bedroom.

"I like your taste. Bright colors suit you." She squeezes a yellow pillow from my bed and tosses it back.

"Thanks." I'm not sure what to say about her breaching my privacy, so I walk to the end of my bed and sit down. Due to the stiffness in my back, it will be a struggle to put my boots on. I'm embarrassed for Beatrice to witness it. I stretch my back, trying vainly to loosen it up. I turn wrong and get a shooting pain, clutching the bedspread on a gasp. My cheeks heat. *Why didn't she stay in the freaking living room?*

The next thing I know, Beatrice kneels in front of me, holding her hand out. "It sucks to hurt all the time. I don't know how you stand it. You must be stronger than I was. When I was about eight years old, I broke my arm. We didn't have money, even if medical care had been nearby, and all I got was a sling. It hurt like the devil." Speechless, I hand her the shoe. "My mother acted like I was faking it and made sure I knew how much trouble I was being." She slips the shoe on and starts tying it. "This boy lived next door; he was real gentle and a little slow. But he would see me struggle and help me out. The arm didn't heal right and always gave me trouble." She rubs her unmarred arm as if it aches. Beatrice grabs my left shoe and starts to put it on. "I never forgot what it was like when that boy would just do stuff for me, like it was no big deal. No judgment, just help-ful." She ties the shoe and stands up. "Want help standing?"

I take the hand Beatrice proffers and stand. "Thank you. Did he ever know the effect he had on you?"

"No. He died when we were still kids." Her voice is devoid of emotion, but a shadow passes over her.

Not knowing what to say, I turn to leave. "So do you want coffee to take, or some yogurt or anything?"

"Ah, thanks, but I already ate."

Feeling like I missed a joke, I shrug. "Okie doke. I'll just grab a bite and we can head out."

The map on my phone shows an accident way down on I-81 South and traffic is backed up above Blacksburg. So, I decide to head over to Route 11 which runs parallel. Generally, it's not as fast but it definitely should save us time today.

I hadn't noticed it when I let her in, but as we leave my apartment, Beatrice reaches beside the door and lifts a long narrow scabbard. My eyes popping out of their sockets, I watch as she handles it like an ex-tension of herself. A by-goddess sword. *She must be a real badass.* Once we get under way, Beatrice con-stantly scans, keeping watch everywhere at once. Be-tween that and the sword now laying across her lap, I'm forcefully reminded that Jo's father is out there, waiting for a chance to get to me.

Despite that, I'm still floating on the high Jo left me with. Funny, every time I think about last evening, Beatrice asks me a question. But the conversation makes the drive go quickly and it's not too hard to navigate to the property once we turn off Route 11.

The whole drive is beautiful. There are only a couple of turns. All good selling points, and I make a mental note to add that to my email to Jenny. The Jeep is a dream to drive once we get off paved roads and I'm grateful my poor old Toyota isn't being put through this. *Score one for Jo.*

The property is deep in the mountains and encompasses almost a full side of a ridge. The whole trip only takes us about 50 minutes and it isn't too far off of the interstate—another selling point. As soon as I stop the Jeep, Beatrice gets her phone, her fingers flying over the screen.

I start to get out, but Beatrice stops me with a hand on my shoulder. "Let me check things out first. Stay here and keep the doors locked. You see anyone, you scream, got it?"

I swallow hard and nod. She eases out and draws her sword. While I wait, I tuck the bottoms of my jeans into my socks, worried about ticks and chiggers. The owner said the open area was bush-hogged in May, but you wouldn't know it now. The grasses are knee-high. When I look up, I don't see Beatrice anywhere.

There are three structures on this fairly level remote tract. Calling them houses is a bit of a stretch, but I see potential, especially for a bunch of hunters. And three buildings means I may not have to find two other properties. I'm anxious to start checking them out.

Suddenly, Beatrice's face fills my window. I stifle a scream, then roll my eyes at her with my hand over my racing heart. She crosses her eyes comically in response, and I laugh in delighted surprise. The badass has a fun side.

I scramble out and pick my way over the uneven ground. The owner said the buildings weren't locked and I'm happy to prove him right. I note the number of rooms and approximate sizes in the small notebook I brought along, as well as my thoughts. Beatrice comments that she felt as if she was playing Goldilocks and the Three Buildings, but none of them were just right, and we laugh and play on that theme for a while.

I'm done less than thirty minutes later. It's not my job to check out the land, only to see if the buildings are worth continuing. Still, I can't help but take in the beauty of the deep woods all around me. Satisfied, I nod to Beatrice and we wade back to the Jeep. She starts texting on her phone while I get us turned around to head back down the mountain. The map shows a clear route on I-81, so we are back in town 10 minutes sooner than it took to get down there. All in all, the trip took just under two hours. Since I'm behind, I decide to go into the office.

"Beatrice, I'm going to go in to work. Where do you want me to take you?" I can feel her eyes on me, and I glance at her. "Okaaay, stupid question."

She laughs her light, bubbly laugh and I can't help but join her. We pull into my office building and I park.

Beatrice nods at me, smiles.

"See ya around." I feel her watching me as I walk inside.

After work, Beatrice and I run home and I trade cars, getting to the meeting in plenty of time. When I walk in, I immediately feel even better. I go up to different people I know and enjoy a little small talk. It's been a couple of weeks and it's good to catch up with folks.

It's a good meeting. I linger for a few minutes, talking to a couple of latecomers before I head to the car. Sarah extricates herself at the same time and I follow her to the deli where we usually meet. We easily find a quiet booth, somewhat set away from others.

Sarah starts us off. "Alright. Tell me everything!" She laughs, spreading deep laugh lines around her eyes. "Seriously, though, you look wonderful. But I know that appearances can be deceiving, so tell me how things are going."

I laugh with her. "Well, things are kind of wonderful right now. But I want to be careful. I'm afraid I'm moving too fast." I catch myself tucking hair around my ear, and she grins.

"Yeah, I thought this was about love. You are glowing. I take it things with Jo have progressed?" She smiles so wide, it lights up her face.

Sarah must have heard about Jo from Dad. They've been friends for almost as long as I've known her. "It's amazing, Sarah. Being with Jo makes me want to be the woman I was before the diagnosis."

Sarah's warm brown eyes sparkle. "I hear a 'but' in there..."

"Yeah, that's where I need perspective. Jo is being secretive about some things that may concern me. But I can't make heads or tails out of any of it, and I'm trying to be patient and let her reveal things when she's ready."

"It sounds like you're trying to give her space to be honest with you. Do you trust her?"

"Even though I know there are things she isn't

telling me, I do trust her. I feel she's as honest as she can be."

Sarah looks pensive for a moment, her eyes searching my face. "What do you think she is hiding? A family? A past? What does your gut say?"

"That's just it. Nothing I come up with fits what it feels like she's keeping from me." I blow air out in irritation.

"So more will be revealed, when it is time to be revealed. The trick is to wait for God's time, not demand ours. And until then, Libby, what can you do?"

"I can keep myself open and trust that Jo will tell me in her own time. In the meantime, I have to say, our relationship is moving pretty quickly. She isn't like anyone I've ever dated. I'm just afraid of...well, getting hurt, feeling a fool."

Sarah folds her arms and sits back, looking at the table. "I loved what you shared in the meeting about remembering to take care of what's yours and not worrying about what others think. So cross off feeling a fool. Anyone who would judge you is too busy worrying about looking a fool themselves. Remember, too, that no one can make us feel anything without our permission. It doesn't sound like Jo's doing anything to show you she's better than you?" When I shake my head, she goes on. "As to getting hurt...well, honey, that's just part of life, I'm afraid. Would I spare you heartache if I could? Hell, yeah. But even heartache teaches us, and you just may find that it's all worth the price. It's even possible that she won't break your heart at all! I know it feels fast, but, well, did I ever tell you about how Bobby and I got started?"

"No!" I can't wait to hear.

Sarah's smile crinkles her eyes as she stares over

my head, lost in memory. "When I met Bobby, he was the best-looking man I'd ever seen. Whew, he just took my breath away. You know, I was much taller than the boys in school, then here comes this tall drink of water. We were so hot for each other, we had to get married right away so we could have sex!"

Shock startles a laugh out of me. This does not fit the image of Sarah I've held in my head.

"Goodness, yes, Libby. We got married because we couldn't keep our hands off each other. We were in a different place than most folks today, you know. Both of us coming up in small-town Southern churches the way we did. But I swear we couldn't wait. We'd known each other about a month when I walked down that aisle, crazy as it seems now." Sarah shrugs. Her face reflects the passionate and impulsive young woman she'd been. Her face glows. "Do I regret it now? Wish I had taken the time to get to know Bobby better, to develop a strong relationship first? No. Not for one second. I knew from the first moment I saw him. He was everything I thought I wanted at the time. And thankfully, he turned out to be so much more. And the sex is still great, by the way. We were lucky." She shakes her head. "Look, yes, taking time with a relationship is smart. It's good to make sure you're both headed in the same direction. But sometimes, you just know. When it is right, you feel it." She points to her abdomen, her breast. "And you have no choice."

"How do I know what I feel isn't just lust, or the love of being in love after so long?"

"Libby, you know as well as I do that there are no guarantees in life. Sometimes, you don't know for a while. But I can tell you this. If it's wrong...well, you will feel that, too. When you're with Jo, when you think of her, does anything feel forced? Wrong in some way?"

I don't even have to think. "No. In fact, things start making sense when I'm with her. The colors are brighter, my senses are heightened, and I physically feel better. The only thing is, she really likes keeping me off kilter."

Sarah's laugh is a little too hearty. "Well, hallelujah! We've talked about this a lot over the years. You do so love to be in control. I'm thrilled you've found someone who can shake your hands off the reins!"

I huff into my water and Sarah laughs harder. But I can't deny the truth. I start laughing, too.

Talking with Sarah banished any lingering doubts I had about moving too fast with Jo, at least temporarily. I just keep thinking about the look on her face when I was in the throes, the way she held me afterwards, as if I was precious. Cherished. Her beautiful words.

I get home in a daze. It's only when I recognize I'm getting aroused that I snap myself out of it. Really, I can't believe how much better I feel. Call it endorphins, call it hormones, call it the sunshine. I don't care why. I'm just so relieved that the pain is gone.

I copy the address from Louis's text on a scrap of paper, and then plug it into my map. I'm surprised to see it is way up in the mountains. It will take about 40 minutes, so I check my ponytail and re-tie my ribbon. I have on a casual knee-length cotton skirt that matches the blue ribbon from Jo's flower. I've paired it with a white T-shirt bearing the lettering *I like to party, and by party, I mean read books*. Though cute, with the T-shirt hugging my curves, it's not a sexy outfit by any stretch. However, since it's so early in the day, I probably won't see Jo. Besides, it's comfortable.

After giving Darcy a few quick strokes, I rush out the door.

12

A MATTER OF PERSPECTIVE

The drive to Jo's place is spectacular. It's such a pretty day, the views just get better the deeper into the mountains I go. *What a thrill it must be to make this drive every day.* I'm belting out lyrics along with Adele as I navigate two fun switchbacks. Then I take a turn onto yet another narrow, heavily wooded road that climbs up so steeply, I wonder if my poor rattle-trap will make it. I mutter encouragements to her, hoping against hope as she groans to the top. Slowing to a snail's pace, her nose finally crests the rise, and what is revealed leaves me so breathless I forget all about my concern for my car. My foot comes off the pedal and I roll to a stop, taking it all in.

The broad mountain top is mostly cleared, though stately hardwood and evergreens liberally dot the landscape. Much of the grounds are devoted to an active meadowland, save for the immediate area surrounding the house and two smaller buildings built in the same style. I'm completely charmed by the blue slate roof and white stone reflecting the sunshine. Jo's home brings to mind fairytale castles, and I imagine it being surrounded by a glistening moat. From what I can see of the sprawling main house, it must contain at least a dozen bedrooms and twice as many windows.

I count ten garage bays in the structure to its right, three of which are open, revealing the Jeep I drove this morning, and what appears to be a fully equipped auto care center. The final building sits on the other side of the garage, and my imagination conjures sword-wielding medieval knights milling around. It stands two stories high and brings to mind a dorm—or barracks—more than anything else. There are large parking areas in front of each building with a number of cars parked in front of the far building. From the main house, an access road curves to the left and disappears behind it.

As I approach, Louis comes out of the first bay in clean khaki pants and a cotton short-sleeved button-up, a shop towel in his hands. This is the first time I've seen him without a suit, yet he looks just as clean and pressed. He waves me in. When I get out of the car, he's there, holding his hand out to assist me. Smiling, I carefully take it. To my surprise, his grip is strong and steady. I take a better look at him. He's extremely fit. Fitter than most men half his age, actually. *Wowzer, I don't know what he does, but I want his training program!* His eyes twinkle with laughter, and it finally hits me I'm still holding his hand and staring like a starstruck school girl. Guiltily, I drop his hand and nervously tuck away a few strands of hair. *No wonder he's laughing at me.*

"Louis, it's so nice to see you, again. Thank you for looking over my car." I look back at it and grimace. My beaten-up little car looks grossly out of place here.

"I know it isn't anything like what you must be used to working on."

"Not at all, *mademoiselle!* These new vehicles are all computer chips. *Dit moi,* tell me where is the challenge in that? Good solid cars like this—" he nods at the Toyota "—this I enjoy. Your trip was not too bad, I hope?"

"Absolutely not. It's a perfect day, a beautiful drive, and I'm grateful you're willing to take a look at it."

"Such graciousness, *mademoiselle.* Now, let us see what your car has to tell us, *oui?*" With that, he pops the hood. I worry about him dirtying his neat outfit, but keep my thoughts to myself.

I am not sure what to do with myself and I stand there, watching him half hanging out of the car. A faint memory surfaces of my dad's father working on a car. I was very small and he gave me the job of holding a wrench. I felt very important. The memory makes me smile. He died such a long time ago that all I have is a lingering smell of tobacco, grease, and coffee, along with bluegrass playing softly in the background.

Louis pops out from under the hood. "*Mademoiselle*, would you do me the great favor of starting your car?"

"I'd be happy to."

"Rev the engine, if you please," Louis yells from under the hood.

I do, and am embarrassed by the sputter and cough. I'm so used to it that I usually tune it out, but now I hear it loud and clear.

"Okay, please turn her off again."

I cut the engine and climb out. "Louis, would it be

okay if I walk the grounds? I won't go into the house or anything."

"But of course, *mademoiselle*. Here, take this bottle of water with you." He opens a wood cabinet. Before I can get a look inside, he grabs a bottle from the door and snaps it closed.

I'm grateful I'm wearing my walking shoes as I set off into the meadow, even though walking paths are cut throughout. The meadow has been allowed to grow pretty wild and I'd hate to run into anything in sandals. I shudder at the thought of what could be out here, but continue on. There's a massive oak a good distance from the house and I make that my destination. I flush a bevy of mourning doves and, startled, jump back before laughing at myself. The scream of a hawk travels to me and bees buzz in the wildflowers all around me. I pause to watch a baby blue butterfly flit around a patch of Queen Anne's Lace.

Happily looking everywhere but at my feet, a distinctive sound hits my consciousness and I instinctively stop in my tracks. *Oh, gods. Rattlesnake. It's a rattlesnake.* I frantically search, finally spotting the thick gray body striped with black zig zags coiled on a low rock not a foot away from my right leg. Its tail rattling, it scents the air with its forked tongue. *It's huge! Oh, gods. Oh, gods. What do I do? Go away, oh, please go away! Help!* I'm desperately trying to think of a way to escape, but I'm scared out of my wits and frozen to the spot. Then the snake begins to draw back its diamond-shaped head. Terror steals my breath, killing the scream building in my throat.

Out of nowhere, a figure appears behind the snake, and I blink, thinking it's a hallucination, before I recognize her. "It's all right, Libby," Beatrice soothes.

Gripped in her hands, that long, lethal, blade glints in the sunlight.

In a flash of sun on steel and a sharp ring as it strikes the rock, pieces of the rattlesnake arc into the air. Beatrice watches me warily and I focus on those huge blue eyes, trying to pull myself together. I glance down at the blade she's holding by her side and watch, fixated, as a drop of gory liquid drips into the grass. Nausea gripping me, I spin around and fall to my knees, retching into the wildflowers. *Gah, I'm such a wimp.*

"Oh, Libby." She sighs heavily. "Really?"

I try not to be offended by her mournful tone as I rock back on my heel, my knee screaming in protest. After wiping the blade on the grass, she tucks it into the scabbard strapped to her back. Then she leans over and grasps my elbows, gently tugging. She's deceptively strong for someone so small. And talk about a badass. *Where did she learn to use that sword?*

Watching her warily, I twist open the sweating water bottle and swill a mouthful of water around before turning my head and spitting it out. My knees want to buckle. I chug about half the bottle down, my hand slightly shaking.

"Sorry to be such a disappointment."

She gives me a half bow, strangely approving of my churlishness. "Don't feel bad. You are too hard on yourself."

I suck in a shaky breath. "Okay then. How did you know I needed help?"

She hesitates. "That's my job, Libby."

I know I'm missing something. As far as I know, I just froze. *Was that it? My immobility?* I shrug. *That must be it.* "Well, I don't know how to thank you. It...I didn't know what to do."

"If I can help it, it won't be me that has to face Jo with the news that something happened to you."

That confirms my suspicion that Jo is a demanding boss. Truthfully, I wouldn't want to cross either of them. Niall either, for that matter.

I study the whitened cut marring the rock. "Aside from snakes, am I in a lot of danger, Beatrice?"

Before she can answer, her eyes slide over my shoulder, and whatever she sees makes her take a step back. She then bows her head respectfully and I have to turn around to see who cows a sword-wielding badass.

Speak of the devil! "Niall!" I'm so startled to see the imposing man, I almost laugh. I must have been so intent on talking to Beatrice that I never heard his approach.

"Beatrice, luv, Jo will be pleased to hear of your heroics. I didn't know snakes could fly!" And he laughs heartily. It's quite something what laughter does to this man's face. It softens the steel, if only momentarily.

Beatrice smiles faintly. It's pretty obvious she's a little afraid of him and it makes me look at him a little more warily. When his laughter runs its course, he focuses on Beatrice again. "You can *take your time* getting back to your post now, luv. I'll escort our Libby back to Louis."

Without another word, Beatrice strides purposefully through the grass towards the house. I watch her go for a minute, musing, then turn back to Niall. "So how come you get to be out here? I thought things were kind of crazy at work."

Niall is wearing what remains of a well-cut suit that looks made for him. Slacks and a crisp pale gold button-up fit his lean body well. The sleeves are casually rolled up and he's not wearing a tie. The top three buttons of his shirt are open, revealing a smooth, strong chest. He really is ridiculously handsome.

He quirks a perfectly shaped eyebrow at me. "I video-conferenced today for everyone's sake. If I'd spent even a minute with those idiots in accounting today, I wouldn't have been responsible for my actions. I was bloody well past my patience when I heard you were in trouble, so thank you for providing me with an excuse to sign off! Jo's arsed not to be here, I don't mind tellin' ya. By now, Louis will have let her know all is well and no harm done."

An all-too-familiar feeling that I'm missing something settles over me. But I just fall into step beside Niall, thinking. I'm back there in my mind, the snake a footstep away, when we flush a rabbit and it explodes into motion almost under our feet. Hysterical laughter threatens to bubble up from I don't know where. I look over at Niall, his hands in his pockets looking all serious, and I let it go. I'm helpless to stop it. It doubles me over and I hug my aching sides. Every time I straighten up and look at him, the surprise mixed with concern on his face makes me laugh harder. It's a full couple of minutes before I finally get control. Hiccupping, I swipe under my eyes for smeared mascara. When I sneak another glance at Niall, he is rubbing his chin, studying me rather comically.

"Whew. Sorry. I'm okay now, really. The stress came out sideways, I guess. But, oh my, you should have seen your face." I fan mine to ward off another wave of hilarity. "It just tipped me over the edge. But don't worry, I'm all good now. Disaster averted, heroes saved the damsel in distress, yada yada, blah, blah."

The humor dissolves as quickly as it came on. I don't like being a damsel in distress. At all. In fact, I'm angry at my reaction of inaction. Forget fight or flight —I froze. *Why did I just stand there waiting for it to strike? Beatrice wouldn't have just stood there.* Watching petite Beatrice take that snake out with one swipe of her deadly blade, well, it still gives me chills, but it also makes me wish I had more courage. *I wish I was stronger. Losing your lunch in the grass isn't exactly the hallmark of a tough girl.*

Niall appraises me. "Come now, luv. What could you have done differently? Any defenseless person would need a bit o' help against such a ruthless foe. Rattlesnakes mean business, and there's no doubt. It was him or you, and as I see it, what does it matter how it happened, so long as you came out ahead?"

His words are unexpectedly kind. "It's all a matter of perspective, isn't it?" I study the ground. "Um, do you suppose it's possible to keep the fact that I tossed my cookies between the three of us?"

Niall laughs again until my cheeks burn. He stops as soon as he notices. "Ah, luv, I wasna makin' fun. Forgive me." His tone gentles. "The toughest of men would feel their tea swill in the same boat. There's no shame in what you did, to my way of thinking. It's just a reaction."

I stare at him, but he nods at me and smiles, and I feel as if we've reached a new level. He is Jo's best friend and business partner. I'd like us to be on better terms.

"Ah, yes, our Louis has news for you if I'm not

mistaken, Libby." He nods in the direction of the garage.

I shade my eyes with my hand and look into the lowering sun. Louis stands just outside of the garage, wiping his hands on a shop towel, though his clothes look as spotless as before. He hurries out to meet us halfway.

"*Mademoiselle!* Oh, *mon dieu*, when I think of what could have happened if Beatrice had not been there..." He actually shudders. "But here you are, pretty as a Degas. Come, I have news to tell you." With that, he turns and walks to the garage.

Grinning, I follow.

13

ON YOUR IDIOTIC HEADS

*A*ll business now, Louis stands in front of me with his arms crossed and his feet spread apart. "It is worse than I feared, *mademoiselle* Libby. You need a new timing belt—you are far overdue; the water pump is on its last leg. There is a hole in the radiator and the engine has a slow oil leak, though I have not found it—" he holds up a finger and his eyes glitter "—yet!" He goes on, and my heart sinks further into my shoes. "All four brake pads need to be replaced, your ignition system is going, and the muffler is rusting through. This is not to mention the need for new tires nor the state of the air filter."

All the brightness I had regained while walking with Niall fades. I've kept up with oil changes, but put off any real work. Still, I had no idea it was this bad. "What absolutely must be done now?" I'm hoping it's something small. And cheap. Despite what Jo said, I'm not comfortable being in her debt.

"Oh, but *mademoiselle*, every bit of it! Any of these could leave you stranded, or worse, *mon dieu*, cause an accident. I cannot let you drive this even a single mile more."

"Oh, but Louis...that can't...I mean, there's no way..." I'm mortified. "I *have* to drive it! I have to get home, go to work..."

Niall clears his throat and Louis looks at him, then at my reddening face. "*Pardonnez moi, mademoiselle*, I thought it was all made clear. Did Jo not tell you she would take care of everything?" A hint of steel comes into his voice. "Jo said she made this perfectly clear."

"Well, Jo did say something like that, but I...this is too much. I mean—"

Niall lays his hand on my shoulder and I bite my lip.

Louis's voice softens. "Do not give it another thought, *petite mademoiselle*. Take Jo at her word. She does not give it lightly. Your safety is my only concern." His kind smile eases my discomfort. Niall steps aside, staring at his phone.

"Okay." I'll take it up with Jo later. "So how long will all this take?"

Louis purses his lips and blows through them as he calculates. "I think a week should do it."

"A...a *week*?"

"Maybe two. Depends on getting parts, of course. No more than three weeks."

"But. But. But." I clench my teeth and try again. "I have a *cat* to take care of. I need to run errands. What am I to do without a car?" My stomach clenches. I can't afford a rental.

Niall slips his phone into his pants pocket. "Don't chuff yourself, luv. Jo has a plan. She always does. For now, I'm a mite peckish. What do you say we leave old Louis to that hunk of rusting metal you call a car, and go to the kitchen?"

I glare at him. Laughing, he sets off, and since I don't know my way around, I'm forced to follow. I thank Louis, then twirl around so fast my ponytail hits me in the face as I hurry after Niall.

I'm still pulling hair out of my mouth as he opens the ornate front door. It's solid wood, at least three inches thick and heavy-looking. But what's revealed inside steals my breath away. A wide staircase with an ornate banister, designed for making a grand entrance, curves upward. The floors are old wood, polished to a sheen. On the pale gray walls are hung Impressionist-style paintings I could spend hours studying. A crystal chandelier almost as big as my car glitters high over the entryway. In the center of the curving staircase stands a magnificent waterfall, complete with a statue of a human-sized mermaid.

Holy. Cannoli.

Niall turns to the right and I follow, my eyes taking in everything. The tasteful colors, the works of art. We pass many doors, including one that stands open, revealing a sizeable bathroom. I make a note of where it is, not wanting to lose Niall. A long hallway ends at yet another door. He opens it to the type of kitchen I have only seen on television.

I walk in reverently, my mouth hanging open. For real. To the far left are deep sinks. Plural. Their high, curved faucets detach. A pair of gleaming stainless-steel refrigerators flank the massive sinks. Each is easily double the one in my apartment. In the far corner, a wide metal exterior door is camouflaged with the same butter yellow as the walls. My gaze sweeps right, and I count—holy cannoli—*four* ovens set into the wall. Under each are two electric and one gas stove tops, and then a long grill. The far-right wall is lined in cabinets. In the center of the room are two long, well-used, but gleaming wood worktables with heavy metal shelves and drawers underneath them. Alongside the cabinets is a beautiful dining table, which could easily seat twenty.

I feel as if I've died and gone to heaven.

Niall is rummaging in the closest refrigerator, but all thought of food has left me. All I want to do is explore. When I wander over, I can't believe how much food is here. Fried chicken, BBQ, and tubs of salads and dips cover the table.

"My goodness, Niall, how many people do you think are going to eat?"

He looks a little sheepish when he hands me a plate. "Didn't know how hungry you might be or what you'd like, so I got it all out."

I look the food over and decide what I want. He isn't making a move toward the food, so I ask if I can fix him a plate.

"Ah, no, luv, I've all I need right here." Turning from the far refrigerator, he lifts a dark bottle with no label and I wonder if it's an ale or something. I've heard some of those malty English beers can be pretty substantial.

"You aren't going to have any of this?"

"No, that's all for you. Listen, luv, I need to tie myself to the computer a bit longer. Will you be okay if I leave you here in the kitchen?"

So this was about getting something in my stomach after I got sick. "Niall, are you kidding? You couldn't have left me in a better spot. Please, go. I'll be fine."

He takes his leave, and I eat my snack while investigating the ovens. Under them are proving drawers. I discover three commercial-grade standing mixers and spend a few minutes dreaming of the baking I could do in a place like this. Heck, a whole bakery catering business could run out of here.

I wash my plate, then put everything back into the refrigerator. I don't see any bottles like the one Niall had in there, and assume the other refrigerator is for drinks. I opt for tap water and find a glass.

After I make my way to the bathroom, I wander the kitchen again. I eventually sink into a dining chair. It's comfortable and I've been on my feet a long time. This kitchen can feed an army and the house is big enough to house them. I wonder where everyone is.

I pull my phone out of my pocket and find a text message from Jo, saying how sorry she is about my rattlesnake experience and telling me she will be home by 6:00. I guess I'm stuck here. I text her back that I can't wait to see her. A check of the time tells me I have well over an hour before I can expect her. I wish I were in my own space.

I keep eyeing the ovens and thinking about what it would be like to bake in such a kitchen as this. It would be nice if I could make something as a thank you to Louis, Beatrice, and Niall. If I find everything quickly, I have plenty of time, so I start hunting for ingredients. The kitchen is laid out so intuitively that I easily find what I need, and start getting the batter together.

Music in my ears thanks to my earbuds, I'm bopping around with a muffin tin I just took out of the oven when I catch a movement in my peripheral vision. "Niall, I hope it's okay, but I just couldn't help myself."

But when I look up, it isn't Niall, it's Jo. A huge smile takes over my face as I yank off the oven mitts and tug out the earbuds. She stands just inside the doorway and is giving me one of her inscrutable looks. Suddenly, I feel shy. "Welcome home. Uh, I made snickerdoodle muffins as a thank you to Louis and Beatrice and Niall. No one was in the kitchen, so I didn't think anyone would mind as long as I cleaned up." She still isn't saying anything or moving, and I resist the need to fidget. "And I did. Clean up, that is. As you can see. Jo? Are you okay?"

With a strangled sound, Jo removes the space between us in a hot second. She crushes me to her in a tight embrace, breathing deeply at my neck. After a surprised squeak, I fist my hands in her hair, my feet dangling.

I stroke her back. "I'm okay, Jo. Everything's okay."

Huffing a gust of air, she kisses me almost painfully. Jo slowly lowers me, sliding my body against hers. She laughs humorlessly, running her hands through her hair. "I have spent the past hours wondering what state I would find you in. *Mon dieu, ma petite belle*." She sets me a little away from her, her eyes sparkling as she wipes flour off my nose. "I should have known. Even Beatrice, who is proudly unimpressed with everyone, says you handled yourself well."

She didn't tell on me. Now I'm doubly glad I baked for her. "Jo, I admit, it was frightening, and were it not for Beatrice...but nothing happened and I'm fine now. Really, I am." Gingerly, I remove the hot muffins from the pan and place them on a cooling rack.

Jo kisses me again, brushes the flour off my cheek with her thumb, and leans over to smell the muffins. I hastily brush at the back of my skirt, sure I have flour there. "These look and smell delicious." Grinning, Jo brushes off the back of my skirt. Mostly though, she just pinches my bottom, making me shriek.

I go up on my tiptoes for a kiss, laughing. "Well, you are surely welcome to them. But remember that I made them as a thank you to Louis, Beatrice, and Niall. Don't go eating them all. Oh, Jo...this kitchen, this house, is unbelievable! Where are all the people that live here?"

Jo tugs my ponytail affectionately. "The staff has Mondays off, so my guests and friends know to fend for themselves."

"How many people stay here?" I think of all the windows I saw from the outside and wonder how many the place holds.

Jo puts her hands in her pockets and cocks her head, considering me. "It fluctuates all the time. Louis is always with me, and Niall keeps a suite."

That doesn't exactly answer my question, but I reason it's none of my business. "Oh, speaking of Louis, have you heard about my car?"

Jo takes my change of course in stride. "*Oui*, Louis called me and told me all about it. He can fix anything; you don't have to worry."

I roll my eyes internally and try not to show my impatience at her nonchalance. "Yes, but it could take weeks before he is done. What will I do without a car all that time?"

"You will take one of mine, of course."

What? "Jo! I can't just take one of your cars! They're too—" I break off when Niall comes in. My cheeks pinken. I'm too embarrassed (or proud?) to finish that sentence.

"I thought I'd heard you come in." Niall nods at Jo. "Listen mate, about Libby's predicament, how about you give her the Mustang? Unfortunately, Louis will have that sad pile of excrement running again. Might as well let the lady drive something with a little class until then." He winks at me as he punches Jo on the arm. "Hey, what's that I smell?"

I grin up at Niall, ignoring his assessment of my car. "Snickerdoodle muffins. Just a little thank you from me to you, Louis, and Beatrice for helping me."

Niall leans on the table and stuffs his hands in his pockets. He stares at me with that laser look before glaring at Jo. "See you don't muck it up, mate. A pretty woman who can actually bake is rare in this day and age."

"I plan to do everything in my power to keep her." I blush to my chest. "The Mustang?" Jo considers me, then she smiles that wolfish smile. "*Oui*, the Mustang will suit you very well, *ma petite*."

Passing Louis, I dart in and tell him about the muffins. The Frenchman is still sputtering when I walk back out to Jo and feel pleased all over again that I thought of making them. Jo leads me down the bays and I gush over the wonder of walking in the meadow —before I met the snake.

She smiles and strokes my hair. "You take such delight in the smallest things, *chérie*. You are refreshingly unjaded. *Dit moi*, how was your meeting with Sarah?" We've come to the last bay, but Jo gives me her full attention.

I dodge her compliment. "It was great seeing Sarah. We had a really good talk. I was able to get perspective on a few things and I am feeling much better about them. Thanks for asking about that, Jo."

Jo nods and turns to the bay door. She opens a panel, revealing a keypad. Beeps sound as she punches in numbers and the well-lubed door silently rises. When it gets about halfway up, I gasp.

Honestly, I *don't* know cars. But years ago, Dad took me to a car show. Right then and there, I decided this was the sexiest car ever made.

"You have got to be kidding me. It can't be. That's a 1966 Ford Mustang convertible. And it's candy-freaking-apple red. When you said Mustang, I didn't know you were talking about a classic. *The* classic. Holy cannoli, Jo, I can't drive this. *No one* should drive this. It should be in a museum. If you want me to drive an old car, put me in something beat-up." I back away. "Please, Jo. Don't risk this *perfection*." I'm muttering now. "Please don't make me drive it."

Then I hear clucking. Following the sound, I watch Niall approach, clucking and flapping his arms. *Oh, very funny. Hilarious.*

"Libby, luv, are you afraid of a wee car?" Niall taunts.

"Oh, ha, ha. You don't understand either. This is your fault." I glare at him, pointing accusingly. "What if I wreck it? What if a shopping cart hits it? What if a neighbor swipes it? Please don't make me drive it."

"Libby, *chérie*, there is nothing to worry about." Jo starts towards me. Instinctually, I take a step back. She shoots me that wolfish look. Unnerved, I steadily back away. "*Belle*, it will be fine."

Niall starts clucking again.

I know I'm trapped and there is no use in me trying to get away, but that glint in Jo's eyes sets my stomach flopping and I can't stop my feet. "Seriously. Put me in *anything* else. What if something happens to it? What if—oof!" Jo grabs me around my waist and hoists me up over her shoulder in one smooth movement.

For a second, I stiffen, worried about my back, but when it behaves, I hang there, defeated, my ponytail bouncing. Thankfully, her arm is pinning my skirt down.

"You are adorable when you get all worked up, did you know that?" Jo inquires of my butt.

"If anything happens to this beautiful car, it is on your idiotic heads." This is met with raucous laughter. *Yeah, that's right. I'm a riot.* "Put me down, you brute. Gah, do either of you even care about this car?"

Niall opens the car door, and Jo swings me down and around until she is cradling me in her arms. "Libby, it will be fine. Nothing can happen that Louis cannot fix. He restored it, after all." She kisses my forehead.

"But—"

"Enough. It is obvious that you love this car. Get in." My feet on the ground, I straighten out my shirt, tug down my skirt, and tighten my ponytail, restoring my dignity. I then lower myself into the driver's seat. Niall slides in the passenger seat and the two of them start pointing out things. I only half-listen, rubbing my hands on the steering wheel and gazing at the wood-paneled, chrome circular instrument cluster. I caress the dashboard and run my hands over the seat.

I don't know stink about what's under the hood, nor do I care. I just know she looks good, and I can't believe I'm sitting behind the wheel of one. With

Niall's help, I get the seat adjusted while they're still going on about the engine or something.

I turn the key and start it. That shuts both of them up. A huge grin takes over my face and I turn to Jo, then Niall. After a minute, I'm still grinning goofily when I turn it off and palm the keys. "Okay."

Later, after I'd made Louis and Niall promise to tell Beatrice about the muffins, Jo follows me back to my apartment in a sleek gray Audi. The Mustang purrs the whole way, hugging the curves in the road and giving me power when I need it. I've never driven anything so exciting, and by the time we get to my place, I'm a little revved up myself.

14

WHERE DO I DRAW THE LINE?

*J*o takes my apartment key, and I stand back while she does her check. When she gives me the all clear, I step in and close the door. Jo swoops me up in a kiss, making me giggle. Darcy comes galloping into the room when he hears me and starts rubbing all over both our legs.

He makes it so hard to walk, I finally bend down and pick him up. He has to be in the right mood to be carried. Apparently, this isn't one of those times. After a couple of steps, cooing to him and scratching, his tail flicks and I don't drop him fast enough. On his way down, he swipes, catching my chin.

"Ow!" He disappears into the bedroom.

I touch my chin and find tell-tale wetness. "Man, he really got me. I better go clean this up before I make a mess of my shirt." Cupping my palm over my chin, I glance up at Jo. A few steps away, she is staring at me with the strangest expression. "Jo? Are you okay? Does the sight of blood make you sick or something?" I almost laugh. That would be terribly ironic —the owner of a blood business squeamish over the sight of it. I take a step towards the bathroom, watching her, and the hair on the back of my neck stands up. She hasn't moved, but there is something menacing—hungry—about her now. And this time, there is no denying it: her eyes are red.

What the heck? "Ah, I'm just...going to the bathroom...to wash this. Okay, Jo? Why don't you sit down? I'll...just be a minute." I'm deliberately soothing, as if I'm talking to a frightened child. But I'm the one that needs soothing because Jo is Freaking. Me. Out.

Suddenly, looking for all the world like she's gripped by intense pain, Jo squeezes her eyes shut and covers her face with her hands. Groaning, she staggers away from me. I'm drawn to comfort her, but gripped by a primal fear I don't fully understand.

I rush to the bathroom and lock the door. Looking in the mirror, I survey the damage. It's a clean cut about two inches long, and a thin trail of blood dribbles down my neck. I wash carefully and, my hands shaking, I apply two butterfly bandages. They close it enough to stop the bleeding, and I wash my hands, watching the water go from red to pink. Blood-red eyes swim in my mind.

I lace my shaky fingers and squeeze them so tightly, the ends go blotchy. I can't stay in here, but I don't want to go out there. It's a while before I finally talk myself down.

I unlock the door and ease it open. Relief fills me when Jo is nowhere in sight. Quietly, I release the breath I was holding. Far from the pink clouds I'd been floating on, darkness looms.

How did we get here?

Hesitantly, I head for the living room, hoping she isn't there, hoping she didn't leave. She's on the couch and I perch stiffly on the opposite corner. Jo watches me, a pained expression on her face. The red haze has been replaced by familiar green, and all the danger I sensed is gone. But it was there. Jo reaches out and I don't flinch away, though I want to. She gently touches my chin and drops her hand.

"How bad is it?" Her voice sounds raw and it pains me to hear it.

"Not bad." I wait a beat, wondering if she is going to offer an explanation or if I will have to do it. I really don't want to. *Coward. Do it.*

"Jo?" I wait for her to look at me. "What just happened?"

She sits forward, her elbows on her knees. She studies her hands, her shoulders slumped. "I did not want to tell you Libby, not like this. I thought I could ease you into my life. Foolish."

Oh, goddess. That doesn't bode well. "No time like the present, as they say. Tell me the truth, Jo." I keep hoping she will just smile and offer up an easy explanation, take me in her arms, and it will all be better. But that's not going to happen. That big thing I've been wondering about deepens to a canyon between us.

Still staring at her hands, she finally starts talking. "You have wondered how I move so fast. You have seen my eyes glow red. You are a clever woman, Libby. Tell me what I am."

My mind recoils. I don't want to even consider what comes to mind. There's no way I'm going to embarrass myself by saying something so absurd. There's got to be a simple explanation. "Just tell me already, Jo."

She looks at me then, her expression challenging.

"You look it in the eyes, but you do not want to see. You do not want to believe what your instincts tell you. Say it, Libby."

I cross my arms defensively. "No. No, don't put this on me. That's not fair. This is your big secret to tell. So, tell me already."

Jo sighs, deeply. She studies me and somehow, I manage not to blink. "How do you want the truth? Do you want to see it for yourself or hear about it first?"

Oh, gods. What the heck? My instincts scream to run, but I have to know. I deserve to know. "Just say it already, Jo. Please."

"Will you hear me out? Let me stay until I have said my piece?"

I force myself to uncross my arms. *I have to do this.* "Yes, yes, okay, as long as...as long as I am not in any danger."

"You are safe with me, *chérie*, regardless of what it looked like a moment ago or what I am about to tell you." There is a desperation in her eyes I've not seen before. My heart goes out to her, but I keep my hands folded tightly in my lap. As much as I want to stop this admission, I need to hear it.

"I was born in the south of France, the only child of the widowed daughter of a marquis in the year 1852." I gape at her but she doesn't stop. "My father is a vampire."

My brain reels. I couldn't have heard any of that right. It isn't possible. *1852? This is some kind of joke.* I stand without even realizing it. *This isn't real. There are no such things as vampires. This is the stuff of books and movies, not real life.* But unbidden, the facts rise. She moves too fast to track. Her skin is pale and cool. Her strength. The red in her eyes. "But you eat food. I've seen it."

"I'm half-human. I must eat food. I must sleep. But I also must have blood. I crave it."

I pace, my hands twisting incessantly. I feel her eyes follow me, but I keep mine on the carpet. *This is absurd. How am I supposed to believe this?* "No. I don't believe it. Look, if you want to break up with me...if, if you have a wife or something, at least have the decency to be honest with me. This...this is just cruel."

In a blink, Jo rushes me, but it isn't the Jo I've come to know. Blood red eyes bore into me, glistening white fangs overhang her bottom lip. Her handsome face has morphed into sunken skin and bones sharply jutting. Instinctively, I turn for the door, but I don't get more than a step away before Jo grabs my arm. When I suck in a breath to scream, she covers my mouth and pulls me against her body.

Her gruff voice scrapes across my skin. "Shhh, Libby. You tremble so. But I will not harm you. Would never. Could never. Just *please*, do *not* run from me. My instincts...regardless of what you see, this is still me. If you can promise not to scream or *run*, I will let you go."

Still shaking, I manage a rough nod. Jo releases me and I stumble away, needing distance. When nothing happens, I gather my courage. *Is she still...?* Hugging myself, I turn. Jo sits on the couch once more, looking as controlled and dapper as I've ever known her. *Gaia help me. I've never actually known her.*

"You would not have believed me otherwise, but I regret frightening you. If there were any other way to convince you of the truth, I would have welcomed it. Now you know the truth." Jo looks up at me, her forest-green gaze pleading. "Libby, I will never harm you. You can trust this. Trust me."

I swallow hard. Oh, how I want to believe her, but I can't stop shaking or envisioning her terrifying face in my mind. My instincts scream for me to run. To hide. *What else has she been lying about? What does she want from me? Other than my blood.* I shiver. *Oh, goddesses.*

But there she sits, looking just like she's always looked to me. And she's had plenty of opportunities to hurt me, so why hasn't she? Can I really believe that Jo feels for me what I feel for her? Can I trust her with my heart? My life? I'd give anything if I could. I start to pace, but then realize I don't want to turn my back to her. *Gaia.*

"I might as well know everything. Go on. What can you do that is different than what, well, I can do?"

"As you have seen, I have superhuman speed. All my senses are extremely heightened. I can read thoughts. I am skilled in compulsion. I heal quickly and I never get sick."

My head starts shaking on its own, and my mind sticks on one thing. "You've...you've been reading my thoughts?"

"You are a particularly clear broadcaster, Libby. Your thoughts are what first drew me to you. Your humor. Your inherent decency."

I back away, holding my hands out in front of me. "No, we're not talking about me right now." I chew my lip. All the times I thought she read my body language or I must have said something out loud without realizing it. "Do you read my mind all the time? Do you know every thought I have? Are you reading it now?"

She is freakishly calm. "I can block your thoughts. I frequently do so."

I cover my face with my hands, then drop them. "You made me second-guess myself." I squeeze my eyes tightly and open them again. *Focus.* All the hair on my body stands at attention. My fingers are icy. "Compulsion, you said. Have you been using that on me?"

Jo goes rigid, her face and voice void of expression. "*Oui*, I have used compulsion on you. To get you to drink, to give you sleep."

"Oh, holy hairballs. Oh, gods. Did you...I mean, when we...was any of that even real? Did you use compulsion on me when we...? What do you want from me?" My voice rises on each word.

Jo leaps to her feet. I flinch, but she doesn't move closer. "No, Libby, no. Do not torture yourself so. Search your memory, your feelings. You know I did not force you or affect your mind. I know you have recognized what that feels like. Our attraction, your sensuality, what we feel about each other, that is all real. I used compulsion only to help you."

"Only to *help* me?" Hysteria bubbles. There was something she said a minute ago. *Oh, yeah.* "To get me to drink? What did you make me drink? Is this about the tea that tasted bad?"

Jo looks pained, but I don't know if I can trust what I see. "The reason for my health is the vampire blood. Influenza ravaged my childhood home. Though I stayed at *ma mère's* side, I did not get sick. My mother died in my 10th year of life. That was over 120 years ago. Not only have I never been sick, I do not have lasting pain, Libby. Most injuries heal almost instantly. A mere drop of my blood brings you temporary relief. The night we met, at the bar, I put a drop into your soda and compelled you to drink it. Do you remember that?"

I remember Niall being mad at Jo for something. And a strange thirst. Now I know what that was about. *"Jo's my magic Kool Aid,"* I told Emma. How perfectly ironic. "Yes, I remember. The pain just melted away." A bitter taste fills my mouth as I think about all the times I was in pain, then I'd be with Jo and, like a puppet, I drank and miraculously felt better. *What a dupe I've been.* I remember the tugging in my mind. "And you kept doing it." She nods. "But I never tasted anything. What was different about the pitcher of tea?"

"That was the day after your extreme pain. I have not done this before, Libby. I was apparently overzealous in my desire to take away your pain. I compelled you to drink a glass, to sleep deeply and dreamlessly. I knew how much you needed rest."

I can't bear to look at her. *Is any of this real?* "So thinking you know what's best for me, you slipped something into my drinks. Then you made me drink them, not of my own free will. You didn't give me a choice." My voice shakes with righteous anger. I'd wanted to know everything, but suddenly, I can't take in any more.

"Libby, that is unfairly oversimplifying things, don't you think?" Jo's hands fist at her sides.

"Seriously? Over*simplifying*? No. No, you aren't going to do this. Leave."

"*Chérie.*"

"Don't. Just. Get out!" The first tears slip down

my cheeks and I know a torrent isn't far. *Not yet.* My head shakes slowly, my eyes seeing nothing. I feel disconnected, fearing that I'll shatter into pieces I'll never put back together.

Jo covers the distance between us too fast and I jerk back instinctively. Her hands fist again, but she lets me keep my distance. "Whatever you need, *chérie.* I will do whatever you want me to do."

My chest tightens. I can't let her guilt sway me. I don't even know if it's real. *How can I trust any of this anymore?* I ache for her arms around me, telling me it's all a misunderstanding. It takes such an effort not to reach out to her, that's what decides me. "Go. I need you to go. I need time." I meet her eyes, see my pain reflected there. *Maybe.*

She nods jerkily. "The danger from my father has not passed. Your protection will continue. I will wait for you to reach out, if that is what you want." When I manage to nod, she goes on. "Contact me at any hour. You have Louis's number, too if you need anything. Goodnight, Libby. I will not allow this to be goodbye."

Before I can protest, she is gone, the door closing silently behind her. On autopilot, I lock it, turn off the light, and drag myself to my bedroom. Though it is too early for bed, I don't care. I succumb to the relief of sobbing into my pillow.

———

I'm on my third cup of coffee, but still feel drained. I stare blankly out the picture window, my eyes gritty. Jo's words keep replaying in my mind, and I wonder if I should have said or done something differently. Her terrifying vampire face still floats in my vision and colored my nightmares when I actually managed to sleep. My heart aches. I feel betrayed. I woke with a throat raw from wrenching sobs. One of my morning pills got stuck on the way down, the bitter powder not helping my throat a bit. However, the scratch on my chin, which prompted her confession, feels fine.

Now that the shock of what she revealed has worn off, the truth stares me in the face. Of course, she's a vampire. How could I have missed that? That nasty voice keeps telling me that Jo fed me blood so I would be normal. That she doesn't want to be with a crip.

Darcy is manic, picking up on my distress. I don't think there are any tears left.

Gods know I need a meeting now. It may be chicken of me, but I'm going to a nearby town to attend one today. I know I look like unholy hell and I'm not ready to answer any uncomfortable questions from people who know me. I just want to sit in the back and listen.

Though it's way early, I decide to go into work. I can't sit around here anymore. My body is full of stress-induced inflammation and my back stiffened to a board in the night. It's going to be a cane day. Whoopie.

I stand on the sidewalk, looking for my car, when my eyes fall on the Mustang. *Oh, Gaia.* Shaking my head, I go back inside and call an Uber. I can't really afford it, but driving something of Jo's is beyond me. Yesterday's fun and excitement taste sour in my mouth.

I relock the building door behind me. The office isn't in the best part of town and I haven't forgotten that Jo's father is out there, somewhere. Thankfully, after a busy weekend of showings, there is a lot of work for me to do, and for a while, I get lost in the distraction.

Gah, I'm tired. I keep wishing I could call Jo and hear her strong, supportive voice. I'm not ready to call anyone else. I wouldn't know what to tell them, anyway. I certainly can't tell anyone Jo is a vampire. *Gaia. Vampire.* I've read my share, and more, of fantasy novels, but that is the stuff of fiction. A month ago, if anyone had tried to tell me vampire exist, I'd wonder what drugs they were taking. But I can't deny what I've seen with my own eyes. And I still just can't take it in. The reality shift is severe.

If vampire are real, what else don't I know about? I shake my head at myself. Do I really want to know?

The rest of my shift goes by in a haze. I'm almost sorry to leave. Another Uber takes me to the meeting and I arrange for the driver to return in 50 minutes. At the meeting, I choose a seat in the back of the room and stare at the floor, avoiding eye contact with anyone.

I can't imagine I will hear anything really relevant today that will help me deal with everything I feel. But then, someone shares about not needing to worry about what his sponsor's response might be to something he says. That gets me thinking about avoiding the very people I need the most. Partly, I remind myself, it is so they won't institutionalize me if I tell them vampire exist. But if I'm honest, the biggest reason is that I'm embarrassed. I feel like such an idiot. I sneak out before the meeting is over to further avoid anyone, but I call Sarah and leave her a message.

When I finally make it home, I sit listlessly on the couch, staring into space, my back painfully stiff. Jo's words last night, and her frightening transformation, run on repeat through my mind. Finally, my phone rings.

"Sarah, hi. Thanks for calling back." I try for upbeat, but know I don't reach it.

"Well, sure, honey. What's going on?" I can hear papers moving and I picture her at her desk.

Gah! I should have been planning what to say. "You know that big thing I suspected, but couldn't figure out?"

"Yes..."

"Well, I found out. And...it turns out, Jo has been...manipulating me."

"Manipulating you how, Libby?"

"Well, like coercing me." I shake my head at myself, wracking my sluggish brain for the right words.

"I don't think I understand. Can you give me an example?"

"Well, it's like..." I flounder. "Suppose...I was hurting a lot, and you didn't want to see me suffer. So, you slipped me...an aspirin when I wasn't looking."

She chuckles. "I can remember crushing baby aspirin into applesauce so my kids would take them when they were little. Sorry, I know that's not the same." She pauses. "Wait a minute, Libby...are you saying Jo has been sneaking you *drugs*?"

"Not exactly? I mean, there are no prescription or illegal substances involved. Nothing addicting. Oh, dang. I didn't get much sleep and I'm not explaining things right." I wish I could be more honest with her, but I just can't.

"Alright, honey, I trust you. Why don't you just tell me how you are feeling?"

That's easy. "Hurt. Betrayed. Stupid. Confused. Sad."

"That's a lot to carry. This...this whatever it is that you can't explain that Jo is doing, is it in some way meant to control you? Is there malicious intent behind her actions?"

Kind of... "I believe she acted out of what she thinks is in my best interest, but she never asked me what I wanted. She didn't give me a choice. And she did it all behind my back."

"Hell, she sounds like my granddaddy. He unilaterally made decisions for my grandma. Like, he bought her cars and never asked her even what color she wanted. Is that kind of what you feel like Jo is doing? Or am I going in the wrong direction?"

"Wow. Yeah, I guess that is kind of like it. Why did he act that way?"

"Oh, it's just how things used to be, honey. Women's lib was a long way off. Anyway, the best thing I can tell you is to talk to Jo. Do you want to be with her if she's going to keep doing whatever it is?"

No. That's what I should say. But do I really feel it? Can I end this if she won't change? Isn't it already over? "No," I say firmly. "I don't want to live like that. My trust is already broken."

"I'm so sorry to hear that. You both deserve to find out if she will keep doing it, or if she is willing to respect your wishes and behave differently." She waits a beat. "And you promise there's nothing illegal and you aren't in danger from Jo?"

Good question. Yet, my instincts tell me I don't need to fear Jo. If I can't trust myself, how can I trust anyone? "I promise." *If* I can trust my inner knowing,

Jo's father is the real danger, but Sarah doesn't need to know about that, either.

"Okay, honey. Look, I've got to run. I have a meeting in a few minutes. Thank you for calling me and talking to me about this, Libby. You've reminded me of something I need to talk over with someone. It takes guts to admit our weaknesses. I love you."

"No problem, Sarah. Thanks. I love you, too."

When I end the call, I feel better. The fact is, right or wrong, I care deeply about Jo. I want so badly to believe she feels the same about me. I think Jo did what she thought was best for me out of concern. That much I understand. I also get that she couldn't tell me without divulging her very big secret. Knowing all that, and being okay with her compelling me and slipping me blood is a different story. And that voice keeps telling me it's all an act anyway. But I just can't figure out why she would bother.

I get up, more confused and more than a little headache-y. As I fix a glass of tea, I'm reminded of Jo's deception all over again. Disgusted, I decide to distract myself with TV. As I flip through possibilities, *Downton Abbey* comes up and I turn off the TV, throwing down the remote in disgust.

Must everything remind me of Jo?

15

I'M A SURVIVOR

I pay for an Uber again today. At one point, I pick up my phone to call Jo about my car, and then stop myself. Am I playing the helpless female? *That's why Jo likes you so much. You are a lonely crip she can manipulate. And didn't I make it easy for her?* I ignored the signs, after all. I can't lay all the blame on her. I was so enamored that I was willing to go along with anything, apparently.

With this unsettling revelation bouncing around my head, I walk into Jenny's office. I sit there waiting for the computer and letting my back adjust, debating. I'm not sure I'm ready to talk to Jo, but I really need my own car. I can't afford to keep using an Uber just because I want to avoid Jo. I consider going through Louis, but that's cowardly and I know it. I need to deal directly with Jo. After much deliberation, I just keep it simple and to the point.

Need my car. Don't want to argue. Tnight?

Within seconds my phone pings Jo's reply:

Anything you want. After 6. Counting the hrs.

Well, that was easy. My stomach is suddenly queasy with nerves. *Ten hours. Right. No problem. I can be ready to do this in ten hours.* Relieved to have something outside of myself on which to focus, I end up working overtime again.

When I get home, I call Emma. "Hey, Em. How are you?"

"Libby, what happened? Tell me you and Jo didn't break up?"

So much for thinking I could ease into the topic. "Wow, do I sound that bad?"

She huffs. "I know you. What's going on?"

I clear my throat and swipe at the tears. "You know how I joked that Jo was like my magic Kool Aid? Well, I found out that she's been putting something in my drinks to help me with my pain."

"WHAT? Like drugs, you mean? Painkillers?"

"No. Well, kind of. Like, nothing illegal or anything. I...I don't know how to explain it, and please don't ask me to. The point is, Jo did this without my consent. Without my knowledge. I only found out because of something else she was telling me. Something else she'd been hiding."

Emma gasps. "Oh, no. How perfectly awful. So deceptive. Sneaky. I'd be livid!"

"I was, a little, but mostly I'm hurt. Betrayed. And I feel completely idiotic that I never figured it out. I think I just didn't want to, Emma. I mean, isn't willful ignorance worse?"

"No. Come on, Libby. What she did was terrible. I mean, what if you'd had a bad reaction to whatever she gave you? What was Jo thinking?"

That's my best friend—always ready to defend me. "Jo says she was trying to help me by removing my pain. I think she meant well." *If I can believe anything she says.*

"Oh, gosh. That's tough, then. I mean, I have to tell you, Libby, if I had a magic Kool Aid I could give you, I sure would. But then, I'd definitely tell you about it, you know?"

"And if I refused?"

"Well, then we'd have a come-to-Jesus and I'd convince you." But she softens her declaration with her tinkling laugh.

I snort and shake my head. "So, but how much is too much, Em? I mean, I keep thinking about women's lib and the way I *should* think, you know? And I don't want anyone to control me, or lie to me, or hide huge secrets that affect me, but I kind of do want to be protected and cared for. And I kind of like when she gets a little domineering. Is that so bad? Shouldn't I want to be an independent, strong woman? Where's the line?"

"Libby! You are...ohmygosh, if you only *knew* how strong and independent you are! Listen, I want my doors opened for me and I want to feel like I am the most precious thing in the whole wide world, but I get to make my own decisions, thank you. And aren't we talking about our bodies here? I mean, my body, my decisions, you know?" She pauses a beat and I mull over her words. "Did you two break up over this?"

My stomach drops at the words. *It feels like we did.* "I don't know. I honestly don't know if we can get past this. If *I* can get past it. If she's even willing to change. She's...old-fashioned, you know? Jo takes care of the one she—" I catch myself. I almost said "loves." I don't know if Jo loves me or not. *Would I even know if she did?* "—the one she is with."

"I have faith in you, Libby. I know you will do what is right for yourself in the end. You always do. If you are important enough to Jo, I'm sure she will be willing to at least try to do things differently. But change is hard. I'm afraid for you to expect too much. Oh, honey, I really hope it works out. I know you care about her."

That's an understatement. "Thanks, Emma." I can always count on my best friend to make me feel better. "Enough about me. How are things with David?"

"He's terrific. I really like him. Wow, like, I really like him. He gives me butterflies just thinking about him."

I put my hand on my stomach. "Oh, I know exactly what you mean."

"Libby, I need you to meet him. With or without Jo, we have to set something up. I trust your judgment and I want your honest opinion. How about dinner Friday night? If Jo is a) still in the picture and b) available, it's a double date. And if not, well, it's—"

"You two and a third wheel!" I interrupt with a forced laugh. "Really, I can't wait to meet him. Look, I'm not sure I'll be up for it Friday, but we can try."

"Oh, sweetie. I'm sorry. I didn't mean to be flip. If David and I were on the outs, I'd be so upset. Hang in there. I just know tonight will turn out great. What time are you meeting?"

"I'm supposed to be out there after six."

"So, starting at six o'clock I will be sending you lots of love and luck and wishes."

"And I will let you know how it goes, and if Friday is a go or a wait-and-see."

———

Restless, I walk to the drugstore about a mile away for a few things. As has become habit, I look around, but never see Beatrice, or anyone else who seems to be watching or following me for that matter. I think it's so weird that I never see any of the guards, but what do I know about security?

When I step out of the store, I'm lost in my thoughts and worry about seeing Jo. I stuff the small bag into my purse and hike it high on my shoulder for the walk home. A man approaches and I groan, thinking it's someone asking for money – I always feel guilty because I sure don't have any to spare. Then I get a better look at him, and fear trickles down my spine. There's something familiar about him for all that he reminds me of the sculpture of David, with his halo of curls and marble whiteness. I shiver.

I catch a blur of movement and jump when I feel a sting on my left hand. I look down and am shocked to see a long line of blood oozing.

What just happened?

From out of nowhere, Beatrice is suddenly forcing me backwards, shielding my body with hers, her empty scabbard pressing into me. "Get the son of a bitch, Dex." She spins and shoves the sword into her scabbard, then she's ripping off the hem of her shirt and tightly wrapping my hand with lightning speed. "Let's go." Beatrice pulls her sword back out and hurries me around the building, forcing me into a near-run with her hand around my back. She yanks open the passenger door of a black SUV and hustles me into a seat. Slamming the door behind me, she leaps, and before I can even process it, she's opening the driver's door. I'm having trouble taking it all in, but my insides are shivering.

Who was that? What just happened?

My phone starts ringing. It's Jo. I debate about not answering.

"You'd better answer that. All I've had time to do is send her the S.O.S. She won't give up until she hears you are okay."

My sense of unreality deepening, I answer. "Jo? Was that your father?"

"*Oui.* Beatrice is bringing you to my home where you will be safest. Louis will look after you."

"I—"

"We don't have to talk if you aren't ready, but I must know you are safe. Were you harmed?"

I look down at the fabric dwarfing my hand. It burns fiercely, but it didn't look that bad. "I...I think so. It's no big deal. It probably just needs a Band-Aid."

Jo muffles the speaker, but I know a curse when I hear one, even in French. "Your wound must be tended. Please allow Louis to tend it. Please."

I doubt *please* is a word she says very often, and she's just said it twice. "Yeah, okay."

Beatrice remains silent, her hands clenching the steering wheel so hard, I'm sure she'll leave finger imprints. But she expertly navigates the curvy mountain road with deadly speed. When we make the turn onto Jo's road, panic sets in about seeing Jo, and it's on my tongue to beg Beatrice to pull over and turn around.

I close my eyes and take a deep breath. *I can do this. It will be okay. Jo may be a vampire, but if she wanted to hurt me, she already would have. If she doesn't care enough to work on this, I can do better. Whatever happens, I can handle it. I've been through worse.* I fist my uninjured hand. *I'm a survivor.*

There are at least a dozen vehicles parked in front of the main house. Beatrice drives to the first bay. Louis walks out to meet us, carrying a first-aid kit.

"*Mademoiselle.* I have been so worried." He holds out his hand. "Here, let me see."

"It's just a scratch, Louis. Really. I'm not really sure what happened."

Louis unwinds the fabric and studies my hand. It has nearly stopped bleeding. He looks up at me over his glasses. "More than a scratch, I believe, but not life-threatening, no. This is not all that troubles you, I fear. You grieve."

"I'm okay." I look away, tears threatening. *Louis, too?* It's just hit me how unblemished, white, and cold his skin is. *And he's so strong. How have I been so blind? Can I trust him? Is it all an act?*

"*Mademoiselle* Libby. Jo may have acted rashly, but her feelings are real. And neither do I pretend. However, I understand this is all a lot to take in and you feel overwhelmed. Time will prove our trustworthiness."

"I don't know what to believe anymore, Louis."

"*Non,* I do not imagine you do, poor girl. Come, let us fix this up."

Louis is gentle and certainly seems capable. I force my thoughts from wondering why he's so good at taking care of a wound. My hand cleaned up and bandaged, I trail him toward the house. We are almost to the door when a car comes zooming up the drive. It comes to a squealing stop, and Jo leaps out. But she stops several feet away.

"Libby."

My heart pounds. I don't know if it's from fear or passion. "Jo." I meet her gaze and can't look away. "Your father...is he...?"

"I am afraid he escaped Dex."

"*Merde. Pardonnez moi, mademoiselle.*" Louis bows, then disappears back into the first bay.

Jo stares at my hand, and I resist the urge to tuck it behind me. When her eyes meet mine again, red lingers. "May I?"

I had a feeling she'd need to check it out for herself. I nod. Jo slowly closes the distance and gently takes my bandaged hand. She sniffs it, then nods to herself. She doesn't release my hand and I squirm internally, caught between wanting to jerk it back and reveling in the feel of her skin on mine.

"As you can see, I have many guests today. I do not want you to be alarmed. You will be respected here. Safe."

"Okay." Dimly, I'd wondered that there were so many cars here. I'm not sure what we are about to walk into, and though I didn't know it was possible, my anxiety steps up another level. I look down at myself. *I'm not dressed for a party.*

Jo chuckles, but then looks contrite. "My apologies. You thought that particularly loudly. *Chérie,* there is no party. This is fairly typical. Those loyal to me come and go as they please, like an extended family."

She opens the door and I'm struck again by the

176

grandness of the interior. I catch her studying me. My cheeks heat and I look at the floor. It's hard to breathe with her looking at me like that.

"Come. I want you to meet Chef, and then we can decide what to have brought to my study."

When she pushes open the door at the end of the hall, I can't believe the change from my last visit. This time, the kitchen is full of life and scents. The chairs around the dining table are full of people talking and laughing. There's a card game at the near end. Someone looks over at the door, and soon, they all rise to their feet facing us, their chairs somehow scooting soundlessly back. They bend their heads respectfully to Jo, and there is a chorus of subdued greetings. I'm unnerved by the collective power in these pale faces. *All vampire.* In comparison, I feel weak, defenseless, and frightened.

Jo slips an arm around my back and holds up her hand. They still instantly.

"Friends, may I introduce Libby Weaver." Almost as one, they nod to me. "Please do not let us interrupt you another moment." I'm taken aback by the formal exchange and the deference they show Jo. Thankfully, they sit, their chairs once again eerily moving soundlessly beneath them, and slowly resume their conversations.

My attention is caught by a round woman hurrying toward us, and by her tall cap and starched uniform, I know she's the one Jo calls Chef. She wears a broad grin showing even white teeth, wiping her hands on her stained apron. She holds out a plump hand. Her dark brown skin is warm and her soft dusky-brown eyes are rimmed with gold. Wavy hair is shot through with gray and she has a welcoming grandmotherly air.

"Welcome to *my* house, Libby. I'm Charlene, though everyone here insists on calling me Chef." She rolls her eyes at Jo as she says this, telling me who is to blame. Charlene turns back to me. "You nearly baked me right outta my own house."

I stammer until I see the sparkle in her eyes, and understand she is teasing me. "I'm not all that. But it sure was a pleasure to bake in such an incredible kitchen."

Her laugh is musical. "Listen now, I had one of those muffins myself. You are being modest. Tell me, which pastry school did you go through?"

Jo laughs at the expression on my face. She turns to Charlene, pride evident in her voice. "Libby taught herself from books and videos, dear Chef. She even bakes her own sandwich bread. I've had it. It is..." and she kisses her fingers in an unmistakably French gesture of appreciation. It fills me with pleasure, even as I question if it's genuine or simply calculated to disarm me.

But Charlene smiles at me. "A natural-born pastry chef? Well, you want to bake here, you come in my kitchen any ol' time you want. The rest of these folk wouldn't know cornbread from grits, and they know better than to mess in my domain. Am I right, Granger?"

"Absolutely right, Chef. No one but Ryan enters your domain. Chef, Libby and I are in need of a light dinner sent to my study as soon as possible. Can you help us?" Jo's tone is as deferential as I've heard yet. Her respect for Charlene doesn't seem like an act, and Charlene takes it as her due.

"Hungry, Libby?" I nod. "Any allergies, or something you don't like?" I shake my head. "Then how about I warm this morning's quiche and throw together some fruit?"

"Sounds perfect."

I might even be able to keep it down.

16

DESPITE EVERYTHING

*J*o takes my hand again as we walk out. We get back to the grand entryway and keep going. Jo points out a den and a game room as we make our way down a long hall. Introductions were repeated in both doorways. My nerves jangle knowing I'm in a house full of vampire.

We pass a half-dozen fully decked-out offices. Finally, at the end of the hall, Jo leads me into a large room. She releases my hand to turn on a floor lamp. There's a long, cushy leather couch the color of roasted chestnuts along one wall and four matching recliners face it, along with a massive corner fireplace. Between the couch and chairs sits a long wooden table set on a huge, fluffy white rug. I want to slip off my shoes and bury my toes in the thick pile. I imagine lying on it in front of a roaring fire with Jo.

Shaking my head, I close my eyes and collect myself. My vivid imagination is so not helping. When I open my eyes, I note a loaded floor-to-ceiling bookcase I'd love to check out, and a sturdy wood desk littered with papers and typical technology. Overall, the look is just right for Jo's study, a perfect contrast of strength and comfort. Jo still stands by the lamp, reading something on her phone. When she lowers it a moment later, her face is apprehensive.

"The room is really you, Jo. I love it."

"I cannot tell you how that pleases me." She gestures to the seating area. "Make yourself comfortable."

Needing distance, I decide on a stuffed chair. I feel Jo watching as I head for it and press my hand into my abdomen, trying to stop the butterflies her nearness causes. Once I get situated, Jo sits down on the couch directly across from me. There's no escaping her now. It's make up or break up time.

"How is your pain today, Libby?"

I shrug. I really don't feel like the litany. "The usual."

She nods solemnly. "*Oui*." She waits a beat, then brandishes her phone as if showing me something on it. "Beatrice feels her honor is in question after my father got close enough to injure you. She wants to make it up to you by staying close."

I get it that Beatrice wants to make it up to me. I picture Jo's father in my mind and look down at the sterile bandage. *Do I really have a choice? What if he comes for me again?* "Tell Beatrice okay."

"This will be a great relief to her, *belle*. And to me. Thank you." She picks up the phone and starts texting as a young man comes in bearing a tray. He's tanned, tall, and lanky—Ryan, I guess—and I judge him to be about 18 or 19 years old. He smiles at me hesitantly, and I smile back. *He's human.* He darts nervous glances at Jo as he sets plates for us and unloads the food. When he steps close to me, Jo drops the phone and leans forward, her eyes crimson. He nearly drops the pie server and scurries away from me. I can't believe the humor lighting Jo's face.

She's enjoying this.

Jo stands. The poor young man grabs the tray and scuttles backwards out of the room.

"You knew he was scared of you and you provoked him."

"Yes, well. Sometimes I am not so nice, *chérie*. *C'est vrai*, I was...having a little fun. But Ryan knows he is safe in this house, I think. Chef would chop me into tiny pieces were it not so."

With that image in my head, Jo insists I make a plate first. I return to the recliner and balance it on my legs. I wait for her to sit before I eat. The quiche looks and smells delicious, but I hardly taste it. The moment of truth looms and I get increasingly nervous.

My hands shaking, I set my empty plate on the coffee table. Jo sits back and rests her ankle on her knee. She stretches a long arm across the back of the couch. Despite her casual appearance, tension shows itself in the rigid lines of her pose and her clenched jaw.

Maybe she's as anxious as I am?

I so don't want to have this conversation. I'm not sure I'm ready, but avoiding it won't make it go away. I brace myself. My stomach rolls and I have to breathe through my nose. I fold my arms across my stomach.

"I need my car."

Jo doesn't blink, but I think I see a flash of uncertainty. "It is not ready, I am afraid."

"I see."

"There is another issue." She waits for me to look up again to continue. "Your safety is paramount. I would like you to ride with a security team."

I blink at her, completely at a loss. "I'm not sure..."

"Beatrice and her partner would drive you around, rather than trailing you. This will allow them to better protect you."

"But..." I try to imagine bodyguards *everywhere I go*. Gaia. "Jo—"

"Please."

Well, crap. I have to admit, what happened today shook me. After a long minute, I nod. "I'll try it." There's no mistaking the relief on her face.

"You have questions, *belle*. Ask them. I will follow your lead."

I start with the first thing on my mind. "What does it mean when your eyes get red?"

She answers thoughtfully. "The vampire within is raised when we feel hunger or extreme passions. Also, if we feel threatened or particularly protective. A little red can be a warning or a tell. Like when you tuck your hair behind your ear." I feel my cheeks heat and I fight the urge to do just that. "Full red means the vampire is in control. Remember this. For when the vampire is in control, our focus is to win. To conquer. To dominate."

To kill? I consider the times I've seen red in her eyes, and what she said makes sense. Swallowing hard before I lose my nerve, I ask what has been haunting me. "Do you...do you only want to be with me if I am... healthy?" I can't help the catch in my voice. Everything hinges on this answer.

Jo tenses, looking offended. "Libby! How could you think this?"

"How? Jo, the first time we met, you gave me blood. And you kept doing it whenever we were together." A tear drips onto my clenched hands. I didn't know I'd been about to cry. I didn't know I still could.

"*Merde!* Libby, my darling, *ma chérie*, I did not mean..." Her jaw clenches. "Forgive me...it was thoughtless and misguided." She rakes her fingers through her hair. "*Ma petite belle*, I could not—cannot—bear to see you suffer. This is why I gave you my blood. No other reason."

I study those forest-green eyes and see only truth there. *Can I trust that? I want so badly to trust that.* "I've been doing a lot of thinking. A lot of thinking. What you did, Jo, it hurts. You betrayed my trust." My voice breaks. She squeezes her eyes closed and I stare, unseeing, at the table between us. "I don't know what to believe, and there is so much I don't understand."

"Tell me how to fix this."

"Niall. He knew what you were doing, and he didn't like it. Why?" Of course, he's a vampire, too. I can't believe I missed it before.

"You are correct, *belle*; *non*, he did not like what I was doing. He told me many times what a fool I was being if I wanted a relationship with you. I wish I had listened to him."

"He is like you, right?"

"Like me? Like only half of me. *Oui*, he is vampire. Niall became a vampire 50 years before my birth. It is Niall who taught me to control my abilities. He taught me to block thoughts when I was bombarded by the cacophony on market days of so many thinking and talking at once. Niall taught me that the blood of animals sated me, which saved my life."

I'm shaking again, but I have to know. "Did you d-drink people before that?"

"*Oui*, gentle one. I cannot deny it. To my great risk. And taking blood can be...pleasurable. Still, the danger of getting caught was great. People lost their heads, or worse, for far less. The need, the drive for blood is so strong." She fists her hands. "I would sicken and die without it. I am only half-vampire, but I inherited much from my father. Food alone is not sufficient for me."

"How...often do you need blood?"

"About every day or two. Though I can have stored blood any time, I enjoy the hunt." She must see the upset on my face. "Libby, I have sufficient control not to do them harm. As with humans, I can create an experience animals do not fear."

I already know the answer, but I need to hear it. "Is everyone here a vampire?"

"Ah, *chérie*, your courage becomes you. You are right to ask. *Oui*. Louis has been with me since my birth. He shielded me and ensured I had a regular supply of raw, bloody meat. I grew more rapidly than human children, and when I stopped aging around the time *ma mère* died, I looked as I do now. He did all he could to protect me, as well as my mother. When I left, he followed me, worried I would be in even greater danger on my own." She shakes her head at the memory. "He is devoted to me as a father should be. He asked Niall to change him so he could continue to look after me."

"Who else? Beatrice? Oh, yes, Beatrice. Of course, she is." *No wonder she's a badass*.

"*Oui*, all the guards are vampire. There is no better protection. My guests are as well, though a few have humans with them—people they care for and desire to protect. Chef, the young man who brought

185

our food, as well as the staff who are gone for the day
—they are all like you. Fully human."

I pluck at the cushion. "What draws so many to
you? Why are they all so afraid of you?"

Jo shrugs nonchalantly. "I am obscenely rich, for
one. My mother died a wealthy woman, and I made
off with everything Louis and I could carry. For
decades, I returned to France, retrieving priceless
family relics. I made that money grow, then started
making more, and then it, too, grew." She lifts her
hands in a careless gesture, then she straightens her
legs and leans forward with her elbows on her knees.
She looks at the floor.

"I was a different person for many years before
Niall saved me from myself, Libby. I was young, impulsive, and furious at my father for what he did to
my mother. He nearly ruined her, leaving her pregnant, and she was forever weakened by it. I sought
out vampire and made it my mission to kill them,
thinking them all cruel like him. I hated myself. I
hated that I survived when my mother did not. Louis
stood by helplessly, unable to stop me. I would hear
no reason.

Word spread to beware the human with unnat-
ural speed and strength. Rumors flew that I drained
vampire and stole their strength. Being born half-vampire is so rare, they did not even consider the possibility. Many tried to kill me, but my vengeance was so
great, they could not succeed. And then came the
night I went after Niall. He was the strongest and
fiercest vampire I had ever met. And he read my pain,
my loneliness, as easily as if I had spoken them. Over-
coming me, he offered me another way. So I began to
change, but I had many enemies. Together, we

hunted, exterminated. And became the most feared vampire in a century."

My heart aches for what she must have gone through. Seeing it on my face, Jo's shoulders relax, and she sits back. "Our numbers grew, as a vampire is safest with others. We offer protection, employment, and collected human blood as well as acres of wild game to hunt in exchange for leaving humans alone and protecting our interests." She looks at me intently. "The world is a more peaceful place even for vampire now. My allies and I are bound by a mutual desire for coexistence. But I protect what is mine, *belle*. I will always do what I feel must be done. You need to understand that."

I swallow hard. "I think I do. This is why you made decisions for me. Out of a sense of protection and care."

Jo nods. "*Oui*. And I understand that my actions made you feel as though I did not value you or your choices. This was not my intent, *chérie*. Vampire are more...practical. We do not see it as heavy-handed. You must believe I wished only to relieve the pain."

"Jo, will you keep doing it? Giving me your blood without my knowing it?" My stomach clenches with dread. I look down at my hands and grit my teeth.

Jo slips off the couch and slowly walks toward me, kneels on the rug before me. She weaves in front of my face until she captures my gaze and holds it steady. "*Ma petite amie*, because this means so much to you, I will try not to make decisions without you. But please understand. I will do all in my power to protect you. My father presents grave danger to you. He clings to the old ways. He seeks to destroy everything Niall and I have built, and will stop at nothing to get to me. Your safety is paramount. I have a century of ruling to overcome. I may make mistakes in my desire to take care of you, but I will try. I cannot promise more than this."

Can I really expect more than her willingness to try? "Okay, I think I can be okay with that. What about reading my mind?"

She purses her lips. "Though at times your mind shouts at me, I will endeavor to block you. Do you feel better about us now, Libby?"

"Rebuilding trust will take time, Jo. Baby steps."

"May I kiss you?"

I chew my lip, warring with myself. Finally, not trusting my voice, I nod.

She moves faster than I can follow, and before I know what happens, her mouth covers mine. Great goddesses, she's good at kissing. With over a century of practice, she knows to do things I've never even thought of.

My whole body responds. Gripping my ponytail, Jo turns my head, her lips grazing my earlobe, her tongue blazing a trail to my neck. She sucks for a moment on my jugular and my heart pounds with understanding. I wonder for a crazy moment if she will bite, and if I'd ever want her to. Then suddenly, she turns my head again and her lips are back on mine, our mouths open, our tongues tangling and no coherent thoughts linger. My nerve endings tingle, my nipples are hard. *Yes.*

All too soon, Jo ends the kiss, resting her forehead against mine. I'm dragging in ragged breaths. My heart pounds. "If I wasn't so brainless, I'd tell you that you're the goddess of kissing."

Jo's laugh feathers across my face. "My sweet Libby."

She kisses my nose. I just love when she does that. Then I decide to test my "loud broadcasting" and think as clearly as I can at her, *I just love when you do that.*

In the only answer I need, she kisses my nose again.

And I love the way you say my name.

"Libby, Libby, Libby," Jo whispers against my ear, and I shiver long and hard. I feel her husky laugh all the way through my chest.

I stroke her face. *Oh, Jo. My Jo.*

"*Oui*, Libby, I am yours and you are mine." Red flashes in her eyes. She blinks and it's gone. "Tonight, I will see you home. Soon, *ma petite*, you will not leave me at night."

With that declaration making my heart pound, Jo holds her hands out and I place mine in them. When Jo pulls me to my feet, she keeps pulling, and we hold each other for a few minutes. Letting go, she steadies me when I sway a little. The emotions and stress of the past two days have left me drained, and I'm suddenly worried about traveling through the dark mountains with Beatrice and a vampire I've never even met.

I open my mouth to say something about it when Jo pre-empts me, her hands holding mine between us. "Libby, how do you feel about riding with me while Beatrice and Dex drive the SUV? They will need to be there to guard you tonight anyway."

"But where will they sleep?"

"Libby, vampire do not sleep."

I take a moment to process that. "How much sleep do *you* need?"

"I need only a few hours each night. I can easily go a couple of days without." Jo squeezes my hands and lifts them. "Now, enough information for this day. Let us leave."

In the end, Jo has Louis chauffer us so she can hold me, and I'm grateful. We're silent during the ride. Our hands tangle with each other, and Jo strokes my back, my hair. I stroke her face, her arm. I run my hand through her hair the way she does, and watch it fall back. She murmurs compliments to me about the brightness of my eyes, the fullness of my lips. I desperately hope I'm not being a fool.

Too soon, we're at my apartment. Louis calls, "Good night, *mademoiselle*", and I wish him good night as Jo unlocks my door and does a quick check of the interior. She takes my hand and draws me in once it is clear, then, with both hands cupping my face, she kisses me breathless again.

"Until tomorrow, my sweet." And with a kiss on my forehead, she's gone.

17

ALL JUST FINE

I wake feeling more refreshed than I have in days, despite pain waking me last night several times. After my shower, I put a couple of butterfly bandages over the healing cut on my hand, throw on a threadbare cornflower-blue robe I've had since high school, and get coffee started. While it's brewing, I dry my hair. I bring a mug back to the bedroom to get dressed.

Jo texts, and we go back and forth a little. She's in a hurry today since she has early meetings in Roanoke, so we don't talk much. Despite feeling so conflicted, it's so nice to talk to her again that I don't even mind. Jo does tell me that she has people looking for her father. The reminder that he's still out there sends a shiver down my spine.

When Beatrice knocks, I let the vampire in with a tight smile. "Good morning."

She adjusts her ever-present scabbard. "Hey, yourself. How'd you sleep?"

"Good."

She wrinkles her nose at me. "Aw, and here I

thought we were going to be friends. It's not nice to lie, Libby."

I blink at her. "How did you...what do you know?"

"I felt your pain all night." She taps her chest.

"You *felt* it?"

"Well, more like, I felt you feel it. See, that's my strength—I'm real good at picking up on what people are feeling. Better than most." She shrugs. "That's why I got picked to guard you."

Wow. *Blessing or curse?* "I see. You said, better than most? Does that mean all vampire can read feelings, too? Can you tune it out like people's thoughts?"

Beatrice looks worried. "I thought Jo told you everything last night. I thought you knew this stuff."

"I do know some. A lot. Look, don't worry, I won't tell anyone if you tell me something I didn't already know." I think for a second. "Wait, is that how you knew about the snake?"

She nods. "I felt your terror. I didn't know exactly what was going on, but I knew you needed help. Most vamps only get a vague sense of heightened emotions. Then I heard what you were thinking."

Well. "So, ah, do you want coffee to bring along, or some yogurt or anything?"

"Di! Mi! You don't know anything yet, do you?" I may not understand her exclamation, but her intent is clear. As if it's my fault I didn't know to ask Jo about all of this last night. "We don't eat. Anything. Some drink a little coffee or alcohol, but it gives me terrible pain." She rubs her stomach. "I can't stand it."

I drop my forehead into my palm. "The muffins. What an idiot," I say under my breath. But I forgot about vampire hearing.

"Oh, no, don't say that. Nobody's made me anything like that before. It smelled so good. I carried one around with me so I could keep smelling it. I'm pretty sure ol' Louis and even Niall did, too. Just 'cause we can't eat, don't mean we can't enjoy it."

I'm struck by this woman's kindness. *She really is a badass.*

Beatrice laughs. "Oh, it cracks me up when you call me that!"

"Beatrice, do you *know* how to block so you *can't* read my thoughts?" I try to keep the irritation out of my voice.

She sobers up. "Yeah, but I'm not supposed to. It's part of your protection. We need to know when something is going on that we can't see."

Geez. "Well, can you block me when it's just us? Like on the way to work?"

"Tell you what, I'll mostly block ya, but I will still check in once in a while. You never know when something crosses your mind that you don't pay attention to. Like when you saw Jo's father out there under that tree? Jo said you never told her, but she caught it when it crossed your mind." She sounds dangerously close to lecturing me.

"Alright, alright." *I didn't know I was dealing with vampire at the time, but fine.* "Fine. Just...stay out when you can." This should make for an interesting drive. "So, what does "dee mee" mean, anyway?"

"Di! Mi! is just something I used to say when I was growing up. Let's see, I know you don't cuss...it's kinda like holy crap."

"Cool. When was that?"

She does a gracefully exuberant step forward and

back, I recognize her movements as The Charleston. "The Roaring Twenties."

That makes her...well. She looks great for a 90-something-year-old.

I meet Dex, Beatrice's partner. He stays in the driver's seat, so I only get an impression of his ebony bulk filling the space. He's all business, but seems nice enough. After running a couple of errands, I am feeling if not good, certainly better by the time I walk in to work. I roll out the chair to find an envelope with my name on it on the cushion. I guess Jenny had left it for me, but I don't recognize the handwriting. Curious, I rip it open. I pull out a pink index card, like what Jenny keeps stocked in the supply drawer, with a clump of soft black hair taped to it. I frown, because I know this hair. It's fur.

All at once, it hits me. The scream is building when the door flies open and it dies in my throat. Beatrice is there, fangs out, eyes red, face sunken in, brandishing her sword. Dex is behind her, watching the hall.

"It's D-D-Darcy's fur." I surge to my feet. "I have to get home! I have to get to Darcy! Move! Oh, gods, my cat. Get out of the way! I have to get home!"

I try to push past Beatrice, but she grasps my arm. Her fangs retract. Beatrice's voice is commanding. "Libby, you have to calm down. Think! This is a trap." Roaring in my ears makes it hard to hear and darkness threatens my vision.

I'm shocked to awareness when Dex lifts me and cradles me in his arms. His eyes are mostly red, but he smiles without fangs. "I've got you now, Miss Libby, don't you worry." We move so fast, my head spins, and I think I may vomit. I turn my face into his chest and close my eyes tightly, trying to stop the spinning. I hear Beatrice beside me, talking to someone, but I don't take in her words. *My dear, sweet, defenseless cat. Please don't hurt him! Please be alive!*

Dex literally tosses me into the backseat of the SUV. I flail, but he peels out of the parking lot before I right myself. *I have to pull myself together.*

A buzzing startles me. I look for the source and am shocked to see my purse on the seat. I drag it closer and scrounge for my phone. I am flooded by relief when I see the display.

"Jo! Darcy! He...he..."

"*Oui*, I know, *chérie*, I know. My people are on their way to your apartment. My father wants you frightened. Do not let him win. I swear to you that he will not have you, *chérie*. You have to trust me. The moment I hear about Darcy, I will let you know."

"Okay." I so want to trust her. "I take it I'm going to your place?"

"*Oui*. You cannot be touched there."

"When will I see you?" I feel weak even asking, but I crave her strength.

"I may be a couple of hours yet. Hold on for me, *chérie*. Can you do that? I assure you I will get Darcy the best care available. Can you trust that, too?"

I toy with one of the bandages on my hand, absently noting that my hand is burning. "Okay."

"I do not deserve such a wonderful, strong woman. But I will do all I can to try."

My throat aches, emotion thickening my voice. "Thank you."

"I must go now, *chérie*. Be safe."

I consider calling or texting my dad, but cannot for the life of me think what to tell him.

Much sooner than we should, we arrive. Louis is there, along with several vampire I haven't met. They all look fierce and ready to fight—what or whom, I have no idea. Louis pulls open my door and looks at me with such sympathy, I melt. He pulls me into a paternal hug.

"There, now *mademoiselle*, all is well now. Here you are, safe, and we will soon hear your dear kitty is fine and no harm done."

I pull back from his hug, not wanting to appear any weaker than I am in front of these strangers. At least my eyes are dry. "Thank you, Louis."

"I have just the thing for you, *mademoiselle*, come with me. We must visit Chef." He turns. "Shoo! Away with you all. You see there is no danger here, *non*? Go!" He winks conspiratorially and escorts me to the kitchen.

When we enter the kitchen, the refrigerator door closes with a snap as Charlene hurries over to us. "Now, you come on in here and sit yourself down, Little Duck. Don't you worry about a thing. Jo's gonna take care of that kitty of yours. Darcy? Is that his name? Where'd his name come from?"

"*Pride and Prejudice*, of course, Chef." Louis turns to me. "*Oui*?"

"Right on the first try. Jane Austen. I'm a big fan." I want to, but I can't muster much enthusiasm.

"Of course. Well, like I said, Jo is gonna take real good care of your Darcy no matter what. Now, can you eat?" Her hands on her broad hips, she looks me over critically.

I manage a weak smile and press my hand into my quaking stomach. "No, thank you, Charlene. I couldn't."

She nods briskly. "Didn't think so. Well, I know just the thing. Sit yourself down and I'll bring you some chocolate."

"Great. Ah, I'm just going to run to the bathroom." I scamper away before either can reply.

I close the door and lean against it for a minute. I'm so scared my cat is dead. And the fact is undeniable; *a vampire is after me.* His threat is escalating. He's shown he can get around my guard, into my work, my apartment, anywhere. Everywhere. I shudder.

How much longer before I hear anything? I study the back of my hand and remember how close he's gotten to me. Realize just how bad it could have been. My heart is racing again and I try to calm myself down. There's nothing I can do right now, except wait. And I hate that. I close my eyes, recite the Serenity Prayer in my head, and step away from the door.

I splash my face with cool water, and wish vainly for a comb or brush. I make do with finger-combing my hair and put it back up. These simple tasks make me feel somewhat better. When I approach the kitchen door, it opens. Louis smiles and bows me in like the butler he was a long, long time ago. I settle into the seat in front of a decadent brownie and a glass of milk.

I spy Louis and Charlene talking across the room, and I do a double take at the naked adoration on Louis's face—as if she is the most precious being he has ever laid eyes upon. I'm so taken by this idea that I almost miss Louis staring at me. When I notice, he winks, then puts his finger against his lips.

You got it, Louis. I won't tell her. He winks again before turning his attention back to the lady.

I almost drop my phone in my haste when it finally pings. I can feel Louis and Charlene watching me as I read.

Long search but Darcy fine.

I send a grateful prayer up. "He's okay. Darcy's okay." I barely take in their vocalized relief as I continue to read.

Must secure apt b4 u return. They will gather items. What would u like tnight & the am?

Ugh. I want to see Darcy for myself. But if I'm honest, I'm not sure I'd feel safe there, and I don't want to put him in more danger by being there. I wish Darcy could come here, but I'm afraid to impose. And the idea of strangers going through my stuff creeps me out. Before I figure out how to say all that, she texts again.

B will collect items.

Beatrice, I can deal with. It's as though Jo read my mind, though I'm pretty sure she can't over such a distance. Gah, I hope not.

Thx 4 evrythng. Ask B to get...

I list several items and have to give locations for them. It turns out to be a text that should have been an email. Oh, well. Maybe Beatrice likes scavenger hunts.

My fear mixes with relief now. Knowing that Darcy is traumatized, but okay makes me feel so much better. Lighter now, I turn back to my brownie. Still, the reprieve is temporary. I have to bake.

"Bread. Excellent choice in times of distress. My mama always said there is nothing like getting your hands in dough to get stuff out of *here*." Charlene points to her forehead, and I know what she means. "What are you making?"

"It's the recipe I use for my sandwich bread—a sort of milk bread. Jo liked it and I thought she might like to have her own loaf." I still my hands. "Oh, Charlene. Oh my gosh. I wasn't even thinking. Am I stepping on your toes? Because you know I can just take this home. I don't want to offend you"

Charlene leans back with her rolling laugh. "Honey, I have plenty to do feeding the staff, and keeping Jo and whatever humans are here fed. Believe me, I don't mind." A timer goes off and she pats me on the shoulder, moving back to her lunch preparations. Ryan starts setting places at the table and Louis settles at the far end, reading a newspaper.

"Louis, how goes it with my car?"

He puts down his paper and regards me, blowing through his lips in that decidedly French way. "I have done all I can until I get parts. Maybe next week they will come." He shrugs noncommittally and lifts his paper again, and I understand we aren't going to talk about it anymore. *Okay, then.* I'm not sure what is going on, but I let it go.

The door opens on a crowd of khaki and black-uniformed people, laughing and talking animatedly. They head for the table, and the sounds of easy banter and scraping chairs permeate the kitchen. As Ryan and Charlene carry in trays of food, a few stragglers come in and the table fills with laughter and talking. I turn back to my dough, not wanting to continue staring at the human staff enjoying their free time together.

The cleaning staff fed, Louis escorts Charlene out back for a walk. I'm staring blankly at the oven when I sense I'm not alone. A few vampire stand around the far refrigerator, holding the door open. Inside, stand rows of dark bottles like the one Niall had the first day I came here. Suddenly, I understand. They nod at me as they exit. The last to leave, a dark-haired stocky fellow, glares at me, malice coming off him in waves. I shudder, unable to look away. The timer goes off, breaking the spell and I automatically turn. When I look back, he's gone. Who was that guy? Why does he dislike me?

Unnerved, I'm just taking the second loaf out of the oven when Beatrice comes in, carrying my battered hand-me-down suitcase and the cat carrier. I'm so overjoyed to see Darcy, I want to hug her.

"I've got your things here, Libby. You sure are organized. It was a cinch finding everything you asked for. Darcy was another matter. Had to haul him out from under the bed and he was none too happy. I'm gonna leave all this here and somebody can take it up for you when Jo decides where you're sleeping. I'll bring Darcy's stuff in shortly." She sets everything on the end of the table and sits down.

"Beatrice, thank you for doing all this. I really appreciate it." I'm dying to take Darcy out and love on him, but afraid he'll get loose. After a few tense minutes cooing to him and checking him out the best I can through the crate door, I join her at the table. My shoulders sag now that I know he's okay.

"Sure smells good in here. You doing the baking?"

"Yeah. I thought it would calm me."

"Did it?"

I consider outright lying, then remember what she said earlier about friendship. "Not really."

"Hang in there. Jo will be here before you know it."

I return her smile. "Thanks, Beatrice."

"See ya around, Libby."

As she walks out, I suddenly have to get out of here. I coo at Darcy and stick my fingers through the gate to scratch his chin, then head outside.

When I step into bright sunlight, I immediately feel lighter. Ghastly hot or not, being outside helps. There's a warm breeze that dries my sweat.

I wander the meadow. I barely notice my surroundings with all the confusion and questions swirling in my mind, though I do keep my eye out for snakes. How much danger am I in? What is going to happen between Jo and me? I want to go home, but I'm afraid. I don't feel like I belong here without Jo. When will Jo get here so I can let Darcy out and check him over for myself?

Ducking through a cloud of gnats, I let my fingers trail the tall grasses. I want so badly to trust Jo, to fit in here. I've already grown to like Louis. Though Beatrice scares me a little, and I guess she should since she's my guard, I'm starting to really like her. And then, there's Charlene, who I can't help but like. Even Dex is pretty cool, though I don't really know him yet. But they all work for Jo. How can I know if they're being nice to me because they like me, or out of fear of or respect for their boss? Like that vampire who looked at me like a bug he'd like to squash...how many others feel the way he does, but won't show it? How many are like Jo's father?

I pause as the shudder rocks through me. Gods, I need to talk to Jo.

Reaching the shade of an oak tree, I prop myself against the gnarled trunk and look up into the wide canopy. It is cooler here under the thick branches, and the sun beaming through the leaves dapples the ground and my eyes. I'm reminded of how small I am. How insignificant in the grand scheme. This tree has seen generations of people. It spans time that my small life will not. But the vampire here have seen generations, will see many more.

Shouting jerks me out of a nightmare. I sit up, brushing bits of bark off of my face. Shaken and disoriented, I struggle up, gasping as pain stabs my back. Bracing myself against the tree, I breathe through it and watch the commotion in front of the house. A short woman with a cloud of golden curls points in my direction, and I wave. Apparently, Beatrice's "feeling sonar" doesn't extend far enough to sense me here. I don't understand why there are so many people outside, but before I can give it any more thought, the tall black-haired figure standing beside her becomes a blur and I stand still in the shadows of the oak, waiting for Jo.

She stops a breath away, not even winded, and wraps me in a fierce hug. "I arrived home and no one knew where you were. My call went straight to voicemail. I thought he—" she stops herself. After kissing the top of my sweaty head, she releases me. "And here you are." She brushes a finger down my bark-pressed cheek. I stick my tongue into my cheek as if I could smooth out the indentations. "Napping. Safe."

I pull the phone out of my pocket. "I guess the battery died. I'm sorry to worry you. I'm sorry everyone had to come out here." I stare at the ground, stab at an acorn with the toe of my shoe. *Great. Just great. They should really love me now.* "But here I am, and everyone can just go back to what they are doing now, right?" I put as much cheer as I can muster into my tone and start walking.

Jo grabs my hand, spins me sharply back towards her. I grimace as another stab hits my spine, but smooth my face as I ride the wave out. She drops my hand. "*Merde*, that was thoughtless of me. Forgive me, *chérie*, I meant no harm. And I wish you would not try to hide your pain from me."

It passes on an exhale. "Oh, Jo. It's fine, really. It's all just fine." The nightmare on top of everything that's happened in the last two days has left me brittle. "Let's just walk back, and everyone can leave. Please. Let them go back to whatever they were doing."

This time, Jo halts me with her voice. "Libby, wait. Please." Warily, I face her. "You are worried. Is there something I should know?"

203

18

I'M GETTING AN IDEA

*H*er voice is deceptively mild, but I hear the steel underneath. However, I don't want to make more trouble for anyone, especially me. I bet Mr. Stocky and Hostile isn't keen on being dragged outside for me. I have a feeling things would not go well if Jo felt the need to reprimand him, and I deliberately avoid thinking about him. Besides, I'm probably misreading him anyway— Jo said I was safe here.

I just blink at her, afraid she isn't blocking me. "No."

Apparently satisfied, Jo raises her arm and, in an instant, the figures standing around outside melt back indoors. Relief washes over me and I begin to relax.

"Louis wanted me to explain things better to you."

"Yeah, you know, that would be a big help."

Jo squeezes my hands, ignoring my belligerence. "He is concerned that I will cause you embarrassment by not preparing you better. He is right. It was careless of me to leave you so uninformed."

"Ugh, Jo. From the first night we met, I've been nothing but trouble for you. You have to have people guarding me, you have to keep giving me rides and cars and putting Louis out. Hell, even Niall had to babysit me one afternoon." She starts to protest, and I tug my hand free and place my index finger across her lips. She kisses it, and I drop my hand. "And now you call all of them out of the house for a freakin' *manhunt* or something. I just needed some air." I tug on my hair in frustration.

Jo considers me, unbuttoning a cuff and rolling up her blue dress shirt sleeve. Her gray suit jacket is missing. She looks so debonair and sexy. I'm sweaty and probably still have bark on my back and acorns on my butt—and I just *cannot* see what she sees in me.

She starts working on the other sleeve. "I must tell you again, *belle*, you are worth every trouble and more to me, for it is who you are on the inside that draws me to your delectable body." I blush fiercely and she smiles wide. "*Ma chérie* Libby, you look at me with your heart in your eyes and how can I refuse you? I have been trying to shield you, but I see now it could backfire. And I will be to blame for the embarrassment you feel."

In an old-world gesture, Jo holds out her arm for me, and I uncross my arms and splay my fingers across her cool skin. She covers my hand with her own, and we start walking. "*Chérie*, you must understand. Most vampire are far removed from their humanity. For them, humanity equals weakness. They find reminders of that life repulsive, painful, some to the point of hating all things human. They hunt those they see as weak, consider it as thinning the herd."

She rolls her free hand. "Obviously, the reactions vary."

"Louis, too?" I can't keep the sadness or horror from my voice.

"*Non*, Louis clings to his humanity, as does Beatrice to a lesser degree. And, of course, I am only half-vampire. My human side keeps me with a foot in both worlds."

Her voice was carefully free of inflection, but I get the sense she feels bitter about her status. I tuck that away to mull over later. "Okay." All I can think is that I am all human and very weak. *Thinning the herd.* Gaia. In terms of natural selection, I've got the short stick for certain.

She cups my cheek with her cool hand. "Thank you for my bread, *belle*. I cannot wait to sample it."

I give her a weak smile, then I ask what has been bothering me. "How did your people get into my apartment today when I had the keys in my purse?"

"The lock was broken, but it would not have mattered. After I stood pounding on your door for 45 minutes that morning, I had Niall make a copy of your key before you were fully conscious. I then made another copy and gave it to the head of security, Commander Thatcher, to be passed from team to team, with strict orders to be used only in case of emergency."

Her admission stops me in my tracks. I pull my hand away. *You've got to be kidding me.* "You made a copy of my key and didn't think you needed to tell me?" I'm too mad to look at her. *Will the surprises never end? Will I ever be able to trust her?*

"Libby, I did what I thought was best to protect you. This was before we talked, I will remind you."

I turn back to her. "But we did talk. You had plenty of opportunity."

A muscle twitches in Jo's jaw. "It slipped my mind. I assure you it was not a purposeful omission."

I start walking again and she falls into step beside me. "Convenient."

"What would you have me do, Libby?" She sighs deeply. "Your locks will be changed. I left the new keys with my things in the kitchen." She pauses. "Will you refuse me a key that would be used only in your security? If yes, I will respect this."

Her clenched jaw testifies to how hard that was for her to say. It's certainly a trust issue for me. I stop walking and meet her eyes. "Jo, I can be okay with you having a key to my home *in case of emergency*. But I know you. Aside from Beatrice, the guards are all strangers."

She nods, thinking. "Is there someone else you could trust to have a key in the event I am detained?"

I give that a minute. "Louis? But isn't he with you most of the time?"

"Except for rare occasions, he does not come with me to work. This is when I will be the least available to you, so, *oui*, I think Louis will be a good compromise." Jo seems pleased, and I'm relieved, too.

We start walking again. "Do you need to be invited inside? Or can you just enter a house like anybody else?"

"No, we are not barred from any building with or without invitations...or crosses or holy water."

Okay, so paranormal fantasies got that all wrong. "Hey, how did you get the management to agree to change my locks?"

"Your locks were flimsy and my father destroyed

them easily. I have had a convincing conversation with the management. Peepholes will be installed, as well as new deadbolts and chains for each apartment. Yours will be taken care of by my own people, as I assured him."

"Wow. That's really great. Thank you."

"Libby, please understand that even these locks will not stop a vampire. However, the manner in which my father broke in suggests that he does not wish to draw attention to his actions. I believe the new locks will make this harder."

I take that in, my fists clenching. "So nothing can stop him?"

"I did not say that, Libby. I increased your protection. Your guards will be closer, more visible to you. And while you are here, you are safe."

I nod, wondering just how visible they will be. I stuff down the fear. At least Darcy is here with me, safe. "What's the plan this evening? Where am I sleeping?"

She has that gleam in her eyes that sets butterflies loose in my stomach. "Ah, *chérie*, at last we come to the important questions. *Ma petite belle*, we can decide together what to do this evening, and later—" she grabs my chin, her scent curling around me making my abdomen clench, "—we will talk about where you will sleep."

Though far from calm, I definitely feel a lot better about things when we walk into the house. Snatches of conversation and laughter drift down the hallway. Jo directs me toward the kitchen. I look around the spotless kitchen as Charlene joins us, but I don't see my things or Darcy.

"I've been waiting for you two. This little duck didn't eat a thing today, and I know you, Jo." She laughs. "You can always eat. So your dinner's ready and I will serve it wherever you want. Just say when."

When Jo looks at me with a question in her eyes, I consider. "I'd love to get a shower. Would 25 minutes be okay?"

"Excellent. The sitting room of my personal suite, Chef. Thank you." Getting her jacket, she hands me the new keys. Her hand at the small of my back, Jo guides me out.

We head up that gorgeous staircase. I keep turning around and looking back at the chandelier over the foyer. After cresting the stairs, she leads me down a hall to the right. Her private suite is tremendous. Like most of the house, it's done in tastefully muted colors. A plush rug spans most of the room. A long, comfortable-looking couch and an equally long table that looks like one wide slice of knotty pine are the only furniture. The largest TV I've ever seen hangs across from them. I glimpsed a massive walk-in closet directly across from the entry. The bedroom is opposite the bathroom.

Jo led me straight to her *en suite* bathroom, and it was all I could do not to squeal like Emma when she sees *the* dress. It is amazing. All buttery yellow and gray marble. Neatly rolled sumptuous striped navy and gray towels fill the open shelves. And oh, the shower. I've only seen things like this in magazines. It's a deep, slate-lined walk-in my entire bathroom would fit inside. High windows show the reddening sky. Adjustable jets jut from the walls.

At Jo's suggestion, I get Darcy set up in here. I sit

on the floor and we spend a few minutes getting reac-
quainted. He's vocal, telling me all about his ordeal.
His tail is missing a chunk of fur. I shiver every time I
look at it. *Gaia.*

After playing around a bit with temperature, direction, and spray intensity, I am soon lost to sensation. I use tons of suds and scrub everything I have,
washing my sweat-dirtied hair twice and spending
extra time to shave. A built-in seat makes it easy and,
wow, I could so get used to these jets. Jo's products
neatly line built-in shelves. Only feeling a little con-
spicuous, I indulge myself by inhaling the scents like
a lovesick puppy. Yummy. But none of them explain
her toe-curling evergreen scent.

Her towels dwarf any of mine. Wrapping it
around myself, I grab another to towel-dry my hair
and sit on a whitewashed chest across from the sink. I
get my wide comb; then, watching my progress in the
ornate free-standing mirror, I work the kinks out my
hair.

I didn't think to have Beatrice grab anything else
for me to wear tonight, so I pull on my sleep clothes.
At least it's evening and, I'm hoping, we're alone for
the night. Since there is only one pair of underwear in
my bag, I debate wearing them now. If I'm honest,
just being around Jo gets me so hot...well, I'd rather
have my panties fresh for tomorrow. I have a morning
appointment with my rheumatologist and can't count
on getting home beforehand. Deciding to risk it, I pull
the faded navy sweats on commando-style. Though
it's early, now that the girls are free, I can't bear to put
even my clean bra on, so I pull the sleep tank over my
head without one. Then I step back to survey my appearance.

And though only Darcy and I are in this bathroom, my cheeks pink to see my nipples so clearly outlined under the blue-and-white flowered cloth. I huff at myself. *Am I being a prude? Am I hoping Jo and I will...nope, don't even finish that thought.* I turn in front of the mirror and view my backside. The thin cut-offs come to mid-thigh and flatter my butt nicely, but are loose enough to not be revealing, so I'm safe on the pantiless front. I turn back around. *Okay, so it's just the top.*

Prudish or not, I can't go out there with the girls announcing how much they'd like to be touched. I look through the clothes Beatrice brought me, hoping for a sweater, and thank the goddesses, I find my black one. The thin, loose cardigan hangs down over my butt, yet hugs my arms. When I experimentally pull the sides together, it camouflages my braless state. At least I don't feel quite so brazen anymore. I pull my damp hair over my shoulder, quickly doing a side braid, and secure it.

Gathering my things, I scoot my suitcase as out of the way as I can get it. The beat-up case looks especially ugly in such a sleek and beautiful room. Pushing up my sleeves—and gathering my courage—I open the door, following Darcy out.

The scent of food makes my stomach growl as I pad barefoot into the room. Jo is watching me closely. She has a nearly empty glass of what looks like dark red wine, and her eyes rake over me, lingering on my breasts. Her expression of hunger has nothing to do with the food laid out in front of her.

Her carnal look gives me pause. I feel an answering hunger of a different kind wash over me. My nipples tighten painfully. A slow, sexy smile lifts her sensuous lips. I risk a glance down at myself and see the cardigan has pulled away. Belatedly, I tug the sides back together. *Okay, this isn't as much help as I thought.* When I start walking again, captured by her hot gaze, I regret to find my knees are shaky.

"Your—" It comes out as a croak, and I clear my throat and try again. "Your, um, the shower is...oh, Jo you have to stop looking at me like that, or..." I trail off, unable to come up with a satisfactory option.

Jo chuckles deep and low. "Or what, *ma petite belle*?" I feel her voice deep in my abdomen.

Flustered, I tuck my hair while I search for an answer, and my eyes land on the food. "The food sure looks amazing. I know I'm hungry, aren't you? Why don't we eat?"

Jo laughs, and there's no doubt it's at me.

Okay, I deserve that. It *was* rather chicken of me.

Jo's voice is husky with need. "*Oui*, I have a hunger, Libby. One that neither food nor blood will slake. But we will do it your way. I am patient. Besides, you may need your energy."

Holy, Holy Cannoli. I fervently wish I had put on some underwear. I hadn't thought about where the moisture would go without any. And thank the goddess Jo must be blocking me because she doesn't seem to have picked up on that thought, though my reddening cheeks likely give it away.

Afraid to sit too close to her, I sink onto the plush couch at the far end from her after helping myself to my plate. Jo chuckles, but doesn't comment, and for a few minutes we eat the chicken pasta salad in silence.

More in control of myself now, I remember a few questions had occurred to me in the shower. I ask the one that bothers me most. "So you said you have heightened senses. Do you think your father can use my smell to track me now? I mean, since he's been in my home, it must reek of me. And he scratched me. Does that help him?" I stab at a piece of ripe tomato.

She looks at me sharply. "*Oui.* I had hoped you would not think of this."

"Quit trying to protect me by omission." She stares at me a minute, then nods, and I take that as acceptance.

"That is how your guards tracked you before. The combination of your scent and the blood I gave you, marking you as mine. But they don't need that any longer. My scent has faded from you anyway."

Why does that make me a little sad?

"Speaking of scent. Sometimes you smell, um, when your..."

My struggle makes her grin. "*Oui.* But I can only give you a limited explanation. All vampire acquire a unique scent at our making. Much like our flawless skin and making us as attractive as possible, it is part of our predatory make-up that affects our natural prey. Scent is used to lure, to calm, to...stimulate."

I'll say. Every time I smell it, I get butterflies. And more. "Ah, so you, like, can control it?"

"To some extent, *oui.* But it also will occur spontaneously under the right conditions."

I nod. I definitely want to give that more thought. Darcy yowls from the direction of Jo's bedroom and we both turn to watch him stalk out. He walks straight past me to Jo and leaps onto the couch beside her. He nuzzles her hand and curls up beside her. She turns to me, bemused, and my heart is that much more hers.

It's an effort to get back to our topic. "Can all vampire read minds, feelings, and emotions?"

Jo leans back, stretching her arms along the back of the couch. Gods, she is sexy. "*Oui*, some better than others. Some are stronger at reading minds than feelings, or vice versa."

"So your father can, too. Read me, I mean."

Her eyes are pained. "I am afraid so, *oui*, as we inherit our gifts from our makers."

"And feelings, emotions? How good are you?"

"I am quite gifted in this, too," she admits somewhat reluctantly.

Great. So he can do everything. I lean back against the cushions and rub my hands over my arms. My damp hair has left my shoulder cold and it raises goosebumps. I tug the edges of my cardigan close.

Jo laughs low, teasing. "*Chérie*, you sit so far away from me and hide as if you are afraid. Are you afraid of me, Libby? Am I the big bad wolf?"

"Yes!" More laughter. *Har, har.* That hungry look she's giving me is proof enough. As much as I want her, there's a part of me that's afraid of taking this relationship further. It's already going to break my heart when she ends this.

"*Non, chérie*, what you are afraid of is not me." She sounds so smug, I could smack her.

I cross my arms. "Oh, smarty pants? If I'm not afraid of you, why am I over here while you are over there?"

"Excellent point." Jo nudges him and Darcy jumps down. Then she starts to scoot toward me. Our gazes lock and she won't let go, the territorial red gleam entrapping me. I shiver so hard, my head shakes and my mouth goes dry. But my nether region is a different story. I feel the dampness, and Jo's nostrils flare and her pupils dilate. "Do you know what you do to me, *chérie?*'

I'm getting an idea.

"I smell your arousal; I see your body react. Though I try to block, I hear the conflicted thoughts and jumble of emotions. You make me wild with need." She lowers her voice to a whisper as she keeps coming closer. "What you are afraid of, *ma belle*, is your own passion. You fear letting go of control. You fear your passion will be too much, it will overwhelm you, and you will be lost." Jo reaches for my braid, toys with the end. Her voice is barely audible. "Lose yourself with me, *chérie*. Let me show you the depth of my feelings. Let me make love to you."

She says the words I hadn't known I needed to hear, and my hand shakes as I reach to cup her face. Yeah, she's going to break my heart, but I have a feeling it will be worth it. "Yes, please." Jo drags me across her leg and seals her mouth over mine. The strength, speed, and agility exhibited as she stands with me in her arms leaves my head spinning. She chuckles, kissing my nose. I think we are headed for her bedroom, but Jo carries me around the coffee table. She drops my legs and slides my body down hers as she stands me on the soft pile of the plush rug, sending shivers down my spine.

She kisses me gently. Pulling away, Jo picks up my braid and pulls off the elastic band. Then she unbraids my hair and runs her hands up the back of my head, and then down, pulling it forward. Her voice is reverent. "Every time I see you with your hair up, I want to take it down and spread it across your shoulders like this."

I lift my arms in invitation. Jo gathers me close and kisses me again. Her hands move in circles on my back before sweeping up to grip my shoulders and pulling me gently down. She guides me to the floor and stretches out beside me. "Much better." I smooth my palm over the close-cropped hair above her ear.

Jo drags me closer. It's achingly gentle, this exploration of tongue and lips. None of the hurry or urgency of our past kisses. Jo presses me onto my back and spreads my hair out. "I've fantasized about these auburn tresses spread around you on my rug." I lift my arms to her and she takes my mouth again. I splay my hands across her muscular back, gripping her shirt in my fists. Her strong tongue dances slowly with mine, explores, drives me wild.

She abandons my lips and rains my face with kisses. She traces my jawline with her tongue and dry lips brush my ears, emitting puffs that give me goosebumps. She suckles on my earlobe and my body lifts in response, a soft moan escaping me. My breathing intensifies and my pulse jumps. Jo's lips and tongue track down to my neck and she laps at my jugular with her tongue wide and flat.

My nipples rub painfully against the fabric of my tank and I wish fervently she would touch them. As the thought registers, Jo's hand skims up my side to cup my breast. Her thumb rubs the taut tip, and I gasp her name. She covers my breast with her palm and keeps it there, not moving. I squirm in protest. "There is plenty of time for that, *ma chérie*," Jo whispers, her lips brushing my neck. I rub my thighs together and my pantiless condition adds to my excitement. Jo stills.

"No underwear?" She growls, which just makes me laugh. Her head hovers over mine, her eyes full of passion. She plants another soft kiss on my lips. Pulling back, Jo takes my hands and draws me into a sitting position.

19

I KINDA ENJOY IT, TOO

 lift my hands to her face and pull her down to me to do a little of my own exploration. I kiss her eyelids, her nose, her cheeks. But she takes my chin and pulls my mouth open, claims it again until I'm breathless. For a while, we content ourselves to explore.

"*Ma chérie.* So beautiful." Her fingers brush one nearly purple nipple and my back arches on a gasp. In my mind, I plead for more. "*Non, belle,* I want to hear it with my ears."

I'm feeling shy and robbed of speech. Jo means more to me already than anyone I've been with before, but I feel so inept. "Please, Jo"

"Please what, *ma chérie?* Let me hear what you want me to do." That husky voice is my undoing.

I can do this. "Please touch me, Jo. Please take them in your hands and your mouth."

With a low growl, she does. Before long, Jo helps me stand and starts herding me to the bedroom. I feel a trickle down my leg, and I slick my thighs together with each step backwards. Jo's nostrils flare and that predatory gleam comes into her green eyes. I get a thrill of fear mingled with the excitement. A too-familiar feeling of being stalked has me putting a little more distance between us. Jo herds me expertly and, in a moment, I feel the bed at the back of my thighs forcing me to a stop.

Her smile widens. All I can see is Jo.

Her hands on my shoulders, I stare up into her eyes, mesmerized by my overwhelming feelings for this woman. Slowly, Jo draws off the cardigan, then the tank. I'm standing before her, naked from the waist up. And she is still fully clothed. I feel vulnerable and anxious, but so excited and very much alive.

I reach up and begin unbuttoning Jo's shirt. Every time I get one undone, she does something that makes me have to stop. Alternating between driving me wild and soothingly rubbing my back, she enjoys toying with me. And, well, I kinda enjoy it, too.

Finally, I get the last buttons undone and push her shirt off her shoulders. I tug the thin white tank free of her waistband and pull up as high as I can reach. Jo takes over for me, yanking it over her head.

For a minute, I just stare. She's magnificent. All solid planes and smooth skin. I splay my fingers wide over her abdomen and push slowly up. I press higher and rub my palms across her rosy nipples. Jo gasps and I look up to find her heated gaze zeroed in on me.

She grips my head and angles it, leaning down to kiss me deeply. Our tongues do their dance and my pulse races. My breasts squeezed between us; I revel in the sensation of her coolness against my heated skin.

Jo lifts me onto the edge of the high bed and nudges my legs apart. She steps into them and I wrap my arms around her once again. I'm gasping and quivering with need when I reach down and undo Jo's belt. She continues her assault. I unzip her pants slowly, watching the fabric loosen from around her waist and slide down her slender hips, revealing navy silk boxers. Fascinated, I push her pants further down and finally over her firm butt. With the weight of the belt, they fall to the floor.

Capturing my mouth again, her hands doing magical things, Jo kicks out of her pants, toeing off her leather shoes. My hands glide over her tight, silk-covered butt and I rake my nails all the way up her back and into her scalp. She shivers under my hands, and I'm struck by the power that I can make her feel this way. She throws her head back and arches her back. There's an answering throb between my legs.

Jo's skilled hands and mouth continue their assault. I'm shaking, my hands moving nearly frantically, my pulse racing. I want. I need. So much.

"Lay back, my lover." Jo lifts my hips, and in one smooth movement, she yanks my sweats clean off. She stands there a moment and just takes me in and I quiver under her scrutiny. I want badly to cover myself up. Her nostrils flare again and red flashes in her eyes.

"So lovely, *ma chérie*. You are so perfect, *ma belle*." My arms raise in invitation. But a feral look comes into her eyes, my brain freaks, and I scuttle back. Her eyes flashing, Jo stalks me to the pillows. At my apex, she stops, dips her nose, and inhales. She blows gently, and I convulse. Her eyes gleam with her smile.

Jo continues her languorous assault up my body and I'm writhing, moaning, my hands roving. She cups my face and kisses me so slowly, so sweetly, I'm almost overcome with it.

Abruptly, the mood shifts. Her mouth devours mine with hot passion, burning a scorching path to my neck, down to my chest. Her nips become sharper and I spread my legs in invitation. In plea.

"Jo. Please."

"I thought you would never ask, *chérie*. Look at me, my *belle* Libby." Jo holds my gaze as she slowly lowers her head. Then with her mouth and long-fingered hands, she expertly drives me beyond imagining, reading my body like a book. When the last tremor passes, I go limp. Boneless.

When Jo eases out, I whimper softly. I feel her shift on the bed, but I can't even pull my legs together. I manage to uncurl my fingers from the comforter, but can't lift my arms. Jo's weight shifts on the mattress and I'm dimly aware when she settles on her side against me. Her arm across my middle, Jo pulls me close. She kisses both of my eyelids.

"My *belle*, you are better than my daydreams. Rest my lover, *mon coeur*. Rest..." she murmurs, brushing hair off my damp face and stroking my cheek.

"But you—"

"Shhhh...*chérie*. We have all night."

And that is the last thing I hear until sometime later. At some point, I turned onto my side, spooned skin-to-skin with Jo, one of her strong arms pinning me there. My head is cushioned on Jo's arm, the top of my head tucked under her chin. Sensing me, she kisses my head. "She wakes."

I smile. Knowing Jo can sense my pleasure, I let it flow out. I feel amazing. Alive. Sexy. More sated than

I've ever felt. Jo loosens her hold on me to make it easier for me to turn. "So I apparently have a G-spot, huh?"

Jo flops onto her back and laughs, her arms akimbo. "Oh, Libby. Despite my powers, you constantly manage to surprise and delight me." She rolls back onto her side and humor glitters in her eyes. She tweaks my nose. "*Oui, ma petite amie*. I am sorry no one found it until now. But not *too* sorry." She tries to look contrite, but is clearly proud.

I squint my eyes and try to look stern. Which is pretty hard, considering I am so completely happy. "We have unfinished business, you and I."

"We do, do we?" She feigns a look of concern but excitement simmers.

Anxiety wars with desire. According to Julie, I'm not very good at this. "I want to give to you, Jo. I want to make you feel the way you make me feel."

Jo pushes her fingers through my hair. "*Chérie*, don't you know? I feel everything right along with you. Watching you, feeling what you feel, knowing I am the reason for your excitement, for your abandon, drives me mad with wanting you. Come, see what you do to me."

She lets me press her shoulder until she's on her back. I take my time exploring her again. I climb on top of Jo and straddle her waist. I lower my face to hers, my hair spilling all around us, curtaining us in our own private world. I may start the kiss in control, but even without using her hands, Jo quickly commands it. There's no question which one of us in the lead now, and for a while, I get lost in it. Jo trails her long fingers up my sides, making me squirm. Wresting control away, I finally break the kiss. *Oh, no you don't.*

Jo chuckles appreciatively. "Mmmm, I like you in this position, Libby. You give me ideas." She grips the back of my head with one hand. I draw her lip between my teeth while Jo squeezes my bottom where it hovers over her stomach. *This is about Jo*, I scold myself. Of course, that just makes her chuckle again. "Oh, Libby, *chérie*, you give me still more ideas."

I mentally roll my eyes at her. I brace myself away from her again as I run my tongue around the outside rim of her ear and nibble on her lobe. Jo skims up my sides and ploys her long fingers. My arms shake and I moan into her ear. "St-stop it."

"Oh, I don't think you mean that. Libby. You really want me to stop doing this?" I moan again and, with all my strength, I press myself into a sitting position. I make the mistake of looking into her reddened eyes and almost lose my resolve. But I know Jo won't hurt me. I return to my exploration.

Jo is breathing hard and her arms reach for me, but I bat them away. Her answering laugh is low and husky, and her eyes flash full red before she lowers her lids and watches me. It blows me away how sexy she is, sweaty and panting, carried away by my inexpert attention to her body. My pulse increases and I feel a swell in my chest. Pride. And something else I refuse to give credence to in a moment of passion.

However, the closer I get to her apex, the more nervous I get. I've gone down on women before because they expected it, but I don't enjoy it at all. I have a moment's panic. *What if she can't enjoy it unless I do? What if she won't see me anymore if I don't?*

Jo bolts upright and slips a finger under my chin, lifting my head. When I look her in the eyes, I remember belatedly that she's reading me. Her breathing ragged, her voice grates. "Libby, *ma petite*, everything you do pleases me. Trust this. Just keep doing what you enjoy, and you will soon know I am truthful."

Disbelieving, I watch her, but she nods at me slowly. I cup her face and kiss her with all the passion I have. Breaking the kiss somewhat reluctantly, I grin as I put an index finger on each shoulder and push lightly. Obligingly, she falls back to the bed, chuckling. When Jo cries out, I feel my center clench at the sexy sound. I can't believe how wet she is.

"Ah, *chérie*. Do you feel what you do to me?"

Oh, Gaia, do I.

Once again, Jo shifts the power, employing her long fingers to further stoke my desire. Our desire feeds off each other, bringing us both to a powerful crescendo, our cries mingling. Jo's face in ecstasy is the hottest thing I've ever seen.

Jo drags me onto her, tucking my head under her chin. My arms flop to her sides bonelessly. Jo wraps her arms around me as our breathing slows. She strokes my hair and kisses the top of my head. Again, I'm spent.

"Ah, *chérie*." I feel it rumble in the ear pressed against her chest.

"Mmmm?"

In that low rumbling voice, she continues. "Thank you. You are the sexiest woman. You respond to me as if we were perfectly tuned."

Her hand still strokes my hair, and I feel almost drugged with sleep. I'm floating, drifting in sated bliss. "Don't you know? You are everything I ever wanted and more."

20

WHAT A MORNING

$\mathcal{I}$n my dream, Jo and I are spooning, and she nuzzles my neck. She explores my body with feather-light touches. Dream Jo whispers, "Wake up *chérie*", but I just want to keep dreaming of her taking me again to those heights I've never been on before. I don't want to wake up and find myself in my bed, alone.

She chuckles, and I smile at the sound of it. With the bravado of dreams, I speak without thinking. "I love your laughs, Jo, but when you laugh like that, you just get me hot. Touch me and see."

"Oh, *chérie*, you are killing me. Wake up, my lover." She pinches my nipple and the sensation is so exquisitely real, I come awake. It takes me a minute to get my bearings.

"Jo?"

"*Oui.*"

It wasn't a dream after all. As in my dream, Jo is spooning me. Hot kisses sear my neck while her hand does amazing things that make me squirm against her. I reach up and run my fingers through her hair. She turns to kiss my hand, then goes back to my neck. Jo nuzzles, inhaling deeply.

"You smell so enticing, it makes my mouth water." Jo's lips tickle my skin.

Between my vivid dream state and reality, I'm already wet and breathing fast. Jo growls low and her teeth graze my neck. The sound scatters goosebumps, tightening my nipples. Again, I wonder if she will bite me. If that is what I want.

"Oh, how you tempt me, *chérie*," she whispers against my skin.

I shiver all over, and Jo sets her teeth wide on my neck. I don't feel the sharpness I would expect of her incisors, but my heart hammers anyway. My breath catches. She scrapes her flat teeth across my skin as she closes her mouth, then spreads kisses all around. I suck in a relieved breath. *Guess that's my answer.*

Jo kisses my cheek. "Nothing happens unless you are ready and want it to happen, *ma petite amie*. But I am quite sure you are ready for this."

All the gentle, leisurely pace is gone. Jo gathers my hands together and holds them. The pleasure-pain she employs gets me crying out, lost to feeling. It shocks me when in a swift, smooth movement, she plunges deeply into me, aided by the flood of my passion.

Jo lifts her top leg, bends it at the knee and brings her heel against my upper thighs, pressing me tightly against her. She starts thrusting against my bottom in her own passion. My thoughts are incoherent, my body moving instinctually. I feel my body gather, my sounds getting deeper and louder, and before I know it's even happening, I shatter into a million delicious pieces.

It takes a few minutes for my brain to come back online. When it finally does, I push the damp hair out of my face and turn awkwardly in the circle of her arms so I can look at her. Her expression makes tears spring to my eyes, and they drip down my cheeks into my hair. *That's how Louis looks at Charlene.*

Concern knits her brow. I swipe at my cheeks, but they keep coming. To my humiliation, I'm so overcome with emotion that I feel a full-on cry coming and I don't understand it at all.

Jo gathers me up in her arms and kisses my hands, my damp cheeks. Some women, like Emma, look cute when they cry, with their bright eyes and pink cheeks. Sadly, not me. I am all splotchy eyes, runny nose, ruddy cheeks. After a few deep breaths, the tears recede. I struggle to sit up, and she helps, joining me against the headboard.

"What is wrong, *chérie?*"

"Nothing? I don't know."

"*Merde, chérie.*" Jo runs her hand through her hair and makes it stand on end, managing to look sexily disheveled. "Do you know what it does to me, seeing you so sexy and vulnerable in my bed?" She runs her hands through her hair again and reaches for me. She holds my hand and toys with my fingers. "Tell me. What troubles you?"

I hesitate, but she's so serious, I decide what the heck. "I think it is several things, really. One, it's kinda been a long emotional day or two, you know? It's partly because what we've done tonight was so amazing and you gave me the most unbelievable orgasms I've ever felt. Plural. And when I had given up on ever having one with someone else again. You are the first person to touch me in over two years, Jo. And

I'm a little embarrassed, if I'm honest. I completely lost control. And you look at me with such..." Tears start streaming again and, frustrated, I smear my cheeks with my palms. The semi-dark and late hour embolden my confession. "And you make me feel things I'd given up on feeling. I don't know what you are doing with me, Jo. I'm so afraid I will wake up and this will all just be a dream. That you will finally come to your senses and disappear from my life." I shake my head. "If you do, what you gave me tonight was so beautiful, I will never forget it."

Jo squeezes my hands. "*Chérie, chérie, ma belle petite amie.* You humble me, you thrill and excite me. Sometimes, you madden me." She lifts my hands and kisses the backs of each before dropping them again. "Libby, no promise I make can force you to believe me. But now that I have found you, I will not let you go, nor leave you. You can trust that. Time will prove that I want no one else. In fact, I find it inconvenient —it is difficult to go to work, because I want nothing but to spend my time with you." I swipe my cheeks again and blink, trying uselessly to stem the tears. "Libby, I know you are frightened. I know I must work to rebuild your trust. But I will not hurt you intentionally. And I will do all within my power to keep you safe."

Unbidden, the menacing image of the vampire from the kitchen comes into my head. I watch Jo anxiously, but she doesn't react.

"Relax, *chérie*. I will not let my father get to you."

Thank Gaia she stopped listening and misunderstood. "You were listening to my thoughts when we were...well."

Jo grins. "*Oui*, I did. And I will again. The first

time I just wanted to make it perfect for you, but your thoughts are so hot." Her eyes flash. "I could not resist listening in again. And again." She raises an eyebrow suggestively, and it makes my nipples pucker. She continues, but her eyes darken so I know she notices. "But I blocked you afterward. Unless you object, I would like to continue to hear you. It not only adds to *my* pleasure, but I can assure you that I will make it add to yours."

Knowing my thoughts did seem to guide her, I shrug a shoulder, aiming for casual despite the blush. "If I'm not comfortable with it, I will let you know. Deal?"

Her grin is possessive. "That is most certainly a deal, my sexy *chérie*. Now, before you fall asleep, I must taste you one more time." With just those words, I respond viscerally and Jo's nostrils flare. Her eyes redden. Mere inches from my center, she looks up at me. "I know you are sore, *chérie*. I will be gentle." And she ever so gently brings me to another Earth-shattering orgasm.

I'm barely awake when she lifts me and places me curled on my side. Cool skin skims me as she spoons me and her arm snakes under my head. I snuggle back into her just before I succumb to a deeply satisfied sleep.

Jo wakes me with such sweet kisses that I almost don't mind how little sleep I got. Especially not when we bathe each other and make soapy, slippery love in the jets. After dressing and taking care of Darcy, I make my way to the kitchen while Jo goes to her study for a little work before she has to head out for meetings. Charlene sets me up with coffee and a bagel, and I happily settle at the table, daydreaming about Jo and our amazing night.

I head to Jo's study for another kiss when a figure steps out in front of me. My heart starts pounding. Mr. Stocky-and-Hostile in black-on-black looks casually rich. And dangerous.

Red eyes look me up and down, and his lip curls in distaste, revealing glistening fangs. "You reek of her, *human*." He sneers, his cheeks sinking. "No one wants you here, little girl. They are all just too afraid of Jo to admit it. What a shame it would be if her father were to just make you disappear." Then he looks over his shoulder and melts back into the office. I stand there trembling, too stunned to move. Yeah. Fight? Nope. Flight? Nope. Freeze. That's me. But I know I can't tell anyone. Right now he's just trying to scare me, but if he's confronted, he'll really come after me.

Just then, Niall steps out of the doorway further down, and I know what the other vampire heard to make him go away. Niall glances my way as he turns toward Jo's office, but it's too late to hide my reaction. Still, I try to pull myself together, as in a flash, Niall stands in front of me, his hands on my shoulders. "Libby, what's happened?"

I force myself to think of flowers. "Good morning, Niall!" I hope he buys my forced cheer. "What could possibly be wrong?" He studies me hard while I envision every shade of pansy I've ever seen.

Unintentionally, I bring up an image of Jo on her knees in front of me in the shower, and Niall jerks his hands away as if I were a blazing iron. "Bloody hell, luv. I didn't need that picture in me head. Fine, you don't want to tell me, I'm off."

I beat a hasty retreat back to Charlene, who can't read my mind, my thoughts whirling. *How much truth was in what he said? Was I making Jo weaker or more vulnerable? Were Beatrice and Louis just being nice to me because they're afraid of her? Either way, I am going to have to be careful. I don't know what Stocky-and-Hostile would do to me if Jo found out.*

"If Jo found out what, luv?" I stiffen. I never even sensed Niall's presence. "You see, I asked myself, what would have wee Libby looking as though she'd seen a ghost, then work so hard at pretending nothing was wrong? And it got me that curious, I tell you, that I had to find out." Standing behind me, he leans in close to my ear. "Who are you afraid of, luv?"

The vampire's sneering face with his eyes glowing and his fangs glistening pops into my head before I can stop it. Niall hisses, and I spin around, begging. "Please, don't. Oh, please don't make any trouble for him. He'll just be worse if you do. I know bullies like that, Niall, please." But I may as well be talking to a wall. He moves in protectively close and gets his phone out, his eyes on the doors.

I'm still trying to deter him when less than a minute later, Jo walks in, talking on the phone, carrying my purse. She looks calm enough, but I can see the hard set of her jaw and stiffness of her body, along with the red tint in her eyes. Jo is seriously pissed. "Louis, Libby is ready...Now, Louis...*Oui*, that will be fine. Beatrice and Dex are your back-up. It is imperative that they know where you are at all times. She is not to be left alone." Lowering the phone, she turns to me, her voice deliberately calm. "*Chérie*, I am sorry, but I must ask you to leave now. You will be safe with Louis. Do not trouble yourself about this matter."

Just then, a slender vampire I only know by sight flies through the door. "He's gone, Jo. We have searched the house and grounds, but the trail ends where his car was parked. He's gone.

Jo curses vehemently in French and English and Niall adds a few from the UK, as well. I feel sick. What have I done? Jo turns back to me, looking fierce and sorrowful. "*Ma chérie*, do not worry yourself. He will not be allowed to get near you. Please, *dit moi* exactly what he said to you."

I chew my lip, afraid to talk, and afraid not to. Jo takes my hand and Niall lays a hand on my shoulder. Strengthened by them, I repeat the hateful words in a low voice, hating how weak I sound. There's quite a lot more hissing and cursing, including from Louis, who walks in partway through.

"Thank you, Libby." Jo turns to Louis. "Do not let her out of your sight for a second."

Louis puffs up indignantly. "What do I look like? *Stupide*? Now, *mademoiselle*, do not listen to a word that *idiot* said. We do not have to pretend to like a brave and kind woman such as yourself."

Charlene bustles over. "Poor Little Duck. As if it wasn't enough having one asshole after you. Here, let me get you a coffee to go." She dashes off, Louis watching her.

"Niall."

"Jo, come on. I know the drill, mate. *Such a shame you were unexpectedly called out of town to address a critical issue at another site. You will no doubt be in touch to reschedule.* You're sure you don't need me to track him?"

"No, I need you covering at the office more. I'm sorry. I know where you'd rather be."

Niall pats my shoulder. "Aye, I'd rather be knockin' around the sodding moron that threatened Libby, to be sure." He leans down to my ear. "By the by, pansies are me favorite. Thanks for the slide show, luv." With a wink, he runs off.

Jo perches on the edge of the table and looks at me seriously. "Libby, we are going to talk about why you didn't think I should know about his threat yesterday. For now, I need you to go with Louis. Louis, Beatrice, and Dex will be nearby at all times. If you need to go to the bathroom, take Beatrice." When I flinch, she presses. "I cannot be worried about your safety while I am doing what I have to do to ensure it. Please tell me I can trust you in this. I cannot impress upon you enough how much danger you are in if this vampire finds my father before we catch him. He has access to sensitive information, and if he confirms our relationship to my father, nothing will stop him."

I swallow hard. "Yeah. Okay."

Beatrice, Louis, and Dex box me in as we make our way to the SUV. After Louis hands me into the back, Beatrice slides in beside me and Dex joins Louis in the front.

Beatrice comes into my apartment with me while Louis and Dex stand guard. I wonder if the front door will get repaired today since there's a hunt on. Beatrice advises me to collect more clothes. Since my suitcase is at Jo's, I stuff a few things in grocery bags. Not sure how many days of my medications I'll need, I drop my prescription bottles in, too.

When we arrive at the rheumatologist's office, Dex stations himself just outside the door and Beatrice perches across the room. She looks for all the world like she's in a trance. Heck, what do I know? Maybe she is. Maybe that's normal for vampire.

After I get checked in, I settle in for a long wait. "Louis?"

He leans in. "*Oui, mademoiselle?*"

Conscious of our privacy, I lean in close to him as well. "Have you told Charlene that you're in love with her?"

He's silent for so long, I wonder if I overstepped. But just as I open my mouth to apologize, he says mournfully, "*Non.*"

"For how long?"

"Far too long. Since we first met."

"Will you tell her?"

He looks at me, a little startled. "Dear *mademoiselle* Libby, it is not so simple, I am afraid."

"Why not?" I'm genuinely puzzled. It isn't like she doesn't already know about vampire.

"Our...differences are too great."

"But—"

"*Non, mademoiselle.* I could not ask such a thing of her."

That makes me unaccountably sad. "Have you ever been in love before?"

"*Mais oui!* I am French, am I not?! But *non*, I jest. I have loved being with many women, it is true, but I have truly loved only one other woman."

"In all this time? Only one?"

"*C'est vrai*, I fear."

"Wow. She must have really been something. Who was she? I mean, if you don't mind telling me about her."

"We met when I was taken on as a footman in her

father's home. Even at fourteen, Josette was a vision. So innocent, so beautiful. I captured her eye, too, being handsome in my youth. It was forbidden love, do you see?"

"How romantic."

"*Mais non! Mademoiselle*, it was bittersweet. As a child, she was promised to another man, as was the custom. The marriage was to come just after her sixteenth birthday. We met in secret when we could. But the danger was great and she had to remain pure, you understand? Or be ruined and sent away in shame, cut off from her father's support. As good as a death sentence to a woman of her station with no skills for surviving."

"That's awful, Louis. What did you do?"

"Do? Oh, *mademoiselle*, what could I do? I continued to love my Josette from a distance. Thankfully, her new husband moved into the marquis' home, so we could continue to see each other. He had a terrible temper, and so we had to be even more careful, for it could mean my life or hers if we were caught. I watched over her as best I could. I became the marquis' valet and, eventually, the *majordomo*. Josette's father died before her husband, though her husband was a few years his senior.

I learned that Josette was visited by Jo's father just before her husband died. The vampire compelled her to take him to bed. She would not for many years speak of it, but I saw her stricken tear-streaked face in the morning, and I knew something *horrible* had happened that night."

Louis pauses, lost in his memories. My heart aches for what he and Josette had gone through. "Josette was finally pregnant for the first time and no matter who was the father, she rejoiced. By the time she could not hide it, her elderly husband passed. This saved her life, you see, *oui*? Her husband had left her bed chamber just over a year after their marriage, unable to perform his duty. If he learned Josette had become pregnant, he would have known she'd been unfaithful. He would have ruined her reputation.

"She became terribly sick, her body wracked with pains. After a month, she could not walk. She required care, day and night. Thankfully, her miserable pregnancy was brief, which helped the staff believe the child had been conceived while her husband had still been alive. Jo was born just four short months later, with Josette draped in the black silk of mourning. My Josette barely survived the birth. Though she was not brought into the world by love, Josette was devoted to only child. I was, too. As *majordomo*, I had the excuse to be in rooms and on floors inaccessible to lower staff. I used this to my advantage, caring for Josette, then Jo, secretly acquiring what I realized they both needed to survive. *Ma belle* Josette never recovered her vigor, but we had happy, quiet years before the influenza took her away from me." Louis shakes himself. "A long, sad tale for a short question, I am afraid."

"Louis, she was so fortunate to have you. What a wonderful thing to have someone so devoted to your happiness, standing by you when things look bleak. Thank you for telling me about her. She must have been an amazing woman."

He blusters a little, but I can tell he is pleased by my words. Then he turns the tables on me. "I believe you may know a little something of love now, *oui*, *mademoiselle*?"

I blush, thinking about Jo. I yawn widely, then laugh at myself. "Perhaps."

He really looks pleased, and we are both lost in thought until I'm called back by the nurse. Beatrice joins me in the exam room, looking bright and alert. She introduces herself as my sister in-law so smoothly, it makes me smile.

After such a long wait, my appointment is shockingly short. But I've been here when the doctor had to take a lot of extra time with me, taking fluid out of a joint, injecting steroids, or just talking to me about my symptoms and what they mean. She tells me that my inflammatory markers are higher than she wants and for me to repeat the bloodwork next month. If they are still high, she will have to switch my medication. My doctor's been patient, letting me put it off, but she reminds me of the irreparable joint and spinal damage that can happen if I don't get on a biologic.

My dejection morphs to embarrassment when Beatrice follows me to the front desk. Thankfully, the doctor won't refuse to see me as long as I pay what I can. Beatrice hovers, obviously listening when they state my overdue balance while watching everyone simultaneously. I have to negotiate them down from $50 and they agree to take $25 today provided I send in $25 next week. She walks away as I pay, red in the face. When I turn to leave, she is murmuring into Louis' ear.

I make my way over to them with all the dignity I can muster. "Shall we go?" Louis' face is smooth, and Beatrice just winks at me before leading us out. By now, I'm hungry and it's nearly lunchtime anyway. I have to go to work in a little over an hour. I stifle a yawn. *What a morning.*

Beatrice and Dex don't say anything, but just surround me until Louis hands me up into the car. The whole way home, I'm beating myself up for money I've spent recently and especially for the big spending spree when Emma and I went thrift and consignment shopping. I'm wondering how much I can put into groceries this week and what I absolutely need. When we get to the apartment, I'm so in my head that I'm getting out of the car before Louis comes around and reprimands me, though he's gentle about it.

"I'm sorry, I just have a lot on my mind."

"And this is how we are made vulnerable to attack, *mademoiselle*. Do not let worries keep you from being careful. Each year brings increased strength and ability to us, and Jo's father is extremely old. We must stay aware."

Gods.

21

GOLDILOCKS

Since I'm out of lunchmeat, I make two cheese sandwiches and a fresh pitcher of tea. *Enough worrying about money.* Louis's right. I have plenty to worry about without letting my embarrassment sidetrack me.

Beatrice is on my couch. Doing what, I don't know. She hasn't had too much to say to me today and I'm trying not to look at that too closely, especially in light of what Stocky-and-Hostile told me this morning.

"Travis," Beatrice calls.

"What, Beatrice? Travis who?" I walk in to the living room carrying my sandwiches and a full glass of tea, ice clinking.

"Travis is the name of the bastard that said those things to you this morning." She's looking at me steadily. "I think you should know his name."

"I forgot you have to read me." I take a deliberate bite and chew slowly.

She waits a beat, unblinking. "You know, if you told Jo how much you owed that doctor and how much it weighed on you, she'd take care of it for you."

239

I nearly choke on a breadcrumb.

Before she can pat me on the back, I scoot farther away on the couch. I recover and finish chewing, taking a sip of tea. "Ah, no, Beatrice, I don't think that's such a good idea."

"Yeah, you're probably right. Good thing I already let her know when I reported in after the appointment."

"Oh, for—Beatrice! Why did you go and do a thing like that? Now Jo will feel obligated to do something about it." I've lost my appetite and set the paper plate down on the coffee table. "I don't need to be a financial burden to her on top of everything else."

"See, that's what I don't get. To folks like you, and how I grew up, what you owe is a shit-ton of money. But to Jo, it's peanuts. Don't you know that?" She looks genuinely puzzled.

"Beatrice, Jo and I have only known each other three weeks. It wouldn't be right for me to ask something like that of her."

"That's not what Louis thinks. He told me to be sure I included it in my report. Jo did say she wanted every detail, no matter how small." She looks so self-satisfied, I want to smack her.

I settle with rolling my eyes at her.

"Look on the bright side, Libby. You have so many much bigger things to worry about, that this will pale in comparison."

"Gosh, thanks." And despite my ire, I laugh with her.

A short while later, after they have checked out the office and hallway, I walk into work and get to it. Beatrice is camped out in the doorway, watching the hall and exterior door. As I'm powering up the computer, I think back to yesterday when I came in. It seems so long ago. So much has happened, both amazing and frightening. I remember the look in Jo's eyes when she got excited and how her face looked when she—

"Whoa, whoa there girl! Okay. Let's keep your little mind occupied, why don't we?" But Beatrice laughs and my embarrassment fades. "So." She walks around the office as I pull up the email. "You have weird hours. So, what, do you, like, clock in or something?"

"No, I just fill out a timesheet like these with the hours I work." I lean over and pull out a stack to show her.

"Where's your timesheet for today?"

I grimace at the computer screen. This should go over like a lead balloon. "Ah, I don't have one for today. See, I'm behind since I missed yesterday. So I figured I'd come in."

"You mean you're working for nothing right now." Her voice is way too calm for my liking.

"Well, see...no, actually. She already paid me to get this work done, and—"

"Louis!" Beatrice doesn't yell because she doesn't have to. *Why do I feel like my sister just ratted me out?* When Louis is in the doorway an instant later, she continues. "Talk some sense into this woman. She's over here working off the clock on her damn day off."

"You see, Louis, what I was trying to tell Big Mouth—" I glare at her and she sticks her tongue out at me, so I roll my eyes at her, "—is that I'm behind in my work, so technically, my boss already paid me to do this." I'm about to keep going until I see the look of dismay on Louis' face. My face gets hot.

"*Mademoiselle*. You are better than this, *non?* Doing this work for free becomes neither your education nor your dignity."

Well, geez, if you're gonna put it that way...

Beatrice nods. "My point exactly."

I ignore her. *I'm ignoring you, Big Mouth.* She just laughs.

I meet Louis's gaze. "Louis, my boss Jenny is willing to let me work part-time and practically set my own hours. I need that flexibility. I need this job. I. Really. Need this job. She's been talking about getting me to go full-time, but I can't do it. If I can't keep up, she'll have to hire someone else."

"And this will not happen today. So...*tout suite!* Close up, put everything away, and we will go. *C'est très difficile* to protect you here anyway. Too much glass." And with that, Louis turns on his heel and walks out.

And that, my friends, is how a Victorian era house steward vampire puts you in your place.

What choice do I have? Chagrined, I shut down the computer. My eyes stray to the work that has piled up, but I force myself to stand and walk away. Beatrice leads me out, and once we get to the exterior doors, Dex falls in beside me. I look up at the tall man.

"Long time, no see, Miss Libby."

Hilarious. "Bite me, Dex."

"No, ma'am, I don't believe I will, 'case Jo decides she needs to bite me back!" He laughs his baritone so heartily, Beatrice joins in.

Everybody's a comedian, I grumble to myself. But then, I can't help but laugh, too.

They insist that the safest place for me is Jo's house. I don't want to make more trouble for them, so I reluctantly agree. I'm sure they all have better things to do than babysit me anyway. When we arrive, Louis carries my stuff in, and I follow him up to Jo's rooms. I piddle around in there for a while and play with Darcy a little. Finally, I decide to walk. It will help my back, and I'm antsy. Hopefully, too, the sun and air will help clear my head. So much has happened that I can barely wrap my head around it all.

When I get downstairs, Dex pulls open the heavy door for me. "Whatcha up to, Miss Libby?"

"Hey, Dex. I was just going to walk. Maybe to the big tree and back."

"Would that be the one you fell asleep under when no one knew where you were yesterday?"

"Uh, yeah, that would be the one."

He winks. "I'll let Beatrice know. We'll keep our eyes on ya."

"Thanks, Dex."

As I wander, I think about the danger I'm in, my fear, money troubles, health concerns, and the incredible night of passion Jo and I shared as well as my trust issues with her. My phone pings, and I pull it from my pocket. It's Jo, checking in on me. I let her know I'm walking to the tree and all is well. I don't want to add to her worry.

When I get under the tree, the shade is welcome. Leaves crunch under me as I lower myself to the ground and lean back against the bark to cool down for a few minutes.

Out of nowhere, a vice-like hand claps over my mouth. I'm yanked painfully across the ground by my wrist, and then an arm snaps around my neck like a cold iron band. I kick my legs and try to scream, but before I can, a cloth covers my face, and my nose and mouth are filled with noxious fumes.

Holding my breath, I recognize Travis's voice. Gods. He's back.

"I've got you now, bitch."

Unable to hold it any longer, I breathe in deeply. As a distant scream of rage echoes, my last coherent thought is, "Sorry, Beatrice."

I come to foggily, but with the awareness that something is very wrong. Slowly, I take stock of myself. I feel sore. My nose and throat burn. There's a sour taste in my mouth, and a burning sting on the side of my neck. I'm lying on an unyielding surface. I can just make out muffled voices.

Footsteps near, and I realize I'm on a floor. "How kind of you to join us, Libby." I don't recognize the voice, but he has a heavy French accent, and my heart sinks. I try to open my eyes as another set of footsteps joins us, but they feel glued shut. "*Mais oui*, Libby. You are correct, but how rude of me. Allow me to introduce myself. My name is François Boucher. I am Jo's father." He waits a beat. "Travis, encourage our young guest to show a little courtesy, won't you?" He sounds bored, just as though he's ordering tea.

I try again to open my eyes as steps near. Following a blur of movement, pain explodes in my chest. I fold in half reflexively. The blow knocks the air out of my lungs, and for a long moment, I'm frozen, my eyes finally open wide and fixated on the layers of grime covering a wood floor. Spots start floating in my blackening vision while panic sets in. At last, my system reacts and I suck in a huge breath.

Unfortunately. When my lungs expand, fire erupts in my chest, springing tears to my eyes. I scream—until the pain it causes abruptly shuts off the sound. Every breath sparks off shards of pain. Wild with panic, I lie as still as possible. Something is very wrong. Trembling all over, trying to take shallow breaths, I rack my brain for how to make the pain stop. Trying to understand what's happened to me. Finally, the pain drives clingy cobwebs of drug from my mind and I catch up. Travis kicked me.

"Oh, *c'est terrible*. It looks as though you have broken a rib or two, Travis." He tsks. "What a shame!" Then he claps, laughing. "Now, Libby. Sit up and look at me properly. This is no time to be lying on ze filthy floor." Then his voice drips with venom. "Sit up *maintenant* or I will ask Travis to assist."

Galvanized with terror, I push myself off the floor, guarding my searing ribs with an arm. Thankfully, I was lying near a wall and I carefully shift back, panting through my nose to control my breathing. Every movement stokes licks of flame in my chest layered atop a steady burn. Finally gaining the wall, I prop against it. At least sitting up helps me breathe a little easier.

I raise my eyes to the two vampire standing before me. They are both in full vampire mode, with bright red eyes, sunken faces, and lethal fangs. François is slender, but I'm not fooled. Being an ancient vampire, I know he's freakishly strong. He has a sharply hooked nose. *Well, at least Jo didn't inherit that* runs across my mind before I can stop it and I clench my teeth, afraid of what he will do to me for the errant thought. He laughs, which doesn't necessarily soothe me. He doesn't exactly seem stable.

"You gonna let her get away with that?"

Ah. They're both listening.

François pats Travis on the shoulder. "I have something special planned for our guest. It will be *merveilleux, oui?* Do not worry. She will regret her thoughts soon enough." He pulls a cell phone out of his pocket and my heart skips when I realize it's mine. "Would you like to talk to Jo, Libby?" I'm too afraid to speak, looking for the trap. He taps the screen and holds it up to his ear. "*Ma fille!*" He laughs. "Such a wonderful vocabulary *ta mère* gave to you, *non?* Listen." And with that his demeanor, does a 180. "You will begin by putting $10 million in an account. I will text the information. If it is not in this account by noon tomorrow, Libby will suffer on the hour, each hour you delay. Though she is delicious, it would be a shame to have to drain her. *Comprends-tu?* Good. Now, just to show I am in good faith, I will let you talk with your little human."

I wonder when he tasted my blood, but I can't hold the thought as he approaches. He holds out the phone and just as I am about to take it, he jerks it back and I peel my eyes from the phone and meet his. "Don't even think you can get away with anything, you little *chienne.* Try it and I will make you both pay." Then he smiles evilly. "On second thought, go ahead! How I would love to hear you scream again!"

My hands shake as I take the phone from him. I pant shallowly, and before I can get a word out, Jo speaks. "Libby?" Relief floods me, just hearing her voice.

"Jo," I croak.

"*Chérie*. Where are you hurt?" Her voice is tight with tension.

I think of the easiest way to convey what's happened with the fewest words. "Kick." Pant, pant, pant. "Ribs."

She curses. "I will find you, Libby. Hold on."

"Try." I manage. When I sat up, I recognized where we are. A word comes to me, and I say it without thinking about it. "Goldi...locks." Then I start imagining all the colors that roses come in.

"Goldilocks, Libby? I do not understand." Though her tone is gentle, there's a note of desperation. Before I can clarify, François snatches the phone away. I slump back with my eyes closed, staring at Midas Touch, my favorite of the yellow roses.

"I warned you not to try anything, Libby." He sounds gleeful, and I open my eyes to see him holding the phone up to his ear. Menacingly he warns. "Listen closely, Jo. Follow my demands or this will only be the beginning." François nods at Travis, who has been standing quietly off to the side. "Travis, her delicate, pointy elbow, I think."

I'm shaking so hard, my teeth rattle as Travis appears beside me. He pulls my right arm away from my side from where I was guarding my ribs and jerks the elbow roughly up. I'm pleading "no, no, no" over and over. My head shakes violently from side to side, terror making my panting faster and more painful.

Grinning at me with his crimson eyes, Travis puts his meaty thumb and index finger on either side of the end of my elbow—and pinches. The pain that small movement causes supersedes anything I have ever fathomed. With the sound of a mortar and pestle pulverizing chalk, bone disintegrates and nerve pain zings down my arm into my fingers like never-ending fireworks. The long, feral scream wrenches out of me, heedless of my burning ribs as this new hell overwhelms me. I think it's more pain than I can bear, and I pray to pass out. Unfortunately, seconds pass, and I don't.

I thought I knew nerve pain, but compared to this unrelenting lightning fire, I've never known pain. I'm not aware of anything else, my entire being focused on my right elbow and lower arm. Not even my broken ribs register. With agonizing slowness, starting with the pinky, numbness creeps in. I can't bend my arm—won't even try. I hug it straight, angled across my torso, gripping high on my upper arm to keep it from touching anything. I begin to notice the rest of my body. My teeth chatter and everything aches from my constant trembling. Pain-filled sounds I don't recognize tear from my throat. Tears stream unchecked and I'm growing cold. I wonder dimly if I'm going into shock. What am I thinking? Of course, I am. Maybe now I'll pass out. *Oh, please, let me pass out.*

I'm not aware of anything else for a long time.

Knowing I have to slow my breathing, I attempt to hold my breath and count, but I only get to two before my ribs protest. My body twitches involuntarily with each nerve pulse down my arm, though the white-hot shots are getting fewer and farther between. My elbow has already swollen exponentially. Cautiously, I roll my arm off of my breast in an attempt to take pressure off my ribs. My swelling hand drags uselessly across my lap, but at least I don't feel it. As my breathing gradually quiets, I listen for any hints about what is going on. I have lost all concept of time. It is still light, but the angle of the sun is lower. I'd place the time as late afternoon or early evening. Not that it matters, but I'm not looking forward to spending a night with these real-life monsters.

Jo. I see the pure adoration in her green eyes. *I'm so sorry I doubted you, Jo.* Because now, I'm sure. Jo and the other vampire I've met—they're nothing like these two. They wouldn't do this to me. I can trust them with my life. *Well, could. It's too late for that now.*

We were followed, because I'm in one of the buildings on the Pulaski property Beatrice and I checked out. I doubt my obscure hint of Goldilocks will filter back to Beatrice, though. I can't count on them finding me. And I won't survive this. There is no way François will let me go. I just hope they kill me quickly.

A seed of thought tickles my brain, something François said. It seems important. But when I try to remember, it fades to nothing. I'm too scattered.

I pray the goddesses find Darcy a loving home, my Dad finds someone worthy of his love, and Emma does, too. I send Louis bravery so he can share his love with Charlene. Badass Beatrice with her easy kindness and delightedly unexpected goofiness. I remember her crossing her eyes at me. I hope she finds someone to share her life with. Even the suave and frightening Niall comes to me, and I send him my wishes for love, too.

But mostly, Jo's face swims before me. Her eyes filled with passion for me, her predatory smile. *I love you, Jo. I'm sorry I didn't tell you.*

Pain jars me awake when I slump forward. It takes a minute for the scorching licks on my torso to recede back to the steady inferno I've become accustomed to feeling. My arm from my elbow down is hugely swollen and darkly discolored. I gingerly explore it with my left hand. It throbs, but other than my elbow, it's mostly numb, and, thankfully, the nerve has stopped zooming lightning down my arm.

The bare bulb overhead is on, blackening the bare windows, now that darkness has fallen. I strain my ears for any sound, but all I hear are cicadas and tree frogs. An owl hoots his mournful call, and another answers.

I find myself reciting the Serenity Prayer in my head, thinking about what I can control and what I can't. While I can't control being in this situation, I can control what I do about it. I'm not ready to give up. Feeling emboldened, I decide to test my boundaries.

All is moot if I can't even stand. I strain my hearing again, and when I still don't detect any sounds, I try getting up off of the floor. I can't use my arms—I need my good left one to hold the injured one steady. The pain in my knee is nothing compared to my injuries. I drag my feet as close to my butt as I can get. Pressing against the wall, I bite my lip to keep from crying out as I slowly push myself up. When my knees finally straighten, I lean against the wall for a few minutes. By now, I know the size of each breath I can take, and pant shallowly while I wait for my body to settle. After years of practice, I know how to compartmentalize pain. Slowly, I succeed in separating from it enough to function.

Straining for any sound, I step carefully away

from the wall, my walking shoes making no noise as I scuffle through layers of dirt—I don't even care that I'm covered in it. I force each step, afraid to make a sound, afraid to stay still. I make it to the doorway, and my heart pounds as I peek around it. The greater room is empty. The vampire could be on the porch; I can't believe they'd leave me unguarded. But I've come this far, and I decide to keep going.

Halfway across the room is another doorway, and I fully expect one of them to jump out and grab me. The tension I hold makes my ribs burn hotter, so I breathe through my nose and try to relax my muscles. I pass the door with nothing happening and, at last, reach the exterior door. I have to release my injured arm to reach out and I do so carefully, letting it fall straight to my side. The elbow throbs with the new position and I sway a little. But I can't stop.

I grasp the door knob, and with my heart pounding in my throat, I pull it open. I'm shocked to find it unlocked. When nothing happens, I take first one, then another tentative step. Clearing the door frame, I take a moment to study the yard for movement. The moon is a crescent, but the sky is clear and there is enough light to make out the yard. There are no vehicles in sight. The only movements I detect come from bats swooping for bugs. Though I know they mean me no harm, I jerk painfully each time one darts close.

It's not far to the tree line. My pace is quick enough to jar my body on the uneven ground, but fear spurs me on. I bite my lip hard to stay silent. When I finally step under the canopy of the trees, I sway with relief. I brace myself against the nearest trunk and let my eyes adjust to the thick darkness inside the woods.

I focus on putting as much distance between myself and the buildings as I can. I sense the ground sloping sharply down and I'm afraid of slipping in the leaves. I sweep my left arm from side to side in front of my torso to avoid running into trees. I stumble often on sticks, limbs, and rocks that litter the uneven ground. My arms and legs get scratched by thorny brambles and rough bark. I'm probably bleeding all over the woods. My feet shuffle noisily in the leaves. On some level, I know I'm leaving a blazingly obvious trail for Travis and François, but am unable to think beyond my panicky drive to escape.

Then it happens. I sweep out my arm and feel nothing, so I shuffle my left foot forward, but it just keeps going down. I don't have the strength to stop it, though at least, I have the presence of mind to lean back in an effort to avoid going down face-first. My slide gains momentum and nearly forces my legs into a split. The left leads the way straight out in front of me, the right leg bent under me. I'm sliding on my back, my head and injured arm bouncing along the ground. I chomp my lip again to stop the scream tearing from my gut as unimaginable agony assaults my senses. I am flying down the slope, praying to just stop. My battered left arm reaches out for anything to grab.

At last, my hand slams against a boulder outcropping and I scrabble for a hold. Gratefully, I grasp a horn-shaped prominence, and my body jerks and swings wildly as it finally comes to a rest, yanking me over onto my stomach. I scream once with sharp torment, then lie there panting. I'm beyond rational thought. It's almost more than I can do to try to stay silent while tears stream unchecked, and let my body settle as much as it will. Roaring in my ears prevents me from picking out any sounds.

Slowly, I unbend my right leg and stretch it out. The muscles protest and spasm, and I curse my body that was once strong, but has been weakened by disease. My foot rests against something. Tentatively, I push down and it holds. I let go of the rock above me, and flex my stiffened fingers and wrist. Sliding my left arm down, I pull it under my shoulder, pressing my palm into the dirt until my arm stretches out, I can get my left knee under me, and flip.

Pausing, I still don't hear anything. The cicadas and tree frogs have even gone silent, but I don't know if that's because of my wild and noisy ride, or the presence of vampire.

I shimmy myself, inch by painful inch, until I'm behind the boulder. Propped against it, facing down the slope, I'm powerless to stop whimpers that escape on every shallow exhale. I landed in a broad patch of boulders that thins the trees. I can see the crescent moon through the canopy. That means I'm not camouflaged well, but I don't have it in me to move again. I know what lives in these mountains, and I don't know which threat scares me more.

Who am I kidding? I'd rather take my chances with a bear or a cougar.

My muscles are spent, quivering in their exhaustion. Goosebumps scatter and I grow steadily colder. I have a pounding headache.

If I survive this, it will be a miracle, but at least I did something.

Oh, Jo.

Nearly consumed by my misery, I drift in and out of awareness. At some point, I catch a faint voice. I

don't bother opening my eyes. I barely have the
strength to, anyway. It's over. They found me. Hopefully, they will just kill me now.

A minute later, I can feel them standing over me.
I can't even brace for the attack I know is coming.

22

YEAH, REAL COURAGEOUS

"*Chérie*, I must pick you up, now. Forgive me."

When I hear Jo, tears start flowing again, relief flooding me. I lift my arm, but all I manage is a few inches before it flops back down.

"Do not try to move." She slides her arms under my knees and upper back, then lifts me in one movement. I chomp my lip to stifle my cries and turn my face into her shirt to further muffle them. My ruined right arm hangs, but someone lifts it gently without bending it and binds it to my leg. I whimper shallowly like a puppy and can't even summon shame for my show of weakness.

This must be a dream. Gods, don't wake me.

Niall's voice floats above me. "Bloody hell, mate. She's hanging on by a thread. Let's get her out of here."

Jo starts moving and I keep my face against her shirt. I reach my good arm up and wrap it around her neck. She feels solid. *Can this be real? Is Jo really here?*

"Good *chérie*, hold on to me. I am real, *ma petite*. I will not leave you. I am proud of you, *mon chou...*"

Her whispered endearments continue in my ear as I fade out.

When the car door opens, I hear Louis and realize I've lost a chunk of time. I hurt so badly; I wish I could just stay passed out. When Jo steps into the SUV with me, there is a collective intake of breath.

Yeah, tell me about it.

My jaw is clenched so hard that my teeth ache and the muscles in my cheek quiver with the effort to stay silent. Though I can't believe any are left, tears still leak, and Jo's shirt has grown damp in an ever-widening circle. I hear Charlene coo "Little Duck" and Beatrice's voice, but I don't catch her words. I'm losing focus again.

"Stay with me *chérie*, just a little longer. Listen to my voice..."

I try, but consciousness is like smoke, drifting through my fingers. I keep slipping away. It is such a relief to just let go. *So tired. Just let me go.*

"Never, *chérie*, I can never let you go. You are so brave, so courageous, so strong. Keep being strong, my lover..."

The tide drags at me, and I drift in and out. At some point, I'm aware of being laid on something soft. Then I succumb for a while. I'm awakened to drink and I choke, my throat too dry and sore to work. Gentle hands move me, and I pass out again. When I come back, I am more aware, a little stronger. Someone gave me something for pain and my head doesn't ache as badly. I can take slightly bigger breaths. I open my eyes and they fall on Louis, perched on a low stool beside me, working on my arm with a pair of tweezers. My exposed skin is covered in thorns and scratches from the bramble, as I knew it would be. I'm dirty, and dried blood is everywhere.

"Do not worry, *mademoiselle*. When I finish pulling these vicious briars from your limbs, Charlene will wash you up."

My voice is so scratchy, I barely recognize it. I feel drugged. After a try, I give up and think at him. *I wasn't worried about being dirty. It must be hard on you to be around my blood.*

Louis regards me steadily. "How very like you to fear for my comfort and not for what I might do to you, *mademoiselle*. But no matter. I fed in preparation for this." He bends back down to his meticulous task.

That's just as well. I realize someone else is in the room and turn my head slowly, the room spinning a little. Jo has a chair pulled right up beside the bed and she reaches for my hand. A slight squeeze of her fingers is all I can manage.

You rescued me.

Her eyes flash red, then back to green. "Not soon enough, *chérie*. I am more sorry than I can express."

I'm alive, aren't I? I'd given up, and then there you were. I guess Goldilocks worked, after all?

From the direction of the door comes a snort, and I slide my eyes over.

"Yeah, when she finally got around to telling me." Beatrice points at Jo. "She kept trying to work it out herself." She looks at my elbow, then back at my face. "That was a high price to pay, but awful good thinking, Libby. You are one courageous chick. I don't know that I coulda dragged my human self down into those woods, hurt like that."

"Here, here." Niall walks in behind Beatrice. "It took tremendous strength to get through what you did, Libby. It's a bloody good thing they underestimated you and left you unguarded."

Louis clears his throat meaningfully. "I don't believe they were the only ones to underestimate her today, including herself."

Niall looks for all the world like a reprimanded schoolboy, and if I had it in me, I would laugh. "Yes, well. I won't make that mistake again, will I?" Then he winks at me.

I turn my gaze to Louis. *Um, Louis, if you have anything for pain, could I please have something?*

He looks at me, then at Jo, who is still holding my hand. I turn to her, the question in my eyes. "Jo?"

With feather-weight strokes, Jo moves her hand across the back of my head, and I wince. "When we saw this lump, we feared a concussion. So we couldn't risk giving you anything. But you were in too much pain and your body needed a break. I made the decision to put a drop of my blood into some water and Louis helped me give it to you." She continues to look me in the eyes.

Thank you, Jo. It was unbearable. I trust you didn't make that decision lightly, but can I maybe have Tylenol or something now? I look at Louis because he seems to know what he's doing. *Am I still at risk of concussion?*

He purses his lips and blows through them. "I think it is a risk we can take. I have better than Tylenol, but you will probably sleep. Are you ready for this?"

More than I can express.

When he takes away the glass and Jo starts to lower me back to the pillow, I look at her. *Can I be propped up a little? It's easier to breathe this way.*

"*Bien sur*. Beatrice—"

"On it." She disappears. Jo continues to hold me upright and when Beatrice comes back, they stuff pillows behind me. When Jo eases me back, I'm already feeling the effects of the pill. I stare up into her eyes as she hovers over me until I am gratefully pulled under.

When I awake, it is daylight, and that is as much as I know as I have no concept of time. Something is in my nose and I wriggle it uncomfortably. I dazedly wonder if I'm on oxygen. Certainly, I feel less like I have to work to get air.

I take stock of myself. I'm groggy and my mouth is pasty, but my headache is gone. My right elbow throbs. My whole arm is encased in a kind of cushioned cold pack. I don't dare try to move it. Just under my right breast burns and throbs. To my left, Jo is still in the chair, still holding my hand, though her head is down and she appears to be sleeping. Louis is gone and I am clean.

I'm on clean sheets, in a loose T-shirt and sweats. No bra, thank all that is. The briars all seem to be gone, at least from my arms, and the scrapes have all been tended to. There are a few bandages. And bruises. Really, I feel like one big bruise, especially my entire backside. My face and hair feel clean, though I long for a mirror. And I don't want to take my hand away from Jo to explore my face. Gingerly, I try to move the fingers of my right hand, but the pain is breathtaking, and I bite back my cry and give it up immediately. Under the sheet and light comforter, I wiggle my toes and move my legs around a little. My bad knee is definitely swollen and it feels as though there are a few bandages on my legs, too.

I seem to be in a hospital room, though I'm pretty

sure I'm in Jo's house. The small room is fully equipped. I take that to mean I'm on oxygen after all. *I'm cold and hungry. And powerfully thirsty. And I want another one of those lovely pills.*

No sooner do I think these things than Charlene and Louis walk in. Charlene has a tray with small containers emanating a variety of tempting smells, and Louis has a blanket and a sweater. "Were you guys in the hall waiting for me to think?" I rasp quietly.

"You would think so, *non?*" Louis' eyes sparkle with mirth. "You are looking much better, though a little gray from pain, I think, *oui?*"

"*Oui.*" I feel Jo sit up, and I smile at her. Her eyes light up, and I get hung up in their depths for a minute. I'm a little groggy.

"There is my *chérie*, looking more like herself. How do you feel, Libby?"

I look at Louis with a smile. "Cold, hungry, thirsty, pain. No particular order."

Jo helps me into someone's thick cardigan, putting my left arm in, and draping it across my back and shoulders. She doesn't move my right arm, which is still in its cold cushion. Charlene drapes a heavy brown blanket across my legs. Louis tells me I have to eat and drink before I can have the pain pill, so I do my best. Since I'm right-handed, I'm awkward, but Charlene and Jo cajole half a bowl of chicken and rice soup into me before I cry uncle.

"Sorry, guys." I wince and ease back against the pillows with Jo's help. "I just can't eat or drink anything more." My voice is still weak. "Jo? Darcy?"

"Darcy is fine. He misses you."

I nod as Louis takes Charlene's place at my side

when she carries her tray over to a table in the corner. He puts the pill in my hand and I knock it back, then take the glass and swallow the pill. I look at each of them in turn. "When I wake up, I will need some answers." Then I hold my hand out to Jo, who takes it as I close my eyes and quickly succumb to the drug.

Soft voices are the first thing I'm aware of. "What time is it?" I don't bother opening my eyes. My throat is dry and scratchy, and I clear it a few times.

"A little after 4 pm on Saturday. How are you feeling, *chérie*?"

Gods. Where did Friday go? I open my eyes and look around blinking, surprised to see the whole gang assembled. I take a quick self-assessment and face Jo. "Pretty awful, actually." I laugh shallowly and am glad to hear my voice is stronger, though that still isn't saying much.

While Jo's smile seems forced, I catch Niall and Beatrice's laughter. Dex leans against the wall at the foot of my bed. He winks at me.

I look around at them all. "What's with the full assembly?"

Jo answers me. "I sensed you waking and called them. You said you wanted answers."

I vaguely remember that, and I'm touched that she took me so seriously and cared enough to make it easy. "Thank you." I turn to the group in general. "Okay, could someone hand me a glass of water?"

Charlene comes from the table in the corner with a small pink smoothie. "Try this, Little Duck." She lays a warm hand on my shoulder.

"Thank you." I give her a genuine smile as I take the cup from her. Jo moves the straw to my lips so I can take a sip as Charlene steps away. The cold strawberry coats my throat and feels good. I set it down on the blanket beside me. "Okay, so we all know what happened to me. What happened here? To...them?"

Jo nods at Dex and he starts. "When you got close to the tree, I realized how far away you were, and I started to worry that we couldn't get to you fast enough. Then when you sat down, I couldn't see you, so I told Beatrice to lay eyes on you."

Beatrice picks up the tale. "I was almost to you when I heard and felt you, and I knew I wouldn't get there in time. I was so pissed, I screamed." Still pissed, it seems.

"I heard it, just before Travis knocked me out. I thought it was in my head and no one would miss me for hours, especially since we'd just checked in." Jo gives me a sad smile.

I look back at Beatrice and she nods. "Chloroform. He left the handkerchief for us to find, cocky bastard."

"They alerted me immediately, and I alerted Niall since he is the finest tracker I've ever known." Though Jo is calm now, I can only imagine her rage and fear.

"I lost your trail at the base of the mountain where Travis put you in a vehicle." Naill shakes his head regretfully.

To flesh out the timeline, I add in what I know. "I didn't come to until just a few minutes before François called you, Jo. How long was that?"

"Little over an hour, and a good thing he did call. We were at a dead end. I was trying to have your phone traced, but they'd shut it off until right before he called."

I look down and pick at the blanket. "François told Travis to kick me since I was just lying on the floor and not getting up to kiss his hand, I guess. I knew he could read my mind and I was scared to think. That was right before I talked to you. I'd figured out where we were and the word Goldilocks came out of the blue, so I just said it, knowing he was going to make me pay for it." My voice cracks and I clear my throat, drinking more of the sweet smoothie to stall and regain my composure. No one says a word, thankfully. "They left at some point. Do you guys know where they went?"

"That's me again, luv. I had a good idea of the vehicle and was making use of a few available cameras. We were able to get Travis, but while I gave him a good chase, we lost François."

I swallow hard. "So." My voice cracks again. I sip the cold fruity drink and start over. "He's still out there somewhere?" I'm ashamed that my hand starts shaking. I put the smoothie down and try to hide it.

Jo puts her hand on my shoulder. "I am afraid so, chérie. We will find him."

Beatrice chimes in. "Jo finally said your clue with all of us around and I coulda jumped her. No disrespect meant, Jo, but, I mean, you know what I mean."

Jo laughs, but not with humor. "Oui, when you understood it right away, I could have jumped myself."

A sickening feeling slowly comes over me. "Wait a minute. You're telling me that if I'd just stayed put in that house, you guys were on the way and I could have prevented a lot of this?" My reedy voice raises an octave before I'm done.

"*Mademoiselle*, how could you have known? What you did, giving Jo a clue at great risk of grievous injury to yourself, then attempting an escape...these were tremendous acts of courage. You humble me."

"Oh, yeah, real courageous when I slid down half the freakin' mountain."

"Enough of this *I am trouble* nonsense. No more of *we waste our time on you*." Louis flicks his hand as if he's brushing away crumbs from the air.

I drink a little more smoothie. "What can be done about my elbow? I'm right-handed. Is my arm ruined?" I bite my cheek and press my lips together to stop them from trembling.

"*Mademoiselle*, it is too early to know." Louis walks to my side and looks at it. "The cold is helping the swelling go down. It will at least need surgery and a long recovery, I fear. But we will talk about all of that. You are gray again, *mademoiselle*, and any fool can see you are in great pain."

He's right, the last pill is wearing off fast.

"Thank you, everyone." Everyone except Louis leaves at Jo's gentle dismissal. Charlene squeezes my foot affectionately before she walks out. Jo turns to me. "Louis here has a degree in medicine and is licensed to practice in several states."

I turn to Louis in shock. "Dr. Louis!"

"At your service, *mademoiselle*. But I prefer cars as patients. You make the rare exception, my dear." His long-suffering sigh caps it off.

That makes me laugh, which causes me untold pain in my ribcage. Instinctively, I stiffen, and that hurts, too, so I try to relax and breathe. I knock over the smoothie in an effort to grab Jo's hand and she rights it before anything spills, taking my hand in both of hers. I curl my fingers around hers and squeeze while I let the tension out of other parts of my body. When it finally eases, I limply relax back, panting. Louis raises the oxygen level, which also helps.

I say what I've been dreading. "I have no insurance."

Jo kisses my hand, then my forehead. Her expression is strained. "You are in a cold sweat from pain, my *chérie*. Your poor battered body needs rest. Please, let us talk about this when next you wake."

Too tired to argue, I swallow the pill. I lift my hand to her cheek before it falls back down and we just stare at one another. Jo strokes my face and plays with my hair. As the pill finally draws me under, I manage, "Jo, I think I forgot to tell you I love you."

———

The next time I wake, I groan. When Jo hovers, I smile meekly at her. "I have to go to the bathroom. And can I have something, and then take another pill?" I'm disappointed that my voice is still so weak.

"Anything. Just ask."

"I'd like a small mirror."

Jo's face is carefully devoid of expression. Louis walks in before I can comment. "She needs to go to the bathroom, Louis."

"Most excellent." He's so pleased, you would think I'd ordered the shrimp dish. "It is quite simple, you see, Jo. Because she is weak and the medicine makes her wobbly, we shall both help her. *Mademoiselle*, it is important that you listen to me. You will be quite dizzy. The blood will rush into your elbow and it will hurt so you won't want to keep going. But remember that this will be quick, and the walking will be most beneficial to you." He stands beside my ruined elbow, freed of its cold casing. "Now I will guide your arm. On three, Jo and I will help you sit all the way up, and then turn you to face me."

The least I can say is it was flippin' awful. I suppose it was good to get out of bed. Louis promised it would never be that bad again. They had to keep pulling up a chair so I could sit down and rest. I thought I'd never get there, but when I finally did make it to the bathroom, Louis brought me my pill so that by the time I got back in bed, I was out in minutes.

23

LIKE THERE'S NO TOMORROW

The sun is up. I spy a little table on my left. My eyes land on the hand mirror and a glass of water with a straw. A quick look around shows me I'm alone for the first time. I'm still on oxygen. My arm is still wrapped in the cold cushion. My ribs still hurt fiercely. But overall, I feel better. Less battered and bruised. For the first time, I feel like I will mend.

I steel myself while I drink some water, and then I reach for the hand mirror. I hold it down for a minute. Gathering up my courage, I flip the mirror. Relief courses through me. It isn't as bad as I feared. I guess if I'd been able to see my face right away, it would have been a different story. I turn my head from side to side and up and down, checking it out from every angle. There are a few bad slashes with butterfly bandages and a gash above my right eyebrow, which will probably leave a scar. The rest of my face is covered in little scabs that are already flaking. My lips are cracked, and my sore lower lip is swollen and purple, I guess from all the times I bit it.

My hair is flat and greasy. I put down the mirror and explore the bump on the back of my head. While extremely tender, it doesn't seem to be as big. If that's the worst I get from banging my head halfway down a mountain, I'll take it.

I set the mirror back on the table as Jo walks in. She seems startled to see me awake and hurries over to me. She presses a kiss on my forehead. I beam up at her.

"What an unexpected pleasure! I did not imagine you would be awake yet. Welcome back, *chérie*. You seem more yourself this morning." Jo leans over me, one hand playing in my hair, the other rubbing my good arm. "What can I get you? How do you feel?"

"Good morning, Jo. I feel a bit better."

"I'm so glad to hear it, *ma petite amie*. Louis will be here shortly. We were...feeding and discussing a few issues." Jo walks around to my good side. "Are you hot? Cold?"

"No, I'm good, though I'd love to get a fresh change of clothes and clean up a bit. Wash my hair." I pause. "I'm glad you ate, Jo. I don't want you to feel you need to hide it from me. It's part of who you are. I accept that."

Jo plays with my hair on the pillow. "Thank you, Libby. I treasure your open heart."

"I wish I could hug you, kiss you. I'd like that very much right now."

She lightly traces my bottom lip with her finger, and I can't stop the wince. "It is as I feared. But soon. For now, put your arm around me."

Jo slides one arm under my shoulders and leans in while I run my hand along her back. After a minute, my arm trembles, and I'm dismayed by my weakness. I let my arm slip off her as she stands, and she takes my hand and kisses it before laying my arm on the bed. But she keeps hold of my hand.

Louis walks in then. "Such long faces. Are you ready to go to the bathroom?" He sounds almost chipper. I'm significantly less enthused.

"I'm weak as water, Louis. I can barely hold my arm up to hug Jo."

He purses his lips and blows out. "*Oui*, this is to be expected. But if you are a good patient and you sit up for a while today and eat, you will become stronger. I have a different medicine for you today. It will help with the pain, but not put you to sleep quite so well, you see?"

"That would be great, Louis. Thank you. Okay. Let's get this show on the road."

Louis is right. This time wasn't as bad, though it was still plenty awful. I only have to stop and rest three times on the way. Go me. When we come out of the bathroom, there is a cushy recliner waiting for me. We head straight there, and Charlene walks in with a tray after I get settled. Louis hands me the new pill and I gratefully take it. He didn't say it this time, but I certainly feel gray around the gills. Charlene brought me coffee and I could have kissed her, I was so happy to see it. She cajoled and pretended her feelings would be hurt unless I ate a lot and she wouldn't let me have any more coffee until I'd eaten what she considered enough. Motivated by the promise of energy, I eat until I'm stuffed.

Louis and Charlene leave, taking her tray with her. I lean back in the chair and rest my head. The new pill makes the pain bearable and I'm just a little sleepy. Louis was right on the money with that one. He has been with everything. I drift lightly for a while, Jo beside me, holding my good hand. My right arm is propped up in its wrap. I stare at it, not really seeing it.

"Jo?"

"*Oui, chérie?*" Jo is reading something on a laptop and doesn't look up. I'm not entirely sure she is paying attention.

"What did you do with Travis?" I know the moment that she stops reading. Her whole body tenses.

Jo closes the laptop and sets it on the floor beside her. She turns to me and puts her other hand over our joined hands. "You do not have to worry about him, *chérie*. He cannot hurt you ever again. I will see to it." Her expression went from reassuring to fierce in the space of a second, and her eyes flared rose.

"Where is he?" I hate the quaver in my voice.

"Somewhere he cannot escape," she says carefully. At least she doesn't look away from me.

"Where is he, Jo?" I may not be able to speak quickly or forcefully, but I put all of my seriousness into that question. I'm sick of the evasion.

"In a secure cell on this property." Her eyes flash.

In spite of my trust in her, my heart rate elevates. Jo strokes my hair, calming me immediately. "Exactly where is of no consequence to you right now. No one put in there comes out without significant assistance from myself or someone I trust implicitly. He cannot escape."

"What are your plans for him?" I ask. "I know you won't let him go."

She looks at me steadily, her eyes guarded. "Travis is paying for his crimes, Libby. He harmed someone under my protection. He betrayed me, and everyone in this house. He took valuable information to my enemy. He is a traitor who jeopardized everything I care about."

"You don't have to convince me that he deserves to pay, Jo. I'm not pleading mercy for him." I've never been a proponent of the death penalty, but I know beyond a shadow of a doubt I could never feel safe, knowing Travis and François are out there somewhere. I decide I'm not ready to know more than that.

I switch topics. "My elbow." I'm sleepy and my ribs burn. I shift a little, and Jo obligingly adjusts the pillows behind me.

When I settle back, Jo picks up as if there hadn't been a pause in our conversation. "Your elbow. *Oui*, we need to discuss your options."

"I don't think I understand what my options are, Jo." My cheeks color.

"*Chérie*, you are under my protection, under my care. You would not incur any personal expense."

I study our hands for a minute, figuring I'm missing something because I feel slow. "Then what do you mean about my options?"

Jo squeezes my hand. She waits until I am looking at her. "Option one, I send you to the finest surgeon. According to Louis, you will have extensive surgery. The joint was crushed and must be replaced. Tendons and ligaments were torn. There is extensive nerve damage. It will require weeks of painful recovery with physical and occupational therapy, if not additional surgeries, and you still may not regain the use of all of your fingers. In addition, the broken and cracked ribs will take about 18 months to fully heal. There is nothing that a doctor can do to help them heal faster."

My head flops back onto the pillow. *Holy hair-*

balls. The idea of losing the use of some of my fingers or even my whole dominant hand horrifies me, and I stare at the arm again. "I knew it was bad, but..." It takes a minute, but I realize she only told me one scenario. *What am I missing?* "Jo, what's option two? That sounds pretty awful, but it's not like I can leave it like this."

Jo tugs my hand to get me to look at her again. Her gaze is intense, and I can't look away. "We can heal you, Libby."

I stare at her a minute before it sinks in. Oh. Blood. "I don't know what to do. What do I do?"

Her face gentles. "*Chérie*, you don't have to decide right now. However, Louis is concerned that the longer we wait, the chance of surgery restoring full functionality lessens."

"Somehow, it feels like cheating to take your blood." My eyes close and I fight a wave tugging me under. With effort, I open my eyes and focus on hers. "Jo, I need to sleep. But I want you to know I got it."

I wake to Louis speaking rapid French with Jo. I can't follow it. He stops abruptly when he realizes I'm awake. "*Mademoiselle*, I am happy to see you awake."

"You don't look happy, Louis. What's wrong?" He turns away from me and looks at Jo. "Jo?"

"*Chérie*, how do you feel?"

I don't have to think about it. "Not much better, actually."

"I was afraid of this." Louis shakes his head sadly.

That's not ominous. Not at all. "Okaay. What does that mean?"

"It means, *mademoiselle*, that your time to decide has run out. I fear already that we may be too late for surgery to preserve any use of the hand."

The idea of what it would all mean...I cannot imagine going through all that surgery and rehab, and still not regaining full use of my dominant hand. I swallow the shame of what feels like my weakness, and meet Jo's eyes.

Blood.

After a second's nod at one another, Louis is gone and Jo leans in close. She seals her lips to my forehead and holds them there in a long kiss, then touches her forehead to mine. "Please do not feel shame, my love. You are choosing to be whole again and there is nothing wrong with that. My darling *chérie*, you humble me with your fortitude. This will all be a memory soon. Louis has gone to retrieve Niall. He is the strongest vampire here, which means you will need less of his blood to heal you. Louis has already factored the amount you will need. *Chérie*, vampire blood clots quickly, so you will need to drink it quickly. Charlene is preparing a syrup to make it easier for you. Just hold on a little longer, *ma petite amie.*"

After a few minutes, Louis comes back, Niall and Charlene following close behind.

Niall winks at me as he starts to roll up one of his sleeves. "This is top-shelf stuff, luv—the best in the house. Just wait. You'll be a changed woman!" He laughs when Jo glares at him. Louis shakes his head at the pair of them.

Tsking, Charlene carries a tall glass about one fourth full of a dark liquid. Translucent waves cling to the sides like a mountain scape in sunset, proving the thickness of the liquid. She shoots me a bolstering smile before she joins Louis and Niall at the corner table, their backs to me.

Jo's voice in my ear continues to bolster me. "It will be over soon. The pain will be a memory that fades in time. You will feel your fingers and bend your arm at will. Your ribs will mend, and you will take deep, healing breaths with ease..."

Louis brings me the full glass with a straw. "*Mademoiselle*, drink this as quickly as you can." He hands it to me, and I wrap my fingers around it.

Without letting myself think, I put the straw to my lips and suck. The first of it clings to my tongue, tasting slightly metallic and so sickeningly sweet that I gag. But I force myself to swallow. Louis, Jo, and even Niall and Charlene all watch me closely and encourage me in fervent voices, like I'm climbing a wall and am *so close* to the top. In fact, each sip gets easier to take. After several swallows, the pain subsides, as if someone has dialed it back a couple of degrees.

Before I get a third of it down, I breathe more easily, and the blazing pain that has been my elbow begins to diminish. The sugar has burned my tongue and I barely taste the concoction now. In my right hand, excruciating pins and needles stab all five of my fingers, but I bear it because I can actually *feel* them. I ask Jo to take the straw out, and she does. I gulp the remaining half, wanting to just be done with the foul liquid. Charlene produces a napkin from a pocket in her spotless apron and hands it to me. I lean forward to take it from her, and I'm wiping my mouth with my right hand before I realize what I just did—without a twinge of pain. Louis takes the stained napkin from me when I just stare, stunned. He pulls the oxygen out of my nose.

Jo places a glass of water in my hands and I stare down into the clear fluid, my tears flowing once more.

I know I need to rinse out my mouth, but I'm so over-come with emotion, I don't think I can manage it. I don't hurt anywhere. I can breathe properly; my arm bends and my fingers wrap around the glass with barely a registered thought. Jo strokes the back of my head and I brace for pain, but it doesn't come.

The relief is profound.

Charlene pats my knee and leaves quietly, fol-lowed closely by Louis after he lays a supportive hand on my shoulder. I don't look at either of them; I'm barely holding it together. I take a deep, deep, painless breath and hold it as long as I can, stretching my rib cage and feeling the strength as my ribs hold. I let my breath out in a slow count of ten. It feels so good, I do it again, and gain control of my emotions.

Jo continues stroking my head. The sensation is so strong, it's as if my hair can feel her touch. Strong smells come into my consciousness. I isolate dried blood, sweat, the clean smells of spicy soaps, astrin-gent cleaners, Jo's shampoo, that titillating woodsy scent which clings to her skin. The lights start to hurt my eyes they are so bright. Even colors are brighter and more vivid.

Niall steps up and claps Jo on the back, and the sound is magnified. I look up at him and he meets my gaze with sparkling eyes. He smiles, showing dimples I've never noticed before. "Let me know if you want any more special sauce. None of us will be far, but we will give the two of you space." He looks at Jo mean-ingfully. "We have a lot to discuss."

As he walks out, I swish water around my mouth like mouthwash, feeling the silkiness of the liquid, then swallow it. I do that once more, and hand up the glass with a movement so fast, the water sloshes. Jo sets it on the table beside me. Even my tongue feels normal again, cleaned of the sugar's burn. I brace my hands on the arms of the chair and push myself to stand. The light strength I put into getting myself up rockets me to my feet so fast, I nearly keep going over and face plant.

"What's going on?" I ask as I regain my balance. I'm looking straight ahead, a flash of fear shooting through me.

In a second, Jo stands in front of me. She takes my hands. "The amount of blood you had to consume to combat the extent of your injuries, has certain...side effects. What are you experiencing?" She strokes my palms with her thumbs. I feel the sensation deep inside, and it turns me on. I lick my healed lips, and Jo stares at my mouth.

I look into her crystalline green-and-gold eyes. How have I never noticed that incredible quality of color? "My senses are sharper. I'm stronger and faster. I feel more alive and vibrant than I can remember feeling in my life." I want her to keep stroking my palms. Or anything else she might want to stroke. The thought sends a rush of hot liquid. *I smell it.* Jo does, too, and then I smell *hers*. It is incredible. Desire flashes through me like quickfire. I want to jump her right now. How does she have such control?

"These effects are temporary, Libby. You are completely healed." She waits a beat, staring at my lips and licking her own. "What would you like while you are experiencing these heightened senses?"

The answer comes without thought. "A toothbrush, a shower, and to fuck like there's no tomorrow."

I'm actually able to track as she scoops me up, and I marvel at the speed with which everything goes by as we fly. She kicks open the door to her suite and we're in the shower quicker than a thought. Seconds after setting me down, she hands me my loaded toothbrush. After a painful start, I quickly, but gently, remove days of ick from my teeth. Jo takes it from me, and I start removing her clothes as fast as I can. In my haste, I rip her shirt before Jo grabs my face and claims my mouth. She kisses me hard, and our tongues dance fast and strong. My hands go to her jeans and I make quick work of the button and zipper, yanking them down. Her boxers ride low on her hips and I skim my hands over her bottom.

She grabs my hands and holds them up high. Jo stops the kiss and whips off my shirt. Her mouth seals over a nipple and sucks so hard that I cry out. I had no idea it could feel this consuming. Not releasing my breast, she tugs on my sweatpants and they pool on the tile floor at my feet. I'm so caught up, I can't even move to step out of them.

Jo lifts her head and lowers my hands, but keeps hold of them as she kicks out of her jeans and turns to start the shower. The sensation of the hot water on my skin is so incredible that I moan and am momentarily distracted. I'm fascinated by the individual drops as they come toward me, splatter, and run down my skin. I don't even care that our clothes are getting soaked. Jo must know I'm captivated because she releases my hands. She does a turnaround gesture and I do, being careful to stay in the warm water running over my scalp and skin. It runs over my face, and I revel in the sensation.

When her hands are in my hair, gathering it up and massaging shampoo into it, I moan again, it feels so marvelous. To be really clean is nearly orgasmic after what I've been through, but thanks to my heightened sensation, her hands gliding through my hair and massaging my scalp is magnified. Jo tilts my head back and directs a nozzle onto the top of my head to rinse my hair. "Don't move," she orders on a whisper, and I gladly stay in the water spray, quivering in anticipation. She steps away briefly and I can literally feel her absence, then sense her return in a way I've never been able to before.

I'm pondering this when her hands slide across my back, slippery with soap. After covering my back, Jo glides to my arms. The dried blood coating my right arm rinsed away when I got into the water, but it is bliss to have her soapy hands wash all traces of the injury from my skin. Jo moves her attention down. She soaps my butt cheeks, slipping around them, and my hips, stroking and massaging so that I have to squeeze my thighs together and get an answering spasm deep within. Jo soaps the backs of my legs.

She turns me and puts my hands on her shoulders. I look her in the eyes. A film of crimson coats the sparkling green and gold, and knowing what it means makes me wetter with need. Jo soaps her hands with deliberate movements, holding my gaze. My skin is alive, and I feel so much *more*. Every touch, every movement drives me wild. Soap runs down my legs, and I slick my thighs together, again. The sensation is exquisite. I moan again.

"Don't make me wait another second, Jo. Please!" Jo drops the soap and presses me back until the bench is behind my thighs. I sit automatically on the cool tile, and the coolness and texture against my sensitive skin makes me squirm. Jo steps between my legs, forcing them wide. She takes my head in her hands and kisses me hard. I kiss her back for all I'm worth. We work in concert to bring one another to bliss. Suddenly I *know* she is, I *feel* it, and the sensation of her orgasm sends me over the edge into my own. The tremors go on and on, and I don't realize I have been yelling out until my voice is hoarse.

Jo picks me up and carries me back under the water. We wash off and she turns off the jets. Already, I can see the effects diminishing. My energy is flagging, and my senses are dulling to their normal levels. Jo scoops me up again and carries me to bed. We lie there spooning, dripping into the sheets, damp skin warming between us. For a few minutes, neither of us says a word. This whole experience has been so intense, I don't have any. I've never felt more alive.

I survived, and Jo loves me.

When I'm nearly asleep, Jo's whisper is barely audible. "Oh, how I do love you, *chérie. Je t'aime.*"

A sleepy, contented smile lifts my cheek against her arm. "*Je t'aime*, Jo."

24

THIS IS INSANE

I wake sometime later, feeling better than I ever remember feeling. A goofy smile feels permanent. Judging from the brightness, I'd say it's nearly noon. My stomach rumbles. I don't feel Jo and I roll over to confirm her absence, but I smile to see Darcy curled up on her pillow. I stretch experimentally. At the moment, I'm still completely painfree. But I use my usual caution as I get out of bed and pad to the bathroom.

I assumed Jo would be in the sitting area, but it appears I am alone in her suite. I take my time in the bathroom, trying to restore what sleeping on my wet hair did to it. I end up having to wet it again, just to get it into a neat ponytail. I pull on some clothes. They aren't exactly fresh—the T-shirt is wrinkly as all get out—but they aren't dirty, either. At least my underwear is clean. It's good to feel like myself again. Well, painfree and after amazing sex, that is. I check Darcy's litter box and refresh his water bowl.

I wander, searching for my purse, my phone. Finding neither, and with my stomach grumbling again, I give up in favor of searching for food. I open the suite door, and nearly jump out of my skin. A shriek startles out of me, my heart hammering before I recognize the looming figures of Beatrice and Dex.

"Good goddess, you scared me to death." I press my hand over my pounding heart.

"I forgot you'd probably be jumpy." She'd be believable if she showed an ounce of contrition.

Dex at least tries for a conciliatory tone. "Sorry, Miss Libby. You sure look better than the last time I saw you."

My heartbeat finally returns to a normal pace. "Yes, well. I wasn't expecting you guys to be out here." I roll my eyes at myself. *Oh, please, state the obvious, why don't you?*

A flash of humor crosses Beatrice's face before it settles back into all seriousness. "Jo isn't taking any more chances with your safety."

I'm not surprised by the flood of relief that gives me. "Okay. Then time to stretch your legs. I'm starving." They let me lead the way. Once we get to the kitchen, Dex stations himself at the door and Beatrice shadows me from a few feet away.

"Little Duck, you look a sight better. How do you feel?" Charlene's face and eyes reflect her concern.

"Believe it or not, I'm good as new, Charlene. And hungrier than I can say."

Instantly, she goes all grandmotherly again. "Of course, you are. You've barely eaten anything for days. I made chicken salad and served it on croissants for the staff. How does that sound? Or, I have soup?"

"The chicken salad would be terrific. Thank you. I know you must be busy, so I don't suppose you would let me make it myself?" The dirty look she shoots me over her glasses confirms what I thought. I laugh and throw up my hands in surrender. "Fine, fine." I walk to the dining table as Charlene starts barking orders at Ryan.

Beatrice takes a seat beside me and I turn to her. "Any idea where Jo is?"

Her face is smooth as glass. "She's nearby, and that's all I'm gonna tell you, so don't even ask." Then she turns and faces forward, her jaw set. What would be keeping Jo that Beatrice doesn't want to tell me?

Oh. *Travis.* And I don't need her to confirm it. Not wanting to think about that any longer if I can help it, I change tacks. "Any idea where my stuff is? My purse? My phone?" Beatrice turns her head and stares at me without saying anything, and it hits me. François had my phone. My face pales. "He has the phone numbers for everyone I love."

"Jo had it shut off as soon as we found you." Her face is still impassive.

Too late. He has their names. He can find them. Panic rises and I start to stand up.

Beatrice lays a heavy hand on my shoulder and keeps me in the chair. "He kept the phone off so we couldn't trace him, remember? He's not interested in your people. He'd sooner take one of us if he wanted to get to Jo."

I look at her sharply. It hadn't occurred to me that they were in danger, too. "Are you afraid?"

She snorts, her face finally showing a little emotion. Her blank face was unnerving to say the least. "Nothing scares me anymore. If he hurts me, I'll heal. If he kills me, I'll die. I've been around longer than I ever expected to and have a better life than I ever imagined."

Her stark honesty shocks me a little. I reflect on

her words until Ryan brings me a plate laden with food. It's delicious. Despite my hunger, I only manage about half of the sandwich along with some of the fruit and a few chips. I guess my stomach shrunk over the past few days. I'm sorry to waste the food and I stare at it mournfully. I want to box it up and take it home for dinner. That reminds me of the contents of my refrigerator and that I'm almost out of cheese. Next up: PB&J. A gloomy feeling bursts the bubble I've been walking around in. *Welcome back to the real world.*

"I know how you feel. I still hate to waste a drop. Spent too many years without enough food or money, I reckon." She looks at me astutely. "I'm guessing your not-enough years have only been recent, though. Am I right?"

"Right. We didn't have much, but it was enough. I do, too, really. I just have to be careful." I point at the plate. "Besides, I'd like to enjoy it again. It's a treat." I pick up the plate with the intention of walking it across to the prep table where I know I can find something to wrap it up with, but Ryan meets me with his hand out. "I'd like to save this for later, if I can, Ryan."

"Sure, Miss Libby. I'll take care of it." He takes the plate, and I don't know what else to do other than to sit back down with Beatrice.

"So what now? Can I go home?"

"That's up to Jo, you know that. All I know is you can't be left alone, no matter where you are." Beatrice shifts around and looks at me. "Do you want to be left alone?"

"Oh, heck no. I know I will feel safe again someday. But that isn't today." I sit with that for a few minutes. Yup. Truth. Underneath it all, I am terrified. I wish I knew how long Jo will be. I feel at loose ends. "What time is it?"

"After two."

I turn to Ryan as he walks up. "Chef says it will be in the refrigerator when you want it. She had to go out for supplies, but she said if you need anything, you are to ask me." He looks a little sheepish and I rush to assure him.

"Okay, thanks, Ryan. I will." After he walks away, I sit there thinking about what I can do. Wishing I had my e-reader, it finally occurs to me that I'll need a new phone. I didn't have insurance on the other one and it isn't time for an upgrade—I was still making payments on it. I can't afford to buy a new phone.

Maybe I can increase my hours. Who am I kidding? Sure, I feel great now. But I know it's temporary.

I drop my head in my hands and groan, thinking of all the phone numbers I've lost. *Oh, gods. I don't actually know anyone's number except my Dad's.* I don't even know my best friend's number. "Crap, crap, crap," I mutter. Beatrice pats me on the back, but doesn't say anything. I know what she would say —Jo would buy me one. *But it's only been three weeks, for Pete's sake,* I think at her deliberately. I know we've been through a lot together. And we love each other. But it's just too soon for something like that, isn't it? I feel so overwhelmed, I don't know what to think.

My thoughts turn to what it was like after drinking Niall's blood. I've never felt so vibrant and alive. Not before AS struck, and definitely not since. Every sensation, the minutest sound or hint of movement, all amplified to my notice. It was thrilling. I felt powerful. And for just a moment, I actually perceived what Jo was feeling. I get warm all over, remembering. What must it be like to have that awareness all the time? How awesome must it feel to be strong and confident in your body's ability? Years ago, when I ran daily and stayed active, I was strong. But nothing anywhere near what I just had a taste of.

And now I'm back to my weak, vulnerable, dull self. My back will hurt again, my knee will swell, fatigue will coat me like a wet wool blanket. All these vampire will have to protect me. Guilt mingles with fear and I drop my head back into my hands. Dread fills me and I wonder again: *what if they can't?*

I feel Beatrice's eyes on me, but she stays silent. *I need a distraction.* Suddenly, I remember the bookcase in Jo's study. I get up and start walking to the door, knowing Beatrice and Dex will follow. I have no doubt Beatrice already knows where I'm headed. She's clearly reading me. I'm trying not to be too upset about my lack of privacy. I get that it's for my own safety. I imagine the bouquet of gerbera daisies Jo gave me, and just focus on that as I walk down the hallway.

When the three of us enter Jo's study, I make several steps in before I pause mid-stride. One side of the massive bookcases is pulled away from the wall, revealing a medically equipped room I am all too familiar with. Walking towards the bookcase hesitantly, memories flood me and I wrap my left arm around myself as though I were guarding the rib pain, my right arm straightens. I don't realize I have been backing up until I run solidly into someone. I recoil, and hands grab me. I'm aware it can't be François or Travis, but the visceral memories have taken my logic offline. Frantic, I slap the hands away and spin around. I feel out of control and panicky. Tears flood my eyes and run off my chin, and I see Dex through them.

His hands are up in surrender. Dimly, I hear his voice, but I can't understand him.

I know Dex. I'm safe with Dex, I tell myself. But my breath is still coming in pants and I back away, spots dancing before my eyes and the edges of my vision darkening.

When I hear Louis' soft voice, I'm curled up on the floor and don't remember how I got here.

"*Mademoiselle* Libby, dear girl. It is daylight and you are in Jo's house, on the rug in her study. Do you feel the softness? What else do you feel? Focus on my voice. Can you hear anything else? You are unharmed. No one here will harm you. You are completely safe in this moment. You must calm yourself, *jeune femme.*" I try to focus as he strokes the top of my head.

"I can't." I hear myself whimper, but don't have the power to stop it. "I can't go through this again. I'm not strong enough, Louis. What if no one finds me next time?"

"Of course, you are frightened. You have been through a terrible ordeal. After such trauma, and then the pain itself was trauma. I am not surprised you are having a hard time. Breathe with me, *mademoiselle.*" I try to breathe with his slow inhale. He keeps deliberately breathing. I find it becomes easier to focus on him, and my heart rate slows. Beatrice hands me a tissue. Finally, I look up. "I'm so sorry, Dex. It wasn't you. I..." words fail me.

"I heard you try to talk yourself down, but panic is

a nasty beast that does what it will. I don't take it personally." His assurance relaxes me further.

"Thank you. I'm better now. I just forgot the...I came for a book," I finish lamely.

"I should not have left you for so long." Jo stands in the doorway. My heart lifts.

Louis helps me stand, and I put the sick room at my back. "I don't understand what happened. I came in for a book and when I saw..." Suddenly, Jo is before me and wraps me in her arms. Drawing on her strength and comfort, I bury my face in her chest.

Beatrice sounds worried. "You took one look at that room and I felt your panic go off like a firecracker, so I took off for Louis."

"It has been a long time since any of us have been human, *mademoiselle*. I am afraid we forgot how this experience would affect you. Just because your body is healed, does not mean your mind has had time to catch up." Louis' voice is laden with guilt.

I fight an urge to make him feel better. It's not like this is their fault—they didn't cause it. But a truth too terrible to entertain comes to me anyway. *This wouldn't have happened if I hadn't met Jo. But Jo is not to blame for her father's actions. No one is.* I can't hold these vampire responsible for the actions of a few. They have been nothing but good to me. *It's not their fault I'm so weak and vulnerable.*

I pull away and Jo lets me go. Raising on my tiptoes, I cup her face and kiss her, keeping my eyes on hers. Releasing her, I take one of her hands and turn to Beatrice. "Thank you for looking out for me. Again." She nods, her face impassive again. I shift back to Jo. "Can we talk in private?"

"Of course, *chérie*. We will go up to my suite." Jo looks at Louis, and he holds up a hand.

"A moment, please. *Mademoiselle*. I want you to consider a light medication to help with the panic. I also would like you to talk with someone to learn techniques to soothe yourself when the panic comes on. I believe what you are dealing with is PTSD—post traumatic stress disorder—and there is help for it."

I appreciate his concern, but I can barely keep up with the medical bills and prescription costs I have. "I will think about it, Louis. Thank you."

Jo stays glued to my side all the way up to her suite. I lead her to the couch and sit down sideways. Her gorgeous eyes are so full of sorrow. I fight the urge to make her feel better and forget my own agenda. *This is about me right now.*

"*Oui, chérie*, it is. Talk to me. Tell me what you need. What I can do." She strokes my arm.

"First, I know you read me down there. I want you to know I don't regret meeting you in the least. You are the best thing to ever happen in my life. And I don't blame you. Any of you."

"You are right. I brought this trauma into your life. I will spend the rest of my life trying to make it up to you. But I will fail miserably, I fear. There is no making up for what you have gone through." My heart hurts to see the pain in her eyes.

I squeeze her hand, trying to communicate with my eyes, the words that fail me. "Can you be honest with me about what you've been doing?"

Jo looks away. When her eyes meet mine again, a crimson haze covers the green. "*Oui*, you deserve to know. I have been with Travis, exacting payment for what he did to you. To all those I protect."

Torture. Right. That's what I suspected, so I'm not sure why the thought bothers me so much. "How long will you keep him alive?" I'm so afraid he will escape and come for me.

Jo's eyes harden and her jaw clenches. "I have gone to great lengths to ensure he cannot get out. I will not tell you what I am doing to him. We are difficult to kill. Our innate healing abilities keep us alive far beyond what our human selves could have survived. However, trust me—he will meet his final death soon."

A shiver of fear goes through me and I tear my eyes away from hers. "What is being done to find François?" I wish my voice was stronger, but a whisper is all I manage. Thankfully, she can still hear me fine.

Jo cups my hands between hers. "Niall is heading a couple of teams of our best trackers. They check in hourly. They last tracked him in North Carolina. This kind of distance is nothing to a vampire. I'm afraid we cannot let our guards down, even for a moment."

"What does that mean? Can I still work? Can I go home?" I realize how sheltered, how normal my life has been up to now.

"No matter where you go, even in this house, on these grounds, guards must be there, close enough to intervene if you, or they, sense anything off. If you are comfortable with them, Dex and Beatrice will be those guards. Only if you can agree to this, will I allow you to go home, to work, anywhere."

I grimace at her uncompromising tone. Every thought I have will be listened to. Everywhere I go, everything I do, someone will be watching. She rubs goosebumps covering my arms.

"*Chérie*, I am sorry it must be this way. Please remember it is only temporary. Once we find him..." Jo's pleading tone softens my ire.

That thing I'd been trying to remember finally came back to me. "Jo, Fran—he said I was...delicious. Did he...?" I can barely think it, much less say the words.

Jo's eyes swirl red. "There were marks on your neck. I'm afraid my father did drink from you."

Gods. My hands automatically cover the sides of my neck. Her words trigger a faint memory of my neck burning, before... "What...what does that mean?"

When she finally bites it out, I wish she hadn't answered me. "When we take blood from a human, we can track them. Anywhere."

Oh, Gaia. "So he can find me. No matter where I am?" Suddenly, I'm relieved I'll have guards everywhere I go. "Okay. Okay."

For a minute, I just let my thoughts whirl around me. What I need to talk to her about next makes me want to vomit.

"Jo, I need your help with something else." My cheeks heat and I take a bolstering breath. "I need a phone and I don't have the money to get one. If I can borrow—"

Red stains all the way down my neck when Jo interrupts. "Oh, *chérie*." She sounds so sorrowful, I know she's going to turn me down. I clench my teeth and stare at my hands in my lap. She places her fingers under my chin, and lifts until I am looking into the forest of her eyes. "I wish it did not pain you so to ask me for help. This is the very least I can do for you. It thrills me to provide for you, to make life easier for you. I have already paid off your rheumatologist bill and arranged for all future bills to come to me. No, I will not hear your protests." My anger ignites. "Why would I allow something to cause you suffering if I can make it go away? You would not have lost your phone were it not for me, so of course I will replace it."

I jerk my head out of her hold. When I look back into her eyes, I don't hide my emotion. "Jo, we hardly know each other. It's only been *three weeks*. It just doesn't seem right. I know you are richer than...anyone, but that doesn't mean you should take on my crappy financial situation. I owed that doctor so much money, it makes me ill. This is insane. If I could just borrow—"

She cuts me off again. "Libby." Jo's face toughens, her eyes taking on that predator cast. "We have talked about this. I take care of the important people in my life. It does not matter to me how long it has been. Should I also bill you for Louis's medical care of you? For Beatrice and Dex guarding you?"

"Oh, for...Jo, now you are just being ridiculous."

Her gaze sparks with anger. "Precisely, *chérie*. I do not want to have to talk about this again. Either I take care of the woman I love, or I do not. There is no half measure in my actions. The choice is yours. Are we in a relationship, or are we not? On this, I will not change. *This* is who *I* am."

I swallow hard and look at my hands. Am I willing to walk away from her, from us, over this ultimatum? The idea makes me nauseous and panicky again. No. I can't imagine life without Jo now. I don't want to. This doesn't make me a kept woman, does it? I mean, wouldn't I do this for her if the tables were reversed? Is this my pride? My need to control everything?

I lift my eyelashes and see the triumph in her gaze, as if the discussion is already won. Heck, maybe it is. But I'm still upset and not ready to just give in. I try to keep the mad out of my voice. "You have to be patient with me, Jo. Give me time. I'm not used to such...generosity. I know I can never repay you. I don't know what to do with that. I already struggle with feeling inadequate when I compare myself to you, Jo. Gah, all I do is cost you money." I pick at the couch.

"Libby, you have no idea, do you? *Chérie*, I have lived a long, long time. I will not lie and tell you that you are the first I have loved, but I have never felt about anyone the way I feel for you. The truth is, I have looked for *you*, waited for *you*, my entire existence. Now that I have found you, I cannot do enough to show my joy. My relief. It is I who can never repay you."

Alarming jealousy spikes through me at her casual mention of past loves, but I tuck it away to examine later. What she just confessed thrills me to my core. Jo lifts my hand to her lips. She kisses each knuckle, repeats the gesture on my other hand. "*Mon coeur*, I am responsible for what happened to you. Paying off a bill, ensuring you are protected, these are easy ways for me to show my love and gratitude. I am humbled by your desire to do things right and not take advantage of me. It may indeed only be three weeks, but I know what I want. You." She tugs on my hands and draws me into a hug. Overcome, I wrap my arms around her and tuck my head under her chin.

She holds me for a while, stroking my back. I can hardly absorb it. Can she love me that much? Already? She's willing to do all that for me? Aren't I willing to do all that for her? In her strong arms I feel loved and cared for. This is my Jo. "*Je t'aime*, Jo."

A satisfied sound rumbles in her chest against my cheek. "*Je t'aime*, Libby."

I kiss her chin. She bends, and our lips meet in a sweet kiss. As I pull away, I wonder how long it will take me to get used to being taken care of financially, too. I am okay with it right now, and that's all I have to worry about.

25

SIGNIFICANTLY LESS SATISFYING

*A*fter gathering my few items along with Darcy and his stuff, Louis takes us to the phone store. Beatrice and Dex follow in another SUV. Louis told me they're all armored. Somehow, that didn't surprise me. Jo leads me away from cheaper phone models to the latest and greatest, and I keep my peace. She's paying, so she gets to choose, though I do pick out the color and a pretty case for it. Thankfully, they are able to transfer my old number and retrieve my contacts, and when we walk out an hour or so later, I have a sweet new smartphone that I'm actually pretty thrilled about. Jo added me to her account, and now I have unlimited everything. It's the fanciest piece of technology I've ever owned.

Before we leave the store, the phone starts blowing up with notifications, and I see several missed calls and texts from Emma. All at once, it hits me. "Jo, what day is this?"

"Sunday, why?" We are in the car and she reaches out to stroke my head.

"Crap, crap, crap! I missed brunch with Emma this morning. Oh, gods." From her texts, she is clearly worried about me. I have to contact her right away. I start to text, then stop and think about what to say. I don't want to alarm her further. Finally, I type:

Sorry 2 miss u & worry u. Long story & lost phone, but all fine now. Dets ltr.

I hope that will be enough to relax Emma a little. "Ah, is this a good time to tell you that Emma wants to double-date with us on Friday?" I look at her hopefully.

She smiles at me. "I would love to finally meet this sister-friend of yours. Friday will be fine. Just let me know what you ladies decide."

"I will." I text that to Emma, too. It feels good to be making plans, to think of a future that isn't spent in fear. A shudder hits along with a flash of memory I'd rather have forgotten. Jo's arm slips around me and she pulls me closer. "I'm okay." I look up at her. "Really, it was just a moment. I'm okay." But she keeps her arm around me while Louis clears his throat meaningfully, though he says nothing. At least not with words.

Louis and I wait in the car for Beatrice and Dex to get into position, and for Jo to check out the apartment. Emma demands answers, naturally, but I put her off again. I'm relieved to walk into my own space again. After letting Darcy out in the living room and setting him back up, I join Jo on the couch.

"What is your work schedule this week?"

Jo's arm dangles over my shoulder, and our fingers dance and play together. I let my head drop back onto her shoulder. "It's kind of up to me. Typically, I would work Tuesday through Thursday, but I'm kind of behind, so I think I should go in tomorrow."

"Are you going to put this on your timesheet?" Her voice hasn't changed, but there's a distinct undertone to it.

Busted, though I'm not surprised. Actually, I'd love her take on it, being a successful business woman herself. "I really don't know what to do about this, Jo. I don't think I can handle working full-time. Jenny's business has picked up since I started, and I'm afraid that if I can't keep up, she will either demand I go full-time or replace me. I need this job."

Jo pauses. "If she is willing to pay full-time, would she pay three-quarters' time? Isn't that about what you end up doing when you put in extra hours? Why don't you talk to her about it? But, *chérie*, if you are going to put in more hours, don't you think she should pay you for them?"

Dang. I've been letting my fear of losing the job take over my common sense. I need every penny of income I can get. "Yeah, okay. I will talk to her tomorrow. Jenny's been so willing to work with me up to now, I don't know why I've been afraid to talk to her." Darcy flops down beside me. I rub his side and, purring, he flips over. Gently rubbing his belly, I hear my own tummy gurgle. I check the time on my phone. "I guess it's dinnertime!"

Jo laughs with me. "So I hear! What shall we eat, *chérie*?"

I'm so comfortable in her arms, I don't even want to get up and check what I have. "Well, I know I don't want to go out. And I don't think I have much of anything here. What are your thoughts?"

Jo lifts me and pulls me across her lap. I laugh

and slap at her hands. "What I want to eat is you, delectable Libby." She cradles the back of my head and cups my neck. The kiss proves her hunger for me, and ignites mine for her. My hands go into her hair.

When she finally pulls away, I'm out of breath and shaken. "What were we talking about?"

Her eyes light up with humor as she hugs me to her once again. "*Ma petite.* You make me so happy." She releases me. "Now, let us see to feeding ourselves, shall we?"

We end up ordering Chinese again and Jo sends Louis to pick it up. We spend the rest of the evening on the couch talking and laughing, and making out heavily. Finally, Jo carries me to my bed and we make love on my sheets, kicking pillows and the comforter out of our way in our haste. I muffle my cries in my pillow, worried about the neighbors on either side hearing. Spent, we lay there for a time, just looking at one another. Jo plays with my hair. It's so easy to forget everything that's happened, and for a while, I do.

It's as Jo is leaving that it comes back to me, bringing fears of being here alone. I remind myself that I won't be alone. Jo doesn't comment, and I can't decide if I'm grateful or disappointed that she's blocking me.

When we get to the door, a thought occurs to me. "When do Beatrice and Dex get to eat?"

Jo turns to me. "They take turns periodically. While they can sustain themselves on packaged blood—"

"It would be like living on MREs or canned meat?" I offer.

She seems relieved. "Precisely. It lacks the thrill of the hunt. Fresh blood is..."

"Fresh. I get it, Jo. I'd hate to eat nothing but processed food all the time. I was just curious how they worked it in." I shrug, showing her it doesn't bother me.

Jo nuzzles my neck. "You have no idea how special you are, *ma petite amie*." Releasing me, she strokes my pink-stained cheeks. "I love that you blush, *chérie*. You do it so prettily." She drops her hand and reaches for the door. "If you need anything, call for Beatrice or Dex. Call or text me at any hour." She pauses, appraising me. "I know you have fear, Libby. And I know you desire to stay here in your own home. You need to know it pains me to leave you. If I did not have complete trust in their ability to protect you, I would not be able to leave you. However, if you wish me to stay..."

She searches my eyes, and I try to stay calm. I understand she has...things to do. I don't want to keep her from her work...and other responsibilities. "I'll be fine, Jo. I'm just going to go to bed." I don't have to fake my fatigue. It's real enough.

I lock the door behind her, appreciating the new locks. I lean against the door for a minute, looking at my bright cheerful colors, and all my...stuff. I am awed by Jo's place and the welcome of Louis and Charlene, but it isn't home.

I push off and pad to my bedroom, turning off lights as I go. I keep the phone in my hand as I go to the bathroom and get ready for bed. I pull on the nightie I stowed under my pillow. When I crawl between the rumpled sheets, I think about Jo and I here just a little while ago. I fall asleep imagining her arms around me.

Red eyes shine in the darkness and I know he has come for me. I start running through the woods, but trip over a root and fall. I fall and fall and fall. When I finally hit the ground hard, my hands and knees are bloodied, and I hear his laughter echo all around me. I have to get up. I have to run. I try to get up, but before I can move, he is on me, lapping at my blood, biting me for more. It's too late. I am going to die. No one can save me now. I scream—and I wake up.

Sweating, breathing hard, and shaking, I'm afraid to move. Afraid he is in my room. Afraid to even open my eyes. My blood pounds in my ears so loud, I'm sure he can hear it, further spurring my panic. Then Darcy purrs in my ear and puts a paw on my face, and my rational side reminds me that he would be under the bed if anyone were actually in my apartment. My hands in my cat's fur, my heart rate begins to slow. My hair is damp with sweat. I've tangled my legs in the sheets and take a second to get them loose. I check the clock—1:46 am. Oh, well. There's no way I'm going to try to go back to sleep now.

I'm not sure if the vamps outside know I'm awake, but I'm not going to make it obvious. And if I can help it, I just don't want Jo to know. I don't want to worry her more. She's lost enough work time because of me. Leaving the lights off, I turn on the shower. I stand under the spray and let the tears wash down the drain. Feeling calmer after that release, I scrub the sweat and fear away so hard, I leave my skin reddened.

Finally feeling clean, I shut it off and step out. Since I have nothing but time, I spend a lot of it on my grooming. I use the citrus lotion, hoping the bright scent will help keep me alert. I don't use the hair dryer, though, settling with a good brushing-out and braid. Still in the dark, I get a fresh nightie, tossing the sweaty one in the hamper. I feel myself flagging, so I make a pot of coffee. I sink into my couch, cradling a cup.

Out of nowhere, Jo's casually tossed out words come back to me, haunting me. *I'm not her first love.* I wonder what the other women looked like. How many there were. *Oh, gods.* A handsome rich aristocrat with a sexy-as-hell accent? I don't even want to think about how many women Jo has slept with. *Gaia!* How can I compete with that? No doubt they were gorgeous. Probably strong, healthy, and well-bred. My mind conjures a beautiful woman draped in sumptuous fabrics, wrapped in Jo's arms.

Cut it out.

The last hours pass by losing myself in a book and nursing cups of coffee. When light filters through the blinds, I head back to the bedroom to dress. A look in the bathroom mirror with the light on reveals dark circles and blotchy red eyes.

I bet the women Jo loved never looked like this.

Irritated with myself, I apply a bit of makeup after I put a few drops in my eyes. Satisfied, I head to the kitchen to make a fresh pot of coffee. The sleepless night, uncertainty, and stress have not helped my back. I don't think it is bad enough to need the cane, at least.

It's going to be a long day.

It was a long enough night.

Jo calls while I'm waiting for my second pot of coffee. I cringe inwardly, but she sounds so pleased when I tell her I slept well that my conscience fusses at me and I feel terrible. I don't want to lie to her, but Jo told me she will be busy catching up today, in addition to making sure Niall's meetings and so forth are put off indefinitely. She told me to call or text if I needed her. Right. There's no way I'm going to bother her today.

I reassure her that I'll call my boss Jenny after 8. She promises we'll spend the evening together. I feel guilty when we hang up, but calmer. It was on the tip of my tongue to ask about her other loves, but thankfully, I kept my absurd jealousy to myself.

Despite my exhaustion, it's a pleasure to be able to do for myself, have time to myself. I eat a little, but my stomach is unsettled from all the stress and coffee. And the guilt from lying to Jo is really working on me. I was so upset when I realized she lied to me about slipping me blood, and now I'm lying to her. There's really no excuse outside of not wanting to be a bother, and I have a feeling I know what she would say about that. I resolve I will tell her about the nightmare and not being able to sleep when she comes over this evening.

Remembering Louis' words, I wonder briefly if I should do something about it. But how will I afford that? And come on, what would I tell a therapist? A vampire kidnapped me and beat me up? I'd be put in a padded cell for sure. If I lied and said it was a person, the police would get involved. Despite knowing better about PTSD, I tell myself it will go away on its own. Soon. If not, I promise myself, I will ask Louis for help.

During my call with Jenny, she is glad to let me work more hours, and grateful that I want to. I'm amazed when she just leaves it up to me to work when needed and put it on the timesheet, regardless of how many hours I work. Suddenly, I can't bear to sit around my apartment a second longer, and I decide to go on in and get some work caught up. I text Jo the good news, then head out.

It's been such relief to have privacy, though I'm not entirely sure they didn't know what was happening. I don't look forward to being read constantly, but know it's worth the price of protection. Beatrice is hanging out by the SUV and Dex comes around the corner as I head down the walkway. He greets me quietly and we walk the last steps together. Beatrice stares at me hard with that blank face, and I try to look awake and alert. Without blinking, she opens the back door. As Dex gets into the driver's seat, I tell them unnecessarily I'm going to work and settle into the seat.

At the office, Beatrice stays just outside the closed office door. I'm a little sluggish, so I buy a soda—with Beatrice trailing me to and from the machine—hoping the extra caffeine will push me through. She is so off-putting, I don't even try to engage with her. I get work done, but I feel as if I'm vibrating. My hands tremble and my heart jumps around. I switch to water and eat my sandwich early, hoping to counteract the caffeine a little. I don't need to be jumpy on top of everything else I feel. By noon, I feel comfortable knocking off for the day. I fill out the timesheet before shutting down the computer and locking up.

Dex is outside the door but there is no sign of Beatrice. "Ready to go, Miss Libby?"

I look up at his handsome face, shielding my eyes from the sun with my hand. "I guess I am, Dex." I wait a beat. "Dex, why do you, and so many others, call me Miss? Louis calls me *mademoiselle*, but I figured it is from all his years in service."

Dex looks back at me steadily. "Like many of us, I owe my life and my livelihood to Jo. You are someone she cares a lot about. It's a sign of respect to both of you. Things are a bit different when you are a vampire, you see. Respect is a much bigger deal than it was when I was human. It wouldn't be right to just call you by your first name."

Beatrice does. "Dex, do you know what's going on with Beatrice?"

"Oh, yeah. She blames herself for your kidnapping. How she thinks she alone is at fault is beyond me. We were both on duty, and I'm the one that let you walk beyond my sight. But Beatrice is feeling real bad about how much you are struggling and she doesn't like it. Not one bit. It's hard to be reminded of feelings, especially guilt. Honestly? I think, too, she's trying to block herself from the enormity of what you feel right now—for your protection, and for hers. She wants all of her focus on protecting you." The SUV pulls to a stop beside the curb. I start toward it, but he stops me with a hand on my arm. "I'm trying hard to respect your privacy, but pretending like nothing happened last night don't help, either. We have to be able to trust you, too."

Dex opens the back door. I climb in feeling like a heel. He's right. Trust goes both ways. Squirming in my head, I know what I have to do.

"I'm embarrassed. About last night. I shouldn't have tried to hide it. It wasn't personal."

I meet Beatrice's eyes in the rear-view mirror. "Fair enough. Don't do it again."

She looks away and I swallow hard. *Okay, then.*

Dex turns around and winks at me. "Where to, Miss Libby?"

Shaking it off, I think. "I need some groceries." Beatrice nods and we pull away.

Though I dread coming clean with her, too, I'm excited to see Jo this evening. I text her, sending her my love and telling her that I miss her. I slump back in the seat and nearly fall asleep by the time Beatrice parks. They both walk with me into the store and, once inside, they spread out a little. After retracing my steps several times for forgotten items, I fish out a piece of paper and pen from my purse to write down what I still need.

Jo tells me in the late afternoon that she has to leave for New England. I keep my spirits up on the phone, but when I hang up, I just sit and stare dejectedly for few minutes. I didn't tell her about last night. She has enough on her plate.

And that green voice chimes in its two cents: *Did she cancel plans on other women, too?*

My typical quiet evening feels significantly less satisfying than it did before. Jo texts when her plane lands and sends her love. We wish each other a good night. The fatigue is like a drug drawing me under, and I wish I could snuggle into the safety of her arms and really sleep. I put it off as long as I can. When I crawl between the sheets, I clutch my phone.

Predictably, it doesn't go well. As I drag myself out of bed and hobble to the bathroom for another middle-of-the-night shower in the dark, I know it is going to be another long day. It goes much the same way as yesterday, minus the trip to the grocery store. I'm exhausted, scattered, and scared. Every sound, every movement I catch out of the corner of my eye makes me jump.

I'm vacuuming the bedroom, which chases Darcy out. But when he comes streaking back under the bed, I realize someone must be at the door. I switch the vacuum off and hobble to the door. The peephole reveals Harry, and I open it with the first smile I've had all day spreading across my face. Those twinges of jealousy and uncertainty that have plagued me evaporate in the fact that Jo sent me flowers again.

"Hiya, Harry," I greet him.

"Hey there, Libby. Gotcha another delivery." He hands me a clear glass bud vase holding a single yellow rose.

I'd know that showy bloom anywhere and I don't know if I thanked him before I closed the door. My hands shake so hard, the vase slips out of them. My mouth goes dry and tears track my face as I bend and retrieve the card.

Counting the hours until you are mine again, delicious fille ~ *François.*

26

THOUGHT WE WERE IN A HURRY

Oh, goddess.

As if from a distance, I hear Beatrice's voice. I'm only partly aware I've got my back to the wall, my arms wrapped tightly around my middle. My vision narrows to a pinpoint, the darkening water stain and the showy bloom, Midas Touch, the only things I can see.

All I can think is that François is going to get me. There's nothing anyone can do to prevent it. And this time, I won't survive.

Beatrice pulls me stumbling to the couch and perches on the coffee table, her knees touching mine. I flinch away, but she puts her hand firmly on my knee, anchoring me in place.

"Feel my hand on your knee. You are in your apartment, sitting on your couch. Feel the couch, your feet on the floor. Dex and I are here with you. You are safe. You can hear my voice. I know you can hear my voice. Focus on it. You are safe, Libby. It's just me and Dex. It's daytime, you are in your apartment, and you are safe."

Slowly, as if I am coming out of fog, everything

comes back into focus. She has a cell up to her ear. Shame washes over me. It mingles noxiously with the exhaustion and I know I'm about to lose it. I barely make it to the toilet before I heave. I tune out Beatrice's voice. When the heaves finally stop, I turn on the water in the sink. I rinse out my mouth, brush my teeth, then just slump to the floor and let the tears come. I can't believe there are even any tears left, but I sob and sob. Spent, I lie down on the plush rug.

After three taps on the door, Beatrice pushes it open. She steps around me and shuts off the tap, then lifts me effortlessly and carries me to the bedroom. When she lays me on my bed, I curl away from her. I don't trust myself to speak. I just want to scream and scream and scream. I want to run. I want to hide. I want to hit something or someone. Hard.

I want to sleep. Oh, my goddess, I just want to sleep. But I can't. I can't. I can't...

I wake to someone stroking my hair and back. I freeze, disoriented, my heart racing. A familiar scent reaches me and I roll over. Jo's gentle green gaze shocks me into a sitting position. My mouth feels like it's filled with cotton balls. The room is dark. *How long have I been out?*

"I am sorry to wake you." Her familiar soothing voice washes over me, and the last cobwebs of fear dissolve.

I struggle to get my bearings. I run my hands over my face a few times and finger-comb my hair. I have no idea how long I've been asleep. I look down at myself and am unsurprised to find myself dressed, shoes and all. In a rush, I remember the rose. Dread fills me, again.

Propped up against the headboard, Jo draws me

in close to her, wrapping me in the comforting circle of her strong arms. I feel so safe here. I wish I could stay here forever.

"*Chérie*, I am disappointed that you lied to me. If you had told me, I would have asked Louis to intervene. This PTSD—you do not need to suffer like this, *petite*. Let us help you."

Snuggled against her side, I squirm uncomfortably. Guilt rises again, and makes a mess in the maelstrom of my stomach. "I'm sorry, Jo, I didn't want to worry you. But who could I possibly talk to about all of this?" *How am I supposed to afford therapy?*

She toys with the ends of my hair. "We have allies. There is one whom I particularly trust. Louis helped her out of a difficult situation some time ago. She owes him a favor, and she is quite skilled." She drops my hair. Sighs deeply. "I wish you had trusted me."

Of course. Why didn't I think of that? "You and Niall have already lost work because of me. I tried to convince myself this fear would go away on its own. I'm just so used to taking care of myself, being self-sufficient. Asking for help, accepting help—this is a huge adjustment. It isn't a trust issue, so much as a..." I pause, gathering my thoughts. "An independence issue, I guess? As scared as I am to be here alone, there is comfort in my ability to do things for myself. I like Charlene and all, but I enjoy making my own sandwich. I don't know what to do with myself at your place when you aren't around."

"And it isn't home."

"Right." I'm so relieved that she gets it. I lift my head and meet her gaze.

She sighs heavily. "I wish I was able to give you

more time. However, I made a mistake sending you home, my father has proven that. Both you and Darcy are too vulnerable in this apartment, Libby. Until this is all over, I cannot allow you to remain here." Her voice is gentle, but brooks no debate.

I hate it, but I know she's right. I did feel safer at her place. Unfortunately, there are plenty of vampire who intimidate the heck out of me. "Jo, when I'm surrounded by so many vampire, I feel vulnerable and weak."

"Your strength is not outside, but inside, as anyone who reads you can see. Not a vampire in my home has missed seeing that after what you have been through, the risks you took, what you were willing to do to survive." Jo kisses the top of my head. "*Chérie*, I am sorry, but the risk of staying here is too great. As soon as you can get ready, we need to leave. Put together anything you think you might want to have."

"How long do you think I will be there?" I try not to put too much emotion in my voice.

"I cannot know, *mon amour*. As long as it takes."

"Okay," I shoot for as bright as I can manage. Jo slips off the bed and I shift around and scoot, grimacing, then stand up slowly. One look at her face and I redirect her. "I thought you weren't coming back until tonight."

She looks at me hard, both of us fully aware I headed her off. After a beat, she acquiesces, and I can hardly believe it. "Louis called once he spoke with Beatrice. I knew my place was here, with you. I was able to find out enough. The remainder will be handled on the phone or, if necessary, I will return to New England after all of this is over."

I clench my teeth to avoid telling her to go back

now. That I'll be fine on my own—which we both know is a lie. She glances at my jawline. I meet her gaze and see those gold streaks I love so much, but which are a giveaway for her. She isn't entirely pleased, either. With that thought, I tuck my tousled hair behind my ear a few times and head for the bathroom.

"Do you think I should bring a dress for our double date on Friday?" I'm in the closet, deciding on how many days of clothes I should bring. I settle on five, figuring I can always do laundry if it takes any longer than that. I hope it doesn't take any longer than that to find him.

"That would be best. What may I do to help?" She comes up behind me as I am contemplating my choices. She pulls a dress out a bit to better look at it. I haven't worn it for her, yet. It's a navy and white polka-dot wrap-around dress, low cut, high hemline. She looks at me with that predator gaze. "This one."

"Well. Okay." I ineffectually shove at her and she just gives me a smoldering look. *Oh my. How does she do that to me with just a look? No! Snap out of it.* I try shoving at her again and she laughs at me. "Now, look. If you want me to be quick, you have to get out of the way. How about you grab me a garbage bag from under my kitchen sink?"

I'm walking out of my closet with my arms full when I almost run into her. She takes my armload and carries it to the bed.

"Thank you." I veer over to my dresser. I start to grab underwear when I realize she is still standing there, watching me. Her eyes are fixated on the panties in my hand. My brain stutters to a stop before kicking back into gear. Hastily, I stuff them back in

310

the drawer. "Jo? Are you going to get a bag for me? I need to pack all this."

"You want to put these beautiful things in a garbage bag?" Her face is incredulous.

Give me a break. I thought we were in a hurry here. I stop myself from rolling my eyes, but just barely. "No. I don't. But my only suitcase is still at your house."

Jo's face clears and she looks contrite. "Ah. I will get you a bag." As she walks out, she tosses over her shoulder, "Bring the blue lacy set."

I turn back to the drawer, shaking my head, but grinning.

It doesn't take long to throw together what Darcy and I want and need. The few hours of sleep must have helped. Jo catches me before I haul the garbage bag of clothes off of the bed and she carries it out to the living room for me. Darcy paces anxiously seeing his stuff disturbed again, and I take a moment to soothe him. Then I scoop him up before he can decide to hide and dump him in his carrier. Jo kisses me soundly and picks up his crate.

I start to pick up the bag of clothes, but Jo stops me with a look. "Let Beatrice or Dex get this, *chérie.* Your back is hurting."

I just shrug, and pick up my purse and Darcy's bag. I'm feeling irritated...*that she's taking control of things?* Jo shakes her head, but she walks out without another word.

"Thank you for helping me out, Beatrice, Dex."

Beatrice's face is a little softer than it has been for days. "You are welcome, Libby."

"No problem, Miss Libby. Anything to keep you safe."

The ride back goes smoothly enough. No one talks much. Jo and I lean into one another. My father reached out to me over the weekend and I text him back, letting him know I'd lost my phone, but all was well now. I text Emma asking if we are still on to double date on Friday. I'm not ready to talk to her yet. I don't know what to say to my best friend, how to explain what has happened to make me cut off communication for days. But I miss her, and know she is worried about me.

Several vamps come out of Jo's house and help us get everything in. Once the suite door closes, I let Darcy out. He struts out of the crate, tail high, king of the suite once again.

I yawn widely. Those couple of hours of sleep have worn off. Jo wraps her arms around me. I rest my cheek against her chest, and she rests her jaw on my head. We stand there like that for a few minutes.

"*Chérie*, come to bed with me." I just nod against her chest.

She loosens her hold and I do, too, reluctantly. When I step away, she takes my hand and leads me to her bedroom. I look for my garbage bag, but don't see it. "Jo, I need to go into the closet to get my stuff."

She tugs my hand and draws me close to her side. Holding me firmly, she smooths her hand over my hair. Her lips move against my forehead, making me shiver. "Your things are unpacked, *ma chérie*. But you don't need clothes tonight. I need you naked in my arms tonight, *chérie*. Let me love you until you fall asleep."

Predictably, her words have the response she is looking for, according to the intake of breath I hear. Worn out or not, Jo's passion ignites my energy. I remember my heightened senses and I'm surprised by a pang of loss. Swiftly, she turns me away from her and raises my arms over my head. My shirt comes off with the speed of a thought, and my bra follows. Jo's hands stroke down my sides, curving over my jeans. They come around to my stomach and she steps closer, her mouth going to my neck, her fingers unfastening my jeans. My arms start to tremble, and Jo reaches up to grab my wrists. She brings them down in front of me, pressing them between my breasts, but doesn't let go. With one hand, she pushes down my jeans and panties and they pool at my feet. I'm panting with desire, shivering with need. I moan. "Jo."

"Touch your breasts the way you want me to, *chérie*. Show me." She releases my hands, and for a minute, I'm too inhibited. I keep my hands clasped together between my breasts where she left them. "Show me what you like, my lover, what you wish me to do." Her own clothes have disappeared, and the sensation of the contrasts in our skin temperature as she presses against me is delicious. Her fingers trace patterns over my stomach, exploring, inflaming. Jo lathes my neck, sucks. I shudder. Suddenly, she drops her hands and backs away from me. Panting, I start to turn around, but she grips my shoulders, holding me still. "You must show me if you want me to touch you again tonight, *chérie*." Her husky voice makes me wetter.

Tentatively, I unclasp my hands. Jo murmurs as my hands hover over my breasts. My heart rate kicks up in nerves, in passion. She steps up behind me, and thankfully, lays her hands over mine. Though she doesn't direct my movements, it emboldens me enough, and I show her. After shadowing my movements, Jo's hands drift down as she tells me to keep it up and her head bends to my neck again. Her teeth graze my pulse and I tremble.

"Jo, please..." I'm not even sure what I'm asking for, but she spins me then and her mouth latches onto my breast. I cry out in relief. She walks us to the bed and lifts me onto it. She drags me to the edge, spreading my legs wide around her.

"Touch yourself again, *chérie*, let me see it while I make you come apart." She watches for a minute, stroking my stomach and thighs, her eyes flashing crimson. Then she kneels and lifts my thighs onto her shoulders. At last, her head dips, and I'm lost to the sensations. Jo doesn't waste time. Her tongue toys with my nub and she thrusts into me, setting up a rhythm that makes me wild. When she curls the tips of her long fingers up, I break into a thousand slivers of light.

She climbs up the bed, then drags me to the pillows. I start to say something, but she shushes me, situating us so that she's spooning me. She pulls the sheet and comforter up over me, murmuring sweetness into my ear as her arms come around me. I drop into a deep and dreamless sleep.

27

I CAN DO THIS

*D*arcy headbutts me awake and Jo's laughter ruffles my hair. I pet him briefly, then roll over. A smile lifts my cheeks. "Good morning."

"*Bonjour, chérie.*" Jo returns my smile and kisses my nose.

I stroke her face, grin at her and start to get out of bed. When she grabs me around the middle, I shriek in laughter. "You'd better let me go so I can go to the bathroom, or we will both regret it!"

She plants a kiss on the small of my back, which makes me shiver, and releases me. I make my way with Darcy winding through my feet. I feed him and brush my teeth, then go back to the bedroom. By this time, Jo is sitting up against the headboard, the sheet pooling around her waist, wolfishly watching my naked progress toward her. The sight of her makes me want to drool and the look in her eyes makes me want to run, but I keep walking toward the bed.

I pause in front of the bed, my nerves getting the best of me, and her scrutiny makes me blush and want to cover myself up. Reading me, she shakes her head and holds out a hand. "Come to me, my lover."

I can't believe how much I want her with just her words and eyes turning me on. I clamber onto the bed on all fours, my breasts swinging as I crawl. My cheeks heat, but the promise in Jo's gaze makes me want to hurry to her.

"Oh, how you turn me on. Climb onto me and straddle my legs, *chérie*. I have a surprise for you."

I do as she tells me, panting and shivering. I'm already wet and needy. "Surprise?" I manage.

"*Ma petite amie*, if you do not like this, we will not use it. But I have the feeling it will suit you."

I look in her eyes, searching. I don't understand what she is telling me.

"Pull the sheet down, Libby." I do and my eyes get big. I look back up at her smoldering gaze. "If you do not want to use it now, or ever, you have only to say, *chérie*. I may seem forceful with you at times, but I will never pressure you to do something you truly do not wish to do."

I look at the dildo she has strapped on. It is smooth and of medium thickness, similar to the one I have in my bedside table. I reach out tentatively and touch it. Instead of the rubber mine is made of, it has a flesh-colored covering that feels more like skin. I briefly study the harness and then look back up at Jo. "What will it do, um, for you?"

She sits forward and cups my forearms. Her voice is husky and she has that look in her eyes. "You mean, besides getting to watch you? The other end has a vibrator. When you are enjoying yourself, I will be, too, in more than one way." I lick my lips nervously and tuck hair behind my ear. Jo looks triumphant. Taking my head in her hands she slants it and kisses me roughly, her tongue moving so fast

I'm dazed. One of her hands drifts down and plays with my breasts, mimicking what I did to them last night. Holy cannoli, is she a good student. She releases my head and I lean back, thrusting my breasts up and out. My breaths come out in pants and moans as she works them with her hands and mouth.

"Raise up to your knees and come closer, *chérie*. You are ready, *oui*?" She is all but growling.

All I can manage is a nod. My cheeks flame, but I'm so excited, I just may come before I even get on it. I brace my hands on Jo's shoulders. I swallow hard.

Jo's fingers tangle in my curls and slide in. It feels so good, I suck in a breath and moan. "You are so ready." I watch as she dips her fingers in my moisture and coats the top of the dildo in it. "Let yourself down, *petite*. I will guide you."

We quickly establish a rhythm, Jo responding to my movements. I watch as green and red fight for dominance in her eyes. She growls low, and I feel it in my abdomen. I quicken my pace, rising slowly and burying the shaft deeper. Jo rubs my nub. The gathering comes fast, and in seconds, I start convulsing with my orgasm. She thrusts hard as she comes apart, too. I collapse against her, still impaled.

Jo lifts the sweaty mass of my hair off of my neck. My pounding heart slows and she holds me close. "Oh, *ma petite amie*. That was better even than I imagined. I will never tire of watching you come apart."

She holds me tight as she flips us, so I am on my back under her. She slowly pulls out, causing deep mini spasms. Jo watches them cross my face and I raise my hands to her cheeks, running them through her hair. "Thank you for giving me an out, for being patient with me. I love you, Jo. *Je t'aime.*"

"*Je t'aime, chérie,* my *belle.* Your love makes me stronger. Whole." Jo grasps my chin and kisses me softly. "Now, sadly, we do not have time to cuddle. I am very sorry. But I promise you coffee by the time you come out of the shower."

Not in a mood to deny her anything, I agree. "That's a deal." After another kiss, she rolls off of me and I make my way to the shower. Flashes of our passion keep me occupied and I hum Prince's "When Doves Cry" as I shave. When I come out, there is a pretty black robe lying across the chest. I pull it on after drying off, the fabric soft and silky against my skin. It doesn't look much like something Jo would wear, with its large blue flowers, and I wonder where it came from, to whom it belongs. I feel a sharp stab of jealousy wondering if it belonged to one of Jo's old girlfriends. The idea makes me a little queasy.

I fix my hair into a high ponytail and add some mascara. The dark circles are nearly gone. Another night of sleep like last night should take care of them. The first thing I smell when I open the door is the promised coffee, and I walk straight for it. Jo is on the couch, Darcy curled up beside her. Absentmindedly, she pets him with one hand while the other flies over her laptop's keyboard. A plain black silky robe, which is clearly the mate of the one I'm wearing, is draped over silk boxers. She's mouthwatering. Jo looks up at me and grins.

"Still listening to me?" I take a sip of coffee and smile to show her I'm not mad.

"Yes. I will stop if you prefer. But you think the

naughtiest things sometimes. It's...mouthwatering." Her green eyes twinkle.

"Mmm. How about blocking me for now? I know Beatrice and Dex will be listening in all day. I'd like a few thoughts to myself." I gentle my voice as much as I can, leaving as much of my frustration and discomfort out as possible.

She looks contrite. "You are right, *chérie*, you have your privacy from me now. But you came out with a question. Why don't you ask it?"

I color, realizing she read my jealousy, too. "Okay, well, I was wondering whose robe this is?"

She smiles. "Yours. That is, if you like it. I have taken the liberty to...fill in a few holes in your wardrobe. I showed my personal shopper a picture of you so she could get your coloring and told her what pieces I had in mind. If there is anything you do not like, it does not matter why, I will simply send it back."

I'll just bet she's wishing she was reading me right now.

Honestly, I'm so stunned by this little speech, I don't even know where to begin. I try to keep my face blank. While I'm floundering, Jo continues. "Come, look at what she chose and then decide." She holds her hand out for me and I take it warily.

She pulls me into her walk-in closet and over to a dresser. She starts opening drawers, and I see my clothes mixed in with pieces I don't recognize.

"Jo, these clothes. They're beautiful, but why? Don't you like what I wear? Do I...do I embarrass you or something?" Unbidden in my mind's eye, I conjure a willowy blond in a silk ballgown.

"*Merde*. Would I do something passive-aggressive

like that? *Chérie*, do you really think so little of me?" Jo grips my shoulders and I lift my chin.

Well, I'm upset, too. Am I not allowed to put together my own freaking wardrobe? Pick out my own clothes? "Well, what am I to think? I'm trying to be open-minded about this, I really am. But I don't understand why you would do this."

She shakes me gently in frustration. "To spoil you, if you want to see it that way. Because I can, Libby. I want you to enjoy fine things. You deserve all I can give you. This is one of the ways I can show how sorry I am for all that has happened."

I give vent to my frustration. "Gah, Jo! You don't have to buy me things to prove your feelings." I look at the open drawers and turn sharply towards them, forcing her to drop her hands from my shoulders. I pick up a folded shirt and shake it out. It's a beautiful periwinkle in thick, insanely soft cotton. The shirt boasts cap sleeves and a sweetheart neckline. It is generous in the bust and tapers at the waist. It's as if it was made for me. My heart goes pitty-pat and I turn to Jo. "I mean, geez, this is perfect. In fact, I love everything I see. And I love that you want to spoil me. Just...take it slow, okay? I love to shop. I like making my own choices. Please don't take that away from me."

With that, Jo swoops in and gives me a relieved, somewhat victorious kiss. "I understand completely. *Chérie*, you see why you truly thrill me?" She kisses me once more and walks out of the closet to get ready.

No, Jo. I don't see why. We are so different. What do you see in me?

I take a breath when the water comes on. *Three-and-a-half weeks and she's buying me a new wardrobe.*

Am I overreacting? I rifle through the clothes. I mean, I love them and there aren't that many pieces, really. If I had the money, I may have chosen these pieces myself. *But I didn't get to choose them.* Am I looking a gift horse in the mouth?

I dress quickly. I don't give too much thought to it, but I pull on the well-made periwinkle shirt with a mild sense of guilt. The mirror tells me it is a great choice with my flared khaki shorts. I grab my walking shoes and walk to a bench on the other side of the closet to put them on. I have to yank the shoelace out of Darcy's claws more than once, and he finally stalks away indignantly. Apparently, he's very happy to be back here. Jo comes in looking and smelling delectable. I smile up at her and she stands there for a moment, taking me in.

"It's perfect for you, *chérie.*" She kisses me and moves to dress. I finish tying my shoes, grab my coffee, and walk out.

I find my phone in the bedroom, and move back to the sitting room to read my missed messages and email. Jenny wants me to go back to the Pulaski property and take pictures she can send to the guys who may want to buy it. My breath hitches and I feel a buzzing in my head. My ears ring. My vision darkens, and I'm grateful I'm sitting because I think I'm going to faint. My lips feel numb when I mumble, "Jo."

I keep getting wafts of something awful right under my nose. I bat it away and open my eyes. Louis sits beside me, Jo standing over him. I'm laying on the couch but can't figure out why. Then it hits me. *Crap.* "What happened? How long have I been out?"

"Jo found you crumpled on the couch. She called for me and it has taken us nearly five minutes to revive you, *mademoiselle*. Now. Can you tell us what happened?" Strain is evident in Louis's voice. The barest glimmer of crimson in his eyes proves it.

He helps me sit up. I find my phone between the seat cushions. "I looked at my email. Jenny...needs pictures...she asked me to go back to..." I can't say it. I swallow hard and Louis hands me a glass of water. I drink it, determined not to flake out again.

"*Enculer*," Louis swears vehemently.

"My thoughts exactly, Louis. Fuck." Jo runs her hand through her just-fixed hair leaving it sexily disheveled again.

I drink some more of the water. "Do vampire get panic attacks?"

Louis looks at me hard. "No, *mademoiselle*. We do not. We feel emotions, particularly anger and passion *bien sur*, but they do not rule us as they once did."

"What kills them? You. Vampire." I stumble over the words, feeling awkward. But I need to know.

Louis answers me, while Jo runs her hands through her hair again and paces the room. I know how she feels. "Our heads must be separated from our bodies, *mademoiselle*. Fire will also kill us, but our entire body must be burned to ash, or we will...regenerate."

Holy hairballs. "Does anything weaken you?"

"*Chérie*," Jo's low voice sounds pained.

"I need to know, Jo. You and I both know this isn't over. He can track me. I need to know if I can survive another attack." My heart races at the thought.

Louis leans in close. Even against my ear, Louis' voice is so low, I have to strain to hear it. "Humans have been hunted down and killed, simply for having this knowledge, *mademoiselle*. It is one of the few vampiric laws that we must abide by—this above all other. Jo is trying to protect you. *Mais oui*, you must know these things now. You are a survivor and knowledge is your best weapon, *n'est pas?*"

I nod, afraid to speak.

"The only thing known to weaken us is Black Tourmaline or Schorl." Jo swears quietly and begins pacing again. "In our earliest days, it was widely known to protect against earthly demons. That means us. For generations, my kind killed those humans who carried the knowledge, but we pass down this information among ourselves. It is my belief that if you were to have some on you, say in a pocket or as a pendant, as long as you had it, we could not touch you."

Louis pulls back and looks at me steadily. I barely whisper. "Where could I find it?"

Jo stops pacing and closes in on us, her own whisper-quiet voice strained. "There is a shop that sells such stones of power. I will take you this evening. You must not tell Beatrice or Dex what you are purchasing. You must not even think of it. And you must not let one of them touch you while it is on your person. Purchase it and leave it in its bag, hidden in your purse. As cover, you will buy a gift of another stone. If necessary, you can let them see that. Tell them...that you bought a gift for Emma as an apology." Jo reaches into her wallet and pulls out a bill. She hands it to me and I stare at the crisp $100. "You will not need to get much. From what I understand, even a chip would do the trick. I can take you, but I cannot go inside. I must not take the risk of being weakened."

I realize what they're saying, and it makes me sad that I can't even trust my guards. "That means I have to hide my thoughts about it, too, Jo. I don't know how to do that!"

Louis interjects quietly but fervently, confirming my thoughts. "You must find a way, *mademoiselle*. Trust no one outside of this room with this knowledge. No one must know you have it." He draws himself up and I take a deep breath. Louis' demeanor softens and his volume returns to normal. "*Mademoiselle*, this PTSD cannot continue untreated. I am giving you a medication that will inhibit the spikes of adrenaline and cortisol that cause your panic attacks. If it does not work or you do not like it, we will try another, and still another. You are suffering needlessly."

"Libby agreed to speak with your friend who owes you a favor."

"Excellent. I will arrange a phone appointment this afternoon. Now, I must ready the car. *Mademoiselle*, if the panic comes on, try to focus on solid objects in your environment. Recognize smells, sounds, anything your senses can grasp. These will all help to ground you in the present." I nod my understanding as he takes his leave.

Jo takes his place beside me on the couch. "Are you well enough to work today, *chérie*? There is no shame in calling in. But you will not return to that place. I will send one of my people out to take the photos."

A weight is lifted from me. "That would be great. Yes, I will go to work. I can do this." I'm not clear which of us I'm trying to convince more.

"The pictures will be in your email before your shift ends. Please." She places her hand on my arm. "Ground yourself before you view them."

"I will. And I will be okay." I look at the time. "And now we're both late. I'm so sorry."

She shrugs. "I am the boss. If I cannot be on time, they must wait."

"Right! Okay. I still have to get food from Charlene." Jo kisses me and I head back for my purse. Darcy is curled up on the end of Jo's enormous bed, and I have to pause and give him scratches under his chin.

Jo opens the door, and Beatrice and Dex bow their heads to both of us. Jo takes my hand and I feel a little like royalty as they fall in behind us. At the base of the stairs, Jo takes her leave of me after a firm kiss and a not-so-gentle pat on the behind. My squeal sends her out the door laughing.

I ask Charlene for a simple sandwich for lunch. I sit down with yogurt, and wash the pills in my pocket down with scalding coffee. Beatrice stays at the end of the table with that trance-like look in her eyes. I walk past her, a little creeped out, and go up to Dex. "I've seen Beatrice do this before. What is she doing?" At the sound of my voice, she snaps out of it.

"That's her way of shutting down when there is a lot of emotion around. She's so sensitive, she gets overwhelmed. You've had so much going on, she's needed to do it more often." Dex nods at her as she approaches.

Beatrice offers me a small smile. "It's not your fault. Anybody'd be overwhelmed with emotions if they went through what you have. I just have to check out of it once in a while. But on some level, I'm still aware. I can still protect you."

"I'm not worried. After all, you are Badass Beatrice. You wouldn't sleep on the job." I give her a quick smile and turn to Ryan, who brings my sandwich. "Thanks, Ryan. Okay, coffee, purse, sandwich. Let's go to work, shall we?"

Work doesn't bring any additional unpleasant surprises. I get a good amount done, and thank sleep and great sex endorphins for it. Just before noon, the pictures arrive in my inbox, and I make sure I notice my five senses before I open the email. With a rapid pulse and nausea, but no other ill effects, I select four views and send them to Jenny.

Jenny loves the additional pictures of the Pulaski property and sends them on to the client. I wish her well. I wonder if my blood mixed in with the dirt on the floor. That thought nearly sends me over the edge, but I focus on the sensation as I clutch the arms of the office chair and smell the remnants of my lunch. The door opens, and I'm able to look Beatrice in the eye, but I take a deep breath before I try to speak. "I'm okay. It passed." After a second, she nods at me and goes back out to her lone vigil in the hallway.

When we get back, Louis tells me a therapist will be calling me within a half hour. After giving my leftovers to Ryan to save for tomorrow, I head up to the suite. Darcy is stretched out, sound asleep in the center of the bed. He doesn't even acknowledge my presence, so I leave him to his slumber.

28

LITTLE LESBIAN ME

*N*aomi Dreyfuss has a soft, flowing voice that draws me in immediately. I find myself telling her everything, the whole story pouring out of me like water. She is gentle and encouraging, and when I finish, I cannot believe how much better I feel. Before I hang up, she advises me to take the medicine Louis recommends, at least for a little while, and to take a shower. So when we disconnect, I head to the bathroom, not even questioning it. The water feels cleansing on more than one level, and as the salt water of my tears washes away, it feels beautifully symbolic.

It all leaves me feeling calm and a little hopeful, and I wonder what kind of creature Naomi is. She can't be just human. It was as if some kind of power washed over me. Benevolent, certainly, and I feel clean and...blessed? Strange.

It feels odd to be in Jo's private space without her, and I text her.

Whatcha doin?

(rolling eyes) Stuck in mtg. You?

Ah. Lucky u. Hanging on ur couch. Miss u.

Miss you. Rather be on top of your beautiful body.
On my couch.

Gasp! Behave!

Or what, Miss Weaver?

Excellent question. I'm grinning goofily while I try to figure out what to say.

Or I may just have to punish you, Miss Granger.

Jo takes so long to answer that I begin to wonder if I crossed a line. But, finally, my phone pings again.

Be very careful Miss Weaver, u may get more than
you bargain.

I swallow hard as my imagination takes flight. I know I should leave her alone to work, but I still feel playful.

Ooo. Is that a promise or a threat?

Both, Miss Weaver. Both.
Enough now. I must focus so I can come home to you.

Grinning from ear to ear like a lovesick puppy, I pick up my e-reader. The hours pass quickly, and when I go in search of a drink, it is after 6. I head to the kitchen with my entourage and am surprised to find Jo there, talking quietly with Charlene. They both look up and meet me a few steps in. Jo looks me over from head to toe a little critically. I try not to squirm under her scrutiny.

"What's going on?"

Jo looks worried. "Chef has just been informing me that you are barely eating."

My cheeks color. "I haven't had much appetite. I guess my stomach shrank."

It's as if Jo doesn't even hear me. "Chef said you didn't finish your yogurt or even half your lunch."

Feeling ambushed, I go on the defensive. "Now, look. I'm not going to waste away." *Let's steep you in some terror and see how much you want to eat.* Beatrice snorts behind me.

Jo looks contrite. "*Chérie*, we are only concerned about you."

I sigh. "I know and I appreciate it. Just...give me time, okay?"

She claps her hands. "Yes, and we will go out for dinner. Didn't you say there was a gift you wanted to pick up for Emma? We can do that, too." She turns to Dex. "You two will follow. We will be out directly."

I turn to Charlene, who looks guilty. "Sorry to put you on the spot, Little Duck."

I lay my hand on her shoulder. "No worries, Charlene. I know you care about me. What if I take breakfast with me and make sure I finish it eventually?"

She brightens. "Excellent idea. I have a few tricks I can add to enhance your appetite and I imagine you have a little nausea, too?" When I nod mutely, she continues. "I can help minimize that. Leave it to me."

We take the yellow sporty car. Our first stop is the stone shop. My nerves ratchet higher the closer we get. Jo remains outside, casually watching the door. Beatrice and Dex spread out on the street. I walk in, my stomach in knots. There are several low tables littered with small baskets of different-colored stones. Along the walls are glassed-in cases showcasing gorgeous stones set in prettier jewelry. Especially in my state, it's overwhelming.

I smile at the woman behind the counter. She scrutinizes me over hot pink plastic-framed glasses perched on the end of her nose. She has wild and short salt-and-pepper hair and sharp brown eyes. "Can I help you find something?"

"Well, I don't really know anything about choosing stones. I need a gift for a friend. And—"

She nods with a soft smile. "You'll know it when you see it. How about you spend some time looking and I will give you direction if you need it." She comes around the counter and joins me at a table. "Each basket of stones has a card detailing its properties." She studies the table and reaches for a card out of a basket of gorgeous teal stones. "Take this one, for example. Among other things, it can soothe emotional trauma, and alleviate worry and fear." I look at her suspiciously. She couldn't know, could she? But the woman laughs, "Relax, I just get feelings once in a while. Apparently, I was right this time. Believe me, I'm not always." Her smile is guileless, and I relax. "Take your time. Choosing a stone is a very personal thing, so I will leave you to it. Ask if you need help."

After reading a couple of cards, I find the black stone I'm looking for and try not to react, afraid to even think. The card confirms it is a stone of protection. I also like that it helps promote rational thought. I could sure use a healthy dose of that right now. I take a little time looking through them, and finally choose a couple of small black chunks that would slip unseen inside my clothes. They feel hard in my fingers, solid black, striated and crystalline. Somehow, I feel better just clutching them.

My eyes keep straying to the Amazonite that the woman showed me. I pick up a few and experimentally weigh them in my hands, the heft, the shape, the rough or smooth edges. One keeps drawing me, and I add that to the small pile on my palm.

At least finding a pretty amethyst for Emma is easy. The stones are all beautiful and I know she will love the purple hues. Jo was right on. I choose one whose shape is reminiscent of a heart. Since it is purported to have healing properties, I hope this gesture will help heal any rift between us. Emma hasn't spoken to me since I put her off Sunday. I'm trying not to read too much into that. Sometimes, that happens, and we go nearly a week without touching base. But I'd be devasted to lose Emma, even for Jo.

As I check out, the woman palms the black stones. "Vampire trouble, hunh?"

I freeze. *What the...* "Excuse me?"

"They're everywhere, looking just like us, just waiting to swoop in and suck us dry. Damn emotional vamps. You have to have strong boundaries with them. Best if you keep them against your skin." She nods vigorously, and I think my heart may never recover its normal rhythm.

I walk out, holding the amethyst in front of me like a prize, a manic smile on my face, I've no doubt from the look on Jo's face. "Have I got a story for you," I mutter under my breath.

The small bag in my purse seems to throb at me, but I keep my attention on the pretty stone in my hand as Jo admires it while Beatrice and Dex join us. Babbling at Jo about how perfect it is for Emma, I drop it into the gift box I asked for and slip that into my purse, too. When I try to hand Jo her change, the dirty look she gives me stops me. I stuff it into my purse, grimacing a little myself.

Misreading the cause of my anxiety, Jo squeezes my hand. "You are safe with me, *chérie*. He will not have you again as long as I live."

Her declaration doesn't make me feel as good as she intends. I can't see how anyone can completely keep me safe. But I squeeze her hand back and smile at her, and the uneasy moment passes.

We arrive at a fine Italian restaurant I've never been to. I've heard the sauces here are particularly good. I guess, too, that Jo is trying to fatten me up. That's fine. My shorts, which fit perfectly a week ago, are loose and I've found myself hitching them up a few times. I'm so used to wearing baggy clothing, it escaped my notice until it was brought to my attention, too.

As we walk up to the door, Beatrice and Dex melt into the darkness. Jo and I are seated quickly. The hostess takes our drink order, and once my request for sparkling water is in, I excuse myself for the bathroom. It is a one-staller, the last door down a hallway shared with employees. I take the Amazonite out of my pocket, enjoying the color and feel of it in my hand. I slip it back into my pocket, and when I walk to the mirror, something tells me to take the black stones out of my purse. I debate it hard. If I do, Jo won't be able to touch me. But I can't get over the feeling that I need them. Now.

I fish them out of my purse. I heed the shop owner's advice and tuck one inside my bra and another in my sock, pushing it below the bulge of my ankle. I'm not sure what makes me put them in those particular places—it just feels right. A last check tells me they are concealed.

A man is in the hall, I assume waiting for the men's room, and I toss him a generic smile as I slip by. I'm totally unprepared when he grabs me and a circle of cold metal presses into my neck. I suck in a breath to scream when his hand claps over my mouth, his hot breath in my ear. "You so much as breathe loud and I will blow a hole through your neck. Got it?" Naturally, I freeze like the rabbit I am. Oh, how I wish I knew how to break his hold on me. *Oh, how I wish Jo wasn't respectfully blocking me.* He presses the metal deeper into my neck. "I said, got it?" Jerkily, I nod. "Good. Now move."

The gun moves off of my neck, but before I can feel any relief it presses into my back, just behind my heart, which is pounding so hard I feel it pulse in my eyes. His hand gripping my arm, he yanks me and force-marches me to the door marked "Employees Only." I drop my purse, but he kicks it into shadows. The gun digging into my back tells me to open the door of a neat dry-goods storeroom with an exterior door. We haven't met a single person, and my only hope is that Beatrice or Dex are patrolling outside and will see us, read my terror. *Help!* is a mantra on repeat in my head.

I try to push open the heavy exterior door, but it seems to be blocked by something.

He hisses in my ear. "Goddammit, push!"

He squashes me against the door, adding his strength to force it open. In the dim light, I realize there is a body blocking the door. Recognition strikes me with horror.

Beatrice lies in a pool of blood, her legs severed above the knees. Layers of camouflage duct tape cover her mouth and her hands are tied up with thin wire. She has almost severed them trying to free herself. Her scabbard is empty. *That must be what he used to cut off her legs. Oh, Gaia. I'm so sorry Beatrice. If he can do this to Badass Beatrice...oh gods. Help me!* Her glittering red eyes rage and she never takes them off of the man behind me. *Dex! Help!* But even as I think it, I understand he would already be here if he could. He is somewhere, already dead or close to it.

Beatrice is painfully white. *Why is she bleeding so much? Why isn't it clotting?* Her wild blond curls are matted with blood. *Oh, gods, she's even been shot in the head.* A thick trail crosses the pavement from the woods, and much of the skin has been scraped from her thighs, telling the tale of dragging herself here. *I'm so sorry, Beatrice. I'm so sorry. Thank you for trying.* Helpless tears fall. Terror. Rage. I want to hurt this man. I want to do to him what he did to my friends. *How did he know what to do?*

Rage starts to clear my mind. Beatrice and Dex weren't looking for a human, they were looking for a vampire. That must be how he got within their defenses, took them by surprise. He continues to herd me, keeping a punishing grip on my arm. *Jo will find you, Beatrice. Hang in there.* At least she will survive. Gods, I hope.

He forces me to a windowless van painted in forest camouflage parked in the deeper shadow of the woods and opens a back door with his free hand. He shoves me into the dark interior and delighted laughter comes from the darker recesses. My hope of escape while my kidnapper drives evaporates as icy dread travels down my spine. I know that voice.

"There you are, my delicious *fille*. I told you we would be together soon. You look so...healthy. Pity the side effects of your cure don't last, *oui*?" François laughs again. "Where is her phone?"

"She dropped her purse inside. You didn't tell me you wanted it and I ain't goin' back in there for it." I hope his belligerence gets him killed.

François speaks as if he is talking to someone a little slow. "We must prepare to leave now, John Boy. Be ready to drive us out of here as soon as I get in the cab. I don't want my daughter to catch on until we are long gone. Libby and I have plans."

"My name ain't John Boy. I done told you before, it's Jeffrey." He mumbles under his breath as he walks away from the door. "It's Jeffrey Damn Davies." I have a moment of hysteria. *That's one heck of a middle name.*

When François laughs, my humor cuts off like a switch was thrown. The idea of sharing a laugh with him sends chills through me.

François' whispered voice comes from inches away. "There is no escaping this time. I've seen to it. There will be no ransom call. Jo will not find you. I have something special in mind, *petite fille*. You owe me."

The door slams behind him and my heart sinks as a lock grinds into place. His words leave me shaking. The van jerks into motion, rocking me on the bumpy metal floor. It's so dark, I can't see anything. I walk my fingers around for any kind of weapon, careful not to make noise that a sensitive vampire's ears would pick up. One after another, I fill my head with every song I know to cover my thoughts. The van doesn't stop. François doesn't come back here to stop me. Guess he doesn't care that I'm hiding my thoughts. I'm not sure if that's a good or bad sign.

I can't believe they didn't search me. I wish I had something more than just the cell and pretty stone in my pockets, but it's not like I know how to use a weapon anyway. Not like Beatrice. An image of her powerful body sliced up and covered in blood fills my vision and rage tightens my chest. That happened because of me. Somehow, I will avenge her and Dex. And maybe even me.

After an agonizingly long time, my fingers discover a screwdriver. Fear makes me want to hurry, and I have to force myself to move just as slowly as I get it into my pocket soundlessly.

It so happens I have plenty of time.

Belatedly, I try to get a feel for where we're heading. I can tell we're on the highway, but I don't know if we turned north or south on I-81. After a while, we leave the highway and head into the mountains. We continue for a long time, up and down steep inclines, pressure building until my ears pop several times with the changing altitude. Switchbacks throw me around, and I breathe through my nose to quell the motion sickness. We travel so long, we have to have crossed into West Virginia. The farther we get, the more my heart sinks. I've lost all sense of direction. Niall can't track a vehicle—that's been proven. Jo will never find me.

So, this is it. François wins.

The thought makes me furious.

All I want is to inflict as much pain as possible before they kill me. Suddenly, it hits me that I also have to protect the people I love.

I draw my cell out of my pocket. Thankfully, the volume is off since I was with Jo, but missed call and voicemail icons flash in the dark. *Oh, Jo.* Fearing François will hear, I don't dare play the messages. I choke back a sob, knowing that would be the last time I would hear her voice. I'm so tempted to send her a text, but fear grips me. *What if he's listening to my thoughts right now?* Resigned, I flip the phone face down and sit on it to keep it from rattling against the metal. Maybe they won't see it in the dark and the people I love will stay safe a little longer.

After what feels like hours, we slow way down and make a sharp turn that knocks me off balance again. We roll to a stop. There's a drone of voices, but I can't make out their words. We start up again, but only go a short distance before stopping again. Then both the driver and passenger doors slam. I blank my face as the back door opens and blink in the widening shaft of light, shaking uncontrollably. I may be mad, but I'm petrified.

Deep in the woods and surrounded by a razor wire-topped wood fence, there is a mix of wooden structures and canvas tents. The camp is fairly large, neat, and there are at least a dozen men in military-style uniforms scattered all over the place. They watch, but don't interfere. Along with the ubiquitous

Confederate flags, American flags flap in the breeze, but they look a little off to me. However, I'm too pre-occupied by François and his side kick leering at me to try to figure them out.

Just great, I think as I belt out "America the Beautiful" in my head. *A militia group. They ought to love little lesbian me.*

29

WILL HAUNT ME

"Enough. Stop singing those *horrible* songs." François brushes imaginary dust from his silk shirt with black gloved hands.

Fastidious bastard. "Better?" I train my face into an innocent mask when he lifts his head to me. I never even see him move before my face explodes in pain with an audible crunch. Startled agony rips out of me. Tears stream unchecked from my rapidly swelling eyes and my whole face aches. I wonder how much more than my nose is broken.

He flexes the hand he punched me with and grins. "Oh, I like the spirited ones. *Oui*, Libby. Much better. I can hardly wait to play more." He turns to Jeffrey. "Put her in your stockade and we will talk about the weapons I promised. And the money you still owe me." He pivots and glides to a small cabin near the front gate.

I'm gasping for breath when Jeffrey grabs my arm, yanking me roughly out of the van. Somehow, I manage to stop myself from face-planting. When I land hard on my hands and knees, I just stare at the ground through my still-streaming, swelling eyes, letting the pain harden my resolve. Blood drips from my nose onto the dirt in splatters. *Make them pay.* He yanks me to my feet and I let the tears continue to fall, my knees aching. He prods me into walking faster, and I stumble. He laughs.

Go ahead and laugh. Underestimate me. You'll never see it coming.

The stockade turns out to be a solid wood structure carved into cells with concrete floors. The doorway opens to a large space. A dented, folding metal chair waits under a gently swaying bare bulb in the center of the room. I shudder to think why a drain is situated underneath the chair. In fact, I'm vibrating like a plucked string. All along the back wall, horrifying items are hung. At least one is a cattle prod, though how I know that I cannot say for the life of me. I don't have to have vampire blood to know the place reeks of feces, urine, sweat, and blood. I catch it even breathing through my mouth. As he pushes me down the center, I scan closed doors. Blue eyes dull with pain watch through a barred rectangle set in one. Though the sickening scent of vomit turns my stomach, I hold the gaze as long as I can.

Jeffrey shoves me hard into the last cell, several down from those eyes. I somehow manage to keep my feet—both my knees are stiff and throbbing with pain. My face aches and throbs with my pulse, and I use that to focus. There's an army-style cot with filthy sheets dotted with what I really hope are blood spots. A chipped, dirty white pot sits against the far wall. *Well, can't say I don't have a pot to piss in.*

Yeah, okay, maybe I'm losing it.

"Quit sniveling. You hardly got anything to cry about yet. Just wait 'til the Butcher really gets hold of ya." Slamming the door, Jeffrey laughs as he twists the lock and shadows fill the room. The only light is that bulb over the chair at the far end of the building. I didn't count, but I'm at least eight cells down and the light barely makes it over top of the high metal walls. Long narrow windows ring the 10-foot-high ceilings. In the corner of my cell, I spot a camera with a red light on. It looks new and the fresh sawdust on the floor under it confirms it was just installed. Just for me. *So much for privacy.*

I turn my back on it. My left foot is going numb. Something must really be wrong in that knee. I'm afraid to even sit on the cot, but the floor isn't any cleaner. I pull the sheets all the way off and drag it under the camera, out of its range. I'm slow going with my knee not working right and because each time I lean down, my face pounds harder. Exhausted, I ease down onto the edge of the bare cot. My knees and elbows are scraped and bruising. Tentatively touching my face, I quickly give up. I wish it, too, would go numb. Hot tears stream unchecked down my cheeks.

Thankfully, I don't have to use the pot, at least not yet. I wonder how long he is going to make me sit here with my knees knocking before he starts torturing me. Who am I kidding, the waiting and wondering is torture in itself. Jeffrey calling François "The Butcher" has been working on me since he left. I swallow hard. I don't want to know why they call him that.

I thank whatever guided me to take the black tourmaline out of my purse and hide them on myself. I just hope he takes off those gloves and touches me when he starts on me. He hasn't yet. Even when he punched me, he was wearing gloves.

341

I pray to all goddesses that they somehow give me an opportunity and I have the balls to follow through. I don't know what my chances are against these militia men, but I have to try to get away. The time for freezing is over. This rabbit has to fight.

Slipping my hand in my pocket, I finger the screwdriver. I don't know when or how, but by Gaia, I'm going to use it.

Before I finish praying, the outer door opens, and I focus on the footsteps as they near. Thinking it is François, I start shaking violently. But the footsteps stop short and a young man's fervent voice wafts to me.

"Why did you do it?"

There is no audible response and I wonder if he is speaking to the owner of those agonized blue eyes.

"You knew the code. You betrayed the brotherhood. Our country."

Still no response that I can hear.

"I've done everything I can for you. I even spoke up for you when the council convened. But they have proof, man. It's out of my hands." There is a pause and I think I hear quiet weeping, but it could just be my own blood pounding in my ears. "I will personally take the flag to your family and make certain they know you died with honor. They don't need to know you were a traitor to our country."

Chills cover my body. These people are serious. They are going to kill that poor guy. I'd heard groups like this existed, but I never imagined I'd end up in the middle of them. And any hope I had that I will get any help here evaporates. As the outer door closes, the sound increases. It's gut-wrenching. My heart breaks for the hopelessness in those tears. My resolve deepens and I settle in, frightened and furious, to await my opportunity.

As it turns out, I don't have much longer to wait.

All too soon, the creak of the outer door comes again on a gust of fresh air. It carries with it male laughter and woodsy scents from the surrounding forest. *Jo.* I squeeze my eyes shut as grief washes over me. The door slams and I nearly come off the cot.

He's suddenly at my door. "Now, now, Libby. Are you afraid of a slamming door? *Mais non!* It is time to play." My heart is a frantic caged bird and I feel light-headed. *Get yourself together!*

The door swings open. François' red eyes glow in the dim light. The truth in his eyes settles over me: I am going to feel more pain than I've ever experienced. I am going to die slowly.

But I'm not lying down for it.

Legs shaking, I stand.

He grins, revealing long glistening fangs. "That's the spirit, *petite fille. Come.*"

I walk forward and follow him without thought. François points to the chair and I sit obediently. On some level, I'm aware that he is compelling me. I clench my teeth and fight the familiar feeling. Amazingly, his control slips and I watch it register on his face.

"Interesting. It will be such fun to break you, child." His movements blur and when he stills, François brandishes a long, curved knife in his gloved hands.

Oh, gods, oh, gods, oh, gods.

"Hmmm, where to begin?" He circles me, drawing out the inevitable. Anger forgotten in the face of despair; I'm vibrating with terror. François strikes from behind, the blade so sharp there's the slightest whisper touch across my cheek. Automatically, I brush at it and come away with bloodied fingers. The deep cut sends blood sheeting down my face, dripping off of my jaw, and seconds later the stinging burn hits. I try to hold my face still, but salty tears create a hell of their own. I scream.

Then François is everywhere at once, too fast to track, slicing my exposed skin. The searing, stinging pain spreads all over my body, tears flowing unchecked in rivulets, my sounds incoherent. In seconds, I'm covered in long cuts, my blood sheeting out of me. He slices over my left breast and blood soaks my bra. Suddenly, the stone hisses and for a terrible second it scalds my skin. I cry out with this new, bewildering pain. The same thing happens with the stone in my sodden sock seconds later and I'm beyond understanding or caring, just grateful there aren't any more stones on me.

The last of my hope fades as I realize they are only harmful to me. François, gloved, remains unharmed. And he just keeps slicing me, crisscrossing previous ones when he runs out of new skin, creating deeper gaping wounds. My clothes are saturated with my own blood, my entire body screeching with pain, and I'm not even sure I have the strength to stand. I pray for it to just be over.

François pauses in front of me, laughter lighting his manic face. "How wonderful! Your delicate skin parts so beautifully. But now—" his face hovers in front of me "—I must have more of your delicious blood before it all goes down the drain." I cringe away, but he keeps coming, crowding me into the chair so much that I fear it toppling over backwards. Then, grinning widely, he does the unthinkable. François licks the entire right side of my face, from my dripping jawline to my bloody hairline. His rough tongue scraping across and opening my cuts is excruciating. My scream has become a croak.

All at once, he hurls himself backwards, dropping the knife with a clatter, and a hideous sound screeches into the night. François' red eyes widen in shock. And pain? His tongue lolls out, half-eaten away.

Is that from licking me? Is that from my blood?

Galvanized, I lurch from the chair and race to him, all but vengeance forgotten. I slap my bloodied hands on either side of François' face. He squeals in inhuman agony, swinging his arm and knocking me across the room. I've slipped so far into my fury, I don't even feel myself land. *Get him! Get him! Get him!*

Heedless of his superior speed and strength, I dive at him. His cheeks are rotting away where I touched him, and I grab at any skin I can reach. Ducking and dodging him, I slap my bloody hands everywhere, leaving smoking craters in my wake. Yet, he still comes at me. Remembering the screwdriver in my pocket, I grip it in both hands and fling myself at him, stabbing him in the chest with all my might. Lurching back, he slips in our blood and goes down heavily. I rush at him, screetching, "Die!" I'm consumed in a white-hot rage. Blood covers both of us, but everything in my vision goes red. As if it were separate from me, I watch my arm arc repeatedly, until bands of steel surround me and yank me off of him.

"No! NO! He won't ever stop! You don't understand! He'll just keep killing! Let me go!" I fight with everything I have to get back to François until I'm enveloped by a scent I never thought I'd smell again and the voice in my ear starts to make sense. "Shh, *chérie*. I am here. It is over now, *ma petite amie*. He cannot hurt you anymore, my little warrior. Shh."

The words register, my vision clears, and all at once the fight leaves me. I slump like a deflated balloon, the screwdriver falling with a thud from my numb fingers. François' desiccated head rolls beside his mutilated body, landing face-up, his eyes forever frozen in an expression of shock.

Niall stands over François' body, Beatrice's bloody sword dangling from his hand. He holds my gaze steadily for a few beats, and then bows to me. Numbly, I watch as François' body dissolves into a pile of ash.

Now that the fight has left me, I feel limp as wet pasta and pain nearly swamps me. My mind scatters. Blue eyes filled with pain swim across my mind. *Prisoners!* In a moment, a couple of men are carried past me. I know those eyes will haunt me for a long time.

I become aware of vampire surrounding us. And every one of them is looking at me. Dazed, I look around at their faces, and they bow solemnly to me and most murmur, "Miss Libby." Many of them have blood around their mouths, down their chins. I sincerely hope Jeffrey's blood is on one of them.

I wonder if those militants tasted better than deer. Snorts and laughs follow this thought, and before I can worry about all of them reading my mind, Niall's dry voice distracts me.

"I don't know, mate. Mine was definitely a little on the gamey side." More laughter.

A vampire speaks up from the back. "Personally,

Miss Libby, I haven't had that much fun in ages." This is met with more laughs and a great deal of agreement.

I've searched the faces and not seen the ones I was hoping to see. "Beatrice and Dex?"

A vampire with the bearing of a soldier steps forward and bows deeply. He has wiped his mouth, though traces are still visible on his chin. "Miss Libby," he begins in a slightly Americanized British accent, "I'm Benjamin Thatcher, the head of JN Securities. I am happy to inform you that your detail are recovering and will be back on duty soon. Louis is attending them." He bows again and steps back to his spot.

Relief floods me. And fatigue. I'm so tired, Jo is the only thing keeping me from pitching face-first onto the floor. Pain threatens to overwhelm me, and my head aches as if it will explode. I wish it would. It might be a relief. But that would be a mess and I'm already enough of a mess.

Smiling, I blink. When I open my eyes, no one is where I remember and I'm on the floor.

Niall sounds weird, as if he's in a tunnel. "She's lost too much, mate. It has to be now."

"*Swallow, petite.*" I do, convulsively, the thick metallic liquid sliding down my throat. The pounding in my face lessons slightly. Some sense of survival kicks in and I draw hard on the skin against my lips. After a couple of gulps, awareness blooms and I stop, drawing back in confusion. I can't stop myself from licking my lips.

"What happened?" I look around, but I only see Niall and Jo.

"You were fading, *chérie*. It was my only choice."

I look at both of them. The pain is somewhat bearable and I no longer feel as if I'm going to face-plant. Yet. "Ah, who..."

Niall shows me his unmarred wrist. "Me, luv. Though there was no shortage of volunteers, Jo and I thought you'd feel more comfortable with someone you knew."

I look down at myself, touch my still-aching face. I look back at them, dazed.

"You only had enough to encourage clotting and replace a little of what you lost, *chérie*. When you are stronger, you can decide if you want enough to heal."

"Okie dokie." And I slump into darkness.

30

PUTTING IT MILDLY

I'm getting sick of waking up disoriented. Still, memory floods me with what I'd just as soon forget. And if Niall's blood helped, I must be in sorry shape. Thick white bandages cover my limbs. I lose count of butterfly bandages after 30. Some of the longer cuts have multiple butterflies. My body aches as though I've been hit by a bus. The throbbing in my head makes me glad I can't take in much light through the slits of my swollen eyes.

Yet, for the first time in a long time, I feel calm. The absence of terror is freeing. Distantly, I hear Darcy scratching in his litter box and the sound is comforting. Home.

Jo walks into her bedroom smiling. "Good morning, *ma guerriere*."

I smile at her. She crosses the room and kisses my hair. "I don't know about warrior. But I need to talk about it?" Thanks to my busted nose, I sound like a cartoon character. But Jo ignores it, so I do, too.

"Of course, *chérie*. Would you like anyone else here?" Jo pulls up a chair and leans over me. She lifts my bandaged hand tenderly.

"No. Just the two of us for now, please." She nods, and I press on. "How did you find me?"

"With help. Yours and Beatrice's." Instinctively, I raise my eyebrows, which hurts more than I expected. My fear is validated when a trickle races for my hair. Jo grabs a tissue and stops it, dabbing at the blood. "You cleverly left your phone on in the van, which allowed us to trace it."

Of course. Duh. I'm too embarrassed to say it never occurred to me that they could do that.

"Beatrice heard Jeffrey say his full name. It did not take long to identify him as a member of a militant group on the government watchlist. So we knew where to find you and what we'd need to get you out. I am afraid that the time we used to gather information and reinforcements made your torture possible. I cannot tell you what I would do to have been there in your place." Jo's pained voice upsets me.

Without a hint of ego, I hold her gaze. "Please don't take this wrong, but you couldn't have done what I did." She raises her eyebrows and her eyes flash crimson. I've offended her. Well, that wasn't my intention at all. I rush to reassure her. "No, wait. He underestimated me. They all did. François kept calling me 'little girl' and 'child.' They never searched my pockets, so they didn't know I still had my phone in my pocket when we left the restaurant, and they didn't know I pocketed a screwdriver from the back of the van. Not one of them saw me as a threat. You would have been searched, tied up, armed guards on you 24/7. They would have expected you to attack and been prepared for it."

Thankfully, Jo sees the truth in that and calms immediately. "We all underestimated you, *ma chére guerriere.* I will not make this mistake again. Will you now believe me when I tell you that you are strong?"

Before I can respond, there's a discreet knock on her outer door. Jo says, "Enter."

A minute later, Charlene comes in bearing a tray with Louis close on her heels. "Little Duck, Louis says you need iron since you lost so much blood, so I made you a liver smoothie, okay?" She looks at me over her glasses and starts laughing so hard at my expression that Louis rescues the tray from her, rolling his eyes. When she recovers sufficiently, she fans her face. "Oh, that was fun. What I've actually made you is a dark chocolate smoothie, some oatmeal with molasses, and you get coffee and orange juice. Food is medicine. Wouldn't you rather that to a bunch of big nasty pills?" She glares at Louis, who has the grace to fake offense dramatically. They really are ridiculously adorable together.

"Sounds great, Charlene. Thank you." She awkwardly pats my socked foot. There aren't many touchable parts of me. Stifling a shudder, I smile at her as she takes her leave. Once the door closes, I turn to Louis. "Hiya, doc. What's the story?"

His eyes soften and he strokes my hair. He and Jo nod at one another across my body. "*Mademoiselle,* you are anemic, despite Niall's blood. Actually, you are depleted in every way. All this adds to your fatigue and general achiness. Your nose and cheekbone are broken. Your swollen black eyes are testament to this. I imagine you also have a headache, *oui?*" He slants his head and I manage a small nod. "As for your knees, besides terrible bruising, a bursa ruptured in your left knee. This is a protective fluid-filled sac. It will take time for it to heal. A few drops of vampire blood will go a long way. More would be far better. The choice is yours."

Is it really a choice? "Somewhere in between. Maybe in the smoothie?"

Louis looks at Jo.

"Yours would be better, old friend, if you are willing."

"*Mais oui.* It is my honor."

The thick chocolate masks the blood perfectly and I finish the small glass quickly. My headache disappears, as promised, and I feel a bit more energetic. The aching in my face fades and I can see better, thanks to reduced swelling. But best of all, the cuts stop stinging and scabs form before my eyes.

"Can I ask you something?"

"Anything, *chérie.*"

"How did they do it? How did they overcome Dex and Beatrice?"

Jo lays a hand on Louis' shoulder. "It was a well-coordinated attack. François must have advised them. Simultaneously, they were shot in the head, temporarily disabling them. The attackers swarmed Dex with machetes and, as you saw, they used Beatrice's sword. Then they fled to vehicles parked down the street."

I ask for the coffee and sip. Unbidden, corroded cheeks swim in my mind. I buck up my courage. "Louis, Jo, I have to tell you something." When they are both looking at me, I cradle the mug in my hands and lower to a barely-there whisper. "When I went to the bathroom in the restaurant, something told me to put the...black stones on. I had one in my bra, here," I pull down the neck of my T-shirt and show them the dime-sized burn, now shiny with some kind of salve.

Jo gasps. I guess she didn't know about it. "The other was in my sock. When blood ran from my cuts to the stones, I heard them sizzle, then become burning hot. I thought they were worthless, but then François... he...licked my cheek." Jo hisses and her eyes go crimson. Louis stays calm, but his eyes go red, too. "It...ate at his tongue. My blood. Then, whatever I touched with my bloody hands started to shrivel away, like my blood was acidic. But it was the shock of it all that let me overpower him."

Louis looks thoughtful, but Jo is still visibly upset. "That explains the condition of his body before he met his final death."

I shudder, remembering the flesh eaten away from his face. "I don't understand any of it, but I also don't understand why Jo could then put her hands on me. I didn't think about it at the time, but I was saturated in my own blood. Somehow it didn't hurt you."

I turn back to Louis. "Do you think, because it is a stone of *protection*, that it only hurts a vampire that wants to hurt me? And, I don't know, blood is needed to activate it?" I think for a minute. "Who cleaned me up and dressed me?"

"I did, *mademoiselle,* with Charlene's help."

I nod. "Do you know where the stones are?"

Louis spreads his hand across his chin and shakes his head thoughtfully. "*Mademoiselle,* when we cleaned you, I found only lumps of ash over your burns. The only stone was the Amazonite in your pocket. I assumed François somehow burned you, but blood is often used in strong magic. Perhaps the stone requires a sacrifice before it will imbue the wearer with its protection. It explains how none of us were injured. We did not mean you harm. I believe you have stumbled upon some ancient knowledge long buried. But we will continue to keep it buried, *oui*? And perhaps provide you with a plentiful supply of little black rocks?" His eyes twinkle.

"Yes, please. Thank you again for all you have done, Louis. How are your other patients?"

"Regenerating limbs is a painful and arduous process, but Beatrice and Dex are coming along. I assembled volunteers from the vampire here, and I am happy to say that most of them showed up to give blood to my two patients. Blood of our own kind speeds our recovery faster than mortal blood could." Louis looks at Jo, his eyes hard. "I have the names of those who did not volunteer, if you want them."

I redirect the conversation quickly. "I'm so glad. I know it must have nearly killed Beatrice to have her own weapon used against her."

"*Oui, chérie*. This part of her recovery will take long, I fear. She blames herself. Though, to be fair, he stole you right out from under *my* nose. I am disgraced." Jo stares at our hands.

I shake them. "You aren't infallible, Jo. So what? Believe me, I don't want perfect. I know you wanted to reassure me, but you boxed yourself into a corner vowing he wouldn't get me. Jo, I feel safe with you, I feel protected by you, but even you aren't invincible. None of us are."

I spend the rest of the day resting, eating Charlene's delicious medicine, and talking and laughing with Jo. I play with Darcy a little, though I'm still exhausted. Jo offers me enough blood to completely heal, but I refuse. I get what they've said about my strength and bravery, but I'm not especially proud of the person Jo's father made me become. I wanted to kill him, nearly did. I was in a blind rage. Two people trying to protect me were gravely injured and won't be right for days. I'm not ready to walk around, all healed up and painfree. I have some tough emotional work ahead of me.

Needless to say, Jo took another day off for me, but I'm letting that go. It's her choice to make. I haven't asked her to miss work, not even once. I decide it's time to stop feeling responsible for everyone else. They're all adults and can make their own decisions. Even Beatrice. She chose to do this kind of work. She knew the risks better than I did.

Toward evening, Niall comes. I've been wondering when he would. He bows to me and we spend a minute assessing one another.

I know you killed François so I wouldn't have to. Thank you.

Niall bows again and winks at me, and somehow I know he will always have my back.

That makes me think of something. I turn to Jo. "Maybe you two can explain something else to me. In the stockade, there were so many vampire that I don't know, and they bowed to me. It felt like more than respect for you. What changed?"

Niall laughs. "You did, luv. We are a violent lot. By comparison, humans are naturally weak and vulnerable. It makes us feel superior. Here we all swoop in to save the little human, only to find you standing over an ancient, him helpless on the floor covered in his own blood." He laughs heartily again.

Rolling my eyes at him, I mull that over. I'm not happy with what I did to win their respect. I was consumed with a need for violence. If Jo hadn't pulled me off...if Niall hadn't beheaded him...

But I can't play the "if" game. "I'd like to talk with Naomi again."

Jo nods in agreement, and maybe a little relief. "Louis will call her."

I shift uncomfortably. "Jo, what is Naomi? Some sort of water goddess or something?" I don't know what made me say that, but something about her voice and her instruction that I stand in water, it just got me wondering. She looks over at Niall, and then back at me.

"What?"

"Once again, you surprise me, *chérie*. Naomi is a rare and special creature. But exactly what creature she is is hers to tell." Jo kisses the top of my head.

After a while, Niall leaves and Jo makes sweet love to me, careful of the scabs covering me. Later, sated, we pad to the sitting room. There's a knock, and Jo answers it. She turns around, bearing a plate with a huge slice of double-decker chocolate cake and a scoop of vanilla ice cream on the side.

"Oh, Gaia. I'll never eat all that!"

Jo tries, but fails miserably to look serious. "Doctor's orders, *chérie*. Remember, food is medicine!"

We both laugh. It feels so good. *I didn't think I'd ever laugh again.* Shaking it off, I focus on the enormous section of cake, really glad to see two forks. The first bite makes me moan and Jo raises an eyebrow. Her eyes get that look.

"Not now, dear, I'm having chocolate." She throws her head back and laughs with abandon.

Amazingly, we demolish the plateful, and I set down my fork and lean back into the couch. She leans back and shifts me into her arms. I snuggle in and rub my full tummy. I am happy, really happy, for the first time in a long time.

"Do you think we should keep our double date with Emma and David tomorrow?"

"What do you think?" Jo rubs my arm almost hypnotically.

"Well, look at me. It's gonna be kind of hard to hide all this. Besides, I feel weird going out and celebrating when..." I trail off.

Jo kisses me, then props her chin on my head. "But you are alive, *oui*? Isn't life itself worth celebrating? And the swelling and bruising are hardly noticeable."

I look at her skeptically. "Maybe you're right. Good. I really want to meet Emma's boyfriend, and I especially want you to meet my best friend. Thank you. It means a lot to me." I look down at myself and grimace. "Though I may have to wear jeans and a turtleneck to cover up all of this."

Jo pats my arm and starts to sit up, bringing me with her. "We will worry about this tomorrow, *ma petite amie*. Now, it is time for you to sleep."

Jo spoons me, playing with my hair. Before I sleep, I get up my nerve. "Jo, are you ever going to bite me?" She stills, and I'm almost sorry I asked. Then she wraps her arm around my stomach.

"Why do you ask this, *chérie*?"

"Because you linger over my jugular sometimes."

Her fingers splay over my abdomen. "Do you want me to?" She is deceptively casual. This must mean a lot to her.

I want to be careful here. "I'm not sure. Sometimes yes, sometimes no. What does it feel like?"

Some of the tension leaves her body. "It can feel

very, very good. Or it can feel very, very bad. But that is not the reason to do it. *Oui*, it can be incredibly sensual, but between lovers it means more. The giving and taking of blood is bonding. For example, I will know from a greater distance how you are feeling. It's more than drinking blood. There is a hint of magic for the bonding, the Claiming, to work."

"Does it have to happen when we're having sex?"

"No, *chérie*, though the act itself is so intimate that they often go hand in hand. For tonight, that is enough. Now, we sleep."

The last thing I remember is Jo pulling the comforter over us. Her arms surround me as she whispers French in my ear and I drift off, cocooned in her love.

I wake up feeling much more like my normal self. Jo has to leave early, and I'm still in my robe getting ready, feeling leisurely after wake-up sex and a shower. She kisses me soundly several times before she finally leaves, looking debonnaire and hot, hot, hot. I can't wait to show her off to Emma tonight.

The day passes quickly enough. I catch up with Dad and Sarah, and choke back tears to hear their voices. Because I have to shovel so much bull about what I've been up to, I'm grateful it was done on the phone. I'd never get away with it in person.

Late morning, I text Louis and ask if I can visit my security team. He collects me at the door and escorts me. The room is huge, bright, and spotlessly clean. Three of the dozen or so hospital beds are occupied. I'm so happy to be able to see Dex and Beatrice, and my smile is broad and genuine. Beatrice returns a faint smile.

"Miss Libby! It looks like you are healing up well!" Dex is sitting up in the bed nearest me. I go to him and he takes my offered hand. After a brief squeeze, we drop our hands.

"How are you, Dex? You don't look too bad." The sheet is pulled up to his chest, so all I notice is a chunk of his left ear missing.

"Don't you worry. I'll be back on duty in a few days, Miss Libby. That is, if you'll have me. I didn't exactly protect you in the end." He looks chagrined.

"Aw, Dex. Like I told Jo, no one is infallible. You did your best and I am grateful. I know you fought. And I'm so glad to hear you'll be out soon, but isn't the danger gone?" I'm a bit confused.

Louis answers me. "True, that particular danger is gone, but Jo has many enemies *mademoiselle*. You will always have guards."

"Yeah, you can bet she won't be lightening up your protection for a long time, Miss Libby. You had all of us really worried. But your quick thinking and bravery—" Dex points at a scab on my forearm and his eyes flash red "—well, I'm just glad you came out of it all right."

I'm not entirely sure I did, at least not for a while yet. But I smile at him anyway. "I look forward to working together again, Dex."

I make my way to Beatrice's bed. Louis stays at Dex's side, busying himself. "Hey Beatrice! How about you? How is it coming?"

While Beatrice's face is impassive, she can't hide the pain in her eyes. I know the damage she suffered, and though I cannot see her legs under the blanket, I know they aren't whole, yet. "I'm real glad you came to see me, Libby. I got something here for you." She reaches to the table beside her and picks up a short wide box, which she hands me.

My finger automatically traces the swirling design carved into the lid and sides of the knotty wood. I shimmy off the snug lid and gasp. Light glints off of the shiny surface of a knife nestled in dark velvet. Maybe three or four inches long, the wide blade is wickedly sharp on both edges and tapers to a pinprick. The handle appears to be wood, worn dark and smooth with years of use. It feels good in my hands—solid, secure, but not heavy.

"This is...beautiful, Beatrice." And it is. Before Francois and Travis, I don't think I'd have seen it that way, but there's an attractiveness in its utilitarian design. "But I don't understand."

She nods a few times. "I've had that boot knife since I was just a kid growing up in West Virginia—guess it had been my old man's or something. I'm too strong for it, and it doesn't feel right in my hand anymore. I'm thinking it's just right for you, though. And it's a damn sight better than a screwdriver." Her eyes dance before dulling again. She looks away before I can blink away silly moisture. "There's a snug leather sheath made to hook it on the top of your boot, strap it on a belt, or tie it on your leg or whatever. I'll have someone get it to you."

"I don't know what to say, Beatrice. I'm touched, which if you are reading me you know is putting it mildly. I'm very glad to have it." I carefully lay the knife on its velvet bed and close the box. Then I shoot for cheerful. "When does Louis say you get to come back to work?"

Beatrice holds my gaze. "I'll be out of here in another two or three days, but I won't be coming back, Libby."

"What do you mean? Won't you heal properly?"

She shakes her head. "It's not that. Physically, I'll be fine. It's just time I moved on. I decided to go back to my hometown. It's been a few generations, and my people need help. I'm going to see what I can do for them." Her face is impassive and her eyes are guarded, but even I can see the undercurrent. She doesn't want to tell me how badly she feels about what happened to me. Twice.

"You have to know I don't hold you responsible," I whisper. "Neither does Jo. No one does." I can't stop a tear from escaping.

In a low voice, Beatrice answers me. "Hell, I know that, Libby. You are too good for that. I just can't explain what it did to me to lie there helpless while that scumbag took you away. I can't protect you. I won't even try." She pauses. "I like you too much. You deserve the best protection."

"But you are Badass Beatrice." Tears blur my vision again, and this time I can't blink them away.

Her gaze turns hard and her eyes flash red. "And *you* are Badass Libby."

The End

Dear reader,

We hope you enjoyed reading *The Warrior Within*. Please take a moment to leave a review, even if it's a short one. Your opinion is important to us.

Discover more books by Brooke Campbell at https://www.nextchapter.pub/authors/brooke-campbell

Want to know when one of our books is free or discounted? Join the newsletter at http://eepurl.com/bqqB3H

Best regards,
Brooke Campbell and the Next Chapter Team

AUTHOR BIO

Brooke Campbell started reading voraciously and writing in childhood. Raised on a Virginia farm, she fostered an abiding love of animals, and calls nature her church. She has been a happy hooker of yarn since a tender age, and she plays well with beads and wire. Throughout her checkered past she shuffled papers, and spent far too much time on computers, cash registers, and phones. Brooke's various and sundry hats include interpreter, English teacher, gardener, full-time RVer, and world traveler. No matter where she and her wife Terri go—along with the felines they loyally serve—they will always call the Appalachians home.

You can find out more about her at www.brookecampbellwrites.com

The Warrior Within
ISBN: 978-4-82410-201-0
Mass Market

Published by
Next Chapter
1-60-20 Minami-Otsuka
170-0005 Toshima-Ku, Tokyo
+818035793528

27th August 2021